OTHER BOOKS BY EDMUND KEELEY

Fiction

THE LIBATION
THE GOLD-HATTED LOVER
THE IMPOSTOR
VOYAGE TO A DARK ISLAND

Poetry in Translation

SIX POETS OF MODERN GREECE (with Philip Sherrard)
GEORGE SEFERIS: COLLECTED POEMS, 1924–1955 (with
    Philip Sherrard)
C. P. CAVAFY: PASSIONS AND ANCIENT DAYS (with George
    Savidis)
C. P. CAVAFY: SELECTED POEMS (with Philip Sherrard)
ODYSSEUS ELYTIS: THE AXION ESTI (with George Savidis)
C. P. CAVAFY: COLLECTED POEMS (with Philip Sherrard and
    George Savidis)
ANGELOS SIKELIANOS: SELECTED POEMS (with Philip Sher-
    rard)
RITSOS IN PARENTHESES
THE DARK CRYSTAL/VOICES OF MODERN GREECE (with
    Philip Sherrard)
ODYSSEUS ELYTIS: SELECTED POEMS (ed. with Philip Sher-
    rard)
GEORGE SEFERIS: COLLECTED POEMS (with Philip Sherrard)
YANNIS RITSOS: RETURN AND OTHER POEMS, 1967–1972

Fiction in Translation

VASSILIS VASSILIKOS: THE PLANT, THE WELL, THE
    ANGEL (with Mary Keeley)

Criticism

MODERN GREEK WRITERS (ed. with Peter Bien)
CAVAFY'S ALEXANDRIA
MODERN GREEK POETRY: VOICE AND MYTH

A WILDERNESS CALLED PEACE

EDMUND KEELEY

SIMON AND SCHUSTER
NEW YORK

Copyright © 1985 by Edmund Keeley
All rights reserved, including the right of reproduction in whole or in part in any form. Published by Simon and Schuster, A Division of Simon & Schuster, Inc., Simon & Schuster Building, Rockefeller Center, 1230 Avenue of the Americas, New York, New York 10020. SIMON AND SCHUSTER and colophon are registered trademarks of Simon & Schuster, Inc.

Designed by Barbara M. Marks
Manufactured in the United States of America

1   3   5   7   9   10   8   6   4   2

Library of Congress Cataloging in Publication Data

Keeley, Edmund.
A wilderness called peace.

1. Cambodia—History—1975–   —Fiction.
2. Thailand—History—1945–   —Fiction. I. Title.
PS3561.E34W5 1985   813'.54   84-23598
ISBN: 0-671-47416-2

Acknowledgments

Though the action and characters in this work are entirely fictional, I have drawn on the following sources in creating an image of actual events in Cambodia and Thailand from 1975 through 1983: conversations with Robert Keeley, Deputy Chief of Mission, Phnom Penh, 1974–75; a report by Sydney Schanberg for CBS News, 1975; *Murder of a Gentle Land* by John Barron and Anthony Paul (Reader's Digest Press, 1977); François Ponchaud's *Cambodia: Year Zero* (Holt, Rinehart and Winston, 1978); Stephen R. Heder's *Kampuchean Occupation and Resistance* (Asian Studies Monographs No. 027, Institute of Asian Studies, Chulalongkorn University, 1980); *Kampuchea Back from the Brink:* The International Committee of the Red Cross reports on its 15-month joint action with UNICEF in Kampuchea and Thailand, 1981; William Shawcross' *Sideshow* (Simon and Schuster, 1981) and *The Quality of Mercy* (Simon and Schuster, 1984); articles by Colin Campbell in *The New York Times,* April 3–5, 1983; news items in the *Bangkok Post* and *Bangkok World,* 1975 and 1979; personal interviews, during my 1982 trip to the Thai–Cambodian border, with Timothy Carney, John Crowley, Kha Sanh, Bun Lay, and several others who are identified in the dedication, no one of whom should be held responsible for what my fiction has created.

Part One of this book first appeared in *Antaeus* 51 and was included in the *Pushcart Prize Anthology* of 1984; two sections of Part Three were selected by the P.E.N. Syndicated Fiction Project; and two sections from Part Four were first published in *TriQuarterly,* a publication of Northwestern University. I am grateful to the National Endowment for the Arts for a creative writing fellowship that supported my work on this novel and to the Virginia Center for the Creative Arts for a residency grant that helped me to complete it. I thank my editor, Donald Hutter—among other friends—for valuable suggestions during the course of my writing.

For Jeff, Keith, Brigitte, Peter, Annie,
and the others on the border

Plunder, slaughter, dispossession: these they misname government; they create a wilderness and call it peace.

Tacitus, *Agricola*, 30

ONE

1975

April 13. The city is waiting now. On the surface there has been no change, even though the Year of the Tiger has ended and we are beginning the Year of the Hare. Our government has declared a state of emergency and so there is to be no holiday, no celebration except in secret, business as usual. Most people have gone to work as on any other day, the healthy children play in the street, the army fights on courageously according to our Prime Minister, the rocket fire from across the river is not much different from what it has been. But the city is waiting. One can tell from the way nobody talks in public about the Americans leaving, out of superstition, as though talk may influence what is going to happen to us and it is therefore better to remain silent and simply wait for whatever the new year brings.

I'm not afraid to talk about the Americans leaving—why be superstitious when there isn't room for choice or argument?—but there's no one I care to trust now, even if talking might help one accept what seems both unacceptable and unalterable. At the same time I feel an urge to record what is happening here, partly for your sake but mostly for my own. Maybe it will give me a certain liberation from the events themselves. Maybe it will serve in ways I don't yet fully understand to put some order into this absurd day-to-day chaos. Whether or not other eyes ever see this inelegant little notebook. I think it will most likely go with me into my next incarnation unread by you or anyone else, and since I'm sure that I will reappear among the lower orders of life—at best as a careless scavenger of a bird, at worst as a tick to suck your blood—even I will not be able to read it after the road ahead turns back on itself. And that too is a certain liberation.

You didn't know I had such Buddhist leanings, you don't take them seriously, not in a woman who could pretend for your pleasure to be so French in her thinking. Why should you understand very much about who I am after knowing me less than a year and knowing best what is now probably the least valuable part of me? My blood is of course very mixed and my loyalties confused—you were quick to recognize that—but what you came to know outside the language classes is mostly the imported part, from my father's side: those English and French and Chinese delicacies that you preferred for a while to your food at home. Yet the stronger, less reckless part that I will need to favor now comes from my mother's side, all Khmer. What can you really know about that, my American friend? And isn't it a shame you couldn't stay long enough to learn?

April 14. This city that I know so well has become suddenly unfamiliar. One grew so used to the shifting feel of danger, the constant movement of those who have nowhere to go, the changing smells of hunger and sickness, that this new activity hangs over us in our spring evening like an unwanted hot mist, bringing listlessness, apathy, disconnection. The rocket fire has increased, but mostly one no longer pays heed to it. The streets are almost empty, and not just because the government has declared a twenty-four-hour curfew in a futile attempt to keep the refugees and army deserters from crowding into the city and blocking all the roads (what cleared some roads this morning and stopped the few illegal festivities was the bombing of the army headquarters by a government plane, they say by mistake). It is as though this terrible waiting for the enemy, this anticipation, instead of heightening fear and vigilance, now lulls us into contemplation. It isn't just the curfew that keeps us inside. We turn more and more into ourselves. The waiting has become almost erotic in the way it induces self-absorption.

And it is supposed to be our New Year (I wonder, by the way, if your Embassy chose the date of its departure to conform with our tradition of cleaning the house thoroughly of the dirt it has gathered before the old year goes out—forgive me if I'm being too unfair). I spent the day at home cleaning my apartment a bit late and with little enthusiasm, because there hardly seemed any point when I don't know how much longer I will be able to stay here. Maybe as a widow of the war I will have special dispensation. And with all this foreign blood in me, I may find some excuse that will counteract my having worked with the Americans in the small way I did (don't laugh; I speak strictly of the French lessons). The Chinese in me is not likely to help after the Khmer Rouge take over the city, because they are said to hate the Chinese merchants first among their local capitalist enemies despite the fact that it is China which has made their victory possible, as you yourself insisted. But maybe my English background through my grandmother will somehow prove useful. Doesn't that carry as much weight as my Hong Kong grandfather? I suppose not, especially since my face and manners reveal too much of what my English nanny used to call "Oriental cunning" whenever she wanted to chastise me for behaving in a way that was less proper and British than she found acceptable. Or maybe the French in me—at least in my point of view. Aren't the French doing their subtle best these days to play the role of neutral? If it weren't for my face and the small remnant of Anglo-Saxon in my blood, I could pass for French, couldn't I? Not that either, I suppose.

Anyway, it wasn't my future as much as my past that kept me so self-absorbed this afternoon—not only our short past but years ago when the three-day New Year holiday often meant a trip to Kampot Province and the lower slopes of the Elephant Mountains by the Gulf of Thailand. My father had a Chinese friend who owned a pepper plantation there, one of those who remained in my father's debt for many years through loans. To go to that plantation was always exciting for me as a young girl, not only for the clear air of the mountains and the green forests, but finding the sea each time, so clean and unlimited, so different from our brown river—the endless free space it seemed to offer, as far as the low sun.

I think it was the discovery of that sea, always for the first time though often repeated, that made me less frightened of going away to France for my university studies when that became my father's plan. It seemed almost natural by then to follow the impulse it had slowly created—I was just eighteen but mature for my age, at least by comparison with my schoolmates in the English-language school here—the impulse to fly clear of this country and to keep going on and on until one arrived at some new and unexplored space beyond the distance another's vision might reach. After I returned from France of course it wasn't the same sea any longer. I was too old and worldly-wise. I went to that region the last time with my husband for a week of vacation just before the army took him from me, a week spent mostly at the beach in Sihanoukville— there was a small but very good restaurant by the beach where you could get excellent oysters from Kep—and I would lie under our striped umbrella or under a palm tree in my very small bikini with the new concrete city at my back, lie there sipping Dubonnet and being very modern, very much loved, and sometimes look out at that sea with a feeling of hatred because I was beyond finding the challenge in it any longer.

It is now midnight. I did poke my head out in the early evening to see if anyone still cared that it's the New Year. Apparently the Khmer Rouge do, because the rocket fire has become the heaviest in weeks. But there was one final absurdity that made me rather cheerful. Against all the rockets some sweet fool sent up a fireworks display from somewhere near the Phnom, and for a few minutes the sky appeared ridiculously to belong to our city again.

April 16. The waiting, which had become as intolerably comfortable as a disease that shows itself with less than the right pain day after day, now is over. We know the end is close, and this brings its own kind of excitement. There are reports that the Khmer Rouge have cut the road to the airport, that they have reached Kilometer 6 in the north and have crossed the Monivong Bridge in the south. We could see fires everywhere in the outskirts yesterday—factories burning, munition depots exploding; who knows if anything is left? They say the last government tanks are retreating to surround the French Embassy.

Now that we are certain a change is at hand, some would say that this new knowledge is better than our continuing desperate lie: the government forces holding on valiantly, reinforcements coming in all the time from unnamed regions—after all, are there any regions left that haven't been "liberated"?—the city prepared for a long fight to the death, etc. Of course few people are fooled by these reports, and most of those who recognize that the government and the army are doomed have already begun to move beyond this certainty. Their direction is toward the uncertain future. And viewing the past we've had in recent months—recent years—some are apparently able to look that way with hope.

I can't, I must admit. Whatever change may come, I now realize that it surely means the end of life here as I have lived it for most of my thirty-six years. Not that what I've known here has been without its trials and complications, as you're well aware. And you're also well aware that I'm not afraid of new adventures. But it's clear that my situation is precarious now. I can't any longer count on my husband's connections—they will vanish with the government. And my connections to the royal family through my mother appear comically remote, as does the Prince himself.

Now that the Americans have gone, it seems even my credentials in foreign languages are not likely to give me a means of support: refugees from the liberated zones report that the Khmer Rouge speak one language only when they speak at all. And other—what shall I call them?—assets and skills that an educated woman with a weakness for pleasure might be thought to have are even less likely to prove useful if this Communist regime turns out to be as ruthlessly puritan as the others in our part of the world. Can you in any case imagine me as the lady friend of some round little guerrilla officer from the northern provinces used to a pound of rice a day and dried fish and painfully boring sexual practices?

I suppose you can imagine it. I suppose from your point of view it is simply a matter of changing one's taste and standard of living and perhaps one's politics a bit in keeping with the reality of new conditions. I did it for you; I can do it again for the next regime. The charm of a civilized woman of the East is her flexibility, isn't that so? And need is ever the mother of invention, as I think your great Anglo-Saxon poet put it. Perhaps, we will see. But I spent yesterday rather depressed by it all—too much so to write about it. Not that I can really blame you for going away; you had no choice. And though you were good enough to offer to arrange my evacuation in one of your helicopters, I think you realized that I had no choice but to stay here, like so many others who worked for the Americans. How could I just abandon my sister and her children, all that's left of my family in this country? And where would I go in yours? You kept saying that we would work something out once we got there, but you never explained how I would support myself without finally becoming a burden to you—not to mention your wife. And I didn't want to embarrass you by raising such a direct and essential question.

I think we both understood the reality of our muddy circumstances here and in your country without having to spell it all out. But what has happened still isn't just, at least not for those of us here who took a road that we can't now reverse, whether by our will or someone else's. And the sudden discontinuity of the life you and I knew will make it difficult from now on for me to look back at our pleasure—yes, I think I can say our kind of love—with very much return of spice or longing.

I tried yesterday. Again I had the whole day to myself at home. And though it has been only five days since you left, I felt surges of desire that I finally had to release. But I could not do it under your image. Not because of any bitterness, just a sadness that came at the wrong moment and made it impossible. Maybe it was from the realization that you and I have nothing more that we can share now, no discovery, no useful remembrance, no irony even, only my one-sided language sent into the void. I suppose if I were a good Buddhist, this might be taken as another firm step toward liberation—not merely the necessary awareness that this is a life of suffering because of the unsatisfied cravings it brings with it but that the way to break the harsh cycle is by turning in on one's self to face the void without illusions. Oh, I wish it were that easy. The cravings, the cravings. They are still too holy for me. And the illusions also.

April 18. The Khmer Rouge began to enter the city yesterday morning, first from the south, they say, but very soon from every direction. I wasn't there to greet them personally. I thought that would be in bad taste. And I guess this bit of decorum is what makes it possible for me to write at all today from my refuge in the French Embassy. I did try to find out what was happening early yesterday morning by way of the radio, but of course the radio was dead, as it had been for hours. News came to me first from my landlady, who went down to Monivong Boulevard as soon as word reached us that the soldiers were arriving, only these soldiers turned out to be the wrong ones. She reported that there was much activity on the Boulevard when she got there. The tanks near the French Embassy moved down to the Cathedral and pointed their guns toward the north. A group of long-haired young men dressed in black marched in that direction and were cheered on their way because the onlookers thought they were Khmer Rouge, especially when some of the tank crews climbed down to applaud and embrace them as liberating conquerors. But their flag had a cross on it, and the soldiers looked too fat to be revolutionaries. It turned out that these soldiers were mostly students who belonged to a new National Movement organized by the brother of your friend the ex-President in a last-minute attempt to replace the current Prime Minister and so perhaps grasp victory from the Khmer Rouge by the power of political miracle, in keeping with our ancient tradition.

The true revolutionaries who came in soon afterward to kill all this celebration were not so fat and much younger, children really, all in black except for a checkered scarf, with Chinese caps and sandals made out of old tires. And they carried large guns and grenades and strange new weapons in belts across their chests. My landlady reported that some of those watching thought these new soldiers looked confused, withdrawn, gaunt, ready to collapse, but she herself thought they just looked severe and determined, especially the girl soldiers—very unfeminine, she said. In any case, they were all silent, and the only time any of them smiled a little was when they found something interesting to steal from a shop that they could share with their comrades: a bottle of soda or a package of cigarettes or a handful of cheap wristwatches. They didn't have time for serious stealing. There was much business to be done. First they had to take over the city from one end to the other, small groups at every crossroads controlling the traffic, collecting all arms, emptying trucks and cars. Then, before the sun set, they had to empty the city itself. Completely.

They began with the hospitals, it seems. My landlady watched them clean out the Preah Ket Melea hospital, and then she decided she had better go home. The hospitals had become so filled with the heavy casualties in these last days since the Americans left that there had been little chance to remove the dead, and those watching the new soldiers at work assumed at first that they were making room for the seriously wounded by transferring those who could be made to walk and then by removing the dead bodies from the corridors. But the dead and the seriously wounded were all that was allowed to remain behind—no doctors, no nurses, no guards even. And those who could walk had to carry those who couldn't or push their beds down the street as though they were carts. It was a slow parade, she said, the crippled and wounded using each other as crutches. One woman had a child by each hand and a third in a blood-soaked sack tied around her neck. My landlady watched a man with no legs thump his way out of the hospital and up the street, picking his way as best he could through the crowd until his arms weakened.

That is when she decided to go home. And that is when she discovered that this bizarre exodus was just the beginning of the great evacuation that long before nightfall would clog every road leading out of the city, because the streets on her way back were already starting to fill with people leaving their homes under the direction of these young soldiers in black. Neighborhood after neighborhood was being liberated to the point of desolation, with only occasional shots fired for encouragement, since the people were told that the Americans would soon begin to bomb the city and that everyone should leave quickly for the countryside, taking only what food they could carry under one arm. They were told to go as many kilometers as they could outside the city by the nearest road and not to bother locking up their houses—all would be protected for them until their return in a few days, after the city had been bombed and then cleaned up a bit. So it seems most people went without argument, tired of the rockets and the shooting, happy that these young revolutionaries had taken over the city without much further bloodshed, ready for any sort of new beginning. Some of the greedier apparently filled up their cars with belongings, but then they found that they weren't allowed to start their motors and had to push their cars through town until they were exhausted. And as more and more people moved into the streets, the journey out of the city became terribly slow, a few feet at a time, much stopping and starting again and always in a single direction after one got going, whatever direction some other member of one's family might have taken in the chaos of this mass departure.

It was my landlady who saved me to begin with. As you no doubt gathered, she always keeps very much to herself—a secretive woman, suspicious of almost everyone in the building, me in particular because of my "French" ways and my questionable foreign associations. So when she came back to my apartment so very agitated with her story about the hospital and her rumors about the streets' beginning to fill with people ordered out of their homes by these armed children, I had to believe the fear in her voice. I packed a suitcase in less time than you are likely to believe—you who became so sullen over what you thought was my vanity when I made you wait half an hour or so while I packed my things for our helicopter trip to Kampot. I took with me only essentials (honestly, very little makeup) and what foreign currency I have collected, and I made my way quickly by the back streets to the French Embassy. I tried to persuade my landlady to come with me, but she just stared at my feet and said, "What business could I have at that place?" So I gave her double what I owed her for rent in American money—the final absurdity—and left her there to gather up all the food I'd left behind.

The situation at the French Embassy was worse than I could have imagined. Of course it was the only place where Cambodians who had worked for the government or the Americans might hope to receive some kind of asylum, but I had not expected to find so many foreigners there as well—hundreds of them—diplomats, businessmen, correspondents, who knows what else, and of all nationalities, American included. It seems that the Khmer Rouge ordered the Hotel Phnom cleared out after they emptied the hospitals, and that eliminated the neutral zone for foreigners that was supposed to have been set up by the Red Cross. So the French Embassy became the only neutral zone, with the foreigners occupying two of the buildings and the Embassy staff the Consulate building. This rather complicated the situation for the Cambodians arriving there, even those like me with a French—how shall I put it?—history. I don't mean only my intimate French friends and my years in Paris. I was counting on my father's past connections with the French community, not least the diplomatic community, which was often in his debt for matters of financial exchange and sometimes information, even in his last years, after he had more or less retired from business. But there was no chance of making a case of this kind at the Embassy yesterday afternoon with more than five hundred Cambodians and an even larger number of foreigners pushing into the Embassy grounds. The staff was simply overwhelmed by this swarming mass—no time for talk; it was all they could do to keep people from striking each other as they fought for space to squat, which is as much space as I found.

My only advantage under such conditions proved to be my face—that and a bit of luck. I happened to catch the eye of a clerk sitting behind a desk just inside the Consulate building. He'd apparently been assigned the duty of recording the names of Cambodian officials arriving on the scene, and the man recognized me. We met more than two years ago at a dinner party given by a friend of my father's shortly after my husband was reported missing. This clerk—a Frenchman maybe thirty years old, a bit short for my taste—was at my table and at one point tried to flirt with me, saying in soft French that I struck him as a ray of Eastern moonlight, with the sort of complicated beauty that he would feel privileged to learn to decipher. But I wasn't in the mood for flattery that night and sweetly told him that though I appreciated his interest, my mind was still very much on my husband, recently reported missing in the war but not yet to be presumed dead. The poor man returned to eat his quenelles with a face that made one think I had emptied the pepper shaker right over his plate.

I had not run into him since that evening as far as I can remember—of course my relations with the French generally diminished after my father's death and especially after you arrived in Phnom Penh. But yesterday he recognized me when I kept looking at him, and once we had exchanged smiles, he signaled me to make my way through the crowd and to put my suitcase among those beside his desk, as though I were the wife of some high official or foreign diplomat deserving such special treatment. I don't know what he wrote in his ledger—there was no chance even to exchange pleasantries—but with another gesture he motioned to me to push beyond him into a small office that already had three Cambodian women in it, all much older than I. And that is where I spent the night, mostly listening to one of them, who somehow got separated from her husband, weep inconsolably about her fate and the fate of her country.

She is right to weep. None of us can say this morning what is going to happen to us. I don't know how long I will be allowed to stay here or what this young clerk who was so kind to me yesterday will expect in return. The one thing we have been told is that our city is now dead.

April 19. One gets to see both the worst and the best of people under these conditions. We in our small office are lucky: we have been spared the fights and arguments that have begun in the crowded corridors outside our cell and apparently in the other buildings too. The problem is food, and it seems of special concern to the foreigners, though not all of them. Some—many of the French, for example—not only are eating well (they are the hosts, after all) but have enough left over for their pets. And the Russians, who arrived today, appear to have brought their own food and drink in large quantities but are unwilling to share what they have with anyone else. This means that the American correspondents and some of the other foreigners have to eat what the Cambodians eat, which is often of poorer quality than what the French pets get and much less in quantity than what the Russians are feeding themselves.

The food problem has created a series of international episodes, and things have been said that simply should not be said in a diplomatic environment. The tension seems to be especially high in the lines outside the toilets, which is where I gather most of the information I get. Those who complain to the French about their pets are called fascists, those who complain to the Russians about their self-sufficiency are called imperialists, those who complain to the Americans about their manners are called sons of bitches. The only true peace is in the toilet itself, where the language is entirely international.

I was visited yesterday afternoon by my clerk, who broke away from his duties long enough to bring me a bottle of French wine and some pastries to supplement my portion of rice. I tried to share these gifts with my Cambodian cellmates, but of course they wouldn't touch the wine and they were either too depressed or too insecure to try the other unexpected luxuries. The clerk was very sweet. He apologized for the spareness of our quarters—the four of us share an empty desk, a chair each, and enough floor space for two people to lie down—but he explained that our situation was better than most and in any case might improve as soon as the problem of asylum was negotiated with the Khmer Rouge. When I asked him what the problem was exactly, he answered that it was too early to define it with precision but that I should not worry. The way he said it was hardly reassuring, and he must have seen my reaction, because he touched my hand gently for a second. I thanked him for his kindness to me and the others. Then he disappeared before I had a chance to ask him the twenty other questions that kept me and my companions awake through most of the night. Mine was spent in a chair, and I woke up from one period of dozing to find the old woman sitting next to me, mother of some minor government official, cradling me under her arm as though I were her daughter. At one point I even let her stroke my face, which she seemed to find fascinating.

Some of the questions we had were answered by talk in the toilet line this morning. A few of the foreign correspondents who did not seek asylum immediately were able to follow the exodus from the city at least long enough to learn from Khmer Rouge officials that the evacuation will be total and that it will probably include other cities as well. Cities have been declared evil, the refuge of capitalist exploiters and imperialist spies. There is a grand plan, it seems, to settle everyone in the countryside, those who have never worked with their hands along with those who have, and to convert all intellectuals, businessmen, technicians, civil servants, everyone with any education into peasant farmers. The "Supreme Organization," the "Angkar," is now in command of the new life we are meant to live. The past and its imported devils are to be wiped away completely—not only the most recent of these, French and American imperialism, but Buddhism too. Can you believe it? The correspondents were told that time in Cambodia begins now. The Khmer Rouge have been storing food on the highways, but there is clearly not enough for the more than two million people who are being forced to take this trip to the countryside. Those who do not have the strength to walk the whole way, wherever the end may be, will be left by the roadside. Those who protest will be executed on the spot. And those who get separated from their families must abandon hope of reunion because families no longer exist. All of Cambodia is now one family, with the Angkar as its sexless father.

What we have seen today leads us to believe that it will be a thoroughly ruthless father, as those of us who found no reason to disbelieve the many refugee stories of past weeks have suspected all along. This morning a delegation of three high-ranking Khmer Rouge arrived at the gate of the Embassy, supposedly to negotiate the question of asylum. There was no negotiation. They simply demanded the exclusion of all traitors, meaning anyone who had served the previous government. When the old Vice Consul still in charge here objected that the people they had in mind had all asked for political asylum on what was after all diplomatic territory protected by international convention, the Khmer

Rouge told him coldly that the land he was standing on belonged to the Cambodian people, not France, and either the traitors were handed over to the people or the people's representatives would come in and take them without consideration for anyone in their way.

I wasn't allowed to witness the spectacle that followed, but I heard from other Cambodians who did that Prince Sirik Matak led the group of departing officials with great dignity—the President of the National Assembly, the Minister of Health, Prince Sihanouk's Laotian wife—thanked France for its hospitality, shook hands with the Vice Consul, and guided his companions toward the jeep that was waiting to take them to their execution. The Vice Consul stood there weeping, quietly telling his French colleagues over and over that he and they were no longer allowed to be men. Of course the Vice Consul had no choice. Does any one of us now?

I imagine even you and your American friends with your bloodbath theory did not anticipate this kind of mass dispossession and the ideological viciousness that seems to go with it. I wonder what the Americans will think when they come to see what is happening. Will they look with new eyes on their secret violation of my country's attempt at neutrality before Prince Sihanouk was deposed? That early intervention surely helped to feed and strengthen this young monster called the Khmer Rouge which is growing fat on Chinese provisions and the blood of its own people. Of course nobody in a way can see clearly enough to do much about these kinds of evil until it is too late, but isn't there some final justice in acknowledging one's mistakes? I wish you were here to debate the issue with me in your rational, unemotional style. I find myself slipping into the sort of irrational passion that encourages hatred. At this moment I could do with a bit of your infuriating objectivity.

April 20. Early this morning two Khmer Rouge officials arrived at the Embassy to extend their greetings to all Cambodians, local Chinese, and resident Vietnamese in the Embassy grounds. One of the officials made a polite speech welcoming these groups in the name of the Revolution, accepting all Cambodians and resident aliens as brothers and sisters, and since we are all part of the same family now, requesting that we leave the Embassy grounds immediately and join the rest of the Cambodian people in rebuilding the country. There was of course immediate panic among those who heard this message. None of the Cambodians I have managed to talk to has any more illusions about what is going on out there. And some of our worst fears were confirmed by a French schoolteacher and his wife who were brought in last evening by truck from north of the city. They reported that the roads were still crowded with evacuees, as far as ten kilometers outside the city in that direction. Many of the sick and the wounded have died and are simply left unburied, creating a terrible stench in places, and many of the old people have had to be abandoned where they collapsed.

The Khmer Rouge are apparently selective in their outright killing: only those in uniform, or those with long hair, or those who complain. This teacher saw several corpses in uniform that had been run over on the highway again and again by trucks so that they were flattened out like cardboard figures left there from a fallen advertisement. And they found a great shortage of food on the highways. When people ask the guards what they are to eat, they are told that the Angkar will feed them, and when they ask who the Angkar is exactly, the answer is "You. The people." One man, also a schoolteacher, tried to argue that this was absurd. The Khmer Rouge cut his throat right in front of his friends and left them his body to dispose of. So most people have to feed themselves by bartering what they have brought with them or gathering up what scraps they can find along the way. And if they are unlucky enough to stumble into a checkpoint, their jewelry and wristwatches are taken away for the Angkar. Then their money, because money doesn't exist any longer in Democratic Kampuchea; the Angkar has eliminated it. People who find a shelter of some kind to settle into for a while are perhaps in the greatest danger, because soon someone comes along to ask them to identify themselves and their profession, and if they admit to having been in the army or the city administration or if they show any connection to the old regime, they are separated out to be taken away nobody knows where. So most people continue to move as they can or find ways of hiding until the roads clear somewhat again.

After the Khmer Rouge welcome this morning, the Vice Consul evidently tried to keep people calm by explaining that the Khmer Rouge had not yet actually entered the Embassy grounds on any occasion and would surely allow the Embassy staff to handle as best it could this new demand that all Cambodians leave. He won his point for the moment, and as it turned out he gained some valuable time by negotiating strenuously with the Khmer Rouge officials.

My clerk brought the news of the latest developments to our office cell. He explained that the Khmer Rouge had set down certain absolute terms: Cambodian men married to French women would have to leave the compound, their wives joining them if they chose to. Cambodian

25

women married to French men would be allowed to stay. That was that. Since no one of the four of us was married to a Frenchman, we collected our things and filed out of our office to join the others outside the building who were preparing to leave, some seven or eight hundred people by that time. My clerk suddenly took my arm in the corridor and pulled me to one side. He told me that the Vice Consul was going to save as many Cambodian women as he could in what time he had left by issuing marriage certificates and passports. He said the situation outside the Embassy was likely to be especially difficult for anybody with a commercial Chinese background, because the Khmer Rouge apparently considered the local Chinese merchants the worst of the capitalist exploiters and were systematically destroying their shops and businesses. The clerk was looking me straight in the eyes, rather tenderly I thought, and despite the weakness from fear that I had begun to feel in my legs, I had a horrible impulse toward comedy. I almost told him, "Surely you cannot mean to propose marriage? I barely know you." He must have seen something in my face, because he said, still firmly holding my arm, "The marriages will of course be fictitious."

What could I say? I let him lead me into a room down the corridor where five or six Cambodian women were already in line, and within less than an hour each of us in there was married to a French name, in my case one Jacques Donnet, who may or may not be fictitious but is in any case not related to me or to my clerk, M. Henri Baudrot. And for what it is worth, I now have a false French passport.

The marriage came just in time. By ten o'clock this morning the column of those leaving the Embassy grounds had begun to move through the gate. As a "French citizen" I was allowed to watch from a window of the Consulate building. I cannot remember an hour of more difficult emotion: the relief from fear, at least for the moment, the feeling of undeserved luck, and to match this, the guilt of my staying behind as I watched my former cellmates go out through the gate, two of them leaning on each other as they wept freely, the third—the old woman who had played mother to me—trying to walk with her head high. And the courage of so many others that followed—for example the mountain troops of both men and women marching out smartly in formation as though invulnerable to history. And the few senior army officers left who must have realized fully that they were doomed but would not let it show, even joked among themselves. And some of the Cambodian men who decided at the last minute to leave their French wives behind to care for the children

26

embracing them too briefly, almost casually, as though trying to pretend they were just off for the weekend.

I don't know what to say about it now. Would you have gone out into that dead city if it was possible to avoid doing so? Was one supposed to survive where one could or join the long march into some unknown countryside and hope to survive that way? Whatever the right or wrong of it, my solution is temporary, since I obviously can't stay in this Embassy forever, even with a fictitious husband.

I now have a proper bed, in a room on the second floor. Yes, it is M. Baudrot's room, but he insists that the bed is solely mine, he will make do elsewhere. I am both too tired and too grateful for much thought as to whether or not I should believe him.

April 22. It has been quiet here since my compatriots left. There are some six hundred foreigners still in the compound, but they are mostly in the two other buildings, and I now run across them only when I go outside for a walk in the grounds (no need to share communal toilet facilities any longer; my new bathroom is luxurious in contrast with the old, and it is open only to a few of the French staff). The city around us is also quiet, except for occasional rifle fire, I suppose from some place where a lone resister has been discovered in hiding or some army officer has finally given himself up for execution. There must be very few such individualists left, because we gather that the water and electricity are cut off in any neighborhood that still shows a sign of life. Yesterday we could sometimes see a cone of smoke rising over the city here and there, today not even that. And the stragglers we could occasionally make out leaving for the countryside beyond Tuol Kauk to the west are not there today. We have had no further contact with the Khmer Rouge except for those who bring us our ration of food—they say it is generous compared with their own— and a few young soldiers escorting some French people who joined the evacuation in the beginning but who have now been brought back in trucks to share our asylum. It seems that we in the Embassy and the occupying forces "protecting" the city are now the only inhabitants of Phnom Penh, and as some have suggested, a few well-aimed rockets directed this way could complete the purification and dehumanization of this once beautifully corrupt heart of our princely republic.

I decided to put the insanity of politics behind me for a few hours yesterday and became domestic (I am, after all, a new, if somewhat soiled, bride). I began by cleaning up this room thoroughly, getting down on my knees and scrubbing the floor with a towel and bucket, dusting the easy chair and the desk—this too must be a converted office—shaking out the rug in the corridor. Then I took up the sheets, which smelled of over-work, and washed them in the bathroom, along with my dirty laundry and what little of M. Baudrot's I found in a bottom drawer of the desk. I spread the washed laundry all over the room, partly because I was too shy to go down and ask for a clothesline and partly to give the room some in-timacy for a while. By the time I gathered up my few things in the late afternoon, I had begun to feel more or less at home.

Of course one pressures oneself into these adjustments. The truth is that I'm still quite nervous about being here. Not that M. Baudrot has been anything but a model gentleman—rather irritatingly so. He came in yesterday evening to pick up some clothes, very effusive in his thanks for my domestic labors, and he brought me a bottle of wine for my dinner but didn't stay long enough to share it. I had a number of questions to ask him. I think he didn't want me to get the slightest sense that he might try to take advantage of my new circumstances. And I felt too awkward to tell him that there was certainly no need for him to run off so quickly, be-fore I had a chance to find out what he now thinks is going to happen to all of us "foreigners" here, married and otherwise. I expect I'll have to be a bit bolder tonight.

I know what you will think: as I was with you. It's very different really. I'm not at all in love with M. Baudrot. In fact, I'm not even at-tracted to him, except perhaps to that rather unexpected gentleness which comes into his face when the news he brings seems to be hopeless, a pre-lude to the very controlled pleasure he takes in offering a way around it. With you it was purely visceral. I had to break you down, crack through that surface of cold intelligence, that assured inaccessibility that you car-ried with you like a diplomatic privilege despite your very obvious attrac-tion to me. In the beginning what I most wanted was to get through to your core, find out if I could bring you out of yourself so completely that you would end up crying like a child after you'd exhausted yourself mak-ing love to me. And I more or less succeeded, didn't I? But what does that prove now?

April 23. I've been given a small radio. I accepted it because I thought it might be diverting, but so far all it has provided is military music and revolutionary songs on the hour, and a horrible long speech by

Khieu Samphan, one of the great leaders now in charge of our lives. I'm sure you've heard of him. He is actually an old politician of the left who went underground, a former professor of political economy who once served in Prince Sihanouk's cabinet and who has always been a cold, sexless fanatic. Especially after he was undressed in public many years ago by the royal police for having dared to offer his criticism of the Sihanouk regime before the People's Assembly, which was supposedly created for that purpose. (Can you imagine the humiliation and misanthropy that would bloom in a man as puritan as this standing in public with his bare bottom and his thing hanging there for everyone to see?) Now he speaks to us about the goals of his revolution in the same language that the guards outside our gate use, as though they had all been made to memorize a new catechism that will magically bring about happiness, equality, justice, and democracy in a country without rich or poor, without exploiters or exploited, where the young are the heroes and where the people enjoy independence, sovereignty, identity, integrity, neutrality, harmony, purity, I don't know what else, under a culture opposed to corruption, reaction, and oppression, especially by the colonialist and imperialist enemy which is still America and its fascist Lon Nol clique, whose culture gave us men wearing their hair to their shoulders like women and who sometimes actually became women in the flesh. Whereas in Democratic Kampuchea there will be no gambling, prostitution, adultery, sexual intercourse outside marriage, or other evil habits of any kind, in particular those stimulated by cities and their corrupt merchants, because those who will now reign like the princes of old will be the peasants and laborers, living not in palaces or even houses but in undefined communities beside their ever-multiplying rice fields and factories.

It seems that one way this new revolutionary program will be achieved is by a process of overnight selection that may soon leave only those without a name or a past still alive. This morning the Consulate admitted a return refugee from the caravan of local citizens who were liberated out of the Embassy and into the empty streets three days ago. This is a woman who was among the two or three foreign wives who decided rather heroically but also recklessly to go out into the unknown with their Cambodian husbands. One night of the new Democratic Kampuchea and both she and her husband reached the conclusion that she should make her way back here on her foreign passport and whatever cunning or bribery might be required to get her safely under French protection again.

From what the woman reported, those poor Cambodians forced out of the Embassy were herded into the Lambert Stadium just north of here and were immediately put through a simple preliminary interrogation that consisted of identifying themselves and writing their names on one of three lists: military personnel, civil servants, people. This woman's husband was a minor civil servant, but he had the presence of mind to sign the list under "people." Those on the first list, junior as well as senior officers, were taken away that night in trucks. The rest slept among the rats on the edges of the stadium, where the military had once set up huts for their families. The next day the Khmer Rouge arrived to read off names from a new list they had prepared overnight, and those on this list—civil servants and who knows what other categories—were also driven off in trucks, one assumes never to be seen again. The remainder were told to go north on foot to join their compatriots in rebuilding the country. Anybody who asked "Where in the north?" was in danger of ending up on a truck going south. Occasionally one of the Khmer Rouge would actually smile and suggest that those on the "people" list head for their home villages as quickly as they could, as long as they could get there without turning south through Phnom Penh, because Phnom Penh was no longer on the map of Democratic Kampuchea for people who belonged to the people. So the caravan, somewhat diminished and quite disorderly by now, moved north through the deserted countryside until it arrived at the rear of the earlier exodus from the city somewhere beyond the ten-kilometer mark, and that is where the woman and her husband separated, with a pledge to find each other again across the border in Thailand. She may be lucky enough for that. It is hard now to believe that he will be too.

April 25. The calm that has come into my life since I moved into my new quarters has begun to prove more unnerving than the restlessness of my first days here when I was sharing the office downstairs with my properly hysterical compatriots. It is not just a matter of being alone day and night. I've known that often before, and with a special flavor of anxiety after my husband was reported missing. Here there is a dissociation that presses in from beyond one's private psyche. It's as though one had suddenly become a foreigner in one's home country, a visitor in the house where one grew up. Only that isn't exactly right, because the objects around me here do not rouse even a sensation of remembered familiarity, and the country outside has come to see the foreign intrusion. Not that the Khmer Rouge have yet actually set foot inside the Embassy grounds. It's the idea of them, their inescapable presence beyond the walls. We are in a sanctuary that has taken on the aura of a prison surrounded by unseen guards, and the silence of these recent days, with only the occasional exchange of greetings in the corridors and little reliable news of the world outside, seems to have shaped us into a community of unconnected, if crowded, cells, of which mine is the most isolated and solitary.

I suppose I may have these feelings more strongly than many of the others here because I am not waiting, however long and uncomfortably, to be repatriated to my homeland. My homeland is still out there where the Khmer Rouge are, whether I like it or not. Or else I have to carry it with me. I can't simply fly home in a helicopter. And what I can't carry with me under any circumstances worries me more and more: my sister and her family in Battambang and my cousins on my mother's side in the northern provinces. My sister is especially on my mind now. I don't want to believe the rumors about what is likely to happen in other cities, but the evacuation of Phnom Penh has been so cruel and thorough that one has to be prepared to believe anything.

Maybe it is our isolation here and my uncertainty about what lies in wait outside the Embassy compound that has worked to undermine my normal self-control, anyway, that has begun to make me unexpectedly vulnerable in my relationship with my—what shall I now call him?—my sweet benefactor. He came to me again yesterday, in the evening, bringing wine and French delicacies—pigeon terrine, goose-liver pâté, triple-crème goat cheese; where he got these only he knows—and this time he stayed. Through part of the night. I cannot tell you how marvelously delicious the meal was, beyond any reality. It has been barely three weeks since you and I last feasted ourselves in our usual uninhibited way, so I cannot say that the special delight of what he brought me last evening was the result of long abstinence. But it may have been partly the reverse of that: knowing that such luxury is doomed and that the great desert lies ahead. Every mouthful seemed to carry a titillation of finality. Of course such definition may all be afterthought. I can't really speak for anything but the intensity of what I felt at the moment, a pleasure that had to be savored in all its corners and no mind for hidden causes. And I know the effect was to put me off my guard, open me to possibilities that in the warm sadness afterward also seemed to lie outside thought or defense.

Henri may have sensed my mood, but he didn't take advantage of it until I gave clear signals. We talked for two, three hours over the Armagnac, talked about what was happening to my country—which he, incidentally, has come to love much as you have and which he knows better than you do—and we talked about France. Henri is convinced that the Khmer Rouge will allow all foreigners to leave the Embassy in due course, though he has no idea just when. He feels that this new regime, like all other new regimes, will want at least some degree of international legitimacy beyond recognition by the Chinese, and if it holds the refugees here as hostages or harms them in any way, it is not likely to get what it is looking for. The fact that the Khmer Rouge have not come into the Embassy grounds uninvited is a good indication, he thinks, though he has no illusions about the ruthlessness of these people.

He actually went out into the empty city day before yesterday with an interpreter to help bring back a group of French people who had turned up some ten kilometers north of the city. He found the suburbs now completely deserted except for scavenging dogs and pigs and a few Khmer Rouge soldiers hunting down anyone still hiding among the litter that fills the side streets. His rescue truck came across a few stragglers evacuating their homes around Kilometer 9 and then suddenly a sea of people spread across the rice fields beyond, hundreds of thousands, the roads clogged except where army trucks forced a lane open, the war-ruined villages covered with people camping under any shelter they could find, the mass of them stretching as far ahead as you could see, as though the whole city had come out at once to gather in the northern market-place for a grim sale that offered no product but themselves. Henri said he could see terror in the eyes of some of those he thought he recognized but who could not respond to any gesture he made because of the guards accompanying him. But he saw no dead bodies. There was no room for bodies to lie on the ground in that section of the highway. The evidence for the killing of former officers and civil servants and teachers came from the French he rescued, each of whom had his own account of some murder seen or heard.

That brief trip outside the city had clearly shaken Henri. His description of what he'd seen was broken at times, and he couldn't bring himself to tell me the stories he'd heard from the French he'd brought back. I also found him too sober when we came to my personal situation, no sense of humor about it any longer, as though he now realized that the charade of my French citizenship had its special dangers if I were caught. At the same time he tried very hard to persuade me that I had no choice but to go out of the country on my new passport when he and the other foreigners were finally released. It was very touching. He insisted on sitting in a chair behind the desk with his brandy snifter square in front of him as though this postdinner conversation were really an official consular exchange about my future, but his hand kept twisting the stem of the glass nervously, and for all his effort to seem impersonal and objective as he argued the case for my leaving with him, his gentle face kept giving him away.

I finally got up from the bed, where I'd been curled around my Armagnac like an indifferent cat, and came around the desk to kneel beside him. I told him that I simply couldn't go with him and the others. It was impossible for me to think of leaving my homeland and the few relatives I have left and wandering from one foreign country to another with a passport that didn't belong to me and no money, dependent on the generosity of strangers, however grateful I was to him personally for the kindness he'd shown and however much the prospect of staying behind frightened me. I was at least half smiling as I said all this, trying not to spoil the honest warmth I felt by the wrong kind of sentiment, the wrong language. But when I'd finished he looked down at me with such sadness that I couldn't resist touching his face. And when he took my hand to turn it so that my fingers crossed his lips, we both knew that one phase of our charade was over.

If I say that he was a quiet lover I hope you won't use that for getting even with me by indulging yourself in some private irony. He gave me what I needed at that moment, that's all I'm willing to say. And if I cried to myself after he was gone, it wasn't any reflection on him but on me for still wanting you, for still wanting the kind of life I'm going to lose, for not having had the courage to survive entirely on my own resources. I can't explain it. And I don't care if I can't. He held me for a while, flesh against flesh, our bodies alive, our breath hot. The rest doesn't matter.

April 26. Just imagine: there were three days of festivities in Phnom Penh to honor the opening of the People's Representative Assembly and we in the Embassy here didn't even know about it. According to the radio the celebration began on April 21 and ended when the Assembly opened on the 24th. I suppose one reason we didn't know about it was the difficulty the new regime had in creating a festive atmosphere and the right kind of noise without any inhabitants to help them and with only hungry dogs and pigs to watch the parades. One of the French officials here did notice a streamer hailing the glorious victory of April 17 and the even more glorious revolution that followed, but one streamer drifting by does not make a holiday. And a few unelected guerrillas sitting in a room do not make a people's assembly. Though of course in time cavils such as these will belong to the forgotten history of reactionary revisionism.

At Henri's insistence I went downstairs this morning to speak to one of the French consular officials about my future. I knew that Henri's intention was to have the official persuade me to go out of the country with him and the others, and though I was quite prepared to resist such persuasion, I felt the least I owed my benefactor was the gesture of hearing whatever arguments he had arranged for me to hear.

It turned out that the official—a rotund, thickly spectacled, rather pompous little man—wasn't as ardent about my prospects officially as Henri had been informally. He said he assumed there would be no difficulty about my falling in with the foreigners when the expatriation was finally arranged, since my "French" identity had already been established, and he also assumed that I would want to take advantage of this escape route which the Vice Consul had been good enough to provide me, since any other course was logically unacceptable, especially in view of my mixed background (by which he presumably meant my once-wealthy Chinese father, apparently still to be counted among the most despised of the Khmer Rouge enemies though dead these many months). At the same time, the official said, he could not offer me any assurance regarding what might happen once the evacuees from the Embassy arrived in Thailand or wherever their initial destination might be. In fact, he felt he had to make clear that the French government could take no further responsibility for my circumstances once I was out of Cambodia since I was not in reality a French national and would henceforth have to be regarded as a displaced person. Henri broke in at this point to suggest that the issue of nationality might be resolved by my asking for political asylum in France. The consular official turned to stare at him as though he had violated some kind of sacred trust by merely raising the question. "That is another matter entirely," the official said. "Quite beyond my personal competence or interest."

I decided to be equally cool in response. I thanked the gentleman and his French colleagues for the generosity they had shown me by taking me in and treating me so well despite my mixed background and my apparently dubious nationality, but I told him I felt I had to make two things clear: first, that I did not consider myself to be a displaced person but a free Cambodian citizen who had been robbed of her native country, and more immediately, of her native city, by a group of murderous fanatics under the influence of an alien ideology and supported by foreign arms, and second, though I was personally fond of France and indebted to her for much of my education, I did not have the remotest intention of settling there while I could still see any chance at all of helping to save my homeland from yet another tyrannical regime under foreign influence after such a miserably long history of foreign domination, not least of all our recent hundred years under the so-called French protectorate. And with that I smiled sweetly, dipped my head humbly, and left the room.

Henri followed me upstairs full of embarrassment, apologies, hopelessness. I drew him inside my—his—room and calmed him with a wet kiss, then sent him back to his desk (he was on duty, so there was no time for further romance). I was strangely elated by what I'd done downstairs, as though some problem of conscience that had been burdening me had suddenly been released. The feeling lasted for about an hour. I spent the remainder of the afternoon brooding over my encounter with the French official. I even began to wonder if that little puffed-up man didn't have a point. What was I if not a displaced person? I may have taken a certain naughty pleasure in becoming eloquent about my free Cambodian citizenship before a French audience, but it was another matter to examine the cold reality beyond that sort of rhetoric. Was there a country out there that I could still belong to? If there wasn't, didn't it become dangerously sentimental to think I should stay behind? On the other hand, how else could I find out what of mine was still there—my sister and her children most of all, and whether there was still some way to help them?

These thoughts were too private and unsettling for me to share with anyone (that is, anyone but you in this unanswerable form). I went to bed early, and though sleep didn't come for some hours, I pretended to be dead out when Henri finally knocked on the door.

April 27. There is a true holiday mood in the Embassy this evening, at least for all those who know exactly where their country is. A group of Khmer Rouge emissaries arrived this morning to settle the repatriation issue. All foreigners, some several thousand of them, are to be driven by truck to the Thai border via Battambang and Sisophon. The first convoy is scheduled to set out in three days. I gather from Henri that the negotiations were rather awkward at moments, especially when the Vice Consul tried to insist that both the French nationals and the other aliens be transported by French planes. It seems this touched a sensitive spot in the Khmer Rouge official who is in charge of foreigners. "We have our own means of transportation," he said, his eyes slits. "We do not need your French planes. We do not need anything from anybody. All foreigners are in violation of the Angkar's proclamation of March last which ordered them to leave Cambodia or suffer the consequences. You are of course still free to suffer the consequences. If we now choose to let you go it is an act of perhaps stupid diplomacy on our part, and I warn you that you question it at your peril." The Vice Consul accepted the offer of trucks.

Since this meeting was among the few contacts that French officials here have had with the Khmer Rouge authorities, much speculation resulted from the encounter. According to Henri, some of his colleagues thought that the idea of using French planes was so distasteful not because the planes were French but because they would give the departing foreigners a clear aerial view of what is happening in Democratic Kampuchea. Others suggested that this did not make sense because the view of Democratic Kampuchea from trucks across an expanse of more than four hundred kilometers would be much more detailed and precise than any aerial view. Besides, everyone here assumes that the Americans are sending over their spy planes as usual to gather whatever information can be gathered from the sky. Henri thinks the arrangement is simply a matter of Khmer Rouge pride, further evidence of their fanaticism. They obviously do not care to hide anything because they fully believe in what they are doing, and it now seems they do not care what foreigners think or don't think or what they can or can't provide—with the exception, of course, of their Chinese patrons. All help that doesn't come directly from China is to be rejected, it appears, including a French plane full of medical supplies that is reported to be still on a runway in Bangkok, after almost two weeks of waiting to be cleared for a landing here, this originally offered in exchange for French nationals housed in the Embassy. The French nationals will now be released as an act of Khmer Rouge generosity, and the medicine meant to serve the sick and dying of the old Cambodia protectorate will apparently go back home with the dispossessed protectors.

I have decided not to go with them. At least not across the border. It is obvious that staying behind in Phnom Penh would be some kind of suicide now that the city has been turned into a graveyard patrolled by vicious children. I don't have a definite plan yet, but my thought is to go with the convoy as far as Battambang and to search out my sister there. I'm sure that she can make room for me; she has a whole house. We haven't been as close in recent years as we once were, not since I went off to France to become the family bohemian and she moved north with her husband to take over the Battambang piece of my father's business and make up for the children I failed to provide (she has three). I don't know whether it was my self-consciousness about being educated and "different" or her bourgeois view of the world that made for the tension, but the few times all of us got together for a family reunion in Phnom Penh, I ended up feeling a failure for not settling down to breed children and promote the family business for its benefit as well as mine.

But much has happened since those days. My sister and I are both widows of the war now, the only family either of us has left in our generation, so we'll have to learn to get along again. And if they make us move out of Battambang, I suppose we can try to settle among other refugees in some new community of the anonymous that those of us in Cambodia who have lost a city and a past will have to create now. Even that isn't the last hope. Should it turn out that there is no such community or no chance of building one, I will simply have to take my sister and her children across the border into Thailand and wait there for a more favorable turn in our history. Given what we've known so far, such a turn is bound to come eventually, and at this point it is hard to conceive of its being for the worse. I don't imagine that it will be difficult to get from Battambang to the border west of the city, where there are mountain forests for cover. It is less than a hundred kilometers.

I'm not going to tell Henri about my decision. I don't feel that I know him well enough to trust him to accept what I have in mind, any more than he knows me well enough to understand my reasons for staying on this side of the border. I'm afraid he'll find a way of trapping me in the convoy so that I can't get away when I have to. He knows even less about my Khmer side than you do. I haven't mentioned my family to him at all since that one remark about my missing husband which spoiled his quenelles two years ago, and I can hardly get him involved in the problem of my sister at this late date, especially after having allowed myself to be led by him in another direction.

Besides, she may be the most important reason but not the only one that is difficult to explain. I'm not sure how I can explain this other reason to you—or perhaps even to myself. It has something to do with being a witness. I can't imagine myself taking part in the new Cambodia beyond what is required for me and my sister to survive, but I may find that I can at least record what is going on in my own words, and I feel there could be value in this record, if only that which makes it possible for me to keep myself from becoming totally displaced. If this seems too self-conscious to you, I could say that there may be a certain fatalism in what I'm doing, a sense that I've been put where I am by events beyond my control and that I'm meant to confront this moment for purposes that may be unclear to me yet, as to so many others who have been identified by their fate as threatened refugees in this cruel century—surely the cruelest of all for the evil man has done by killing or displacing his brothers in the name of some ideology. So let us say that like you, I find I simply have no choice but to do what I am doing.

April 29. Yesterday—the last of my days in the Embassy that I'll be able to record at leisure—was among the oddest of my long visit here. It started out feeling the freest of all, as might be expected when one has been released by a decision that seems both inevitable and right. My early-morning euphoria was very evident to Henri, who responded to it by becoming more openly playful and flirtatious than I've seen him, and this despite a rather exhausting night together (before carrying up our breakfast he grasped the excuse of some quite innocent irony on my part to chase me around the room and then hold me prisoner on the bed, pinned there with surprising violence until I was willing to buy my freedom by suckling his nipples in turn), but of course he completely misread the causes of my mood. During breakfast he told me that he would make sure I went out with the first convoy, the one that is supposed to leave tomorrow, and though he wasn't certain when he and the other French officials might follow, I was simply to wait for him at the first camp set up to accommodate us on the other side of the border, and whenever he arrived he would take charge of me for the rest of the trip home.

The absolute confidence with which he pictured our reunion and what would follow assured me that he had no idea at all of what was really in my head. And for much of the rest of the morning he was irritatingly domestic, helping me gather up all my things for a final wash, hovering around the bathroom while I was in there working, then reorganizing our room so that I could hang things up out of the way at one end on the length of clothesline he provided, all of which made me feel that he had actually begun to see our presumed reunion beyond the border as the first stage of a trial marriage. I finally told him that he was making me nervous hovering around like that and sent him downstairs. Then I began to feel guilty. He was probably just trying to be helpful, solicitous, and the domestic aversion he had generated in me was no doubt my own creation to compensate for secretly planning to betray him.

This thought killed my euphoria. And it led to an afternoon of self-absorbed reflection. I lay on my bed gazing at the laundry spread on three levels across the opposite end of the room, thinking not about where and when I might next have a chance to display my clean things like that but about why my life seemed to depend so often on a delicate balance between loyalty and disloyalty, why my obsession with holding on to what I believed in was constantly threatened by a passion for adventure in unknown and sometimes dangerous places. You were such an adventure. And just when you had become among those things I believed in and needed to hold on to, another adventure came along to undermine my commitment to you and your American view of the world.

I never told you about that episode, of course—which was also disloyal of me. Anyway, it was too brief to prove really dangerous. And I suppose there is nothing lost in telling you now, since it was among my preoccupations yesterday afternoon and must therefore still gnaw at my conscience in some way. Do you remember the trip you took with your Ambassador to survey the Mekong north of here and the situation around Kompong Cham? I had a visitor during that time. A young soldier who belonged to a government battalion originally stationed in Siem Reap but deployed to this area when the Khmer Rouge began their January offensive. He had deserted when his unit was overrun south of here, and he drifted into the city with other army refugees looking for a place to scratch out survival until the war was over. He came to me after tracking down one of my husband's cousins who was a minor official in the city administration. The soldier said he'd had some documents to give this cousin, some letters and a picture that he'd been carrying around for months, ever since one of his former officers failed to return from a patrol up north and the foxholes they were in had to be abandoned. I think the soldier hoped to sell his documents to my husband's cousin, but when the cousin saw what they were, he simply sent the soldier to me.

He was a boy, really, no more than eighteen, absolutely filthy, very uncommunicative, what you would call spaced out by the war. He stood there in my apartment holding his envelope of trophies, unable to speak more than a few words. I think I frightened him out of any cunning he may have had left. Anyway, I had to go over and take the envelope out of his hand, and what I discovered in it was letters from me to my husband and a photograph I'd sent him from my bikini days. I tried to interrogate the boy about the circumstances of his finding the envelope and what it might tell me about my missing husband, but he wasn't any help: the officer had disappeared on patrol and the soldier had found the envelope among the things he'd left behind. My being the lady in the photograph clearly unnerved him, ruined the whole sale for him, destroyed all his expectations, especially when he saw how much it upset me to leaf through those letters. A rush of words finally came out of him. He begged me to keep the envelope—all he wanted was to deliver it to me safely, unless I might have a few cigarettes to give him for his fellow deserters from the battalion, and even that didn't matter since the missing officer was my husband. I finally ended up smiling at him through my tears because he looked so desperately pathetic. And so hungry. I told him I'd be happy to get him something to eat in a moment, but before we got to that, I suggested he take a bath. The poor boy just stood there thoroughly miserable. So I finally went over and started undressing him, unbuttoning his torn shirt, trying to get him to help me. He wouldn't move. And I could feel him tremble every time my hands brushed against him. Who knows how long it had been since a woman had touched him, even through his clothes? I had to undress him completely, then take him by the hand into the bathroom and give him a bath.

He stayed with me the three days you were gone. I was both mother and lover to him, but more than this, I used his body to try and find my husband again. That was the way I betrayed you most. And when that vicarious pleasure failed to work anymore and I finally sent him away with enough money to keep him going for a month or two, I was left with the same old quiet absence, only now there was something new to go with it: I recognized that I could no longer trust my feeling for you to take the place of what I'd lost. At least not in the long run. And as things have turned out, the gods were on my side in teaching me that.

I've put off my packing until now, really the last minute. Even without a firm sense of my purpose in keeping this diary, it seems to have become what I take up first, sometimes to the exclusion of all else. Don't let that go to your head. Though you are my first audience, the living image I address my voice to, I now think that I would keep on writing even if that image were to vanish. I don't want it to, I'll give you that. But it will not be easy for me to write regularly from now on. I suppose I will find a way as long as it remains essential. And that is what it seems to have become—maybe the one presence in my life beyond any possibility of betrayal.

April 30. I'm in the prefecture at Kompong Chnang. We had a good dinner of rice and fish about an hour ago, and since we're scheduled to leave at dawn, most people have already gone to sleep. I'm writing this under my pocket flashlight, so I can't be sure it will be entirely legible, but to worry about that seems rather precious in these circumstances.

This morning about twenty-five trucks arrived at the Embassy, some of them American GMCs captured from our army and the others Chinese Molotovas. More than five hundred of us crowded into the trucks. I can't say that it was even reasonably comfortable, but once we left the Embassy grounds, everything assumed a new relativity, so that in the end we had to see ourselves among the fortunate. We didn't head north as we expected to but west along Highway 4. We went through the empty suburbs, patches here and there wiped away by fire, and past the airport, where we could see the few planes left behind, skeletons burned clean. It was raining hard. At the edge of the city we came across a new cemetery, but only for cars, every kind of car you could think of, abandoned at all angles along the borders of the highway, some on their sides with bent doors open like broken wings, others overturned with their wheels in the air, most stripped of their tires, I suppose to make Ho Chi Minh sandals for the army of liberation. Every large settlement we entered today had its cemetery of cars. It seems the rotting dead have now been gathered up from the roadsides along our route and disposed of elsewhere, but the cars are to stay indefinitely where they were abandoned, chaotic markers of the capitalist evil that has been expunged from the new Kampuchean paradise along with capitalists, intellectuals, and those classless peasants trapped on the wrong side of our capricious history.

We saw something of the new paradise after passing through Thnal Totung, where there was nothing left but a few ruined walls and cement staircases leading to the open sky, the sugar palms beheaded and stripped by our bombardments or burned to spikes by napalm, nothing alive to be seen, the landscape barren, all creatures now dead or gone off as they could elsewhere. We turned suddenly northward then, by design it seems, because that brought us through territory "liberated" by the Khmer Rouge several years ago, and there has been time for the villagers to learn to smile again. That was very refreshing. But the landscape they lived in was alien, the houses not on stilts as you would expect but built on the ground the way the Chinese and Vietnamese do, and the fields cultivated with yams, the Viet Cong crop that grows fast and travels well: guerrilla food. At one point we saw an army of the young, hundreds and hundreds of them, working on dikes, and later some Buddhist monks rebuilding a bridge. Eventually we stopped for a meal, beside a pagoda, and some villagers working nearby were allowed to come up and stare at us, we the curiosity now, especially awesome to them when they found out we had live Americans and Russians among us.

I had to act as interpreter for the group in my truck. Only a few of the villagers—smiling men—actually spoke: those in charge, it seemed. They talked easily about the war, the horror of the B-52 bombers and the government bombardments but especially the T-28s with the stubby wings, flying in just aboveground so that they couldn't be seen. They said one could occasionally hear the B-52s coming over, certainly the bombs they dropped, so there was usually a chance to hide, and anyway the bombers spent much of their time bombing the forests aimlessly. But the T-28s were too fast and unseen; anyone who heard them was already dead. They smiled at that. Now they were happy, they said. Now the war was over and they could live like normal people. And they said it in a way that made you actually want to believe them.

We drove north again in heavy rain, the heat steaming the water over the countryside, the sky black. They took us through Amleang, I imagine to show us that the Khmer Rouge command post which had been there for years still stood untouched for all the bomb craters scattered in the neighborhood, proof that their new gods had diverted the Americans from the most important target in the bombing. Beyond was forestland, kilometer after kilometer, the green of it heightened by the rain but finally oppressive in its abundance because it was so uninhabited, so silent, no sign of people or animals or even reptiles, as though it were too early in the Creation for living things. And then we suddenly found the living, thousands of them with their oxcarts on the road ahead, moving slowly toward us, refugees from somewhere in the region going God knows where else, pans and bits of clothing and a few old people or children piled in the carts like rubbish, skeletons really, the rest walking almost without visible motion, their faces—some of them—burned to dark leather by the sun, the eyes sometimes vacant or bewildered or openly terrified but never curious and most often afraid to look in our direction as we passed between them. That seemed to take hours. And all you heard in our truck was versions of "Mon Dieu" and "My God"—no talk, nothing to mute the despair of it.

We didn't reach Kompong Chnang until well after dark because there was a long stop at Romeas to visit—like tourists—the great cemetery of revolutionary soldiers buried there. It was impressive; those in charge of us made their point about how many had died fighting on the Khmer Rouge side for the liberation of the New Kampuchea. But it didn't work to quiet the image of those oxcarts, any more than the special meal provided our convoy by the Angkar could fill the desolation of Kompong Chnang when we finally settled here for the night. I remember this place as a small town on the river with a pottery works that I visited with my father the year before he sent me off to France. It became a city because of the refugees who swarmed in from the liberated zones late in the war. Now it's a desert as empty as Phnom Penh. Are there no cities left? Will those who lived in them have to keep crossing back and forth between one desert and another until there are no refugees either? I don't want to think anymore about what I may find in Battambang tomorrow. I have to sleep.

May 1. I must have a secret source of luck—maybe those ancient Khmer spirits that have guaranteed long life to my mother's side of the family for generations (though they didn't quite manage to keep her from dying ahead of her time). We left Kompong Chnang on schedule at dawn—a clearer day, actually bright at moments—and since the road took us through the same empty spaces between one deserted town and another, we traveled at a good speed. I began to worry about how soon we might reach the outskirts of Battambang. I still hadn't figured out how I was going to escape from my truck without getting myself shot, or at the least without having to leave my suitcase behind. It was tricky. One couldn't help feeling exposed in the truck, watched all the time by somebody, either those in charge of us or people one had never seen before who might prove to be enemies. So there seemed little chance of my finding someone I could take into my confidence if that became essential.

I tried to smile at the paradox of my situation: the sense of danger one is made to feel even before attempting to escape from the best opportunity for survival. Yet I was sure the danger was real. To be caught trying to leave the convoy would bring my identity immediately into question. If I admitted who I really was, how could I explain my false passport and my days in the Embassy without becoming totally suspect? And if I succeeded in passing for a Frenchman's wife, what was I doing running away from the other foreigners and the road home? My best hope was to slip away unnoticed at some point after we entered the city and make my way to my sister's house like any other refugee from Phnom Penh. That wouldn't be too difficult once I was clear of the convoy; I knew the city fairly well after having lived there with my sister for a month—a rather unhappy month—shortly after her husband was killed early in the war, so I was sure I could find her place again from any major intersection. But clearing the convoy with my suitcase seemed an almost impossible obstacle. At least my imagination didn't come up with a secure plan this morning, and I began to wish Henri would suddenly arrive on the scene with his gentle expression of hopelessness and the possible solution he would have hiding behind it.

I suppose if you are born lucky there is always an Henri. In any case,

43

my solution arrived at noon when we reached Pursat and apparently entered a new military region. Without warning we were ordered by our
young drivers to disembark from the American and Chinese trucks that
had carried us for two days and to board a line of buses that would be
driven by their replacements, soldiers who looked generally older and
more relaxed and who were under the authority of the Battambang committee chairman. Our new leaders handed out food liberally and told us
before boarding that we could help ourselves to any fruit that appealed to
us in the neighboring orchards because the trees were now the property
of the people, which in the Battambang region appears to include even
foreigners. The people who once owned the orchards were of course nowhere to be seen. House on house along the road stood empty, abandoned
by those who had been ordered somewhere else to gather what fruit they
could in the wilderness while they waited for the Angkar to bring forth
the new Eden.

I was quick to see this change of the guard as an opportunity. I still
had no specific plan, but it struck me as a chance to move closer to the
rear of the convoy, where it might be easier for me to slip away. And it
also struck me as a chance to find a seat beside somebody I felt I could
trust. So I joined the others to pick some oranges from nearby trees,
working my way down the road. Don't be unnecessarily flattered if I
admit that I was looking for an American. My thinking was mostly objective: an American would be the least likely of my fellow aliens to create
difficulties for me if I asked for help because he himself would feel among
the more threatened. Also, given our particular nationalities, he might be
among the more generous. In any case, the one I ended up pursuing
turned out to be a Canadian. Very blond, with a thick reddish mustache,
big eyes, beautiful teeth. I spotted him under a mango tree as I was edg-
ing my way toward the last of the buses. I developed a sudden craving for
mangoes. So I put my suitcase down by the side of the road, took out a
new kerchief, went over to his tree to see if he might share some of the
fruit he was picking.

We became friends quickly after settling in a seat near the back of
the last bus—there was no time for normal reticence—and by the end of
the afternoon, we were co-conspirators. He turned out to be a journalist-
photographer representing several Canadian and one provincial British
newspaper—I don't remember which—and I think what started out as his
merely flirtatious interest in me, no doubt livened by my audaciousness,
became more serious when I told him I was planning to leave the convoy
as soon as I could work out a safe way of doing so. I had to make up a bit

of biography to explain myself. I told him that besides being a Cambodian war widow who had worked for the Americans and who was now posing as a French housewife, I had some years ago been a stringer for several French newspapers and considered journalism my first profession, which was why I felt both a special opportunity and an obligation to record what was happening to my country as long as I was healthy enough to keep a record, and I planned to stay healthy first of all by tracking down my sister in Battambang and then, with her help, by making my way to a village near the border on the Battambang–Pailin road so that we could cross into Thailand quickly if that became a necessary route to survival.

I think Nicholas (that's what I'll call him: the closer I come to going out on my own, the less secure I feel about putting real names in this diary)—I think Nicholas actually played for a while with the idea of coming along with me, my white lie maybe stirring a jealous reporter in him, whatever else I may have stirred. But the more we talked about the problems I might run into getting clear of the convoy and merging with what were after all my people speaking my language, the less sense that idea must have made to him. And of course I wouldn't have permitted it, blond beauty though he is—for both his sake and mine. Still, I found his boyish enthusiasm for my plan rather touching. And of course useful: he's now in charge of my suitcase.

The first scheme we worked out was to make ourselves a couple when we reached Battambang, where we assumed we would spend the night in some sort of official quarters. Then, at the right moment, maybe during the dawn washing, we would simply take a lovers' stroll into the open air with the suitcase between us, and I would disappear down the first safe street we came to. It was a scheme that obviously appealed to Nicholas because it meant our spending the night together in some kind of intimacy, but the Khmer Rouge spoiled even that touch of romance. Our convoy stopped short of the city center, in the outskirts by Battambang's graveyard of cars, and our shelter for the night has become our bus. Nicholas is now sound asleep beside me. I haven't been able to sleep at all. We held hands like adolescents for hour on hour, until he finally dozed off and I eased myself free to write in my notebook, hoping that would tire me. It hasn't. Now I'll stay awake until dawn.

Our new scheme is to go our separate ways at the morning washing—we'll surely be allowed one trip into the fields—and I will simply remain behind whenever they let the women go for their bit of privacy. Nicholas is to take care of my suitcase: he will leave it hidden behind one of the abandoned cars by the roadside where I can pick it up when the convoy has gone on its way. That seems to matter less to me now. I feel so near the edge of a beginning, the presence of some new confusion of good and evil, that it almost seems right for me to go into Battambang to find my sister and her unfamiliar children without any of my recent past to burden me.

May 7. It has taken nearly a week for me to come back to my notebook. I am in Treng, on the Pailin road, with my new family, waiting to be given a piece of forestland to clear and cultivate. There are thousands of us between here and Boeung Trasal waiting for the same thing, so I expect to have time on my hands for a few days. I spent yesterday resting from the trip here. Today I'm less exhausted but also less preoccupied, and images from Battambang and the long walk here crowd my mind uncomfortably. Battambang first of all. It was empty. More than Phnom Penh even, it seemed a ghost town, because I discovered only a few familiar landmarks to locate my memory of what had been. It had the feel of a great vacant set for an abandoned film, without actors, now partly dismantled, much of the expected landscape taken away. On the road going in I did come across some carts, the people with them death walkers mostly, too tired or terrified to do more than glance at me. So getting to my sister's place proved even simpler than I'd anticipated—too simple. There was no one at home. The house was open and all the furniture in place—the heavy overstuffed easy chairs and sofa, the grand buffet and dining table, everything I used to detest because of its pretentious bourgeois provinciality; worse, its domestic complacency, which I had come to see during my irrational month there as a silent accusation. Now it seemed funereal, and it touched me at a level far deeper than that of taste or even of pride.

As I looked around the house it became clear that my sister and her children had left in a hurry and taken very little with them. The dishes hadn't been cleared from the table and the kitchen looked as though it had been burglarized. I went through every room in turn looking for I know not what, and then I sat down in the living room and gazed at that pathetic furniture I had hated so passionately until I felt myself beginning to cry. To put a stop to that I got up and cleared the dining-room table, washed the dishes, went upstairs and made the beds. I couldn't stand having the place look as though life in it had been suddenly terminated in mid-course by some quick and violent interruption.

The work calmed me. I decided I would simply have to determine

what route they were most likely to have taken when the city was evacuated and try to catch up with them. That meant first of all getting rid of
my suitcase. Nicholas, dear boy, had done his task brilliantly: he'd left the
suitcase by the roadside in the open trunk of an abandoned car, a new one
turned on its side, where it apparently seemed so at home that nobody
took notice of it in the short time it was there. But it occurred to me that
it might now become a dangerous liability: both too heavy to carry as far
as I might have to go and making me too obviously out of place among
those I would now join on the road. So I made another careful selection of
my belongings—this time only what I considered truly essential—and
transferred them to a rice sack that I found in the kitchen. I topped the
sack off with a few tins of food my sister had left behind and a box of British biscuits.

There was no one in the street outside or anywhere in the neighborhood to help me decide which way to head, but as I studied the situation it
still seemed to me that the Battambang–Pailin road was my best route,
since as far as I could tell at that moment, it would have given my sister
her nearest escape exit from the city, and it was also the route that I
thought led most directly to the Thai border. So I headed for the Pailin
road, and I reached it without incident, my walking much aided—alas—
by the lighter load I was carrying.

A few kilometers along that road I began to encounter remnants of
the exodus that had apparently cleared the city overnight the previous
week. The accounts were all the same. People had been told by loud-
speakers in cruising military cars that they had three hours to make their
way out of Battambang if they wanted to avoid being shot. Everything
still alive in the city after the deadline would be killed where it was: citizens of all ages, dogs, other domestic animals. Nobody argued. People
took what they could and fled for the outskirts, men and women, old and
young jamming the roads in every direction, because this was only a few
days after the reports had come in about the massacre of officers and noncommissioned officers belonging to the government army, and nobody
had any illusions about who were now in charge and how they planned to
maintain their authority.

The officers had been called in by radio the day the Khmer Rouge
entered Battambang. The radio asked them to lay down their arms and
assemble the following day in order to offer assistance to the new government in unspecified ways and to promote unity. So they gathered in front
of the prefecture on the morning of the 18th and waited for further
orders. When there were no further orders, they went home. They gath-

ered again the next day and were marched first to the university and then to the Sar Hoeur primary school, where they stayed four days waiting for orders that never came. Then someone arrived to read all their names off a list that had been prepared for the occasion, as though they were to receive a special commendation for cooperating with the new government, and they were told to go home, put on their dress uniforms and all their decorations, say goodbye to their wives, and return to the prefecture to be transported to Phnom Penh to greet Prince Sihanouk on his arrival there from China. Of course there was no Sihanouk or even a ghost of Sihanouk. Six trucks loaded with officers in dress uniform moved slowly out of Battambang in single file, and that was the last anybody saw of them in that city or any other. Witnesses from the region of Phnom Thippadey reported that there was a mass graveyard of unburied officers in a field there, clearly marked by its stench. The noncommissioned officers were transported to Bat Kang, near Thmar Kaul, where they were lined up on the sides of Highway 5 with their hands tied behind their backs, shot one after another, and left in piles along the highway for any traveler to see. The ordinary soldiers were sent elsewhere—some say to reeducation camps in the region of Phnom Sampeou, some say to the river.

Battambang is now the cleanest of the military districts. What war couldn't quite do in five years for all its dead, wounded, and still missing, peacetime has completed in just over five days—at least in the case of those who chose the wrong army. Now the ordinary citizens in the Battambang region find the question of choice much simpler: there is only one army left, and when that army gives you three hours to pack up and find a new life, you find a new life or none at all.

Mine began about thirty kilometers into the Pailin road, just beyond the Anglong crossing. I arrived there late in the third day, exhausted from two wet nights of little sleep spent on my rice sack by the side of the road under a yellow umbrella. I was lucky even so; most of those camping on the roadsides had to take the rain as it came because they hadn't managed to get out of Battambang with anything so luxurious as an umbrella. During my first day on the road I inquired constantly about my sister and was greeted constantly by silence or suspicion. Nobody knew anything about anybody, and nobody wanted to talk except in general terms about what had happened. The mention of specific names, even specific streets, was somehow threatening. The talk—except for the storytellers—seemed to be confined within families. And I suppose there was something in my way of speaking Khmer that showed me to be an outsider.

All I learned that first day was that people had left the city in all directions in their hurry to get out, and some routes had proven more accessible than others at certain moments, depending on which of the main streets was the least crowded at a given time. Those I questioned turned out to come from various sections of the city, proving the point. So my sister could have taken any one of several routes. The farther I got that first day, the more hopeless I became about my prospects of finding her easily. And the more cautious I became about asking direct questions. The second day produced nothing new. I spoke less and concentrated on passing from one group to another in the hope of hearing anything that might give me a clue. I was worried that something I might say would reach the wrong person and cause trouble. By the third day I'd become as silent as the others. And almost as self-protective.

But of course when you're exhausted from walking and not sleeping you let your guard down. I did the third night, which I spent among refugees some of whom had been camping by the roadside for several days, waiting for a new rumor that might help them decide where to go next. They took me for a stranger to that region—I suppose not hard to do given how relatively fresh I must have looked to them—and the more courageous asked me if I had any news. I offered those nearest me some oranges from my convoy supply, but sharing news seemed more important for the moment than sharing food. So I told them what I could about Phnom Penh without revealing too much about myself, and I was repaid by an account in full detail of the Battambang massacres. The later it got the more we crowded in together, gradually forming a tight circle against the dark and the dampness. It turned out that the people gathered there had come to the crossroads from three directions and most were as much strangers to each other as they were to me. Everybody new kept testing his neighbors with questions, small bits of personal history, never enough to prevent a retreat back into silence if it seemed one had suddenly become too exposed.

The talk opened out again when we began dividing up what each of us had to eat that wasn't likely to last. We picked over rumors and opinions from wherever they may have come from to see if there was any consistency in them that would help to tell the future. Those from the north, outside the towns, had heard that all population centers were being evacuated because the Khmer Rouge were afraid of spies left behind by the Americans, this after discovering secret radio transmitters in several cities. Others thought it was the Lon Nol government officials and certain conspiring military leaders they were afraid of, and that was why they had decided to kill everyone in uniform or government service either by murder or by gradual starvation, and since they didn't have a new administration service to replace the one they destroyed, the cities had to be abandoned. Some of those from Battambang said that it was the Khmer Rouge hatred for Chinese merchants and their capitalist exploitation that had caused them to close the cities and make everyone a farmer, as was proven by the way they had destroyed the market overnight by changing the cost of rice from 150 riels a kilo to 3 and pork from 300 riels to 12, thus clearing the market of food, emptying pockets of whatever money there was, and driving the Chinese merchants mad. But most from the city thought it was the problem of controlling so many people with so few soldiers, especially when it became apparent that there wasn't enough food for everybody. Some said they'd been told by the soldiers themselves that city people had to be sent into the country where the food was grown in order to prevent mass starvation. But those from villages didn't see how that explained why the Khmer Rouge were burning what they could of village houses and emptying the rest, even isolated farmhouses, why almost everybody in the newly liberated areas was made to move elsewhere even if a farmer at work on his land, why the rice fields everywhere were deserted and so little cultivation was under way when it should be nearing its end. The more we talked the more it seemed the Khmer Rouge had in mind destroying absolutely everything that had been, so that they could start the country entirely over again from the beginning. But what would the beginning be like? And what were we to do until we came to it?

These questions hung depressingly over our circle, and since there was no answer to them, we turned to things we knew, things actually seen or heard from witnesses who were beyond any need to lie. The stories built a horror too large to seem possible outside the world of myths, and places one had never heard of or seen only on the map became suddenly essential in the imagination's landscape, as though planted there by clever new fables meant to twist the mind. Mechbar, for example, an experimental farm in the north where a full company of soldiers was executed in front of their wives and children, then the wives were executed, and when the children began to cry they were told to stop crying over these enemies of their country or they too would be executed beside them. A man among us had traveled for a while with some people who had come down from the Mechbar farm. He said one of them talked without stopping, telling the story over and over again, but the others couldn't talk at all, as though their tongues had been cut out. And Pailin. Two trucks carrying government troops wearing the Black Cobra insignia crossed from Pailin into Thailand on April 17 but came back a few days later to surrender to the Khmer Rouge because the Thais wanted their weapons. They said they had told the Thais that their weapons were Khmer and would stay Khmer, and now they wanted to join the Khmer Rouge to fight the Thais. So the Khmer Rouge gathered up their weaopns and then drove their noncommissioned officers out to Trapeang Ke, near the first bridge on the Pailin–Battambang road, and shot them all dead. The ordinary soldiers were sent to found a War Prisoners' Village somewhere near Samlaut, as though they were permanent enemies of the new Cambodia they had hoped to defend. And it was at the Samlaut crossroads that a family from Pailin had to choose between going into the forest to face evil spirits and turning back to face the Prince of Death because they couldn't continue on the main road past the smell and disgrace of the slaughterhouse they found there in the shape of a mass open grave for officers and officials who had once run their city.

This is the family that has now become mine. The father is a mechanic who worked in a garage in Pailin, maybe forty years old (it is hard to tell because the cracked dark skin of his face seems much older than that, except around the eyes). His wife is a simple woman who looks both older than he and better fed, and she is evidently in constant terror of spirits. They have a daughter who is somewhere between a child and a woman, delicate, with the possibility of being beautiful—she could be fifteen or sixteen and simply undernourished. It was the daughter who brought me into the family. She was next to me on my left in our circle that third night on the road, and I could tell that she became increasingly upset by our talk because she ended up squatting there beside me with her head between her legs as though to hide from the sound of our voices. I could feel the whole of her body tremble at moments. Her mother, squatting on her far side, was apparently too frightened by different voices coming out of the darkness to pay attention to anything but her own silent dialogue with the invisible. I finally drew the young girl in close to me and put my arm around her. She wouldn't look at me, but at the same time she didn't resist, and she stayed that way through the night. After I fell asleep I would wake up every now and then and feel her cheek against my breast and her warm breathing, feel it with both more tenderness and more sensuality than I want to admit.

The next morning, as I was gathering my things to move on toward the Pailin hills, the father came over to me and shyly asked where I was planning to go. I told him I wasn't sure exactly: in the general direction of the border, where I hoped to find some safe place to settle while I tried to figure out if there was still any way I could trace my sister and her children. He squatted beside me and asked my permission to tell me something he preferred the others not to hear. Against my better instincts I gave him permission. He said softly that he was afraid his wife had gone mad. She hadn't been right since they'd come out of the forest beyond the Samlaut crossroads. Angry spirits had reached her during that passage through the forest, so near the unburied dead, and now he was afraid they would get his daughter as well. I told him the only spirits that I thought truly dangerous were those that living men carried in the dark half of their selves. He gazed at me without comprehension. He said that I had to help him with his daughter now that her mother was mad, I had to give her my protection as I had through the night. I kept shaking my head, but he went right on in his soft, desperately intense voice, breath close and vile. He had heard as they passed through Treng that the new government was going to distribute forestland to the people for clearing and planting, as much as three hectares to a family depending on its size, and if I agreed to join his family to act as mother to his daughter and sister to him, he would be willing to turn around and head back for Treng, fearful though that was, and I could freely share in whatever lot came his way for as long as it served my needs.

Of course the idea was grotesque. But as he gazed at me with those unblinking eyes of his it suddenly occurred to me that, unlikely as it may have seemed in that wretched, desolate, absolutely godforsaken setting with that tattered, vile-smelling demon of a man squatting beside my rice sack, it was just possible that I had found myself a new Henri. And that is why I am now at Treng, still very tired, still waiting with my new family, still not sure whether it is angry or benevolent spirits that have guided me here, but quite certain now that I will have to be more lucky than I deserve to be if I'm ever going to find what is left of the real family I once had.

May 10. Today I have a new identity again. I am no longer Francine Donnet, wife of Jacques Donnet, as my French passport had it, but Phal Sameth, sister of Phal Saren, auto mechanic from Pailin, where I have lived with my brother and mentally sick sister-in-law to help care for their daughter since abandoning my profession of schoolteacher in Phnom Penh two years before Prince Sihanouk was overthrown. This is what I wrote in the autobiography that each of us in our ten-family group of "new people" was required to submit before we could qualify for our allocation of forestland in one of the settlements to be founded northwest of here.

The autobiography was to cover the last five years—since the Lon Nol coup deposed Sihanouk. I had not planned to mention anything about Phnom Penh, just pretend to have been a member of Phal Saren's family since leaving school, but my new brother convinced me that I had to create some excuse for my manners and my way of expressing myself if I wanted to avoid suspicion. And there has been much suspicion in the air since we reached Treng—though as far as we know it has not yet touched us personally. We were told by those already camped here that spies have been planted everywhere and that we must be especially wary of children who are not attached to families—and even those who are. Now that the Angkar has disposed of the official enemy, it is apparently training the children to report on the hidden enemies among us, and every evening certain people have been summoned to meet with the Angkar Leu only to disappear into the night. There is still much weeding to be done, it seems, yet there is little time for official concern about what belongs in the new Eden and what doesn't. Word has spread among us that it is best to surround one's house with kapok trees and one's person with silence.

I began the process of insulation yesterday by disposing of everything alien in my rice sack, everything that might be regarded even remotely as capitalist or imperialist luxuries: the last of my makeup, two books, my one beautiful blouse—everything that once seemed essential. What I have left now fits into the bottom of my rice sack, which demonstrates how lavishly foreign and intellectual I've allowed myself to become these fifteen years under French and American influence.

I tried to be lighthearted about separating myself from this past, tried to cover my feelings with appropriate irony, but I wasn't very effective. What I found especially painful was ridding myself of my French passport, the most dangerous thing I was carrying—except, perhaps, for this notebook. The so-called luxuries I simply left in a gully by the side of the road, and I'm sure that bundle has been picked clean by now so that nothing I left in it can ever be traced back to me. But the passport and other papers that might have served for identification, both false and real, had to be taken care of more subtly, and that became complicated. My first plan was to rip everything into pieces and dispose of it in one of the toilets we've created here, the farthest I could get to. That worked for everything but the false passport. I simply couldn't bring myself to tear that up and watch it dissolve in filth. I didn't have time to understand whatever irrational hold it had on me, so I decided to exorcise the thing by making a small ritual out of giving it up. In the middle of the night I buried it in the earth under my head with a handful of my rice ration. We are camped under a stilted house, many of us packed in close, so it took me an eternity of careful scratching to clear the burial place, and when I had finished I discovered that Phal Saren had been watching me with those unblinking eyes of his—for how long, I don't know. My scratching that way must have made him think I'd suddenly gone as mad as his poor wife.

But this morning he didn't say a word about it. Nor has he yet asked me about my scribbling in this notebook, which he and his daughter, Thirith, both pretend not to notice at all. I'm sure, though, that they realize it will do none of us any good if those in charge of us should find it among the few things we will be taking with us to our new home, and of course it would have been prudent of me to bury it with the passport. I couldn't do that. This little notebook and the simple clothes I wear are all I have left outside myself from my other life, and this now seems to have become an essential part of me, like an implant. There is only one place to hide it that is safe, that I have to believe is safe: in my panties, flat against my belly. That is also where Phal Saren's wife keeps several rubies she must have rescued from Pailin, wrapped in a dirty handkerchief that she brings out and opens to explore whenever her mind's eye frees itself from whatever threatening presences inhabit her darkness.

Tomorrow we go northwest toward one of the mountain ranges that is supposed to stretch to the border. We have been told that each family in our group will be expected to clear a tract of land and build a bamboo house, then cultivate the land with cassava and yams. None of us in the group knows how to do that, and there are no animals to help. When someone asked our leader how we are to manage without the help of animals and tools, he smiled and showed his hands, the way a priest does.

May 26. Our village has no name, and it has no streets. It is a village only because we have decided to call it that as a defense against total anonymity. It consists of random huts that we have made with our own hands out of bamboo and branches in the area at the edge of the forest assigned by the Khmer Rouge to our group of families. The men go into the forest every day at 6 A.M. with hatchets to clear the land as they can. They return at dark. The women are planters in fields already cleared and in new land the men make and then plow in teams of eight because there are no oxen. The leader of the women in my group is a man, a Khmer Rouge veteran with one leg, who goes along ahead of us on his crutch and makes holes with a stake for us to drop our seeds into. We cover the holes by scraping earth over them with our feet. We have no tools. Our work also begins at 6 A.M., but unlike the men, we are given a recess between 11 and 2 so that we can return to the village to husk rice for our families. Sometimes, when we are not being watched too closely, we go into the forest to gather bamboo shoots, leaves, roots, anything edible we can find to supplement our daily ration of a half-tin of rice. Only the evenings are free for rest—most evenings, that is. Two so far have been given over to lectures by the village chairman, a stupid man, one of the few "old people" in the village, a reformed drinker and gambler who has been cured of his sins by our new religion. He has tried to teach us the catechism we are meant to know by heart, but his speech is not always clear, and it is hard to avoid laughing at him. Nobody does laugh. Laughter at a village meeting is taken to be a kind of complaint, and complaints will be allowed only at special meetings for self-examination which have been scheduled for sometime in the future. To complain now is to take a trip at night to the rice fields far from here, where there is apparently much need for human bodies to serve as fertilizer.

I got the catechism by heart in three languages today to keep my mind from fading out during the morning's planting. I give you my English version. The people are to become masters of earth and water, masters of rice fields, forests, and all plant life, masters of annual floods, masters of nature, masters of the future, masters of revolution, masters of factories, masters of both rainy and dry seasons. The four guiding principles for achieving the ideal society are independence-sovereignty, self-reliance, defense of the country, taking our destiny into our own hands. To arrive at the new society, justice must be simplified. For every crime, there will be one punishment: death. For those who do not want to be part of the new society, there will be one alternative: death. For those who protest the system of justice, there will be one satisfaction: death. We are told that the new code of justice has to be simple enough for a child to understand. And it is mostly children who are called on to administer it, young soldiers nicknamed "A-ksae nylon" or "A-ksae teo" because of the nylon rope or telephone wire they use to tie your hands before they break your neck with an ax handle to save ammunition.

Our life in the new village was almost good at first. After the long hours of waiting in Treng and the uncertain nights on the road, there was relief in arriving at a place that we could think of making into a kind of home, and even some pleasure in work that created a certain privacy and a shelter against the dampness. But the work in the forest and the fields has become cruelly exhausting for those of us not used to such work. After the first days, Phal Saren would sometimes come home from the forest with his hands bleeding, but we had to keep that hidden so that he wouldn't be transferred to the plow, where they say the blood eventually comes into your throat. Fortunately I had some of your first-aid cream among the things I had kept from my suitcase—there is no medicine of any kind in the village, and to ask for any special treatment is to raise suspicion or hostility. Our problem now is Phal Saren's wife, Hoon, who has a bad fever. No one wants to say that it is malaria, but our chief at work, who normally abides no suffering from us ("Think how we suffered during the war," he mumbles, baring his stump and pointing it at anyone who complains), is superstitious enough about malaria to raise no objection to Hoon's staying home from the fields. Since there is no quinine, we can do nothing for her but try to keep her warm when she shivers and cool when the fever begins to make her delirious. Thirith has been frightened deeper into silence by the noises her mother makes. She works beside me in the fields and husking rice and never says a word to me, but at night, after her father finally gives up attending to Hoon and falls asleep on the far side of the room (a manner of speaking, since there is only straw on the ground, as in a stable), she edges over next to me and I take her in my arms and hold her until she no longer hears her mother's hard breathing. I try to disengage myself after she has fallen asleep, but there are times when I can't, when I don't want to, and we stay that way until the light comes.

I spent the anniversary of your leaving on the road west of Treng. I was going to write something about it there when we camped for the night, but I found that I had a block. It seemed so remote, so sentimental to make something out of a past that has broken into too many fragments even in this short endless time. But I did think of you then, as I do now, and if it is without enough sentiment, that is no fault of yours. It is a measure of the road I've taken, quite unwillingly, away from what I was.

May 28. Hoon died on Tuesday. It took less than a week for the malaria to kill her. Others in the village have died too, all quickly. They are buried in the forest in the middle of the night—the village men help each other, our one voluntary communal project—so that a death doesn't become an excuse for the Khmer Rouge to move the survivors in the family out of their hut and away to some place unknown. We have heard that they transport people from one place to another on any pretext, supposedly to avoid epidemics but also to wear out the weakest, and the prospect of moving seems to have become more frightening to many than staying where one's fate is at least partly visible.

I don't know how Phal Saren feels about remaining here. He hasn't talked since Hoon died. When he comes back from the forest at the end of his day, he lies down on his side of the room and just stares up at the lattice of branches that we have made into a roof, his eyes rarely blinking, no response when Thirith or I speak to him. I think he has given up. It is as if he knew now that all of us in the village are going to die, it is just a matter of time. If it isn't the malaria, it will be starvation, because they are already cutting down our ration of rice, and there is little hope that we can last with this kind of exhausting work until we have the benefit of what we have planted—or whatever portion of it is meant to be shared by "new people." He must feel that if he talks, this is all he will be able to say to us, so he stares at the roof. And once in a while he glances at his daughter.

I have to tell him sometime soon that I've decided to leave. Maybe he already knows that too, which would explain why he never looks at me. Maybe he suspects that I want to take Thirith with me when I go. I wouldn't do so without his permission—at least, I don't think I would. Of course he could come with us, but he probably can't bring himself to leave his wife, not so soon, and I can't wait. He must realize how dangerous it is not to go now, yet I'm certain the poor man won't move, just like most of the others. I don't know whether Thirith would be willing to leave him behind. And I'm not sure how best to persuade her.

June 1. A few lines before I put this away in its secret place and take up my rice sack again. Phal Saren has vanished. Deliberately. He finally spoke to me yesterday evening after he came in from the forest. I was asleep, trying to save my strength for today, and he must have noticed that my things were packed. He was bending over me as I woke up— cheeks hollow, eyes holes—and when he spoke he nearly scared me out of my skin. "You'll take her with you," he said. It was a statement, not a question. Thirith was watching us. She said "No." That is what she said to me when I told her I was planning to try to cross through the forests and mountains into Thailand and wanted her to come with me. She said "No" both times in a way that left no room for argument. I'm sure she realized that it was her only chance to survive, but nothing I could say budged her one bit, so I'd made up my mind to go on without her, to-night, when the village would be asleep. And Phal Saren must have seen that she wouldn't move unless he went with us. Since he couldn't do that, he disappeared into the forest. When he didn't come back from work this evening, Thirith and I went out to see what had happened to him. Those who had been working with him said that he wandered off during the midday recess and simply didn't return. They thought he was gathering things to eat. Now Thirith says she has to go into the forest to look for him, and of course I will go with her. I think we both know that we're not going to find him, and she knows we won't come back, but in this way she can go with me without being disloyal. So we will leave with what we have left: this dying flashlight, my yellow notebook, the handkerchief with rubies that Thirith inherited from her mother, food for maybe a week, her youth, my luck. It isn't enough. But at least now neither of us has to worry any longer about questions of loyalty and choice.

TWO

The evacuation hadn't been his responsibility in any but the most technical sense, so its coming back to work him over like this after four years gone from Cambodia was almost as disturbing to Macpherson as the thing itself had been. The sudden advent of another Cambodian visitor—refugee, job seeker, what-have-you—surely wasn't reason enough: there had already been four or five Cambodian visitors of one kind or another who'd managed to track him down in Foggy Bottom since he'd begun his new Washington assignment. What must be getting to him was some harsh afterglow from the irony that had moved in gradually to color his image of what had happened out there.

Those on the outside were bound to think that the irony was self-defensive, and no doubt that was partly true. But the fact of the matter was, the evacuation had turned out better than he or anybody else in the Phnom Penh Embassy had expected it would. And that had been the essence of his draft report at the time. From a logistical point of view, the image he'd created was perfectly accurate. The first three choppers came in at 9:07, almost exactly on time, easing down on Landing Zone Hotel in a triangular formation to squat dead center in the soccer field, the marines out and running in all directions even before they'd had a chance to see clearly what kind of country they were in. And as the first three choppers lifted off, three more had come in right behind them, then another three in turn, the marines moving out quickly to secure the periphery of the landing zone, soon outnumbering the curious onlookers gathered there. Everything had gone smoothly. Within the hour all three hundred and sixty marines were dug in around the soccer field with their M-16s and their grenade launchers, and no sign of life from the Khmer Rouge camped along the far side of the river.

The one hitch Macpherson remembered admitting in the report was the concern some at the Embassy had expressed when no member of the Cambodian government appeared for evacuation by the 9 A.M. deadline, but he'd suggested that this was not a consequence of some flaw in the operation itself, just a miscalculation of probabilities. The Prime Minister had not overslept that morning as some feared he might, and the final letters from the Ambassador had indeed arrived by special messenger as planned. The problem had turned out to be one of principle. The Political Counselor they'd dispatched to check out the situation reported back that he'd found the Prime Minister presiding over an emergency meeting of his cabinet and that his cabinet had decided to a man not to go out with the Americans. "We'll stay here and fight on," he told the Counselor. "You just continue to send the rice and the ammunition." And when the Counselor said, "What rice and ammunition? You don't seem to understand. There isn't going to be any more rice and ammunition," the Prime Minister had gazed at him silently with no evident sign of grasping the truth.

But of course the principle wasn't absolute, as it rarely is in Southeast Asia. The Acting President of Cambodia showed up at the Embassy more or less on time with a family larger than he was legitimately allowed, which meant that a compromise on that score had to be quickly negotiated. Then one other minor Cambodian official arrived, this one presumed to be connected with the CIA, and at the very last moment the Minister of Youth and Sports. But the decision of the Cambodian cabinet not to join the evacuation had its positive side from the logistical point of view. None of the choppers was overcrowded, and in the end only twelve of them were needed to get everybody out who had a right to get out. The whole operation had been completed ahead of schedule, so that the last chopper was off the ground and out of there by the time the first mortar fire came in from the Khmer Rouge on the other side of the river to disperse the onlookers, causing just one civilian casualty.

That was about all Macpherson could remember of the quick draft report he'd submitted to the Ambassador after they'd settled in on the rescue carrier in international waters. Just the essential facts, no strong shading this way or that, no indulgence in overt irony. Of course the facts had to be somewhat selected for him to pull that off. You couldn't mention all the CIA agents left behind with radio transmitters to go on doing their job and incidentally to find they'd given themselves easily away—a piece of cake—as soon as the Khmer Rouge moved in to take over Phnom Penh and close the country. And there was no room to mention the clear misunderstanding of events that had divided the onlookers at the soccer field, some so certain that those evacuating marines were the first wave of a rumored army that the Americans were planning to send in for the city's defense, others more in the know or more spaced out waving goodbye like children at a parade. And naturally his report hadn't covered the hysteria of competition in his escape chopper, the departing news photographers and TV cameramen stumbling over one another even after takeoff to grasp a final picture of confusion and disbelief in the crowd below before the chopper moved out of range.

Cambodia was gone now for all practical purposes, hardly anybody's concern unless you counted those few specialists in Southeast Asian affairs and voluntary-agency types who still held on to their past in the country with a mixed aftertaste of bitterness and nostalgia. The truth was, he himself hadn't thought about the place in some months and might have been spared this latest review of the saddest chapter in his Foreign Service career if he'd made a point of warning his secretary to be particularly ruthless about protecting him from unfamiliar visitors whose names she usually got wrong on the first try and ended up calling "Oriental." But if this gentleman had in fact been a stringer for the Baltimore *Sun* in Phnom Penh, the very least he deserved was a warm meal under State Department auspices after what must have been a horrendous journey to freedom via Thailand. Probably all the poor fellow was looking for was a simple job reference on the basis of some now-dim encounter they'd had in the bar of the Hotel Phnom. But even that wasn't an unreasonable expectation on the part of a former ally in the business of political predictions who had no doubt been all too accurate in calling the demise of a five-year intervention that had ended up costing the stringer no less than his homeland, at least as they'd both once known that extraordinary place.

Macpherson decided that given a chance now, four years after the fact, he might be less reticent with his irony. Now he'd report all the relevant facts, and not only those he'd deliberately left out initially but some of the juicy details that emerged in dispatches from the few journalists who had stayed behind after the Khmer Rouge crossed the river to take Phnom Penh. The clearing of the cities, for example, the forced migrations, the starvation and the murder, all that had ended up justifying the very worst predictions he and his colleagues in the Embassy had cabled Washington during those last days.

Even the relatively secure circumstances at the French Embassy, where the foreigners and their friends had taken refuge, offered facts that could have been taken for clues to the bloodbath ahead: the forced departure of Cambodians seeking asylum there, the last-minute marriages arranged by the French to save some of the Khmer women who otherwise would have been ordered out of the compound, and—what had brought home the reality of things back there with a vengeance—that wirephoto of Sihanouk's old rival, Prince Sirik Matak, stretching his arms back in despair toward the French Embassy gate as he was hauled away in the street outside by his Khmer Rouge executioners. And the note the Prince had sent our Ambassador in response to the Embassy's evacuation offer, which the Ambassador had brought out to Thailand in his pocket and had handed over to Macpherson for translation.

How had the thing gone? Something to the tune of "My dear Excellency and friend, thank you sincerely for your offer to transport me to freedom, but alas, I cannot leave in such a cowardly way. As for your great country, I never believed for a moment that you would abandon a people that has chosen liberty. You have refused us your protection, and we can do nothing about it, but I still hope you and your country will find happiness under the sky. Yet note well that if I die here in my country that I love, it will be too bad, even if we are all born to die one day. I have made only this mistake of believing in you, the Americans. Please accept, Excellency, dear friend, my faithful and friendly sentiments . . ."

There had been no time for an answer to those princely sentiments by the Ambassador or the political section or anyone else on his way out of the country. Even now, after four years of brooding over the issue, what could one really say? "Dear Prince and lost friend. The issue is a delicate one. However right and honorable your choice, the question of faith that your note raises cannot be settled so simply for all the parties concerned. What does one do if one loves both your country and one's own, though fully recognizing that there have been terrible mistakes made by both? And not of a kind that can be so easily blamed on the other (may I be so bold as to mention just two: your coup against your cousin Prince Sihanouk, and our secret bombing of the sanctuaries)? And how does one act when there is no heroic way out? When choosing not to abandon your country, dear Prince, finally becomes a betrayal of one's own?"

So be it, such unanswerable questions were the best Macpherson could offer at that point. If four years of thinking about Cambodia and the aftermath of that evacuation hadn't settled the issue in his mind, he could serve no purpose by turning the thing over yet again. Cambodia was Cambodia still for those who remembered, even if you were supposed to call it Democratic Kampuchea these days. And now that the Khmer Rouge had been pushed back to the border jungles, it was up to them and Sihanouk and Son Sann to fight it out with the Vietnamese invaders to whatever new political resolution might save that poor country at least temporarily from yet another cycle of internal chaos and outside domination. The French and the Americans were out of it now. So was he. Washington was rich with blossoming cherry trees, he had finally settled into his home assignment after what his less friendly colleagues still insisted on calling his "rehabilitation tour" in The Hague, and Democratic Kampuchea was simply very far away.

Macpherson squared his back. The disk was acting up again. He decided to fit in a quick swim at the Shoreham pool on his way home even if it might mean having to face his wife's frantic pre-party outline of the tragic flaws in his character while he tried to set up the bar coherently before the doorbell started ringing.

"Yes, Miss Leonard."

"The gentleman with the Oriental name."

"Good. Send him in."

Macpherson recognized the Cambodian immediately, though the man had lost twenty or thirty pounds: he was one of the reporters who had come in regularly for briefings at the Embassy during the final two months before the fall of Phnom Penh, one of the few who had vanished without trace during the last days, before arrangements might have been made to include him in the evacuation plan. Some of the man's colleagues in the press corps had suggested that he had his own means of protection via the CIA; others took him to be a rather sentimental patriot with a predilection for suicide, despite his American training. Now he stood there smiling thinly, waiting for Macpherson to make the first move.

"I'm delighted to see you," Macpherson said, motioning him to a seat. "I really mean that."

"Yes," the Cambodian said. "It has not been easy."

"I bet it hasn't."

"I mean for both of us," the Cambodian said.

Macpherson studied him. "Are you finally settled in now over here? Place to live? Job of some kind?"

"Oh, yes," the Cambodian said. "No problem. I have many friends here."

"You've been here awhile, then?"

"Not in this city. I just came to Washington a few days ago. I came to see you, in fact. But I may stay awhile."

Macpherson was having trouble keeping his eyes squarely on him. He rarely had that trouble.

"Well, how can I be of help to you, my friend?" Macpherson said.

"Maybe I can be of help to you," the Cambodian said. "Or we to each other."

"How's that?" Macpherson said, a bit sharply.

"For a beginning, you can help me by taking this. It has really been something of a burden. I've had to carry it from Bangkok to Paris and then to New York without misplacing it, and at times that has not been easy."

He handed Macpherson a small notebook with a soiled yellow cover. There was nothing on the outside to identify it. The writing inside was in English script, and the first page was dated April 13.

"Do you recognize the handwriting?" the Cambodian asked.

Macpherson glanced over at him. "I can't say that I do."

"You will, I'm certain," the Cambodian said. "After reading just a few pages to refresh your memory."

————

Tim turned the leather so that its rough side was up, nailed it to his cutting board with a tack in each corner, then pinned the pattern to the leather and carefully followed the edge of the pattern with his knife to make a line deep enough to show yet not beyond repair if it came out less true than it had to be. He'd made plenty of sandals in his day, but moccasins, he decided, called for more sophisticated craft. The tongue section had to be cut to fit the main body exactly, and the stitch holes had to be punched through the two parts at the exact same intervals if you were to come out with both a tight joining and a piece of work pleasing to the eye. He studied the cutting board with the pattern still in place. The marking looked true, so he unpinned the pattern and took the knife to the leather, working with pressure but also with a steady hand so that the thing didn't ease away from him under its own impulse.

It struck him that there was a wonderful simplicity to a moccasin even if it was a job to make: just two pieces of leather to be stitched together and a cut to be stitched at the back, with overlapping sides punched through so that the whole of it could be held together by a single leather thong. No tacks anywhere, no glue, beautifully self-sufficient, especially if you did the stitching with leather also. The Indians had a ge-

————

nius for simplicity and self-sufficiency, no doubt about it. Very practical yet very sophisticated for a so-called primitive society. But try and tell that to the Department of the Interior. Try and tell that to Tom and Ismini while you were at it. You got the impression that from their point of view giving yourself to making moccasins and chairs and leather jewelry in peacetime was about like avoiding the draft by heading for Canada in time of war. Not to mention growing vegetables in your—okay, their—backyard with real manure so that you could get some taste into the things you brought in to eat. What was it the old man had finally said about his six-month self-training project when he decided he'd better get it all out into the open? Too artsy-craftsy for his taste, a throwback to the Sixties, all right for your spare time but not a very sensible way to prepare yourself for making a living these days when you had college potential and plenty of opportunity still to give college a second try. Sure a throwback. Like Vietnam and Cambodia and Watergate were a throwback. Time to forget all that bad history and settle down to an honest nine-to-five living in God's country now that you didn't have to worry any longer about getting yourself too involved in somebody else's war on the other side of the world, right?

He took up the punch and chose to work on the tongue section first, because he figured if he screwed that up, he wouldn't lose all that much leather. Once you decided to go for broke and do the stitching with leather too, there was no turning back to start over if you punched the holes out of line. He got himself squared on his chair and went to work with a hand so steady he had trouble watching it stay that way without getting tense.

Ismini he could understand in a way. She came out of a different culture, light on the issues, laid back politically, your basic Mediterranean society type who wanted to see everyone happily married to the right kind of person but one way or another married and hot at it raising a nuclear family. That made her more affectionate than some mothers, more caring most of the time and God knows easy with her spare cash, but pure cocktail circuit when it came to questions of politics and lifestyle. It was old Tom the supposed Ivy League liberal he couldn't figure out. The man seemed to have a conscience about some issues, talked a good line on Vietnam, for example, but was way out of it at other times. Mostly he made things seem so complicated you really couldn't talk about them at all. No clear lines, no direct answers. You wouldn't want to call him cynical or indifferent, just wishy-washy, as though you could always find two sides to a question if you looked hard enough. In this world? The way Moscow and Peking and Washington had been pushing people around at least as far back as Kennedy?

Never mind the Bay of Pigs and Vietnam, just take Cambodia. Old Tom had been out there for a year or more, right up to the end, seen what was going on before and after the evacuation he himself had helped to organize, and yet no real outrage over what his country had done. At least none that showed. Of course he was official government, so maybe you couldn't expect him to speak his mind in public, but inside the family? Never even mentioned the place as far as he could remember after that one time the old boy had wriggled out of an argument about America's role over there under Lon Nol by saying bad as the situation had turned out, the whole thing was more complicated than it seemed on the surface. Complicated? What's complicated about bombing people who aren't even in a war and then sitting back and watching several million of them get murdered by the crazies you helped to bring out of the jungle and into the open because you were bombing the shit out of them and everybody else in sight?

The punch wasn't working the way it was supposed to, failing to cut cleanly through at times—or he wasn't giving it what it needed. He decided to pack it in for the time being and have another go after lunch. His hands were probably too tired for this kind of precision work after almost five hours of putting chairs together. He crossed to the mattress on the floor under the dormer window and lay back with his arms behind his head to give his shoulders a rest.

There was no getting around it, they had their world and he had his. People thought it cute that he called his parents Tom and Ismini, very intimate it seemed, but in truth it was the opposite, even if he himself hadn't seen it that way in the beginning: a strategy for getting yourself a little distance, like the change from Tom Junior to Tim that he'd manipulated through buddies at school when his old man's shadow had become just a little heavy. He'd never really been able to fit the two of them under the heading of Mother and Father or Mom and Dad, not even when talking to them as a kid, and he'd always had trouble finding an easy way of addressing them in a letter when he was away at school in Switzerland those god-awful years, tried all kinds of things including Cher Papa et Maman, very classy, and finally settled for Dear Folks, which was just as phony. But finding something to write to them about was the real problem—the old failure of communication, which hadn't really gotten better over the years, however much he tried and maybe they tried as well. That was one problem that was surely going to take a turn for the worse when he got around to telling them his travel plans for the immediate future.

He got up and went over to the refrigerator to pick out some zucchini and carrots to fry up for lunch. He cut up the zucchini into thin, coinlike sections, and the carrots to match as best he could. The butter beans from the night before were floating in a pool of vinegar, but he decided to throw them in anyway. Then he chopped up some kale and sprinkled a handful in. He studied the gathering he'd made, then ended up dropping in a couple of cloves of garlic as a peace offering to Ismini, wherever she might be spending her day. As an added gesture he chose olive oil in place of corn oil for the frying.

She was all right, really generous and affectionate most of the time for all her pressing him to get a steady job and hinting that it was time he found himself the kind of girl he could marry—whatever that might mean in view of his not having had enough cash to take anybody's kind of girl out in weeks. No more unemployed typists on the make, right, Mom? And no dark strangers coming into town to work for somebody's government and bringing in God knows what kind of venereal diseases from unknown places abroad either. Just live-in types from a family somebody had heard of and maybe a degree in psychology to help her handle what she was getting herself into, right? At least Ismini still had her bridge games to turn her on, and her TV series. What was it that turned on old Tom? Who could tell—unless it was checking out the latest dispatches down at the State Department and putting on his sentimentally royalist wife with the latest news of rising socialism in Athens. Living at home those first six months after Tom and Ismini came back to town may have been a lot lighter on the pocket, but it was also like living in an underground cell with a vacuum cleaner for companionship while you listened through the floorboards above to long silences mercifully broken every now and then by violent debate. At least with his own place on Capitol Hill, however empty, he could think of building up a domestic situation that had less mothering and forced feeding and more sex in it, even if the building had to be pretty much on the installment plan for the time being and interrupted for a while by the foreign travel he had in mind.

Something had gone very wrong with the olive oil while he had his back turned. It was dark now and smoking, no doubt the result of the hot plate's staying too hot. His next project would definitely have to be getting more variation into the thing or digging himself up a decent stove. He decided to dump the olive oil down the toilet and start over with corn oil—to hell with sentiment, especially when you no longer had a manure garden to make your vegetables reasonably edible without having to fry them half to death.

The major problem he had left with Tom and Ismini now that he'd moved out from under their sometimes noisy private life was persuading them to back his personal Peace Corps plan with some hard cash to cover his transportation costs. If he could get them to fork up enough for his trip over, say as far as Europe, he'd take it from there, pick up odd jobs until he got himself some place out in Southeast Asia, where he'd heard there were several international agencies seriously looking for paid volunteers to help clean up the new mess out there that was at least partly the result of the war he'd missed by the pure luck of being a few months too young as the thing petered out. Reading about those thousands of boat people coming out of Vietnam only to be sunk by pirates or left to float barely alive where they weren't allowed to land made you wonder all over again what that war had really been about. And now the Vietnamese had invaded Cambodia and were sending thousands of refugees across the border into Thailand, which hadn't figured out how to cope with the refugees already camped out there for years to avoid being murdered by Pol Pot.

It was a mess all right, but that wasn't going to make it any easier for him to sell his idea, at least not to Ismini. There was no way he could argue a political line with her when her politics didn't extend any farther east than the evil regime in Ankara. The only way to approach her was via some sort of domestic line—maybe tell her how much he was looking foward to settling down any day now on his own piece of land with a wife and a family and enough know-how to make the several hundred acres he had in mind not only entirely self-sufficient but actually profitable, at least on a small scale. And the best way he could think of to pick up that kind of practical knowledge without anybody's having to pay for it, now that he'd given up on the university route and failed to make the real Peace Corps for lack of college credits, was through the kind of training you picked up working for one of the voluntary agencies over there whose job it was to teach people all different sorts of ways to become self-sufficient. And there was more than a half-truth in that line even beyond the educational argument. Who wouldn't look forward to settling on a piece of land in the Shenandoah Valley, with the Blue Ridge Mountains on one side of you and the Alleghenies on the other and green hills spotted with horses rolling out and away from you in any direction you might care to look? And who wouldn't want a wife and kids to fill the empty spaces? But all in good time. First he had to beat the Peace Corps at its own game, as a matter of personal pride.

The corn oil was about ready, but he took the frying pan off the burner while he figured out how to pace the various parts of his ratatouille, or whatever it was called, so that he ended up with a fairly consistent texture. Then he decided what the hell, the carrots were healthy cooked or raw and the butter beans were already partway cooked through marination, so he'd just fry the zucchini a bit to keep it from being completely insipid and then dump everything in together and let the combination cook long enough for the oil to be eaten up so that he didn't come out having to shovel down tasteless half-cooked vegetables floating in grease the way he generally seemed to since he'd taken up cooking for himself.

The trip he had in mind wasn't just a question of pride, either. There was plenty of principle involved. Whatever the old man might see as the other side of the question, Southeast Asia was still the place where Uncle Sam had a few debts to pay. And it happened to be one place where the Peace Corps didn't operate these days as far as he knew. So even if they had turned him down despite the skills he could have offered them, now that he thought about it he didn't really want to go where they might have sent him anyway. Africa, South Asia, Central America was all fine territory for traveling around in, South America too, and no doubt there were people in trouble out in those places who needed as much help as they could get. But Southeast Asia was the forgotten territory as far as he was concerned, even if it was only four years since the American war over there had ended. Thailand, Cambodia, maybe even Vietnam itself, that was where the main action ought to be because that was where we'd done our bit to fuck things up royally and that was where the refugee problem was even worse now than when we'd pulled out of the area and headed home. There was no getting around it, this was the line he'd have to take with Tom even if it led to another infuriating argument. And who knows, it might just turn out that the guy really had a conscience hiding away somewhere behind that Foreign Service shirt and tie he seemed to wear even in bed.

Macpherson had decided against the State Department restaurant for his second meeting with Tan Yong, primarily because he felt something more intimate and luxuriously appropriate was called for. But the protocol of arranging the change at the last minute had required some delicacy: he didn't want Tan Yong to think that his decision to drive from Foggy Bottom to a Chinese restaurant in Georgetown was motivated by a wish to keep his Cambodian friend hidden from State Department colleagues. He wondered if he hadn't made too much of an issue out of the thing, putting down the State Department food unnecessarily, pretending the place was too crowded for honest conversation when that was hardly the case, and so on. But the talk of food seemed not to have influenced Tan Yong's placid expression one way or another; what the man ate these days was evidently of no consequence to him. On the other hand, where he ate clearly was, because the argument for intimacy had settled the question at once. Apparently the man had things to talk about that he wanted to keep as private as Macpherson himself might.

He had to admit that whatever unease he felt in Tan Yong's presence had little to do with Tan Yong himself. The man had behaved with perfectly reasonable discretion from the start, excusing himself as soon as he could do so with grace after delivering the diary he'd evidently been carrying around with him for well over a year and waiting for a good ten days before calling back to follow up on his delivery. And if his manner all along had remained a bit stern for Macpherson's taste and his tone something close to accusatory at a few points in the phone conversation when he may have taken Macpherson's hesitancy for evasiveness, he hadn't yet let anything of that kind come into his look or his bearing while the two of them were together.

What had Macpherson off balance was really Chien Fei, or Sameth, as she apparently now called herself. After four years of finding ways to accommodate the remnant memories of the year they'd more or less lived together and the quick, cruel separation—obviously more cruel for her but no easy ride home for him either—she had come back now to stir it all up in him again in a form that he'd thought at first he could handle with reasonable objectivity but that had finally got to him where he could still be hurt. And this for all the cool facade some people, including his own son, seemed to think was a natural reflection of his character. He'd tried so often, and with no little difficulty, to make people understand that it wasn't really coldness that allowed government officials in his kind of work to turn away from one disaster and begin to prepare as best they could to face the next. It was professionalism, the capacity to put things in context so that you could go on doing your job, to sacrifice when necessary the luxury of feelings that let others without the same responsibility indulge in self-pity or hatred or even excessive compassion following the event. You simply had to be able to pick up and move on to the next country and the next crisis. But of course professionalism had its limitations when it came to governing the heart's secret territory, even four years after one had been forced to return to less passionate regions.

He'd started out trying to read Chien Fei's diary as he might a work of documentary fiction, not taking it as a personal record by somebody he'd been involved with intimately but as the story of a place he'd known and loved, of a city's disappearance and a people's agony, both of which he'd so far heard about only by way of official reports and press dispatches. Here was a detailed eyewitness account of brutal history in the making that couldn't help being of interest to someone who'd been as concerned as he'd been about the consequences of a disastrous Southeast Asian policy of which he'd been a part. But that stance had begun to break down early on in his reading, and now he could actually pinpoint its final collapse: when Chien Fei, turned Phal Sameth, was settled in her new village that had no name in the area west of Battambang. That was when she'd made it clearly evident that the role of the silent American who was the audience to her drama—his role, in fact—was finally over, killed by inconsequence.

There was no doubt a touch of egotism and maybe self-pity in the awareness that had come to him then, a degree of hurt pride in his being set aside like that, but the truly devastating thing he'd realized was that her capacity to survive at that crucial point, the reaffirmation of her will that was necessary in order for her to go on despite the humiliations she'd suffered, seemed to depend on her being able to see her fragmented past without sentiment. What that moment in her diary had made him recognize was that along with his own increasingly fragmented image of her and her doomed country over the past four years, he'd lost his own capacity for sentiment—personal, political, whatever. And his loss was hardly earned the way hers had been. So in a sense, his son, Tim, was right after all.

Of course that recognition as he read the diary not only had brought sentiment back with a vengeance but had occasioned another painful review of those last days in Phnom Penh when he'd tried to persuade Chien Fei to fly out to Bangkok or Paris or wherever she might feel most comfortable waiting until the Embassy had put its evacuation plan into effect and he would be free to join her—had even told her more about the plan than strict security permitted, in case she changed her mind and decided to go out by helicopter at the last minute. And she had obviously, by her own admission in the diary, taken that as a serious offer. Yet what he hadn't wanted to admit to himself at the time and what she had just as obviously sensed—he saw no other way to interpret her remarks in the diary about his wife and his "muddy circumstances" in the United States—was that he hadn't really had any clear idea about what he would do with her if she decided to abandon her sister and her country and go out with him. They would work something out, that was what he'd told her, what he'd honestly believed at the time. But either she'd read some ambiguity in his assurances that he himself was incapable of seeing or else she was simply wiser than he was.

Anyway, her decision not to leave—if it was still fair to call it entirely her decision—had certainly made it easier for him to rationalize his not having attempted to get in touch with her in the months and then the years that had followed, futile as any attempt would have been from her own account of things. The trouble was, it wouldn't do as a rationalization any longer, and his instinctive sense of this, along with a general confusion about how to cope with what might now be opening up as a result of the "document" that Tan Yong had handed him in his office two weeks ago, must have been responsible for the nervousness he'd felt the minute Tan Yong reappeared to meet him for lunch. He still had no idea just what Tan Yong might be after now that Chien Fei was apparently safely settled into the same camp in Thailand that he'd emigrated from over a year ago. The man was obviously still feeling things out, taking his time before showing his hand.

Macpherson decided he would simply have to lay his own cards on the table when the moment of truth arrived. Tan Yong was not the only one who had a legitimate personal interest to promote. And Chien Fei wasn't the only one with obligations beyond her own well-being, whether or not she'd legally adopted the daughter she'd inherited in Cambodia. He had his own family interests to promote and protect. After four years, he was finally getting his personal life back into some order, making the compromises he had to if he was to keep his marriage from falling apart and his son from giving up entirely on his—how would Tim put it?—his basically uptight and politically uncommitted parents. He wasn't about to let anything upset the delicate balance he'd managed to establish recently, however much his conscience had been stirred by Chien Fei's story.

Getting himself into the right frame of mind had been another unspoken reason he'd chosen Georgetown for lunch. He'd thought the ride there might actually give both him and his Cambodian visitor a chance to warm up to their necessary conversation by chatting about irrelevancies such as the landscape and the weather, given the roundabout route he'd chosen to Wisconsin Avenue, past the spread of tulips, daffodils, pansies, azaleas, and all else that had been trucked in from foreign places to create spring around official Washington. But Tan Yong was still sitting there beside him gazing straight ahead, not a word yet, not a flicker of emotion to show what might be going on behind the set sober face he'd brought in with him that noon through the office door. Even the sight of kites playing hide-and-seek behind the Washington Monument hadn't served to crack the man's apparent single-minded self-absorption. But when he did finally speak, his voice, though quiet, whipped into the silence between them with cutting directness.

"I'm sure you understand now why I had to come to this city as soon as I could," he said. "Those fortunate enough to find a place in your country have a moral obligation to help those who have had to stay behind."

"I understand, of course," Macpherson said. "I just don't quite know what I can do to help you."

"I'm not the one who needs the help," Tan Yong said. "My friends here in the journalism community have been most generous. There is even the chance of a possibly permanent job in the Baltimore-Washington area. It's Phal Sameth and her daughter."

Macpherson stared out the window at the Mall. "I find it difficult to get used to that name. I knew her as Chien Fei."

"In any case," Tan Yong said.

Macpherson decided to swing around the Tidal Basin and past the Jefferson Memorial to take in the cherry trees. Tan Yong was looking sideways at him now, steadily, as though waiting for something.

"You're absolutely certain she's all right," Macpherson said. "I mean not only healthy but as settled as can be expected under the circumstances?"

"I'm certain she was. At least in a manner of speaking. But that was well over a year ago. Before I moved on from the camp in Aranyaprathet to Paris and before Vietnam invaded our country. Who knows what conditions along the border are like these days?"

"And the daughter?"

"The daughter was of course living with her. But not always well. At least psychologically. Rather too silent at times, as you can imagine."

Macpherson decided to take the 14th Street bridge to the other side of the Potomac and then cross back over at Rosslyn. There were sunbathers already claiming the grass outside the tennis courts as he slowed to enter the bridge—mostly tourists, he guessed, in makeshift undress. A puff of loud music from a cassette player wafted through the car as they passed. Tan Yong was still looking at him.

"I'm sure you understand that my options are limited," Macpherson said. "However urgently I may want to help."

"One's options are always limited," Tan Yong said, turning to look up the river. Then he turned back suddenly. "Nevertheless."

Macpherson glanced at him for any evidence of irony. The face was the same stern mask.

"Well, exactly what do you think I can do?"

"That surely isn't for me to say. You have the resources. And the personal interest."

"You don't have the personal interest?"

"Of course," Tan Yong said. "But not in Phal Sameth only. She was one among many refugees I met in person who are still there. And of course she made a particular impression on me over a period of time. But there are still hundreds and hundreds in her situation."

"But she gave you her diary. She trusted you with it."

"The diary was meant for you. She trusted me with it because she thought that was her best chance of getting it to you, to whom it was addressed. As we both know."

Macpherson felt that he had somehow allowed himself to be worked into exactly the kind of defensive posture he'd meant to avoid. His tone was going wrong. The man was obviously not about to let up on him, especially if he sensed too much resistance. Macpherson decided his best hope at that point was to show proper concern while trying gently to postpone the issue until he'd had a chance to think it through more thoroughly. He focused on a softer tone.

"I'd honestly like your advice on what you think might be done. You're so much more in touch with the situation over there these days than I am."

"There are a number of things that might be done. The question is how far you are prepared to go."

"I really don't know at this point," Macpherson said. "It's all too new. I mean not only the diary but learning that she made it out of Cambodia alive and is now presumably still in Thailand."

Tan Yong seemed to be fascinated by the river now. His head turned slowly to explore it in a sweeping pan shot.

"I imagine you think it beyond possibility now to bring Sameth to this country to share your life," he said to the river. "As you once did."

"You know my situation here," Macpherson said. "I still have a wife. And a son more or less out of work. Besides, who says she would want to be part of my life here at this point?"

Tan Yong turned back from the river. "I suppose you're right. But the daughter may be another matter."

"The daughter? You mean you think I could bring the daughter here to live with me and my wife?"

"For a while perhaps. Until you can safely send her somewhere to be educated."

"Educated?"

"To a university. I think that would please her mother like nothing else. Her mother so to speak, I mean."

"But that's absurd. I've never even met the daughter. The so-called daughter."

"Many things seemingly absurd are not so absurd. You who have known events in Southeast Asia surely understand that."

Polk had a hunch that things might be about to turn his way again. The feeling had started coming on strong that morning for no particular reason, unless it was the change in the weather, news that spring might be in the nation's capital to stay for a while. But what had really given life to the feeling was catching sight of old Macpherson sitting over there on the far side of the restaurant with some Oriental type, the two of them talking serious business from the look of it, no doubt international business of a coloring that wasn't likely to do the country the greatest good, you could count on that. The point was, Macpherson might do him some good—more than might, in fact. It was nigh on to five years since he'd last seen the man, yet for all his gray hair he still had that golden-boy appearance which had gotten him voted most likely to succeed in the high school poll, to nobody's surprise. Though now he was getting a touch heavy in the midsection and a touch loose in the jowls like the rest of humanity his age.

It was funny how some people were born with success written all over them while others with reasonably good looks and the same brains could drift along for years without getting anywhere to speak of or maybe moving up where it was finally worth heading only to find themselves knocked down halfway there. Of course it wasn't really funny at all if you considered how some people got all the breaks along the way, Macpherson at the top of the list.

It finally came down to a question of luck—and luck was a thing he sorely needed of late. Not only were his Capitol Hill contacts getting thin, but those still active under all this so-called post-Watergate hysteria that should have died its natural death back in the Ford administration were just not bringing in the kind of business he used to be able to take pretty much for granted on a week-by-week basis. It had been almost a month since something solid enough to sink his teeth into had come along. And that made him begin to think the time had finally arrived to move on out of Washington, and maybe even out of the country, in search of new terrain where his skills in administration and public relations might finally bring in the kind of profit they deserved.

Macpherson could be useful in that connection if he wanted to be, there was no doubt about that, and Polk had to admit that coming across him the last time he was in town had brought on a run of luck as strong as any he could remember—anyway, for a spell. The problem was getting to the man in a way that wouldn't give him the idea somebody was out for special favors again. Macpherson wasn't as easy as he'd once been, far from casual these days, a bit in love with his position in society one might say, and a bit uptight about people who'd known him back when he was really no better than anybody else in the Western High crew that used to drift into Sam Tehaan's in Georgetown once in a while.

Polk stood up tall to give Macpherson a full six-foot-four target in case the guy took it into his head to look over his way and give him some sign of recognition. The man was clearly too deep into whatever policy debate or arms negotiation he and his Oriental contact had been rapping about since they'd first sat down. Polk decided to angle across the room and come up on Macpherson from behind to see what a surprise approach might bring out in him. As he moved in, he smiled down at the Oriental gentleman and winked, then gave Macpherson the old grip on the upper arm. He could feel Macpherson go rigid.

"Well, look who's here," Polk said. "What's the news down at your end of Foggy Bottom? We gonna survive as a world power?"

Macpherson was still looking at the hand on his arm. When he glanced up at Polk, the look on his face made Polk loosen his grip.

"Polk," Macpherson said finally. Then he held out his hand.

"So mind if I sit down a minute?"

Macpherson was still staring at him. "What happened to your hair, for God's sake?"

Polk pulled out a free chair and sat down. "Shaved it all off.

78

Thought it was time to try a new image. See if it might bring on a change of luck. So how the hell are you?"

"Great," Macpherson said. "Great."

"You look great," Polk said.

Tan Yong reached for the raincoat he'd laid over the back of the other free chair.

"I think I'll excuse myself now if I may," he said.

Polk crossed his legs. "Don't go on account of me. I'm leaving myself in a minute or two. Just wanted to say hello to my old pal here."

Tan Yong sat down again. "In any case," he said, "I really must go."

Macpherson was on the edge of his seat now.

"So how long you plan on being in town?" Polk asked Macpherson.

"Just as long as they'll let me stay," Macpherson said.

"That's good news," Polk said. "Real good. You're still down at State, right?"

"Still at State," Macpherson said.

"Well, I'm sort of on sabbatical," Polk said. "At least as far as government service goes."

"Is that right?" Macpherson said. He glanced at his watch.

"You might call it that anyway. Only it's a kind of indefinite sabbatical at this point."

"That's the best kind," Macpherson said, looking around for the waiter. "If you can afford it."

"Yeah, well, that's the thing. I can't really afford it. So I'm putting in my time these days as a free-lance lobbyist for semi-noble causes. So to speak."

Macpherson let a smile begin to take shape. "What exactly is a semi-noble cause?"

"I don't really think that's the kind of thing that would interest your friend here," Polk said.

"Please," Tan Yong said, standing. "You can speak freely. I am definitely on my way."

As he reached for his raincoat again, Macpherson stood up. "Well, I'm on my way too. I'll take you back downtown wherever you'd like to be left off."

"I won't allow that," Tan Yong said. "I'm sure you two gentlemen have much to say to each other. And I believe you and I have said all we have to say at this point."

"Well, I'm not going to let you go back downtown by yourself," Macpherson said.

"You must," Tan Yong said. "I will be most unhappy if you don't let me have my way."

Macpherson studied him. "All right. I'll take you at your word. And you can count on me to be in touch again as soon as I've given the situation a little more thought."

"I do count on you," Tan Yong said.

Polk watched the two of them cross to the door and shake hands. Macpherson signaled the waiter for the bill as he sat down again. Polk was studying him with a steady half-smile.

"You two were going at it heavy there for a while," Polk said. "You looked as though you were dividing up the Far Eastern provinces between you."

"As a matter of fact, we barely got into politics," Macpherson said. "And it was all old history."

"Old history, huh? What kind of old history?"

"Various kinds," Macpherson said, looking around the room again. "Mostly personal."

"Is that right?" Polk said. "Don't tell me the gentleman has an arranged marriage in mind."

"To whom?"

"Your daughter maybe?"

"I don't have a daughter," Macpherson said.

"Is that right? Yeah, I remember now. You've only got a son. Well, I hope you aren't after his."

"After his what?"

"His daughter. Or wife. Or whatever."

Macpherson stared at him.

"What's the matter with you?" Polk said. "I was only kidding. Don't tell me you've gotten so important these days that you've lost your sense of humor."

———

Macpherson did not consider himself a man given to superstition except maybe in the old Greek sense of watching out for hubris, never letting yourself get too settled in your security or too arrogant about how well things in general might be going for you, because that was a sure way to bring the gods out of hiding to restore the balance by giving it to you

———

80

for a while. Superstitious in that sense he'd surely become of late. It wasn't exactly the same kind of modern Greek superstition that made Ismini cross herself three times before heading out on a pleasure trip or pretend to spit discreetly on beauty and good fortune to keep the evil eye at bay when complimenting somebody, yet it wasn't that far off either. Anyway, he'd begun to feel that the easy ride he'd been enjoying in his new job down at State and the aura of abundant well-being that had come in with the Washington spring were beginning to cost him dearly. First Tan Yong and now Polk, two messengers out of the unsettled past come back into his life so close on each other's heels, evidently set on making him pay his dues for having been too complacent, too relaxed, too content with his reasonably comfortable circumstances these days.

Polk was certainly the more threatening of the pair, being less of a gentleman about making clear what he was after and not likely to be a gentleman at all about trying to get it. He apparently wanted help in finding a job abroad, no doubt as far abroad as possible, because he knew damn well he couldn't get a serious job in Washington, D.C., after the mess he'd made of the last one he'd had in the Department of Transportation during the second Nixon administration. If Polk had been working in a town less tolerant of influence peddling and gross favoritism toward special interests and more fully in charge of itself, the man would be in jail now instead of out there hustling again.

The truth was, he didn't owe Polk a thing and never really had. If he'd given the man what was probably a crucial recommendation for the job in Transportation during his earlier Washington assignment, that was partly because he felt Polk had done the state some service in two wars Macpherson hadn't served in himself and partly to get him off his back once and for all. It had seemed to him the man deserved at least one chance at getting ahead legitimately in this town after having survived what he'd been through both during and after the army, including all the post–Korean War disaffection that had come over many of his high school compatriots. If you wanted to be charitable, you could call them war casualties left from the last wars in which they had known at least the possibility of clear-cut heroism for some cause they could actually understand. But one bad favor was charity enough for a man like Polk. Macpherson had no remorse at all over having cut his old classmate dead in that restaurant once he started hinting about what he was really after. The man hadn't even bothered to get up and follow him out the door.

Macpherson decided to head down to the Potomac and circle back gradually to Georgetown University. He still had a half-hour to kill before his appointment with Father Grigorian, and he needed a chance to settle into his normal relaxed form before facing what was bound to prove another sort of awkward encounter. He could see at least one canoe out on the river when he came to its open view, new evidence that the weather was turning toward summer early this year. He watched the canoe pick up speed as the two paddlers seemed finally to be working as a team, managing to keep the thing headed more or less parallel to the shore against the pressure of the river's current and their deficient skill. As it angled in closer, he saw that the paddlers were male, though their hair was as long as that of the girl stretched between them, her shoulders bent over the gunwale and her head dipped way back so that her dark hair nearly touched the water.

They were high school kids, he was sure of that, cutting out for the river the first afternoon in April that the sun was hot enough to justify the cost and the trouble of faking an excuse note from home. Of course that could be just another swig of middle-aged nostalgia. What did he really know about the habits of high school kids in any generation since his own, having flubbed his one chance to learn something new in that area when he allowed Ismini to talk him into sending Tim to the American School in Lucerne rather than fight it out *en famille* wherever his next transfer might take the three of them?

He finally had to accept, and thereby maybe begin to accommodate, his relationship with Tim as another Foreign Service casualty along with most other relationships that had lived their brief interlude in one or another of the three-to-four-year posts that constituted the shifting map of his career. Of course the cost of such an itinerant lifestyle—as Tim might put it—wasn't only in the instability it brought to the younger generation. The older generation suffered its own measure of unsettling emotional strain. And not only from the bittersweet partings, but also, it seemed, from the sudden return of apparitions out of the forgotten past—ghastly resurrections such as Polk, men envious of your having gone off to what struck them as some brave new world and then coming back with a view of things they could never reach by clinging to the same old neighborhood.

Then, on another level of emotional strain, what Tan Yong had brought back with him out of hell. Not only the agonies that came with reading Chien Fei's diary but now these cloudy, inchoate needs of a daughter who wasn't even hers, let alone his, but who had somehow become old Macpherson's responsibility in a form not yet entirely clear—

though one that would surely prove less than palatable to his unknowing wife and son. He wondered if some part of Tim might not actually enjoy the irony of where his old man now found himself, given Tim's rather righteous view of the world. You worked constantly in your professional life to strike a balance between divided loyalties that in the end would permit you to serve your own country's interests without severely damaging those of the host country to which you were assigned, but in your personal life there was apparently no balance that held, no way finally of escaping a sense of loyalties betrayed. Even if others didn't impose it on you, you ended up imposing it on yourself.

He decided to take off his jacket and stretch out on the bank to give himself a few minutes of sun while it was still high enough to have some bite in it. As he got himself settled, the girl in the canoe spotted him spread out there on the bank and waved one hand in a slow arc. He sat up to wave back. She looked cool, her shirt unbuttoned and tied in a knot at the waist, so that she showed a large triangle of white to the sun, her legs dangling over the gunwale on the side facing him and one foot teasing the water. She seemed to be wearing a white bikini. Then he realized that it was white panties, because she took her folded jeans from the bottom of the canoe and used them to cushion her back. She tilted her head to take the sun full face.

There was something about the image of her between the two paddlers that disturbed him—though the audacity of it struck him as more amusing than sensually stimulating, her manner too innocent really to be provocative. He wondered if it was a signal that another apparition was on its way, some gray-haired version of the golden girl he'd once taken out on that river for an afternoon of love in the open air only to find that everything below shoulder level was strictly out of bounds. Was this girl in the canoe an image of lost possibilities that mocked the hardening in his capacity for sentiment about what could no longer ever be? Or was the disturbing thing something less precious: the contrast between her seemingly healthy and natural American openness and the mental picture of turned-in, wounded silence that Tan Yong had conjured up for him in describing Chien Fei's adopted daughter and that had been at the back of his mind all day? Whatever it was, he found himself putting on his jacket and standing up to brush off his pants as though he suddenly needed to get out of there. As he angled up the bank, his eyes on the canoe, the girl waved again, but he let the thing go with a vague gesture she probably didn't catch and headed off for the University.

Father Grigorian was waiting behind a spare, immaculate desk in his office near the college library. His face—a bit rosy but unlined—made him a younger man than Miss Leonard had led Macpherson to expect, somewhere between forty and fifty, though his hair was even grayer than Macpherson's and cropped close to undercut its natural curliness. He was smiling—rather stiffly, Macpherson thought.

"I'm sorry I'm a little late," Macpherson said. "I got caught up in what you might call a nostalgic tour of Georgetown."

"So you're a graduate of this University?" Father Grigorian said.

He was already getting set to take notes on a yellow pad that he'd brought up from a drawer to signal business without further delay.

"No, I used to live in the neighborhood and graduated from Western High School. That is, what used to be called Western High School."

"And now that you're back here on a Washington assignment you want to enroll your daughter in the special orientation program for foreigners, is that it? Even though she isn't technically a foreigner?"

"No. Not my daughter. A friend's daughter. And at this point I just want to explore the possibility. Which I have to admit seems a bit remote to me."

Father Grigorian looked up from his pad. "I'm confused," he said. "Why am I interviewing you instead of your friend? Or better still, the candidate herself?"

"That's a long story," Macpherson said.

The smile appeared again, with what seemed a pinch of irony. Father Grigorian sat back in his chair.

"You look as though you're about to confess to me," he said. "I assumed from what your secretary told me that you wanted to see me on strictly official academic business."

"In my line of work the official and the personal get mixed up sometimes," Macpherson said. "Anyway, I count on you to be discreet."

"That I can be. But I can't act the confessor in this office."

"Well, I'm not going to confess to you in any way that will embarrass you in your priestly capacity," Macpherson said. "I'm afraid I'm a lapsed believer. From way back."

Father Grigorian's smile disappeared. "And I'm not easily embarrassed. It's just that in my line of work I constantly run into people who think they can absolve themselves by talk, without ritual. I have to protect myself against the casual talkers. Because I am not a psychiatrist."

"You can relax, Father," Macpherson said. "I'm not looking for absolution. Just some practical advice in a rather awkward situation."

Father Grigorian studied him. Then he bent down suddenly and opened the bottom drawer of his desk to bring out a bottle of sherry and two stemmed glasses.

"Maybe this will help both of us relax," he said. "It's reasonably close to cocktail time, isn't it?"

"Reasonably," Macpherson said.

Father Grigorian passed him a glass. His hand was absolutely steady.

"Now," he said. "What is this awkward situation?"

"Put in its simplest terms, the daughter in question is in Thailand at the moment, and I have no way of knowing what her academic training amounts to at this point. Or even the quality of her mind."

"And the parents? Wouldn't they know?"

"Well, the parent, the mother, is in Thailand too. In a refugee camp near the border."

"And the two of them are presumably on their way here, is that it?"

"Not exactly. A friend of theirs is here, a fellow refugee. And I think he hopes I will sponsor the daughter in this country. Which I assure you is a very complicated business."

"I'm sure it is," Father Grigorian said. "But wouldn't one begin by sponsoring both the mother and the daughter? I mean they would presumably come together."

"Well, the mother isn't really the girl's mother. They're from separate families that merged at some point. Whereby lies another long story."

Father Grigorian was studying him again. "There seems to be mystery on mystery in this case. It would be easier for me to understand the issue if you were to begin by telling me why the refugee friend of theirs in this country hopes that you in particular will sponsor the daughter. Unless that is among the questions that fall under the category of confession."

"I think I can say that he feels I have some obligation to the mother. The mother so-called, that is. As a result of my period of service in Cambodia before the American evacuation."

"I assume you mean not just in the sense that all Americans may have an obligation toward refugees in Cambodia. Because then of course the so-called daughter would be an obligation quite aside from her still-unexplained connection with the so-called mother."

"Your assumption is correct," Macpherson said.

"I see," Father Grigorian said, his glass poised for a second like a chalice in front of his lips, before he began to twist it slowly. "That does rather complicate the issue. Especially if you already have a family in this country."

"A wife and a son," Macpherson said. "A wife who would not be very understanding of that bit of her husband's history and a son maybe old enough to understand but impossible to talk to. So you see my situation."

Father Grigorian stopped twisting the glass to take a sip. "Indeed. And exactly what sort of practical advice do you think I might be able to give you in your situation?"

Macpherson decided to take a second sip of sherry after all. "How I might be able to help the daughter begin some sort of educational program in this country without getting myself too involved. I mean if she were somehow to qualify for residence here."

"But it seems to me you're already involved," Father Grigorian said.

"I suppose so," Macpherson said. "In a manner of speaking. But I'm still hoping to spare my wife anything that might put a serious strain on our already rather shaky marriage."

Father Grigorian lowered his glass. "I'm afraid we're getting into an area where I can't offer advice. At least not in this context."

"Well, damn it, I have to talk to somebody about it. I mean I've got to decide to do something one way or another."

"I understand," Father Grigorian said, raising his glass again. "If I may make a totally unofficial and informal suggestion, maybe you should at least try talking to your son. Just in case you find that he can become an ally."

"My son an ally? You don't know my son."

"Yes. Well, I don't know you either. But in these things one has to start somewhere. I mean when one hasn't the benefit of what you've allowed to lapse."

"The point is, I don't have the benefit of my son's trust either. Haven't for some time now."

"Well, maybe the time has come to try building it up again. By sharing your problem with him. Showing some confidence in his advice."

"I think I have a pretty good idea what kind of advice he'd give me under the circumstances," Macpherson said. "And I expect I wouldn't find it very pleasant to carry out, let alone useful in solving the problem at hand."

Father Grigorian sighed. He reached for the sherry bottle and poured himself a second glass. Then, without asking Macpherson's permission, he filled up the other glass as well.

"Look," he said. "Behind this collar I'm still an Armenian. I know how to strike a bargain."

"I couldn't be more willing to bargain," Macpherson said. "Just give me something to work with."

"All right. I'm ready to try and find a place in my program for your friend's daughter and no questions asked about whose daughter she really is or how she got herself to this country. But at the same time, I have to have some assurance that she's qualified to undertake university work after an appropriate period of orientation and that she'll not become dependent on me or my program over the long haul. Either financially or psychologically."

Macpherson smiled. "You call that a bargain?"

"Well, have you had a better one today?"

"I suppose not," Macpherson said, sipping his sherry. "So how do I give you this assurance short of bringing the girl over here untested and making her part of my family?"

"Maybe you can arrange for somebody to check her credentials before she actually comes over to make sure ahead of time that we're dealing with a feasible case. But how you arrange the financial and psychological matter once she's here, I'm not prepared to suggest."

"I see," Macpherson said. "So I guess that is that."

"The point is, if I had an easy answer to that problem, I wouldn't have to make it a condition."

"And if I had an easy answer, I wouldn't be asking for your help."

"Which brings us to the only satisfactory conclusion one can ever reach in an Armenian bargain," Father Grigorian said. "Neither buyer nor seller is fully satisfied, both feel they have somehow been cheated of the best possibility. So they end up having to divide the embarrassment in half."

Tan Yong had hardly been enthusiastic about the restaurant the last time he'd been there—Chinese food as one usually found it in America was not his favorite cuisine in any case—but it was certainly the simplest place to meet this Mr. Polk once it had been established that neither had access to an appropriate office at that time. And meeting there had to be despite the several reservations that had come with the sound and the look of the man during that first encounter—a man given to a rather suggestive way of speaking that Tan Yong couldn't quite grasp well enough to judge except superficially, but with something clearly sinister hiding behind the eyes—because one was not in a position to dismiss an offer of assistance on the basis of untested intuition or personal taste when one's own circumstances were relatively secure and the fate of others still in balance. And though he'd felt a twinge of disloyalty in agreeing to the condition that the two of them meet without Macpherson's knowing about it, a condition he hoped to have explained before this meeting was over, that too seemed an excessive sentiment in view of his purpose. There was simply no excuse for failing to explore all avenues that might lead somewhere. Sameth, who had every excuse to have given up on him by this time, might forgive him out of her natural generosity for his having failed to turn up anything substantial, but he wouldn't be able to forgive himself if he let any possibility slip through his fingers, first of all regarding her case but also that of the others at the camp who had put their hope in him.

If there was some small justification for his feeling awkward about Macpherson, the truth was that Macpherson himself had reason to feel awkward about evidently not yet having done anything that might clarify Thirith's situation. The two of them could thus share the guilt with regard to Sameth, as they had shared her affection, however disproportionately. Macpherson had been very shrewd in playing on his intuitive sense of there having been some sort of personal relationship in the camp, in fact had appeared ready to make use of it somehow in his defense or at least in his attempt to withdraw from a continuing relationship; but Tan Yong was fairly certain he'd closed off that escape route without rousing the man's suspicion dangerously. His own relationship with Sameth was not the issue at that point and must not be allowed to enter the current rather delicate state of affairs in any way that might confuse the case for Macpherson's helping Thirith. They both owed Sameth whatever assistance they could give her, and that inescapably included assistance to the girl she had taken on as her charge. If for the moment he himself had what might be considered the advantage of knowing the basis for Macpherson's debt without having revealed his own, that didn't alter the urgency of their common obligation, regardless of whether or not Macpherson was ready to acknowledge and act on it. And until he was, no other possible avenue of assistance could be discounted simply because it might prove a waste of time to explore it.

Tan Yong wasn't at all sure that it would prove a waste of time. Often it was people like this Mr. Polk who turned out to be the most useful in solving the kind of problem he hoped to bring before him if things went in the right direction—someone in touch not only with government officials like Macpherson but perhaps also with the unofficial government on the periphery of the bureaucracy, where a stateless refugee might have more chance to maneuver on behalf of equally stateless friends. One gathered this was the principal area of the man's expertise from the way he'd answered that no doubt rather blunt question about how he'd managed to track him down after their single brief meeting in Georgetown that day. How had he put it? "I have contacts all over this town. You might say it's the business I'm in." And a bit later in their quite strained phone conversation: "I have certain connections that might prove useful to you, and I think you have some that might prove useful to me." Even if all this contact and connection talk seemed rather pale when examined in the open light, perhaps amounting to no more than a minor functionary here and there and a gullible secretary or two—of whom Macpherson's could well be one—there was at least a distant chance that their obviously separate interests might intersect profitably at some point. The question was how to lead the man to specific cases and still allow room for a graceful retreat.

"Ah, here we are," Tan Yong said as Polk came up to the table and stood over him, shoulders hunched, smiling broadly. "I'm afraid I arrived here a bit early because I wasn't certain I would be able to find this place so easily after only one visit."

"No problem," Polk said. "You found it is the thing. And I guess you and I both have some spare time these days." He pulled out the chair opposite Tan Yong, then changed his mind and sat down catercornered to him, his back turned a fraction away, his eyes surveying the room from one end to the other.

"I feel a bit awkward about something," Tan Yong said. "So may I be excused for bringing it into the open immediately to clear the air? I don't quite understand why it is so important that I not mention this meeting to our mutual friend."

"That's an easy one," Polk said, turning, smile gone. "Our mutual friend works for the U.S. Government. Officially. You and I don't, right? At least not any longer."

"You used to work for the government?"

"For a spell," Polk said, looking away again. "In the Transportation Department. And that's not counting my army time in the Pacific and Korea. But in the end the government didn't get along with me and I didn't get along with them. Still very useful for contacts, to be sure, but I prefer to free-lance it, if you know what I mean."

"What sort of free-lancing do you do, Mr. Polk? If you'll forgive me for asking a direct question."

"At the moment mostly lobbying on Capitol Hill," Polk said. "But

I'm getting ready to branch out a bit. Hoping to move out on the international scene again. Say, how about something to eat?"

"Please go ahead and order," Tan Yong said. "I'm quite happy for the moment with my tea."

"You've got to eat something," Polk said, studying the menu. "It's on me this go-around. I've had a pretty good week, all things considered."

Tan Yong watched him read the menu, trying to decipher what it was he sensed behind the man's eyes. Something akin to the indifferent brutality—anyway, the brutalization—he'd seen in young guerrillas who'd spent too much of their youth in the jungle along the border fighting for one faction or another.

"The connections you mentioned," Tan Yong said softly. "These are on Capitol Hill?"

Polk closed the menu. "Mostly," he said. "But elsewhere too. I've done my country some service over the course of time, as they say. And you don't live in Washington, D.C., for close on to fifty years without picking up a friend here and there who owes you something. What say we get the waiter over here to break the code this thing is written in?"

He tilted his chair back and signaled for the waiter. The waiter was taking an order at another table. He nodded in Polk's direction and went on about his business—a young Chinese, maybe twenty, wearing a dinner jacket that was too big for him. He was taking his time, writing down the order slowly, checking against the menu. When he finally came over, Polk sat there looking at him.

"I really don't want to eat anything," Tan Yong said. "I have another appointment in a few minutes. And I'm not yet used to eating heavily at noon."

Polk was still gazing up at the waiter. "Well, I hope you don't mind if I go ahead and have something to eat. That is, as soon as we can get ourselves a little service."

The waiter stood there holding his pad and smiling, as though he hadn't heard. Tan Yong took up the menu and studied it. Then he glanced up to smile back at the waiter.

"I suggest the gentleman try number three," Tan Yong said without looking at Polk. "Neither too spicy nor too mild, a nice combination of meat and vegetables."

"What do you think?" Polk asked the waiter. "Is number three our hot combination today?"

The waiter smiled. "Number three good dish," he said. "Not too spicy, not too mild."

"That's what Mr. Young here said. So fine. We'll make it number three."

Tan Yong made a gesture to signal the waiter that he was content with his tea, and the waiter gathered up the menus.

"Anyway, since you're in a bit of a hurry, I wonder if I can get right down to a few questions about your line of work," Polk said.

"I don't want you to be misled," Tan Yong said. "I don't exactly have a line of work yet. Just some prospects."

"Well, I assume you must be in some line of business that brings you in touch with people like our mutual friend. He's not one to waste his time on just social amenities. In fact he's never even invited me over to his house once in all these years."

"My business with Mr. Macpherson is essentially a personal matter," Tan Yong said. "By profession I'm a journalist."

Polk sat back and studied him with something like a smile.

"All right, Mr. Young. I'll come clean with you. We can play cat-and-mouse right through the lunch hour, because I'm in no hurry, you're the one who has another appointment. But I prefer to let it all hang out in the open. I mean if we're going to be of assistance to each other, there's got to be a little trust. And you've got to give me a little something to work with."

"Forgive me," Tan Yong said softly. "It seems we have increasing difficulty understanding each other."

"Let me put it as simply as I can," Polk said. "I did some scouting on you through certain government channels because I thought it would save us time. My contacts tell me you've come from Cambodia recently."

"Thailand, to be exact," Tan Yong said.

"Thailand. Good. For my purposes it amounts to the same thing. And my contacts also tell me you were in some kind of refugee business over there, right?"

"I'm afraid your contacts are mistaken," Tan Yong said.

"No refugee business? Please, Mr. Young. You can't tell me you managed to get out of there safely and make it all the way over here without some connection with the refugee business."

"Not unless you mean by being myself a refugee. Which in a way I still am."

"Aren't we all, Mr. Young? That isn't really what I meant."

"In any case, the only business I am in now is trying to help people like myself who are still over there. Through the various voluntary agencies, among other things."

"And you don't think that counts?"

"Not as a business, no."

Polk leaned toward him a fraction. "Well, maybe I can show you how it can become profitable business for both of us if you'll spare me a minute or two of your time."

"I still don't think we understand each other," Tan Yong said.

"Maybe we can both try a little harder, then. I mentioned my Capitol Hill connections to you?"

Tan Yong nodded.

"Well, let's just say a few of these connections have been known to help out in the business you're now in. Follow my meaning?"

"I think so," Tan Yong said.

"And I've been known to help them get their help to the right people. Still follow me?"

Tan Yong sat up just enough to be comfortable for the first time.

"Please feel free to tell me what you think might be done," he said. "But slowly and specifically, if you'd be so kind."

"Now we're talking business," Polk said, leaning back in his chair. "Because if my connections can be of help to you, maybe your connections in Thailand can be of help to me."

———

Macpherson figured he hadn't been to Capitol Hill since '71, when he'd been called in to testify before the Foreign Relations Committee regarding the evils of the Greek junta and the idiocy of America's continuing a friendly attitude toward those fascist slobs. The residential area beyond the Capitol was clearly a different place these days, another Georgetown, or rather another new Georgetown, just about every other house on a given block transformed from its slum remnant into a showpiece of Federal-style architecture that surely few in the federal government who were reasonably honest could afford to buy. Just how long Tim would be able to stay on in that kind of territory after he was through helping with the renovation of the building he was in remained a question Macpherson felt he might want to raise as an expression of parental interest—if not of parental self-defense. But of course that was just the kind of question likely to stir up the old fire under ashes both of them had spent some time in recent days carefully banking against the contingency.

And what was even more likely to stir up some fire was showing Tim the diary of his father's onetime mistress in foreign parts. That was the one concrete course of action that had emerged from his rumination over Father Grigorian's advice, a risky course whose practical consequences remained anybody's guess. His assumption was that it would simply further complicate his relationship with Tim and in no way advance Tan Yong's interest. But if that proved to be the case, he would simply have to arrange a final short meeting with Tan Yong to tell him the essential truth: he'd looked into the matter of Sameth's daughter—he was ready to use that designation as a gesture of courtesy—and had learned that there was no chance of getting her admitted to an educational program in this country, however special, without evidence of her capability and solvency. That was something Macpherson couldn't provide at this time for obvious reasons, nor could Tan Yong himself, since he hadn't seen the two of them in over a year and was now in the wrong country. So the only hope he could see that either of them had for helping the daughter—an increasingly remote hope at that point—was through one or the other of the agencies that had worked to get Tan Yong where he was now, and even then there would be the problem of arranging some sort of continuing support over here, assuming the girl qualified for residence in the first place.

He was fairly certain Tan Yong would try to get around this by suggesting that Macpherson might himself want to arrange the necessary status through his channels and himself provide whatever support might be needed, at least at the start, and so on. And to this he would have to respond that he couldn't very well try to arrange for the girl—who was, after all, a woman now—to come to his country without first of all finding her and then looking carefully into her situation, an aspect of which would be the rather vital question of whether Sameth actually wanted her adopted daughter to come to America, a thing he wasn't ready to take for granted, especially since it would presumably mean the two of them separating indefinitely. And even more to the point was the question of whether the daughter herself wanted to come. If it turned out both questions could somehow be answered positively, one still had to determine exactly what auspices they themselves would consider appropriate, quite aside from what Tan Yong or Macpherson himself might think.

This strategy would naturally open him to the charge of further procrastination, and indeed there would be some legitimacy in the charge, but he still had his own immediate family problems to cope with first. And it wasn't only a matter of testing the ground to see if Father Grigorian's advice had any possibility at all of taking hold propitiously. Something else besides his own preoccupation was out there just waiting to drop down and complicate the easy ride he'd been having with Tim since the boy had moved out of the house how many weeks ago to live on his own. You simply don't get a call out of the blue from Tim Macpherson unless something serious has occurred in his life: dropping out of college, or a "close friend's" pregnancy, or having to change jobs again.

Whatever it might be, you could be sure it meant an outlay of cash on the old man's part—never very much, so one couldn't really make an issue out of it, but still irritating when you stopped to think that the only thing you were ever called on to offer these days was what the boy himself had spent much energy in the past claiming to despise. Precious little advice was sought, almost no time allowed for man-to-man banter, God knows no overt affection demonstrated. What it usually came down to was a hearty handshake by the old man that seemed grossly out of place, and when the small talk was over a sort of embarrassed, hangdog statement from the boy that things being what they were, he could use a little extra pocket money to tide him over. And then it could be weeks before you heard from him again, except during those few really tough periods when he chose to live at home and when you sometimes heard from him more than you wanted to. Maybe in the end a cash tie was better than no tie at all. Someday—someday—it might serve to lead the two of them out of their emotional labyrinth into less complicated and constricted territory. And who knows, Father Grigorian might have pointed toward a possible route. Letting Tim have a look at that very personal diary could be the sort of gesture that turned out to be the necessary first step in the right direction. Just as it could turn out to be exactly the opposite.

Macpherson backed off from the house, a three-story affair still needing much work, Tim's room obviously somewhere on one of the unrenovated floors, since his place had yet to merit its own bell. He backed up further and yelled "Macpherson." That brought a "Yo" from the top floor. Tim appeared at one of the dormer windows and signaled to him to come on up. They were working on the stairway between the second and third floors: half the steps had been replaced by beautifully rounded but still untreated treads. He remembered Tim's saying over the phone that he put in most of his time these days on carpentry work, both at home and at other places under renovation on the Hill, which was why he'd chosen to settle in that part of town. Macpherson suspected that another reason was the distance from his parents' place way out there off Connecticut Avenue, presumably beyond convenient reach except by car—and the only car in the family was Macpherson's own after their second car had spent what appeared to be its last healthy season vaulting precariously back and forth between his wife and his son.

"So what do you think of the place?" Tim said, motioning him on in. "Your standard small and not-so-cozy pad, right? Anyhow, it will look a lot better when I get some furniture in here besides these chairs and the mattress."

"It's fine," Macpherson said. "All a man really needs."

"Anyway a man without a woman, right?"

"You said it, I didn't," Macpherson said. "I'm not in league with your mother on the early-marriage issue. Your living up here by yourself is perfectly okay as far as I'm concerned."

"Well, I've got me this old refrigerator and a hot plate. What more do I need? Especially when I only have to cook for myself and can't afford anything fancy."

Tim suddenly remembered that he had something sitting on the hot plate and went over to look into it. Macpherson took advantage of the break to cross over to the dormer window. He could see a corner of what appeared to be the new Senate Office Building beyond the end of the street. Most of the buildings across the way were newly renovated and looked expensive with or without the local inflation.

"What happens when you've finished working on this place?" he said, still gazing out the window. "Will they give you an option of some kind on your room?"

"I don't plan to be around that long," Tim said.

"No? Where do you plan to be?"

Tim came over and handed him what looked like a cup of hot water.

"Southeast Asia probably."

Macpherson studied the cup of hot water. There was some kind of herb floating in it.

"Southeast Asia?"

"Probably," Tim said. "Why? Something wrong with that?"

Macpherson took a sip of the herbal tea. He resisted the thought that it tasted like weak dishwater. "No, there's nothing wrong with that. What exactly would you have in mind doing in Southeast Asia?"

"There's plenty to do out there, God knows. You realize what kind of destruction those people suffered? The number of refugees over there? And it's still going on."

"I have some idea," Macpherson said. "What particular people do you mean?"

"Take your pick. Cambodia, Vietnam, Laos, Burma, Malaysia. Who knows where else?"

"Well, as I understand it, you can't just wander into most of those places freely these days. No American, anyway."

"I haven't got in mind just wandering in there," Tim said. "I have in mind working for one of the voluntary relief agencies."

Macpherson took a second sip. He focused on trying to identify one or another of the mixed tastes in his mouth to counter an almost uncontrollable urge to spit the stuff back into the cup. Tim was watching him.

"What particular agencies do you have in mind?" Macpherson asked.

"Well, I've been looking into that. One reason I wanted to talk to you. The Quakers. The Mennonites. UNICEF. They say there are several agencies that have Americans working for them even in Cambodia and Vietnam. I thought you might be able to check a couple of them out for me. Through your normal channels, I mean."

Macpherson put his cup down on the floor. Tim brought over a chair and set it beside him to serve as a coffee table.

"Now, let me get this straight," Macpherson said. "Your latest plan is to go over to Cambodia or Vietnam and work for a voluntary agency?"

"It's an idea," Tim said. "And you don't have to say it as though it's like all the other plans I've had or like joining the Foreign Legion or something. It's the least we owe those people over there after what we did to them."

"Not to mention what some of them did to themselves."

Tim raised his hands as though Macpherson had pointed a gun at him.

"No, I'm not going to argue politics with you," he said. "You look at things your way and I look at things mine. This is just something I feel I'd like to do and I don't care whether you approve or not."

"I didn't say I disapproved," Macpherson said. "I'm just trying to get used to the idea."

"Call it a matter of conscience if that helps," Tim said.

"I understand. I'm just trying to get the details straight in my head. So you figure one or another of these agencies will pay your way over there to do volunteer work, is that it?"

"Not exactly," Tim said. "Hey, how about some more of this tea? It's a special blend I made up myself."

"Just a touch," Macpherson said, handing him his cup. "My stomach is a little queasy from lunch in the State Department cafeteria, where they make sure the poison has no name or country."

Tim took Macpherson's cup. It was still almost full.

"Getting there is another thing I wanted to talk to you about," Tim said, working over the hot plate. "If you can spare the time."

"Shoot," Macpherson said. "Plenty of time."

"I wondered if you might stake me to the trip over there. You and Ismini. Once I'm over there, I'm on my own."

"Pay your way over and back, you mean."

"Just over. I'll worry about the trip back once I get there."

"Well, maybe you'd better worry about it right from the start," Macpherson said. "In case you get over there and change your mind."

Tim put Macpherson's cup down on his coffee-table chair.

"I guess you just don't understand me and never will," he said. "I'm dead serious. Once I get over there I'm not turning right around and coming back."

Macpherson decided to let the cup stay where it was, what the hell. "Will I offend your sensibilities if I ask how much a plane ticket costs?"

"That depends on how you go," Tim said. "They say there's a cheap fare via Europe to Thailand because of all the tourist traffic going that route. I wouldn't mind checking out Thailand while I'm at it anyway."

Macpherson got up to look out the window again. Without turning, he said, "I'll have to take the matter under advisement, as they say down at State. That doesn't mean I'm against the idea, understand. But if it's all the same to you, let's for the time being keep the thing between you and me. I mean let's not get your mother all stirred up unnecessarily."

"I'll have to tell her at some point that I'm taking off. And why I'm doing it."

"Of course. I just mean the matter of your ticket. And where you may be heading exactly."

"You mean because she may think it dangerous?"

"That among other things. Let's just keep the question open until it's definitely settled, okay?"

"Like what other things?"

Macpherson reached into his jacket pocket and brought out the soiled yellow notebook. Tim stared at it as Macpherson held it out to him.

"What's that?" he said, still not taking it.

"You'll see. I think it's pretty much self-explanatory. But when you've had a look at it, give me a call and I'll try to fill you in on anything you find difficult to understand."

―――――

Since he was already likely to be in hot water with old Tom over having kept the car through the morning rush hour, Tim figured he didn't stand to lose anything by adding another hour or so to his delinquency and heading out to Connecticut Avenue while he still had wheels under him. He'd pay Ismini a short visit, then cut back through the park to deliver the car to the old man's parking place down at State so that he could return the yellow notebook to him personally, as he'd promised to do. His late date out in Falls Church the previous evening and a long, easy morning to recover had been worth whatever it might end up costing him—which, given the recent change in the old man's attitude, might prove to be no more than reimbursement for the taxi ride that must have gotten him to work that morning.

It wasn't just that Tom had been generous enough to make his car available for an evening—it was his deciding of his own free will to hand over that diary for background even though he must have figured it wasn't likely to rouse a great deal of enthusiasm for some of the things he'd been up to out there in Cambodia while his wife was under evacuation orders in the country next door. That gesture demonstrated more trust than he could remember from old Tom since he'd dropped out of college. On the other hand, his showing that diary to someone he no doubt expected would disapprove of his involvement with another woman clued you in on how seriously he still took that bit of past history, despite his fairly cool explanation in their one phone conversation on the subject as to why he'd decided to let Tim have a look at the thing and what he hoped might be possible once Tim got himself to Thailand. So where did you draw the line on how far you let yourself into another man's basically private business, even if he was your own father? At least in that part of the business which was strictly personal and still secret from Ismini.

The general idea of helping Tom out by trying to find the woman once he was over there and checking out the daughter's credentials, or whatever, wasn't really any problem, in fact gave him that much more reason for spending some time in Thailand besides what was needed to see the Buddhist temples in Bangkok and visit a few of the wats in the countryside and maybe look into job prospects among the international agencies in the border area. At least the trip might end up showing the old

―――――

man something about the ability of his supposedly indecisive son to see a thing through once he'd set his mind to it, not to mention some good coming out of it for at least one miserable and forgotten refugee. The problem was how to handle Ismini and the implications, first, of Tom's not having come clean with her and, second, now that he himself had read the diary, of his having to conceal much of what he knew.

One thing he naturally couldn't tell the old man to his face was that his initial response on getting into the diary was Wow, who would have thought Tom had a woman like that tucked away in his past, and not-so-very distant past either if you considered how long he'd been married to Ismini. But it was one thing to find a lively hidden side to your father that you wouldn't have dreamed he had in him and another thing to let yourself get involved in some new phase of an old intrigue that had gone on behind your mother's back. The man had brought him up against a moral dilemma that he could see no easy way out of. On the one hand he didn't want to turn a cold shoulder to his father's good intentions after this first sign of real trust that he'd seen in years, but on the other hand, taking the man up on his request for help under these terms meant a kind of disloyalty to a woman who had her peculiarities, God knows, but who had given herself to both of them for more than twenty-five years and hardly needed new complications coming into her life at this late stage. So where in the moral wilderness of his nation's capital did that leave him? He decided he'd just better keep clear of that particular thorny territory until it became absolutely necessary to enter it. He was going to have problem enough getting Ismini to live with the idea of his going over to Southeast Asia for any purpose, let alone the hidden one he and the old man seemed to be getting themselves into.

Offering Ismini his memento suitcase for storage while he was gone might ease the way a little. She'd like that idea, especially if he ended up handing over its key so that she could look through all the photographs and other odd souvenirs he'd collected in it over the years. She was a great one for family history, keeping her own albums of pictures, invitations, tickets to this and that, postcards from friends, God knows what else, year after year from the day of her marriage through every stage of his childhood and on up until the idea seemed to peter out somewhere around the time he went off to school in Switzerland. Maybe she'd been obsessed for a while with keeping such a detailed record of her marriage and his childhood because she had no record at all of her own childhood as far as he could tell. She never even talked about it. All he knew was that her father had been killed by one of the factions in the Greek resistance and her mother had died soon after of an unnamed illness that sounded a lot like tuberculosis but that Ismini said was basically a broken heart. And the only way he'd been able to distinguish between her father's faction and the one that killed him was via Ismini's rabid anti-Communism. There were the good guys and the bad guys, it was as simple as that, and no good guy could be a Communist or even a Socialist unless he hated Communism. And no argument that whatever the Greek experience of Communism, you couldn't apply that history to every other place in the world where there was some kind of conflict between the right and the left.

Of course it wasn't that simple, even in Cambodia or Vietnam, though he had to admit, especially after reading the diary, that it was hard to see anything more than true horror having come out of the so-called revolution that the Khmer Rouge brought in to devastate those people over there one more time before the Vietnamese moved in to have their go at it. He wasn't likely to find out just what it all amounted to these days, what was really behind it all, until he actually got over there to see for himself. But you could be sure there would be no room for discussing the subject ahead of time with Ismini. In fact, any talk of politics at home had become a definite no-no some time back. Except when old Tom got it into his head to play games with Ismini's prejudices, which after all grew out of an insecurity that might not be so hard to appreciate if you'd lost your parents and who knows how much more of your family during one war or another.

From Ismini's point of view, family were all there really was, which you might call the positive side of her insecurity, even if it could sometimes make her a pain. Not that he himself had anything against marriage, God knows, or raising a family. What else was out there worth aiming for in the long run? But it was a little hard to get worked up over your own family history, let alone somebody else's, when one half of that history was dark space filled by made-up images of men and women he'd never seen or even heard a full description of.

At least on Tom's side there was the concrete memory of a white-haired old geezer of a grandfather who had a thin little mustache left over from his days as a World War I aviator and who used to threaten jokingly to "pulverize" him over the slightest infraction of rules he himself made up on the spot during the few times he'd run into him in the early days, before he went off to the home in Rochester, New York, with his equally white-haired and endlessly talkative wife of close to fifty years, your classic warm if scatterbrained grandmother. On Ismini's side, there was a country of stark mountains, white villages, the bluest sea you could imagine, all out of picture books, and no recognizable figures that he could relate to personally. It was as if one half of him had sprouted out of upstate New York and was as all-American as you could stand with a hero in the family going as far back as World War I, and the other half had sprouted out of an unknown foreign country that had fought strange internal wars and was pure refugee. Which made Ismini's own insecurity at least comprehensible—after all, she really had been a refugee in a way—if sometimes a little hard to live with on a day-in, day-out basis.

He decided to leave the car parked in the street even though he still had a key to the garage, because to drive in there at that hour of day might scare the hell out of her, especially if she was in the so-called family room on the ground floor watching some morning TV show. TV was another obsession of hers that he'd never quite understood, probably a throwback to her maybe deadly silent childhood when even listening to the radio was apparently some kind of luxury. But he suspected she kept it on most of the day just to have a voice somewhere in the house, especially now that he'd moved out and Tom was putting in his solid eight-to-seven down at State and some extra time on weekends. Too much silence indoors seemed to drive her crazy.

He glanced in through the ground-floor window: sure enough, the set was on, but no sign of Ismini. She was probably upstairs in the kitchen, or maybe on the top floor taking a bath, or even more likely already outside on the patio back of the kitchen up there taking in the sun, which was the one thing you could count on to get her out of the house and away from the TV set before the bridge circuit took over in late afternoon. She could just sit there on that patio for hour on hour with her naturally half-tanned face tilted toward the sun, long black hair with a few streaks of gray in it laid back behind her in a full spread and her eyes closed, the expression on her face truly relaxed as if that were the one source of peace left in the world. It broke your heart even to interrupt her with a question.

His ring of keys was getting ridiculously heavy, but he never seemed to find the time to sort them out, maybe because that too was a way of carrying your past around with you, all the places you once had access to that were now closed off but that you might want to remember anyway if you could only figure out what key came from what door in what house. He finally found the one he was looking for and let himself in, then called out "Hello" as he started up the stairs so nobody would get the idea he still thought he lived there and had free run of the place. No answer.

She was out on the patio all right, but she wasn't sunning herself.

She had a pair of jeans on and was weeding out the single patch of flowers she'd managed to plant in time for spring along the edge of the brickwork out there: azaleas, crocuses, who knew what else. She looked good; no fat on that lady except a little around the hips, and some good muscle going for her in those bare arms.

"Ho," he called through the open French doors off the dining room. "Need any help from a guy with a black thumb?"

"What's that?" she said, looking startled. "Oh, it's you. Why do you scare me like that?"

She was smiling now. She put down her trowel, wiped her hands on her jeans, and came over to hug him. She smelled of expensive, exotic soap. She always did. When she let go of him, she studied his face and gradually lost her smile.

"What's the matter?" she said.

"Nothing's the matter. Why?"

"It's eleven o'clock. Why would you come here without warning at eleven o'clock if something isn't the matter?"

"Well, the old man let me have the car last night after he got through down at the office, so I thought I'd make use of it while I still had it this morning to stop by here and say hello."

"He isn't an old man. Why must you call him an old man?"

"It's just an expression, for Christ sake. An American expression, like 'daddy' or 'papa' or whatever."

"Why can't you call him 'papa,' then? And don't swear at me."

Tim turned away and went over to flop down in one of the canvas butterfly chairs they had out there passing for garden furniture.

"Hey, let's not get started on the same old stuff right off, okay?" he said. "I'm in a reasonably good mood at the moment and it would be very nice to just keep it that way. So no arguments, okay?"

"What has happened? Why are you in such a good mood? You were with a girl last night?"

"Right. Finally. I mean it's been a long time, I can tell you."

"What kind of girl?"

"Come on, will ya? Nobody you know. Just a girl. A woman, that is."

Ismini wiped her hands on her jeans again. Then she came over to stand beside him, above him. Suddenly she ran a hand through his hair.

"Are you going to tell me what's the matter?" she said. "I promise not to argue with you."

"There's nothing the matter. I swear. Things have been going very good for me lately. At least in a manner of speaking. I'm just getting a little restless not having steady work all the time. You know, no clear set aim in life and that kind of thing."

She was still running her hand through his hair, very slowly, lightly. It felt good.

"Your father thinks you should go back to school," she said. "He thinks you're not going to get very far without a degree from college."

"I know what he thinks. We've been through all that in the past. I mean someday I may go back to college, but not right now."

"Well, one thing you don't need to go to college for is to get married and settle down to make yourself a family."

Tim stood up abruptly and went over to study the flower bed she'd been working on.

"I'm not quite ready for that either," he said, his back still turned. "Not yet having found a woman I'd really like to marry, let alone one who might like to marry me. Which would seem to me a necessary beginning."

"That's because you don't give yourself a chance to meet people. You know, people in our circle. It's as though your father and I belong to one world and you to another."

"What are people in our circle?" Tim said. "Refugees, you mean? People on the move all the time from one country to another?"

"You know what I mean," Ismini said. "Don't be so smart."

"Okay," Tim said. "I'm sorry. I did not come out here to get in a debate about my future. I just wanted to let you know that I'm planning to take off for a while and do some traveling. Which they say is one way of getting an education without going back to college. Even for those who've already had as much traveling under their belt as I have."

"So," Ismini said. "That's what is worrying you. And just where do you plan to travel?"

"Europe. Southeast Asia. It's all still a little vague in my mind."

"Is that right?" Ismini said. "And have you discussed this with your father?"

"Just a little. The basic outlines."

"He didn't mention anything about it to me. Where in Europe and Southeast Asia? I mean Europe is one thing, but Southeast Asia is very far away. On the other side of the world."

"I know that," Tim said. "But it isn't so far away that a lot of Americans weren't sent over there to get involved in a way that cost a lot of lives on all sides."

"Well, the war is over now," Ismini said. "It has been for four years, I believe."

"Yeah, but do you know what it left behind over there? The destruction of agriculture everywhere and the refugee problem they still have on their hands? Actually, for your information, the war is still going on along the Thai–Cambodian border."

She'd come over to stand beside him and was looking not at him but at the flower bed as though seeing the weeds in there for the first time.

"And you want to go over there and get yourself into a war that isn't any of your business, is that it?"

"No, I don't want to get myself into a war. I just want to help out over there in some way if it turns out there's some way I can. Do my bit after all the damage we caused."

"We didn't cause the damage," Ismini said. "The Communists caused the damage. They were the ones who started it. You had better learn a little history before you decide to go over there."

"Okay, okay," Tim said, turning with his hands raised. "It was all the Communists' fault, one kind of Communist or another—who can keep them straight since they all look alike over there anyway, right? I've got to cut out now and get the car back to Tom. I'm very late already and he's not going to be happy about it, you can be sure of that."

"I mean if you have to travel somewhere, why don't you go to Greece, where you have some roots at least? Why do you have to go to the other side of the world?"

Tim sighed. "I don't know. It's a gut thing, I guess. Maybe I'll stop in Greece on the way over. Would that make you feel any better about it?"

"No," Ismini said. "Not if you just keep going on to Southeast Asia."

"Well, we don't have to settle the thing this minute. I mean I've really got to get myself down to the State Department. So what say I stop by again in a few days and we can talk about it some more when the idea's had a chance to percolate a little, okay?"

"You're leaving now? Just like that?"

"I'll be back. I swear. Anyway, I want to drop off a suitcase of valuables here for safekeeping as soon as I can get myself organized, if that's all right by you guys."

"Of course it's all right," Ismini said. "How could it not be?"

"Well, you know," Tim said. "I just thought I'd check it out."

They stood there looking at each other. Then she put her arms around him again. He returned her hug, hard.

"You really have made up your mind, haven't you?" she said.

Tim nodded.

"And can you tell me just one thing?" she said. "Why didn't your father even mention this to me?"

"That's a thing I'm afraid you'll have to ask him," Tim said.

Macpherson was up again, pacing in front of the photograph of Cyrus Vance behind his desk.

"I don't mean to sound unreasonably critical," he said. "It's at least partly my fault. The fact is, you met the man through me in the first instance."

Tan Yong nudged the paperweight so that it lined up exactly with the pencil cup on his side of the desk. "And I for my part want to assure you that I did not tell the man anything that might be taken for a betrayal of your confidence. Just the names and addresses of a few people in Thailand who are working with the international agencies."

"I should have warned you," Macpherson said. "The man was simply not to be trusted in any way. It didn't occur to me that he would get in touch with you on his own. And by the time I found out he had, there was of course no point any longer in warning you. He was up there on the Hill wheeling and dealing in all directions. That is, until he came up against somebody who decided he'd better give the FBI a call."

"Please," Tan Yong said. "I knew he wasn't to be entirely trusted. I was very careful. At the same time, I couldn't afford the luxury others may have of not exploring questionable possibilities that nevertheless might help the people who have put so much hope in me."

"But what possible help could that man have been to you?"

"He told me he had connections in your Congress. People who could arrange immigration of unwanted refugees. Of course for a price."

Macpherson shook his head. "I'm sure I could have put you in touch with people on the Hill who might have found ways to help you without it costing you a penny."

Tan Yong studied the paperweight. "Forgive me. You appeared not to want to get involved. And in this business your Congress has not been open and generous to the degree one might have hoped for."

Macpherson sighed. Then he crossed to look out his window toward the Lincoln Memorial.

"I was just trying to make it easy for my family. Trying to find a way to handle this without burdening them with a thing that's really my responsibility. For all the good it did me. All it's succeeded in doing is getting some of the less sympathetic Congressmen up there on my back again. Apparently Polk had no compunction about using my name right and left."

"I'm very sorry," Tan Yong said. "I wish there were something I could do."

"There's not much either of us can do at this point," Macpherson said. "The man's somewhere out in Southeast Asia by now. Who knows exactly where?"

"So you think he's gone there already?"

"That's what some of his friends in Georgetown say. The few still willing to talk once they'd found out the FBI was after him for trying to influence the wrong people in the wrong way. They told me he'd been planning to head out to that general area on business through some contact I had presumably set up for him."

Tan Yong looked up. "I suppose that refers to me."

"That's what I finally figured out. Though nobody was willing to say exactly what business he had in mind. If they knew."

"I assure you I don't know either," Tan Yong said.

Macpherson came back to sit down at the desk again. "Anyway, you'll be happy to know that I managed to vouch for you so that your name is now clear of any questionable involvement in what he was up to on the Hill. And the whole thing doesn't seem to have done me any serious damage, professionally speaking. At least not yet."

"There are things to be grateful for, then," Tan Yong said. "That pleases me."

"I suppose that's one way of looking at it. Only I feel a little awkward about having brought my son into this business. Not to mention my wife. Unfortunately the investigators got hold of her before they could get through to me."

"You brought your son into this as well?"

"He was out at the house when they got hold of my wife. And I gather he was there to drop off some of his personal effects, because he's clearing out of his room near the Capitol in anticipation of a trip to Thailand. At my expense, since once he's over there he's supposed to do a personal favor for me."

Tan Yong studied him. "I don't understand."

"I had thought he might look up Phal Sameth's so-called daughter while he's in the region. Check her out, as they say these days."

"And now you think his mother won't want him to go? Or he won't want to himself?"

"No, he wants to go all right. It's just that I wonder if it should be up to either of them to worry themselves about what is really my concern. I suppose you can say I think it's time to begin settling my own debts."

"You consider it a debt? How interesting."

"Whatever," Macpherson said. "Call it a moral obligation if that suits you better."

Tan Yong was smiling gently now. "So what you are telling me is that you are considering going to Thailand yourself?"

Macpherson glanced at him, then shuffled through the papers on his desk.

"At some point maybe. It depends on several things. For one, when I can reasonably put in for a little leave."

"I see," Tan Yong said. "This possibility pleases me more than I can properly express. Especially since it is so difficult for me under my present status to think of returning to Thailand myself."

"I certainly wouldn't advise it," Macpherson said.

"And just when do you think you might be able to go?" Tan Yong asked, his whole body suddenly relaxed.

"Hard to say," Macpherson said. "I've only just begun my new assignment here. I'm supposed to take an official orientation trip to southern Europe during the fall with or without leave, so maybe I could combine the two trips. Or maybe next winter."

"I hope you won't have to delay it that long."

"We'll see," Macpherson said. "You've got to realize, I'm not a completely free agent."

"No, of course not. Nobody is."

"I mean, all I can promise is to do my best."

Tan Yong stood up suddenly and offered his hand. "In any case, I'll have some messages to send with you," he said soberly. "Or with your son if you decide he can in fact be of help to us sooner than you yourself may be able to be. That is, if I can assume you don't mind his acting as my personal messenger as well."

"Why should I mind? If I decide to let him go ahead and help me, the least I can do is ask him to help you too."

"I have in mind a message for Phal Sameth in particular."

Macpherson had met his look head on. Then he found himself suddenly lowering his eyes.

———

Tim felt he had the whole job plotted now. The thing was to get the measurements absolutely right from the start, four sides so that they would match exactly, then the outline of the dovetailing along the two edges of each side. Once you had the markings as they should be, the shaping of the tenons was a matter of steady hands, of getting yourself in the right mood so that no extraneous thoughts came in to mess up the atmosphere you needed for handling the saw and chisel. The same went for the mortises, though that was more a question of just taking your time, easing into the thing and staying with it at its own pace, giving the wood a chance to let you know how fast it wanted you to keep going so that you weren't ever forcing your effort against the rhythm natural to the thing you were working with.

Of course the people down at the shop thought he was out of his mind not to use the dovetailing machine when there were that many joints to be made and the box you were constructing was only meant to hold dirt. But there was no way you could explain to people in a hurry that there wouldn't be any point in using the machine to make a box you planned to give somebody as a parting present, even if you could be certain that the thing would come out looking halfway decent and hold itself together long enough to get your plant out to Ismini's place. How could a thing made mostly with the machine end up feeling first of all really yours and second worth giving to somebody else? The thing had to have a little care and sweat in it to be of any value. Not that Ismini was likely to understand everything that had gone into it—the point was, you understand.

Tom would no doubt think he was out of his mind too when he got up there and had a look at what he was working on, but he'd probably pretend otherwise. The man was not just conciliatory these days, he was really openhanded, not only with the car but with his cash. He'd also at least tried to explain what even he, in his too well-trained way of seeing reasonable motives behind just about any action people might take, still couldn't explain so that it was understandable beyond a gut level.

Like that crazy influence peddler spreading the old man's name around town until it prompted that call from the FBI. And others where that character came from, according to Tom's testimony—guys they'd gone out to interview in Georgetown, either spaced out or still fighting a forgotten war or trying to live like old-time Washingtonians in territory surrounded by outsiders of various shades who were moving in to dispossess them. Talk about a lost generation. From one point of view, you had to say it was to Tom's credit that he'd managed to escape from all that in time and had worked his way up in an entirely different direction. But from another point of view, you had to wonder if the man was ever going to free himself from these weird things in his past that seemed to be coming in of late and threatening to turn his life around, not to mention that of his immediate family.

Still, whatever the local problems and Ismini's unhappiness over an unmarried college dropout going off into the unknown, he wasn't about to renege on his promise to try to help Tom out with his problem overseas. Washington was one scene and Thailand was another. Now that he'd made up his mind to head out there, he wasn't going to change direction, and once he was there he still planned to do whatever he could to track the woman down and have a conversation with the daughter on a preliminary basis. No commitment, no detailed involvement, just enough contact to let the old man know what was up these days with the lady and her charge, then out of there for more serious work with one or another of the voluntary agencies in whatever devastated region over there would let him in. But none of this behind Ismini's back. She had to be clued in on what he was up to or the whole deal was off. And that really had to come from Tom.

He took the five sections of planking that he'd brought up from the shop and stacked them on the bench he'd made out of two of the chairs and a discarded door from one of the renovated rooms. He decided to go for a trapezoid shape even though that made the work more complicated, because it would give the eye an angle to follow as it took in the gentle rise of the thing, some opening out. And he would leave the wood natural and highlight it with a bit of polishing so that not just the wood's grain but the linked pattern of the joinings would show. If he'd had time, he would have looked around until he could pick up something a shade more unusual than mahogany, much as he liked what you could bring out in that if you gave it what it wanted—something a little more exotic like tulipwood or teak or amarynth or primavera or rosewood, something with a name and a place in it that you could talk about along with what you were showing off.

Of course if he waited to track down wood like that, he'd never get the rest of his stuff out of the pad before the place was rented, let alone clear the city with one hand free and a clean conscience. It was nearly June already; the summer would be half over if he didn't get himself moving east pretty soon. He figured while the old man was not only staking him to the trip but adding a little pocket money, there would be no harm in taking some time getting where he was going—maybe a stopover in London to check out the museums there, talk about good-looking furniture and what it could do to put your heart at peace, and then possibly Rome for a short detour into that hill country to the north he remembered from his school excursion out of Switzerland as one of the great turn-ons nature mixed with architecture could give you. And then maybe a brief stopover in Athens so that he could tell Ismini he—

"Hey there," Tim called out to the doorway. "Come on up. I guess I didn't hear you with this saw grinding away."

Macpherson stood in the doorway and loosened his tie. "I hope I'm not interrupting anything."

"Not a thing," Tim said. "Just making myself a box. To hold a plant."

"Well, I'm sorry it took me so long getting down here, but anyway I won't take more than a minute of your time."

"All the time in the world," Tim said.

"I don't know exactly when you have in mind heading over to Thailand, but I wanted to make sure I got to you before you left town."

"I wouldn't just leave town," Tim said. "I mean, do you think I'd just leave town without saying anything?"

"I don't know," Macpherson said. "I can't say I know what I think on that subject any longer."

"Well, relax. I wouldn't do a thing like that. No matter what."

"I'm not suggesting you would," Macpherson said. "One just never knows."

"Well, one ought to know by now," Tim said.

Macpherson went over to look out the dormer window. "I can see you're busy with your work so I'll come to the point. I have a list I'd like to give you of the names and addresses of people over there who might be helpful to you in getting yourself set up."

Tim took up the section of plank he'd sawed off and held it against the light. "What kind of names?" he said.

"Some people in the Embassy I used to work with. And some people attached to the U.N. operation out there."

"I appreciate that," Tim said. "I really mean it. But I'd just as soon not get myself hooked up with any government people."

Macpherson glanced at him. "I'm not suggesting you get yourself hooked up. I just want you to have the names in case they prove to be useful to you while you're traveling around over there."

"Whatever," Tim said. "You can leave the list if you want to, but I can't really promise I'll follow up on any of it at this point."

"I mean I don't know whether or not you read the newspapers regularly, but if you do, you'll know that things are getting a little tense these days on the Thai–Cambodian border."

"I read newspapers," Tim said. "As much as I get the chance. And I really think I'm capable of taking care of myself whatever might be going on over there these days. But I appreciate the thought, and I'll keep the list in mind if it makes you feel any better."

Macpherson turned away from the window and looked around for a chair. There wasn't a chair. The place seemed to have been cleaned out completely except for the daybed. He decided to sit on that.

"Let me just get this door off of here and you can have one of these chairs." Tim said.

"This is fine, " Macpherson said. "I can only stay a minute. Really."

"How about some tea? I'll brew up some tea."

"I'm fine," Macpherson said. "The point is, I hope when you do make it out to the border, you'll have a chance to deliver these. I don't expect you to do any more than that at this point, because I'm still hoping to get out there myself sometime next fall or winter."

He took two envelopes out of his jacket pocket and passed them over to Tim, then took out a list of names, folded it twice, and left it at the foot of the daybed. Tim studied the two envelopes, one with a typewritten name and address, the other in almost illegible script. He turned them over to see if there was a return address on the back of either, and when he didn't find any, he turned them over again to look at the names and addresses on the front. He decided finally that they were both addressed to the same person. Then he handed them back to his father.

"I don't think I can deliver these," he said.

"Why not?" Macpherson said. "I thought the idea was that you'd be heading out to the refugee camp in Aranyaprathet at some point one way or another."

Tim went over to his work kit to get some sandpaper. "I agreed to look up the woman and her adopted daughter if I managed to locate them out there. But delivering messages makes me really uncomfortable. I mean behind Ismini's back."

Macpherson sat there smiling stiffly. "Who said it was behind her back?"

Tim crossed to his workbench and began to go at the piece of sawn board with the sandpaper. Macpherson shivered from the sound of it.

"You mean you've told her about it?" Tim said.

"Not yet. It doesn't strike me that this is quite the right moment."

"But you're planning to any day now, right?"

"That's right," Macpherson said. "But you don't have to say it in that tone of voice."

"Well, how am I supposed to know what's really going on between you two? I mean I can't just wait around until you've finally decided it's time to come clean with her."

"Then I guess you'll just have to trust me," Macpherson said quietly. "For once in your life."

Tim studied him. Then he put down the sandpaper and went over to take the letters out of his father's hand.

THREE

1979

January 21. Phnom Penh has fallen again. It seems to take the loss of our city to still another enemy to make me open a new notebook (this one a bit larger than the last) after so many months of telling myself that any writing outside my class roll book and my ledger of accounts would simply be a self-indulgent way of escaping from the reality of life on this border. Now I begin to feel something near the opposite: to write here, even if it proves to be for my eyes alone, may be the only way I have of grasping that reality and holding on to it before it too becomes part of the life we have lost. News came to our camp two weeks ago over Thai radio that the Vietnamese had entered Phnom Penh, what was left of it, and now new refugees from Cambodia have crossed the border to our camp with more details about what has taken place in this latest violent shuffle of political absurdities inside our vanishing homeland.

The Vietnamese have apparently set up a new People's Revolutionary Council in what they still call "Democratic Kampuchea," this Council to rule our country on terms acceptable to Hanoi. The Khmer Rouge command and most others belonging to their administration have fled once again toward the jungle forests and the mountains. They tell those they encounter in their flight that they will struggle on relentlessly wherever they can until our capital city is liberated again, the city they themselves had emptied overnight except for a few hungry dogs and maniacal snipers when I last saw it four years ago. Our Prince Sihanouk is back in China now asking the world to ignore the puppet government of the invading Vietnamese and to recognize the fleeing Khmer Rouge instead, the very regime that was responsible for killing his own sons and then for turning him into a bourgeois husband under house arrest for three years. They say that he weeps for his sons at the same time that he pleads for the Khmer Rouge cause.

This, my dear Tan Yong, is the latest turn in our country's fate. I address you as I come back to this notebook because you more than any of the others who have found refuge outside Thailand would want to know what is now happening on the other side of the border beyond our camp, and you would also be the first to appreciate the ironies of it. For my part I will feel more at ease recording these latest political idiocies and their cruel consequences if I can imagine a familiar and sympathetic audience listening to me, especially since it still seems wise for me to write in the English language you and I would turn to in our moments of secret dialogue after we came to trust each other in those early days here.

I don't really expect you will ever read this. It is now over a year since you left us for America, and still no word from you. I don't mean that to sound like a complaint. As you well know, I am not the kind of woman to exploit sentiments of trust for some emotional advantage. I don't know what part of my very mixed Sino-Khmer blood makes that impossible—perhaps a legacy from my Scottish grandmother who apparently governed my father's childhood in Hong Kong with quiet Anglo-Saxon terror. Or perhaps the sternly moral English nanny he later imposed on me. In any case, I'm sure you've done what you could to help those of us here who put our best hope in you. That is what makes me feel we are not likely to see each other again. Your pride would not allow you to get in touch with me unless you had something useful to offer, and that means the obstacles have proved too complicated. We are well aware that the quota of those found acceptable for immigration into America is becoming ridiculously small compared with the number of those here who are hungry to go, and it seems to most of us who came across the border as long ago as you and I did that our time has now run out.

I myself am no longer hungry to go to a third country. If it weren't for Thirith, thoughts of America or France would no longer clutter my mind. I know that preference is given those who once worked with the Americans, but I can't bring myself to use that experience when I look back on it with such ambivalence. And from such a distance. I even begin to have difficulty remembering exactly what our mutual State Department friend looked like, let alone imagining what may now be going in and out of his head and those of the people he serves. No, my work is here. And my future, at least for the moment. It is not only that I continue to see the work as important, essential even. It also has its privileges, its conveniences. I'm considered part of the regular staff now—not quite equal to the "foreign" staff, of course, but with the right to go to Aran when I please and with my own room in the administration section, much more spacious than what you and I knew in our early days here, those squares of platform in the barracks partitioned like prison cells only open in too many ways to communal noise and stench. Our room is actually comfortable for two if one divides the space with discretion, and Thirith and I are allowed to use the staff kitchen facilities for our meals. Also the staff toilet facilities, which are short of water for bathing but a great improvement over the bamboo-sided horror we had to cope with in the past.

But this place is not right for Thirith. She is still so young—not yet twenty; she deserves another chance to live some kind of normal life. And though I inherited her from the rain on the highway outside Battambang, she is now my daughter as much as any I might bear, and I worry about her as much. Not possessively. Her future obviously has to be free of my need, and I have to survive without the hope her youth carries.

I'm not afraid of that. If I learned one thing in making my way with Thirith through the forests and the mountains that now lie behind us here, it is the simple virtue of stretching what little one has to the limit while looking no farther ahead than where it seems one can safely place the left foot after the right without stepping on a mine or on somebody's shattered corpse—that is, except when it might shield one against a possible hidden danger underneath.

And another thing I learned was to look with deep suspicion on whatever abstractions might come into my head to give me a sensation of hope. In the jungle west of Battambang one doesn't find political or philosophical refuges to help the mind survive the damp nights, no erotic retreats, no easy place for ideological excursions, no comforting images of America or France. There are only the trees with no name and the sharp bamboo and the bushes covered with thorns, the poisonous plants, the treacherous open grassland. There are the snakes and the malarial mosquitoes that turn out to be nothing beside the imaginary wild animals, the tigers and leopards and bears that they say actually live there but that never quite show themselves. And there is the unseen enemy who has stretched wire between two stakes with grenades at either end and buried boards holding spikes that can penetrate rubber, leather, anything one has left to wear on the feet. And of course the waiting patrols, heard and unheard.

Still, even when you are frightened so that the perspiration pours down your face at the coldest moments and every new noise seems to signal an ambush that could leave you dismembered but still alive to crawl, like the half-bloated bodies with bones exposed that one sometimes came across in clearings near a pond or water hole—even at the very worst times, I found no room for mystery. There was only thought for the next meal of young leaves and the next sip of your own urine if the water holes proved to be dry again.

I remember one time—did I ever tell you about this?—when Thirith and I came to a sudden clearing in the trees that may have been man-made but looked more like a natural defect in the forest, very frightening as one moved across it because the brush and grass were taller than what the eye was used to and the pattern of sounds different, so that every hidden thing one stumbled into seemed at first a part of something unburied and the whole place an unmarked graveyard. I was leading Thirith as usual, keeping just enough ahead of her to create a kind of path and to anticipate any trouble if I had time and luck enough, and about halfway across the clearing I lost her. I turned to find that she'd vanished out of sight behind me, as though she'd fallen into an open pit. I went back and finally spotted her off to one side, squatting on her haunches behind a bush, her eyes wide, fierce with terror, her lips in motion but not shaping anything I could understand around the same low moan her real mother used to make in her madness when talking to the spirits that haunted her during our nights on the highway. I didn't give Thirith any argument. With one hand I held her shoulder and with the other I struck her face as hard as I could, then struck it again, almost knocking her over. When I raised my hand again, she screamed at me in rage, but that ended the moaning. And I never had to hit her again, because that pause in our journey to the border apparently ended all conversation with the unknown.

I'm sure you know what I'm talking about. You had your own jungle to get through south of ours and at a time when crossing the border to our camp was dangerous beyond anything Thirith and I had to face. If you came out more of a believer in the unknown than I can be, I think we still share the same unsentimental knowledge of this particular godless reality which appears to have chosen our country for a playground, entering from more directions since we lost our neutrality than even the godless-

118

ness of politics can justify. At least I hope that is one thing you and I still share, because I need to assume it now.

February 11. The new refugees have begun to arrive at our camp in large numbers, several hundred this past week. Some are Khmer Rouge fleeing the Vietnamese, but most are ordinary Khmers fleeing the Khmer Rouge, who have begun to gather up what civilians they can in their retreat and are driving them off to the mountains to make guerrillas out of them. A new mass migration is under way in "Democratic Kampuchea," with the Vietnamese invaders urging the Khmer citizens they find herded in work camps to return to their former villages for the winter harvest, and the Khmer Rouge trying to intercept the returning villagers before they make their way back to whatever homes they still have left. The invading enemy plays the liberator and the retreating defender plays the enslaving enemy—a familiar game that is of course not a game at all. The very young and the very old again have to fend mostly for themselves, because those with any strength and cunning seem determined to use this latest disruption to make their way across the border. As of course you and I would have done.

The stories they bring with them are also familiar—the forced labor, the ideological ruthlessness, the ever-present spying, the sudden disappearances at night—though it seems the threatened Pol Pot government grew increasingly paranoid in recent months and the killing became capricious beyond what even you and I knew. The invading forces have apparently uncovered new mass graves full of blindfolded skulls and wired wristbones, and also new evidence of school buildings used for reeducation by torture, all of this now rich food for Vietnamese propaganda. And there are the usual accounts of betrayal and revenge and separation. I don't have to tell you these stories. Still, though one hears yet another version of personal loss and family death from each of those arriving, the familiarity doesn't change the fascination we give them, the attention to some new detail of horror, some new confession of a child sacrificed because it began crying too loudly at a dangerous moment or of a wife left behind because she was too pregnant to go on walking fast enough. And we continue our almost ritual participation in everybody else's sorrow by recounting our own again, as if the only communal faith we have left in this green refuge were our shared knowledge of cruelty and our shared guilt in having successfully escaped it, at least for the time being.

The dark side of this faith is suspicion of one's new neighbor. Most of us who have become firmly settled in here do what we can to take in the new arrivals and make them at home, but some of us have begun to see them as a threat. There are rumors that the Thais will not allow more refugees to enter if this latest exodus keeps bringing them into the country at the current pace, that they will try to force those entering back across the border, just as one hears that some of those arriving by boat have been forced back to sea. And since they can't possibly keep everyone out who is determined to cross over, the talk is that they may eventually have to come into the overcrowded camps and remove the new refugees. If that happens, who will be chosen to distinguish the old from the new—that is, if anyone still cares to make the distinction by then? So some here have begun to speak of the new arrivals as possible Vietnamese spies, or Khmer Rouge agents pretending to be guerrillas, or collaborators with one or another former enemy—the old system of defense through accusation that I thought I'd left behind with the one-legged Khmer Rouge leader who bullied us into creating a village out of the forest west of Battambang. But of course there are all kinds among us now, and this undercurrent of insinuation not only has changed the mood in our camp but may signal a true danger to us from our hosts after so many months of almost boring—what is the phrase the Americans would use?—domestic tranquillity.

I try to keep all this at a distance by occupying myself with more teaching, not only the larger classes in English and French that I've accepted, but now informal history as well—modern history, unrevised. I can see you smile at this, take it for my last stand at the ramparts of our dying civilization. And there may be something in that. But to the extent that I can understand my own motives, I think it is a thing less pretentious. I simply want a few of those who go out of here to another country to have some notion of what their own country was in this century, who owned it when, the good that was brought into it from foreign places and the evil that came along at the same time, how it was corrupted by the war and how its treasures were damaged and sometimes annihilated before many here were old enough to know them. And I'm not referring only to things like Angkor Wat and the other monuments that have suffered but to the Khmer tradition of living that my mother grew up with and my sister and her children and that I myself used to be so ready to disparage.

If all this strikes you as hopeless nostalgia, let me offer another excuse: I want to keep the history of our generation fresh in my mind so that I don't let myself slip—it is so comfortable sometimes, so entertaining—into easy cynicism. I want the hatred this history generates, the anger that comes with its harsh ironies and absurdities, to keep my own sense of location from dying while I'm still capable of passion.

Outside the classroom I occupy myself, no doubt too much, with trying to keep Thirith out of trouble. And by that I don't mean keeping her a virgin—I long ago gave that up as a futile and meaningless business. She is, after all, close to twenty years old now, and though she is younger than that in some respects, her body is as ripe as one could hope for in someone brought up on what she had to eat while she was still growing. I mean trying to keep her from getting so caught up in the—how shall I put it?—fecund aura of this place that she gets pregnant and then has to marry somebody who complicates her chances of leaving Thailand when her luck begins to work for her again. Before you left, breeding children had perhaps not yet become the leading business of our camp and its best recreation. Now it thrives more than our handicrafts, our weaving and sewing and carpentry, our gardening and trinket making. And the native instruments and dancing we sometimes provide for entertainment can't compete for musical exercise with what goes on behind our thin partitions any time there is enough darkness to suggest privacy.

This must surely influence Thirith. Lately she spends less time on her language studies and less time on her vegetable garden—last year's great obsession—and more and more time where I can't find her. I'm certain she has a lover. And I'm certain she will do everything she can to keep him hidden from me. Again you may smile. What else would a daughter—especially a daughter found on the highway—do with a substitute mother like me? And why shouldn't God's lucky children be fruitful and multiply? That's fine for you to say from the security of your brightly lit New York, or wherever you are in America. But what about those of us who have nothing but the future of our young—even if adopted young—to give us an image of possibilities? The trouble is, if Thirith does finally come to me to reveal what you may think she shouldn't, I'm afraid I will have made myself unacceptable as a person to offer her healthy advice. I now have a lover too.

March 4. The past few weeks have been unsettling. We had "important" visitors from the Thai government recently, and you know what that means: they come to a place like this only on the dark days, when they sense trouble or hope to cause it, never when the sun is strong on our planting and the air mildly perfumed.

The problem seems to be gold. One wouldn't think that refugees who arrive the way these are dressed would create a problem of gold, but hiding gold and jewels from the Khmer Rouge—hiding them sometimes very uncomfortably, as I'm sure you know—has apparently continued to be a means of private resistance in the years since you and I escaped. Anyway, those arriving these days have come out with enough gold to establish a black market with Thai traders all along the border, from Aranyaprathet south to Trat, it seems. The refugees are of course hungry for the simple things that they've been denied during the past four years, things which now strike me as so ordinary that I have to recognize how spoiled we've become: needles, soap, candles, nails, matches, sugar, salt, hats for their heads and sandals for their feet and maybe a necklace of flowers to celebrate their successful conspiracy with benevolent spirits. These things are all available now in our camp market, but the refugees are too angry and wild in their deprivation to wait until they arrive at the outskirts of this oasis—and I can call it that with somewhat less irony than I could when you were here.

The Thai traders are taking in refugee gold in such quantities and spending it so freely in Bangkok that it appears the government has become concerned enough to investigate not only the camps near the border but much of the forest in between them. One rumor is that they merely want to collect their share of the gold. Another is that they want to eliminate not just the black market but all traffic across the border by planting new mines and heavier patrols. And the worst rumor of all is that the true purpose of their activity in our area is to establish routes that will supply the retreating Khmer Rouge wherever they settle in near the border. This would make them agents of the Chinese on behalf of Khmer Rouge guerrillas, but of course for the patriotic motive of defending Thailand against possible aggression by the Russia-supported Vietnamese. And we Cambodians without a country or an ideology would end up trapped between one enemy and another. As usual.

I may soon learn from an authoritative source what the Thai government is really up to. I told you I had a lover. I didn't say more not because I was being coy, but because I didn't know exactly what tone to take in telling you about him. That disturbed me then and it still does. Tone was never an issue between you and me when we were together. In serious matters we were simply candid—at least I always was with you, and I'm prepared to believe you were with me until you candidly tell me otherwise. And beyond our personal feelings for each other, we managed to hold on objectively about the situation around us, see it for what it was and talk about it truthfully, never allowing personal feeling to jeopardize the work we did together organizing the classes in the camp. I think we were also very careful about the boundaries of our intimacy—and I don't mean to put aside our one tender excursion into more dangerous regions under my persuasion. That you followed me then was as important to me as your not pressing for more in the days thereafter, when we both knew you would be leaving and when I think we both became especially sensitive to the damage that might come from letting our friendship take that route again in our last days together. And strangely, I remained celibate for many months after you left, feeding myself off other resources, some of which—perhaps the more selfless kind—you were responsible for discovering in me and nurturing.

Is that why our friendship has remained strong enough—in my mind, anyway—to make you my necessary audience here? And if so, why is there a problem of tone? Because for all this candid accounting on my part, I still have a sense that talk of a new lover is bound to make you uncomfortable, maybe a little jealous (is that bold of me?), maybe a little suspicious of where my thoughts seem to be directed these days, so that no tone would be quite right. Especially so when I tell you that he is not a Khmer but a foreigner. Anyway, since I can't speak to you directly, I'll simply have to let questions of tone answer themselves. The facts are these: he is a large Dutchman, reasonably handsome—blond, square-jawed, thick brows and lips—reasonably intelligent, evidently in love with me. He works for one of the international relief agencies under the United Nations, a new one that has come into our area since you left it. His headquarters are in Bangkok, but he travels to the camps once or twice a week—and that is about as much of him as I need. We are discreet. I would never let his—shall I call it his courting?—compromise me with my students here, and I don't mean only the children but the older ones too. He has a small covered truck—the foreigners here say "van"— that he uses for his rounds, and this is our pleasure boat, carrying us as far as we need to go to be safely private.

I won't deny that I delight in him most of the time—he is considerably younger than I am, and his body is still untrained yet wonderfully receptive, wonderfully malleable. But there are times when he is quite boring. Especially when he proposes sociological theories—German and French theories on the whole—about how refugees are best handled in an area of conflict between Marxism and capitalism. I have to shut him up then and not let his babble ruin my taste for his ripeness (which in this climate sometimes makes him sweat too much). In his defense I have to say that at least his theories have brought him out here to the front line. And the way things have begun to move along the border, that may soon demand more courage than even he expected to need. In any case, he says that his work in Bangkok brings him into contact on occasion with certain government sources that may prove useful in determining just what is going on.

Oh, yes, by the way, his name is Maarten. He calls me Sameth, as you did, because I haven't yet told him my real name nor much else about my past. And we also talk English when together because his French is insufferable.

March 18. It has been only a month or so since the new refugees began to cross into our region in large numbers, yet what we see in them has already begun to change. They now arrive more exhausted, thinner, less animated. That may be because they have come from greater distances and have been on the road longer, but it isn't only a physical thing. The mind too seems to have changed. The substance of the stories they tell about what they've been through remains what it has been all along—the mass killing under the Khmer Rouge, the cells for torture, the leg irons, the clubbings, the endless work, the hunger—but it comes out of them with less passion, almost indifference. It's as though the horror of it all became so routine at some point, so ordinary, that those who had to watch it day after day where they were living and then take to the highways again finally came to look on their own past as they might someone else's drawn-out death by sickness or, worse, as the slow imposition of fate.

This lack of passion they show, this acceptance or fatalism or whatever it is, now seems to me as appalling in its way as the stories they tell. Maybe it's a process by which the mind protects itself against indelible wounding, but I don't care what it is. I can't bear to see this happening, people treated as these have been now losing too much of their anger, their hatred of what has happened, their unforgiving recollection. The inhumanity of others now eats away at their own humanity; the tortured gradually become as callous, it seems, as the torturer. And if it goes on, that is how the Khmer Rouge will finally win. Memory will eventually die and blame along with it, fate will become the evil that replaces the one these people have known, and before long, time will have purified the enemy of their crimes so that a new round can begin again. As has happened so often in our century.

I work to keep memory alive wherever I have influence, but the effort is hopeless sometimes. In my French class for the youngest earlier this week I got myself so wrought up trying to find a way of explaining Sihanouk and his talent for accommodation that I apparently frightened some in the front row and suddenly two little girls began to weep. It occurred to me finally that those who came out of "Democratic Kampuchea" at the age of five or six have no clear idea who Sihanouk is, and since very little in the past four years has educated them about him, he is a name with no specific shape. I must have portrayed him in a way that made him seem the kind of evil spirit who goes after children when they haven't behaved properly. I ended up trying to sweeten my language so as to calm the front row, but it was too late. In that class Sihanouk is now a forbidden subject. And in the classes for adults, I find that history in the abstract is the easiest way to bring a dull mist into the eyes of my listeners in the back rows of our YWCA school building. They all have their own versions of history, their own personal demons, and what memory remains seems to be confined to the lost family and the lost village that for most now begin to fade into a private mythology that has little to do with the country's fate and the old stories of political disaster that brought us where we are. Instead of inspiring my fellow refugees to remember with emotion as I talk about their common past, I seem to bring myself under suspicion for talking too little about the sister I lost and not at all about the village I never had—at least not until the Khmer Rouge invented one for me.

I became so depressed after the Sihanouk episode this week that when Maarten came to visit he felt he had to take me away from here not to make love to me but to have a serious conversation. We went on a long excursion yesterday, through the plain of rice fields west of Aranyaprathet and then south to the mountains called the Khao Soi Dao Tai. I'd never been half that far. We left the highway and walked toward the base of the mountain range, and this was exhilarating even though it was hot. We ended up in a place that was very green, a table of grass between rocks where we could look up at the mountains, and we spread ourselves on a blanket under a coconut palm.

Maarten hardly said a word on our way there, I think hoping to calm me down by leaving me to myself, and when we were fully rested and the sun was getting low, he still kept to his side of the blanket. He said that he had been worried about me for some weeks, actually from the time Phnom Penh fell again. At first he was worried because that news seemed to put me at a distance from him, since I hadn't wanted to talk about it with him very much even though it was clearly on my mind (what would he say if he knew that is when I started to write in this notebook for your eyes alone?). But eventually he found his worry becoming less personal; he began to sense what he called "a deep melancholy" in me that didn't have to do with him or even so much with myself but with the way of the world around me. I almost laughed when he said that, but I managed to hold myself back because I knew he wouldn't understand my amusement (he doesn't have your keenly sharpened sense of irony, nor your talent for appreciating understatement). He went on to say that he didn't want to pry into why things had suddenly turned so sour for me, and though he knew it didn't have to do specifically with the camp, where my work still appeared to keep me fully occupied and generally content, he wondered if it might not be good for me to get away from the camp for a while and move with him to Bangkok.

I was tempted then to reach over and take his hand and say, "Sweet young fellow, how is it possible that the milk of human kindness hasn't curdled behind those pink cheeks of yours even after what little you've seen of the way of our world since you've been on this border?"—but I was too shy or despairing or self-protective. What I said was that I felt grateful for his worry, it showed that he was sensitive to my nature and cared for me, all of which was very touching, but I couldn't possibly leave my work at the camp and my responsibility for Thirith and just pack a suitcase to go off with him to Bangkok. He answered that he meant for Thirith to come with us, that he had in mind finding work for me which would be just as important as what I was doing in the camp at Aranya-prathet. I pressed him on that point, really out of curiosity more than any-thing else, and he said he saw no reason why, in view of my knowledge of languages and my Anglo-French education and my general experience (that made him lower his heavy-browed eyes), I wouldn't qualify for a po-sition with one of the international refugee-relief agencies, perhaps even his own.

So there it is, dear Tan Yong. I was made an offer that would have seemed two months ago the next-best thing to emigration to another country or repatriation to the old Cambodia, and all I could do was shake my head and touch the man's hand gently to thank him for what I couldn't possibly accept. And of course that made him suddenly as de-pressed as I must have appeared to him in recent days. I tried to bring him back the one way that had always worked with us, but it was no good. I'd managed to lead him into the circle of my own hopelessness, and there wasn't anything so obvious that would ease him out. We drove back to the camp in silence, and now I'm not even sure I'm going to see him again.

He has forced me to think about my situation, though. I now see that the camp has become my excuse for not looking closely into myself. I hide in my work, concern myself with what others don't see out there so as to avoid what I can't bear to see under my own roof—that is, I keep from facing my own situation at the same time that I complain about how insensitive others are to the larger view. I turned forty this month. That is a fact that I haven't confronted. My childbearing years will soon be gone. And even if Thirith were not almost twenty and so ready to fly off on her own, I'm not really her mother. Do you understand where that leaves me? I'm certain you do understand, but what good is it to me when you aren't here to tell me if I'm being foolish not to grasp Maarten's offer while there's still some warmth left in both of us?

April 1. I'm going to Bangkok, it seems. Anyway for a week. Maarten convinced me that I owe him at least one trip there, for my sake first of all but also for his because he apparently feels that our life together has become too much a matter of brief exercise in green places with too little shared experience of ordinary daily living, meaning his ordinary daily living. I don't know whether this domestic impulse of his emerges from naiveté or indicates strategy—some deeper plot to get me to settle down with him in Bangkok. In any case, I think I'm old enough to resist whatever subtleties he may have in mind, and the truth is, I'm willing to believe a few days away from this camp not only will do me good but will prove a relief for my students as well. So he comes on Friday in his white van to carry me off to the city of new cement towers and new gold, and if it were not for my worrying about Thirith, I would begin to let myself enjoy some of the same nervous excitement that I knew as a schoolgirl waiting for my first trip from Phnom Penh to Paris—which perhaps shows what has happened to my psyche after almost four years of confined simplicity.

Getting permission from our leaders here for a week of leave required much persuasion on my part—first because they tried to tell me that the Thai authorities are becoming difficult not only about the new arrivals who are officially designated "illegal aliens" but about those of us who settled in long ago as displaced persons with recognized refugee status. I wasn't convinced by this line of argument since, displaced as I still may be, I would be under at least unofficial United Nations protection, one step closer to the lowest form of actual citizenship.

But their stronger argument was that I would be abandoning my classes, going off when I was really indispensable, etc., a thing that should have flattered me, I suppose, but that actually brought me close to tears. It is the first time in recent months that I was made to feel trapped in this place, not only condemned to the daily routine by my own need and what I sense to be the need of my students—which of course includes Thirith—but trapped by those in charge of our life here. It brought out the old impulse to escape, to head for the sea, for open country, anywhere to break out of intolerable boundaries, that which once took me to France so easily when I was still a girl and divided me from my family when I got back and finally saved me from the Khmer Rouge. Only now there is no open place nearby, and the more distant regions one might think of going to—were there a choice—sometimes seem even more threatening than where one has again entered the circle. Anyway, I won my case in the end by offering to solicit larger provisions for our camp from any of the relief people Maarten may introduce me to during our week of free domesticity.

Getting permission from Thirith proved simple by comparison—too simple, I'm afraid. At first she didn't say anything when I told her about Maarten's plan, just stared at the ground. I thought that was her shy way of responding to the news that Maarten and I had an intimate relationship and that he and I would be living together under the same roof for a week. But when I tried gently to explain the full character of the relationship, she looked up to say, "You don't have to tell me about it, Sameth. I understand." She said it so dryly that it was clear to me she'd known about our meetings all along. And her saying it that way didn't leave me much room to tell her that she had no reason to see Maarten as a threat either to her or to me, if that's what was on her mind.

But what truly unsettled me was how readily she accepted the idea of my going to Bangkok and being away from the camp for a week. "Why shouldn't you stay that long?" she said. "If it's me you're worried about, please don't be. I can take care of myself perfectly well." Again her tone made me feel that she was saying less than she could. I was very much tempted to ask her if she was so easy about my going to Bangkok because she had a lover of her own and would be just as happy to have me out of the way for a while, but instead I tried to be light about it, less direct. "You don't seem at all sad about getting rid of me for a week," I said.

"Am I that much in your hair?" Thirith looked at the ground again. "Why should I be sad? I'm envious. I would give anything to go to Bangkok for a week. Or longer." "Would you?" I said, smiling. "I hear it's now more than half a modern city and full of danger for young people. Especially for young women. They sometimes kidnap them and put them to work doing unimaginable things." Thirith shrugged—a new gesture someone has taught her. "What do I care about danger? There's no danger for me anymore. Not since I died the first time four years ago."

One could of course take that kind of remark for late-adolescent cynicism or mock Buddhist fatalism of what have you, but I've seen the attitude too often in this camp and among some who are older and more mature than Thirith. There are those who carry a seemingly endless burden of depression, as though a tap in the brain had opened at some point on the road here to leak a steady dull fluid that causes lethargy and indifference with as much consistency as the juices that stir appetite. And then there are those who seem ready to risk anything because they feel they have risked everything already, so they begin with insolence toward anybody in authority, including those who may want to help them, and sometimes they go so far as to run off through the forest and cross the minefields along the border just for a show of reckless will.

Thirith now seems to be moving from the one state to the other. My worry for months after we came here was her almost unbreakable silence. Now she talks, but what she sometimes says makes me wonder if soon she won't be quite beyond anything I can do to help her. And that puts the pressure of time on my hope to get her out of Thailand and away to a place that will turn her sudden new energy and lack of care into something healthier than this camp or even Bangkok will ever allow. That is, dear Tan Yong, if it isn't already too late. I'm obsessed now with the thought that it may be, and that brings a fear as cold as any I knew in the jungle. Too late for both her and me, not to mention our country.

April 15. I'm back in Aran, not yet adjusted to my demotion from liberated tourist to more or less legitimate refugee. Bangkok proved to be a wonderful change, at least in the first days. Maarten made it possible for me not to have a care about anything and to feel courted in a way that might have seemed almost old-fashioned were we in another time and country. He has a fourth-floor apartment on a Soi off Sukhumvit Road, a comfortable little nest with an undistinguished view mostly of new hotels and apartment buildings, but with the sort of casual furniture and modern kitchen that gave me the sensation for the first time in four years of being in rooms where someone actually lived a normal, regulated life of the kind I once knew in Phnom Penh. And I exploited that sensation by staying put in his apartment from Friday night through the weekend, for all of Maarten's efforts to get me out of the place and off on a tour of temples and klongs. To be fair to him, he didn't really become restless until Sunday afternoon, when he had every reason to be tired of my insatiable domesticity, my puttering around his kitchen and my cleaning up the mess of his living room, which was at least partly an excuse to create some intermission between our hungry use of each other in his rather narrow bed.

We finally managed a walk at sundown that evening—part walk, part ride in a tuk-tuk. From one point of view, his section of the city must be as ugly as anything one can find in civilized Southeast Asia, a terrible mixture of street markets and fancy modern shops, faceless cement office buildings and wicked hotels, what look like temporary shacks beside walled-in villas that are often attractive but that require impudence to be seen, here and there an abandoned waterway that is really an open gutter clogged by every kind of natural waste and every kind of plastic debris that can't be identified any longer but still won't disintegrate, and the worst air for walking I've breathed anywhere because the traffic fills both main and side streets with its fuming and simply doesn't move. But from another point of view—let's say the refugee view—there was sudden freedom there, an openness to pleasure, to forgotten luxury, frivolity, excess, call it what you will.

Walking by those shops made me completely bourgeois again. I stopped every chance I got to gape like a schoolgirl at the silk blouses and high-heeled sandals and imported purses, at the cosmetics and household machinery and even the displays of food. Fortunately most places were closed, including the bookstore I ravished through the glass so long that Maarten finally dragged me off by the arm to show me something he found more entertaining and exotic: an elephant standing on the pavement across the street with a laundry basket and a garbage can tied to its back (he forgets—or maybe doesn't know—that I see elephants all the time bringing new refugees across the border from Cambodia as regularly as trucks bring Thai soldiers into our area from the opposite direction). I failed to show proper enthusiasm for feeding the elephant dried fish, so Maarten loaded me into a tuk-tuk for a broader tour of the city's dusky streets, including the Patpong section, where the go-go bars and massage parlors were just beginning to light up for their evening carnival and the pimps to hawk their girls, animals, and fruit in the various combinations they imagined might appeal to the traveling voyeur. We moved on to a fish restaurant in that neighborhood for Tom Yam Gung soup and a whole lobster each; then we walked down to the river and had a brandy at the Oriental Hotel.

I don't know if it was a delayed bit of postcoital tristesse or a momentary relapse into my "deep melancholy," but as we sat in the tasteful extravagance of that hotel I found the tears streaming down my face. I tried to tell Maarten that it was just unfamiliar happiness, the pressure of joyful release after so many weeks of stifled tension, etcetera, but I didn't really fool him or myself. He took me out into the garden around the swimming pool and just stood there holding my hand, not saying anything at all, a clear signal that he knew I was still balanced on an emotional tightrope, and then the tears finally stopped so that he could lead me to a taxi and take me home. When we made love that night, I think I surprised him by my energy and persistence (I started to say "awed" him, but that sounds self-congratulatory, and I have to be careful how I sound when I speak about these matters to you—you in particular). I suppose this was the other side of the same crossed emotions, the unstable current generated by too much compensation too quickly realized, only now I was on the side of gluttony, as though this might be my last free meal. I don't want to try to explain it so long after the moment. All I know is that I filled myself beyond reason during the weekend and especially that night.

We slept late the next morning, almost until noon (Maarten gave himself leave that day), and I got up rather light-headed, feeling cleansed. I made breakfast of boiled eggs and warmed brioche—imagine that, will you?—then let Maarten carry me off to the Grand Palace to play the tourist, along with a group of some fifty Oriental visitors heavily armed with cameras and airplane bags who turned out to be from Hong Kong. That unsettled me a bit, mixing nostalgia and incongruity, and so did the Throne Room with its Western balustrades and Eastern steeples and the gathering of temples outside the palace where one finds steep Thai roofs beside those phallic domes that someone from our country left behind. Still, I won't pretend that I wasn't impressed by the lavishness of the place. Whatever irony you hear is from my French training, brought in now to protect myself from seeming foolish in this cooler aftermath. Beyond the glitter, the aesthetic surfeit of too much glass mosaic and bright tile and Buddhas in gold, you come to those frescoes in which history and its mythology have stirred some human spirit, maybe over generations, to paint quite impersonally but magnificently. And that is when you realize that there is unspoken glory behind those long white walls that hold in the glittering temples, a thing that persists even while you find yourself kneeling barefoot in front of the emerald Buddha with no more religious feeling than the hollowness in the pit of your stomach for not being able to believe in anything that the Buddha and his monuments represent.

Later in the afternoon we went to the river beyond the palace walls and had beer and dried squid sitting on a platform over the water. The river was covered with grass around us and looked like a field you could walk on. It was the hour when people living along the klongs were going home from their work in the city, and we watched the long-tailed river-boats speeding by until, like a child at the fair, I couldn't stand not riding in one. So we went up the Klong Bangkok Noi for almost an hour before turning back, past the royal barges and wat gardens with temples and enough houses on stilts to make another city. We went so fast at times that I was sure we would cut right through one of the slower flatboats steered mostly by old women and full of cabbages and melons and other things that looked like human heads through the spray our boat was making so that I half-expected we would have to end this romance in a wet filthy grave surrounded by bobbing skulls. I kept my lips sealed the whole way out for fear some of that thick brown water would spray its diseases on me, which tells you how delicate and provincial I've become since my days in the jungle. And of course Maarten the Innocent just mocked me with his camera, taking snapshots not only of my discomfort but of every woman and child he could find bathing in that water and one of a man squatting in it to shave. When we finally got back to our landing, he bought a bottle of sweet Mekong whiskey and ceremoniously washed my forehead and cheeks and lips with it. And then he took me across the river on a slow baht bus so that we could see the sun go down over the city from the Wat Arun.

That is a good place to study the split personality of Bangkok. From across the river you can clearly see all the brilliance that has gone into those golden bell-shaped domes and intricate tile spires, but you see it beside all the commercial energy that has gone into new towers of cement. And in the foreground you find elegantly prowed water buses carrying girls in uniform across the path of heavy barges carrying crates of beer and Pepsi-Cola. The incongruity of that place opens out in front of you without embarrassment when you survey it from a high point in the Wat, and maybe that's because you can't really conceive of that city's having the one face without the other. Each would appear excessive on its own; together they seem to display an inevitable human limitation—maybe even a necessary limitation in our part of the world, at least among cities still alive and free.

Maarten felt he had to go back to work the next day, so I had a delicious six hours by myself to give to the shops, most of all to the bookstores near his apartment, especially the one with foreign books. That morning he'd given me one hundred American dollars to spend as I wished, dear boy, and after I treated myself to a burgundy silk blouse and some face cream from Paris, the remainder went for Thirith—first a silk dress made of delicate blue flowers with a scarf to match, then as many books in English and French as the money allowed. The woman running the store must have taken me for a maniacal and somewhat retarded student, because I believe I looked through forty or fifty books while I was there, all kinds of books, flipping the pages of some with barely a look just to get the feel of good paper and reading whole chapters in others because I couldn't let go even after I'd found out I should. The woman was actually very sweet. She came up several times to ask if she might help me, if there was something in particular I was looking for, and I would just stare at her without recognition because I was caught up madly in what I was reading or mumble her away with gentle incoherence while I moved on frantically to another shelf. I finally bought some history books and a few new novels that I could share with Thirith and some Jane Austen and Thackeray and Flaubert to begin her serious education. I would have stayed there into the evening, but Maarten had invited some friends of his to go out with us to dinner, and he was counting on me to play hostess in his apartment when they came there to meet us—an unfamiliar role that made me more nervous than I'd been since facing my first classes of emaciated students at the camp.

The friends were a Thai couple. The man worked for one of the government ministries as a liaison with the foreign relief agencies, which is why Maarten wanted to make an evening of it—for my sake really, to allow time for us to learn anything useful that I might take back with me to the camp. The couple were nice enough, though I can't say I got to know the woman very well since only he spoke English and so did most of the talking. And he wasn't nice the whole evening. Late in our dinner (of "Home-cooked European Cuisine" at a little place called "Bay Leaf" off Sukhumvit Road), Maarten asked the man bluntly if there had been any policy developments on the refugee question after the recent changes in the government, and then the man wasn't really nice at all. He said that frankly, in his opinion, the refugee question was getting more and more complicated—that is, the "new"-refugee question—and he bowed slightly toward me and smiled to make sure all of us at the table understood that what he had to say did not pertain to "old" refugees like Maarten's dinner companion. The problem about the new refugees, he said, was that nobody could be absolutely sure any longer who these refugees were. Many were obviously Khmer Rouge guerrillas who came in and out of Thailand to escape the Vietnamese army, some were Khmer Rouge entourage, and some of course were ordinary Khmers trying quite understandably to escape the Vietnamese occupation. But others, he had to say in total honesty, were simply economic opportunists. And still others were Vietnamese soldiers out of uniform or members of the puppet regime acting as spies. So the refugee question, he said smiling rather stiffly, depended on who was a real refugee and who wasn't.

I tried to smile back at that and keep my mouth tightly closed, but of course I couldn't, and Maarten knew I couldn't, which was why he didn't dare look at me or anyone else. I asked quietly if the gentleman would regard those Khmers who came across the border in order to get more rice to eat as economic opportunists, because that was what brought in most of the new refugees I'd spoken to at Aranyaprathet. "Naturally that is what all of them say," he answered. "And for many of them it was true. But now that the Vietnamese are threatening my country from across the border, one cannot be sentimental about those for whom it is not true." I tried to keep a smile in place. "At least you still have a country to be threatened. The Khmer refugees have no country at all."

Maarten called the waiter over at that point to see what there was for dessert. Then a strange thing happened: I'm certain I felt the Thai gentleman touch my hand with the tips of his fingers, as delicately as the brush of a bird's wing. "I understand your point of view," he said, when I glanced at him. "I hope you understand mine. Especially after what has happened to your country." I studied him. "The only thing I don't understand," I said, "is what your government plans to do with these new refugees if they can't decide which ones are real and which are not. Push them all back across the border? Deal with them the way they're dealing with the so-called boat people?" The man was silent for a moment, gazing at his plate. "I wish I could answer that," he said finally, and he said it in a way that made the blood run out of my face, because it seemed to me he knew the answer all too well but just wasn't ready to share it.

We had a piece of the answer the following day. Maarten was already gone when I woke up the next morning, so I just lay in bed feasting myself on the books I'd bought. He called during his lunch hour to arrange to pick me up that afternoon in time to visit the Oriental art collection in the famous house of a onetime American spy, a place that he said we mustn't miss. Unfortunately we had to miss not only that but the rest of our days in Bangkok, because he called about an hour later to say that the gentleman we'd been out with the previous evening had just gotten hold of him to pass on some news that he was afraid might alarm me but that he thought I ought to know nevertheless: the Thai military in the region of Aranyaprathet had received instructions from the government to transport some 1,500 new refugees by bus to the camp in Trat that is maybe 250 kilometers south of ours. Can you imagine? The camp in Trat must be as overcrowded as all the others. Where were the new refugees to go? And how could one be sure that only those now classified as illegal entrants would be put on the buses going so far south?

Of course I gave way to panic. Hearing the news from that particular source was enough to convince me of the danger in this sudden and apparently unannounced decision by the new government under General Kriangsak. I got dressed immediately and began packing up, my mind full of wild images of Thirith, especially one of her face against the back window of an unidentified bus, hands pressed against the pane, eyes searching frantically to find me or anyone else who might save her from vanishing into the anonymity of wherever she was being taken. And when Maarten arrived with his van, he had nothing but a sort of forced calmness to offer for reassurance. There was no mention of the government's plan in the English-language newspapers that he brought with him. The only refugee story there had to do with a freighter carrying some 500 Vietnamese that had managed to sail right up to Samut Prakan, at the mouth of the river south of Bangkok. The captain and the navigator who had brought the ship that far in without permission had been arrested and were being held without bail to face further "tough legal action" if those investigating this surprising arrival discovered that the two of them had taken bribes from the Vietnamese, who were of course detained on board in the filthiest of circumstances, though provided with food and water by local "church organizations and charity groups."

While I was getting the last of my things together, I asked Maarten why the United Nations High Commission for Refugees wasn't down there in Samut Prakan to help those poor people, or his agency, or somebody else with the kind of foreign connections that might put pressure on the Thai officials. He said that was another development he hadn't wanted to bring up in view of everything else that was happening these days, but the UNHCR and the other international agencies were now having some difficulty getting around the red tape that the Thai government had begun to introduce from various directions to make sure the so-called refugee question remained entirely under its control. And when I asked him just what this "red tape" consisted of, he shrugged and said, "Anything they can do to keep us from getting too close to the refugees. Permits. Who is in charge of operations where. That sort of thing." I tried to pretend I was amused by the way he'd put it. "Of course 'us' includes you but not me, correct? So where exactly does that put the two of us from now on? Not to mention Thirith." This made him come over and hold me at arm's length. "If you're worried about the government keeping me from getting to you, forget about it. That would take a tank battalion. All this business is just a bit of international politics. They feel other countries aren't doing enough to solve the refugee problem, so they're going to make a show for the world by getting tough."

That ended the discussion. Nothing was said about what we were to do next. He knew I had to go back to Aran to see what was going on there, and maybe he felt he had to himself. He just picked up my suitcase and my package of books and stood by the door waiting for me to get myself completely pulled together. I tried to ease more information out of him during the drive back to the camp, but he kept telling me not to worry about the situation, everything was going to be all right. Either he knew more than he felt was healthy for me to know at that point or he was drawing confidence from somewhere I couldn't. And of course it was difficult to talk about future plans when there was so little one could say about the present. So we talked about things that had happened during our time in Bangkok—some of the things, those that might have made us laugh freely in another mood—but we mostly didn't talk at all. And he drove faster than was really safe, with only one hurried stop for pork on a stick and Mekong whiskey mixed with Pepsi-Cola.

Even before we got into Aran there was evidence that the military had moved in to seal off the region, because we came to a new roadblock well ahead of the usual one. Maarten must have expected something of the kind, because he tried to get by on the identification documents he normally used, and when those seemed not to be good enough, instead of arguing he brought out a letter in Thai. "Our friend," he said to me when the soldier took it away to show his officer. I assumed he meant our friend of the previous evening, but I didn't ask him what he meant, and when the soldier brought the letter back and signaled us through, Maarten tucked it away in his shirt pocket without another word. That was the first time since we'd been together that I felt awkward about asking him something impersonal, something about his professional connections, that it might have done me good to know.

There weren't many military in Aran itself. They were all out on the road guarding the buses they'd lined up as though they were military transports. They hadn't actually started loading the new refugees on the buses, which is the only thing that kept me from losing control of myself when I couldn't find Thirith anywhere in our camp. I had to assume that she was off somewhere with her lover, taking her own little vacation while I was off on mine, but of course I couldn't be sure. When the Thai soldiers started loading the buses, those in charge of them saw to it that they were efficient: no exceptions allowed. If you didn't have identification to show that you were a refugee from the period before January 1979, the date of legitimacy in this border wilderness, you were put on a bus, whether or not that meant leaving some relative behind among the "older" refugees, even a husband or wife. Watching one of those separations made me feel what I'd felt in the French Embassy compound in Phnom Penh when some of the men left their families to go out into the unknown to rebuild our country under the Khmer Rouge—though naturally these people were told that they had nothing to fear, the separations were only temporary, just until the refugee question was finally resolved.

The Thai government had obviously done everything it could to keep foreigners and reporters away from the area, so it fell to Maarten and two UNHCR officials who had somehow gotten through to try and put reason into the military authorities when they insisted that all new refugees in the local hospitals join the departing parade. They meant even those who had to be carried in on stretchers—hardly among the group one might choose to identify as economic opportunists or spies. The military were adamant; they had their orders. Maarten and his friends won the argument only in the case of three patients who were so ill that doctors on the scene insisted they wouldn't survive the trip south—too much danger there of bad publicity, I guess—and several other patients who could show that they were suffering from leprosy.

I didn't find Thirith until the following day—yesterday—long after I'd made certain she wasn't put on one of those sixteen buses by mistake and after I'd sent Maarten back to Bangkok—against his inclination—because I thought it important that he let his people there know exactly what had happened. I tried to send him off as though it were just the end of another of his routine visits, but I could tell he felt some new distance had come between us, and since neither of us knew just why that was so, we couldn't talk about it. I finally promised to get one of our relief workers to phone him news of Thirith as soon as I had any. She came home a little before noon, full of excitement, apparently quite unaware that she'd caused anybody the slightest anxiety. She'd been on an excursion, she said, an excursion with some friends to Ban Nong Chan, not far from here really, where there were many new refugees in a makeshift camp, including some from her home district in Pailin. She'd actually found a few old schoolmates who'd survived the Khmer Rouge and were now ready to fight the Vietnamese invaders, and she'd also run into many Sino-Khmer who told her they'd felt under great threat from the occupiers of Cambodia because they were now being forced to leave the cities again and settle in the countryside, which they considered just a step toward their extinction—this a bit of news she thought would especially interest me. And one couple she'd met had pedaled on a single bicycle all the way from a village east of Phnom Penh through the retreating Khmer Rouge and the Vietnamese army and the minefields right up to the border.

It had all been such fun, her getting away from the camp and meeting new people and finding old friends, and the whole group would have stayed longer if word hadn't reached them that morning about something involving the military going on near the Wat Koh camp. So they'd come back. She said she was surprised to find that I'd returned from Bangkok already and hoped that it wasn't because something was really wrong. What could one say to her? I gave her a brief account of the forced bus ride she'd missed and let it go at that. The news seemed to upset her a little, but only a little, and in a rather impersonal way, because of course she now belongs to the veteran refugees in the camp and, like most of her friends, considers herself in a different class from the recent arrivals. Which she no doubt is after all she's learned here. I still haven't told her about my time in Bangkok for the simple reason that she hasn't asked me about it. But it isn't only her rather casual attitude these days that bothers me. What I'd like to know is how she and her friends got permission to leave the camp for so long. You don't just go wandering out of here on an excursion along that section of the border. Unless of course your friends have certain other friends.

April 21. Well, dear Tan Yong, I have things to report that I'm sure would raise your spirits to hear after what I've had to offer recently in another direction. There's been some activity this week on our strip of the border. It began with a visit by an important American official who has promised to try to persuade his country to take more refugees from

Thailand. I didn't see him, but others said he was actually here on his way to several other border areas, and when he got back to Bangkok he saw the Prime Minister, General Kriangsak, to make his pledge personally. Then he collapsed in the Prime Minister's office as "the overpowering heat got the better of him" (I have all this from the package of English-language newspapers that Maarten sent me by special courier yesterday in lieu of actually visiting me himself). This American gentleman is reported by the press to have been highly gratified before his collapse by an assurance he received from General Kriangsak that the Thai government would continue to allow Cambodian refugees temporary asylum in this country and that no refugees would be turned back against their will.

It seems the heat in Bangkok must also have affected the Prime Minister's grasp of reality, because these reassuring sentiments by him were expressed on the very same day that his soldiers in our military region tried to drive thirty-seven Cambodian refugees, including many women and children, back across the border at gunpoint, this near the village of Thaprik. The soldiers failed to follow their orders only because a redheaded Australian working for the United Nations High Commissioner came up and placed himself between their guns and the refugees. And when his pleading seemed to no avail, he took up one of the young children and protected the child with his body. The paper reported him as saying: "I am following the rules of the United Nations. If you have to shoot me, I am willing to die. You have your duty, but I have mine as well on the basis of human rights and the nations I represent." Can you believe it? In these days? The soldiers were apparently stunned, and in their confusion they decided to let the women and children return to the village. Then this redheaded gentleman argued with the authorities late into the night until they agreed to release the male refugees as well. And before he was through he sent a message to the Military Commander in Aran apologizing for causing him trouble and accepting full responsibility for his action, at the same time explaining that it was necessary because the refugees had made it clear to the soldiers and villagers alike that they would be killed if they were forced to return to Kampuchea.

One can of course become easily cynical about the value of this sort of thing when one learns that the very next day twelve Cambodian refugees, again including women and children, were actually escorted back across the border into the war zone in our area despite their weeping and hugging the feet of the soldiers driving them out and their pleas that they would be killed in Cambodia by one side or the other. The only change brought on by what happened the previous day was that the soldiers did their messy work beyond the sight of reporters and UNHCR officials, so that now the testimony comes from unofficial accounts by villagers in the area. But I choose not to be cynical—not quite yet. What our redheaded friend did still exhilarates me. And of course its consequences could not be practical in the long run, that goes without saying. There was an item in yesterday's paper announcing "a difference of outlook between the Thai Government and the U.N. High Commissioner for Refugees" that has prompted the government to decree that the UNHCR will no longer have a hand in determining the fate of Cambodian refugees who flee their country as a result of the war beyond Thailand. We are told in this piece of news that "the UNHCR has slated too many rules for the government to follow," so the rules will now be simplified. Under the new policy, the U.N.'s role in looking after refugees who arrived before the first of the year will not be affected, but all the other illegal entrants are now to be strictly under military control. General Prem of the Interior Ministry reaffirms that the Thai position regarding Cambodia will remain neutral. New refugees arriving will be given medicine if they are sick, will be fed if they are hungry, and when they have recovered, "will be pushed back across the border."

The fighting has been intense all week. Those close to the border south of here can sometimes hear the machine-gun fire from around Poipet. It seems the Khmer Rouge guerrillas have been driven out of the town by a Vietnamese counterattack and are now regrouping to the north and south. This means that the civilian refugees trying to escape both the Vietnamese and the Khmer Rouge have nowhere to settle except in the mined forests along the border, or if they are lucky, near Ban Nong Chan or farther north near Ban Nong Samet, where they are given several sticks of bamboo and a plastic sheet to make a kind of shelter in the fields on the Cambodian side of an invisible frontier. And if they are especially lucky they can listen to the radio and hear our old friend Khieu Samphan make speeches celebrating the fourth anniversary of the Khmer Rouge liberation of Phnom Penh. He came out of hiding the other day to accuse the world of having remained silent while Vietnam swallowed Laos "like a boa constrictor swallowing a chicken." He now sees Vietnam with its fourteen army divisions and its Soviet aircraft trying to swallow Cambodia as well. Of course our country, having been slaughtered, eaten, and fully digested some time ago by Khieu Samphan and his revolutionary regime, must be a rather less pleasing meal even for a boa constrictor. But the old gentleman is probably right to suspect that the new monster is as ravenous, if less obviously so, as his was, and that just creates another argument for irony.

One tries to remain aloof from the politics of our situation, but of course that is impossible when the roots of it continue to be one or another kind of political fanaticism. The issue has come home to me again this week. I discovered, as I had suspected all along, that the excursion Thirith took to Ban Nong Chan was not simply a pleasure outing. She went there with a Khmer Sereikar group from this region, and their purpose was recruitment among the new refugees. I know the leader of this group. He has a long history as a scoundrel, going back even before Lon Nol, who put him in jail for stealing from the state—imagine what it means if Lon Nol had to do that!—and then forced him underground with other bourgeois "resisters" who had originally hoped to take over the country from Sihanouk before Lon Nol brought off his coup. Now he is pretending to be a heroic liberator of his country, and unfortunately he has made enough as a smuggler since he came out of Cambodia to have his way, more or less, with the local authorities in this area. Anyway, it seems he and his lieutenants can move freely from one refugee settlement to another and can try to recruit the young of both sexes who are not already recruited by others. They say that he has also begun to receive aid from some general who arrived here recently from Paris representing Son Sann, the old businessman who was economic adviser to Sihanouk.

The long history of confused loyalties and corruption and failure that these ghosts bring with them is enough to frighten me, but learning that Thirith is somehow involved in the activities now being organized alarms me thoroughly. I found out because she told me the other evening that she was going out to an important meeting and might be late. I said, not very subtly, "You mean an important rendezvous." That made her draw herself up rather stiffly: "No, I mean a meeting. A political meeting," and then she explained that she had decided to join a group of "old" refugees mostly her age who were becoming the core of a new movement to help free Cambodia from the Vietnamese. When she told me who was in charge of the group I'm afraid that irony got the best of me again. I let her know that this "movement" of hers was hardly new, that I was quite familiar with its origins, which went back many years, and that as far as I could tell it still represented the old feudal, bourgeois interests that had failed the country ever since the French colonials went away and left us to our own devices. Thirith said, "What's wrong with being bourgeois? You're bourgeois, aren't you?" That made me smile. "I suppose I am in some ways," I said. "But not in my politics." Thirith shrugged. "I didn't know you had any politics." I said, "Well, at least I know what I don't believe in. And that happens to include your new friends."

I lost her with that. She went over to her bed and took up the silk scarf I'd brought her from Bangkok and tied it around her neck with a knot so tight I couldn't imagine how she'd ever get it undone again. "At least I'd rather believe in something than nothing," she said finally. "I'll die of boredom if I go on not believing in anything at all." And then she walked out of the room as though I were no longer there.

I don't think I can do anything about this, Tan Yong, even if I knew what would be best. She has a right, after all, to make her own mistakes. I've certainly made enough of my own, and worse ones than supporting a decadent politician. Of course the stakes are higher now than when I was her age, but there's nothing one can do about that either.

May 4. Maarten was here on Tuesday. That apparently took some cunning, because his agency is now under severe restrictions along with the others distributing supplies in our area, this a result of the stand taken the other day by our redheaded Australian friend and the new government's reaction. The UNHCR supported their representative by declaring that the Australian did what was required of him as a U.N. official, and General Prem of the Supreme Command has answered them by further limiting UNHCR activity along the border: "They feel we have to assist all incoming refugees and we feel we have had enough trouble with refugees already and do not need to add to our burden." So the lines have been drawn more firmly, and it may be increasingly difficult, Maarten tells me, for him to visit me in Aran, though he hopes that once things settle down, his agency, as a voluntary organization supported mostly by funds from Holland, will be considered harmless enough to be allowed to go on doing its distribution work at least in the established camps.

I don't think this is a way of his preparing not to visit me at all any longer. At least there's no reason yet for me to think that he's not being honest with me, and there are signs that he still cares. For one, he has promised to take me on a trip to the coast south of here as soon as he can break away from his work in the city, this to make up for the days in Bangkok I had to miss. I don't think there will be any difficulty getting permission from my end, because I will soon be expendable here. Did I mention that official language classes in English and French are no longer allowed in the border camps? The new Thai government considers such classes just a way of unsettling the recent refugees—that is, a way of feeding their hope for resettlement in a third country when there should be no hope for them now except "repatriation" to Cambodia. So what teaching I do now is done informally, and I don't know how long I can go on with that.

This news inspired an idea that will bring Maarten back early in the coming week, if luck is with us. He says he wants to rent a room in Aran that can serve as his agency's base of communication with our area of the border while at the same time providing Thirith and me with a means of escaping the camp when we please now that it is becoming crowded beyond all reason and now that I will not be needed there in an official way. Maarten thinks this plan of his will give me added security and also a useful purpose, since I can act as his agency's contact in Aran. He expects to arrange an appointment of some kind for me that will provide for clearance with the authorities here, I suppose again through his friend in the government. And there will be a phone so that he can talk to me regularly whether or not there is business.

Though I can't take this so-called appointment very seriously, my inclination is to accept his offer of a room in Aran. At the very least, it will give me some privacy. More important, it will give Thirith some, whether at the camp or in the new room. Since our confrontation over her new political enthusiasm, it has not gone well between us, and I think that is partly because of the totally unpolitical tension that has been growing in our quarters for some time. She is simply too old now to have to share a room day and night with the woman she once looked on as her mother. Even a room as relatively spacious as ours, with all its little partitions and its strategies for dividing what we have equally. I must inhibit her, get in her way, just be there too often when she would prefer to be by herself. It's easier for me. I have ways of shutting her out when I have to. But she hasn't yet tasted enough independence to know how to turn in on her own resources with another adult—even a well-meaning adult—there, always there.

We'll share the room in Aran too, but never together if I can help it.

May 15. I'm in Aran now, on the edge of the town, in my spare quarters among new arrivals working for the International Committee of the Red Cross. What Maarten found for me turns out to be two rooms and a bath—small rooms, but actually separated from each other by a solid wall and a door. And though the bathroom has only the usual hole in the floor as a toilet and a cement tub that one dips water from to wash or flush, it is absolutely private, completely my own. I can't tell you what a feeling of luxury this gives me. Yesterday, during my first afternoon and evening there, I washed three times—no, four times—which really means that I stood naked in the middle of the cool bathroom floor and just poured basin after basin over myself until it seemed obscene to spend more water that way, and still I went on. Then, without drying myself, I'd go in and lie on the bed with my arms and legs spread out to let the warm air play over me, and when I was quite dry and feeling very sensual, I'd go in there and pour water all over myself again.

I have very little furniture so far: the bed and a table in one room, a table and two chairs in the other. And there is much bare green wall that needs to be decorated. But there is all the space I need to write in this journal at my leisure, and just lying on the bed yesterday looking around at the privacy I now have gave me a sense of freedom that had become quite unfamiliar. At the same time, I don't have to be alone here when I don't want to be. There is the radio Maarten left behind, and a telephone in the communal room where meals are served. And next door there is an Irish nurse who has a warm red face and a delightful accent. She's trying to learn Thai, but every time she attempts a sentence she ends up throwing her arms back and raising her blue eyes toward the heavens to say "Fock it all, I'll never larn this blodey language."

I needn't have concerned myself with the question of how best to share this new gift of space with Thirith. She's apparently not much interested in my making it possible for her to come here when she chooses. In fact, I get the impression that she would consider it inconvenient, maybe even a bit treacherous, to associate so closely with foreign relief workers, presumably including nurses with no politics she might understand. At the same time, her face couldn't quite hide the relief she felt when I told her that I would be spending as much time as I could fixing up the new quarters in Aran and that our room at the camp was essentially hers for the days ahead. Not that she herself is there much any longer. Twice last week she disappeared overnight on another of her excursions, I suppose to Ban Nong Chan. It is a sign of how things are between us that I was afraid to ask her where she'd been. But I've convinced myself that it's better for her to be involved in something she seems to take at least half seriously and to be with others her age than to wander around that camp alone with nothing to do.

The situation there is becoming more and more intolerable, and that is another reason I take such pleasure in the simple private extravagance of this place. Some four thousand new refugees came into the Aranya-prathet area during the past week, and our camp has had to accommodate many of them in the fields where our vegetable gardens used to be. Others are in makeshift camps in the fields nearby, with no protection at all against the daily rains. Most of the recent arrivals are Sino-Khmer whom the Vietnamese first drove from the cities and then tried to herd together and isolate outside Sisophon. Some say these new moves are the result of tension between Vietnam and China, but whatever the larger cause, these people see it as another turn in the familiar road to doom that the Chinese minority in Cambodia was forced to set out on under the old regime. Now they simply prefer to take their chances here. And of course the arrival of so many economic opportunists all at once, especially with that coloring, has made the Thai authorities increasingly nervous.

Those who can observe this situation on the border objectively—I myself can't, no doubt because of the unwashable Chinese in me, but Maarten apparently has begun to—these objective observers view the Thai predicament with some sympathy. Why should the Thais be the ones to bear the full weight of the problem simply because of their geographical location and because they've been lucky enough or shrewd enough to remain relatively neutral? Why doesn't the rest of the world, at least the rest of the Western world that has had its own long experience of displaced persons, do more to help the refugees? All good questions, fine questions, but how do you ask them with a straight face in front of people squatting in a muddy field drenched to their bones, sometimes even smiling, the older ones anyway?

It seems the nervousness of the Thai government has reached out beyond this country at least as far as the headquarters of the United Nations, because day before yesterday our camp was visited by Secretary-General Waldheim. You can imagine what rumors that created. Secretary-General Waldheim was moved. He called the fate of our refugees "a great human tragedy," according to the newspaper, and he said "the basic problem is how to stop the influx." Of course that is not the basic problem at all. The basic problem is how to stop human cruelty and human political idiocy. Mr. Waldheim had nothing to say on that subject, though the newspaper reports him telling our people that he was "deeply touched and shocked by this horrible situation." Fortunately one of our camp leaders did have something more specific to say on the subject, and Mr. Waldheim had no choice but to listen. Our leader, a young man of thirty-three, asked His Excellency to appeal to the countries of the world to open their doors to the Cambodian people before they all died in Cambodia. He said acceptance by the countries of the world would encourage the Thai government to be more generous toward the refugees. Until that happened he felt he had to protest the forcible expulsion of so many into the mountains along the border "where there is little food, no medicine, and where many will die." Mr. Waldheim promised to bring the matter up at his dinner with General Kriangsak.

I gather from the newspapers that the dinner, really a banquet, was not an unqualified pleasure for everyone there. General Kriangsak reaffirmed Thailand's "strict adherence to its obligations under the U.N. Charter and its firm commitment to pursue U.N. aims and purposes," but at the same time he complained that the present level of assistance from the U.N. "is not sufficient to cope with the magnitude of the problem" and that there had been severe delays in the provision of what was supposed to be forthcoming from the U.N. Then he begged to point out that Thailand was a developing nation like any other, with its own economic and social problems, and that it had "borne the brunt of the refugee problem for many years." He left the impression that Thailand did not plan to bear the brunt much longer. The General concluded his remarks by stating that the situation in Cambodia raised grave implications concerning peace, stability, and security, but "in this tense and often confusing situation," Thailand was determined to maintain its "consistent neutral policy of noninvolvement." I read that to mean more "forcible expulsion" of Cambodian refugees, as our young camp leader would put it, but Secretary-General Waldheim apparently didn't receive that message, because he finally thanked the General and the Thai government for their humanitarian response to the refugees despite Thailand's own economic difficulties, and he promised to send a coordinator to help solve urgent refugee problems as they arose. I wonder if he's been introduced to our redheaded Australian friend.

Reading this sort of rhetoric does bad things to my blood. I begin to think the way Thirith seems to these days, and I do so despite my more sober conviction that such violent thinking only leads to deadly politics. The one conversation I had with her recently that wasn't entirely about trivialities brought out a rage in her that she's been keeping secret for months, maybe years. She has a new belt that someone gave her, a khaki belt that I find unattractive on a girl her age for obvious reasons but that I simply suggested might be dyed a brighter color so that it didn't look quite so military. Thirith was getting herself ready to go out at the time and whirled on me to say, "That, dear Sameth, is the whole point." I tried to smile. "Do you just mean it goes with your new organization or do you plan to use it someday to carry ammunition or hand grenades or something?" Thirith shrugged. "Something." She looked quite serious. "Well," I said. "That's rather alarming news. When did this idea get into your head?" Thirith studied me. "You've been down to the far end of the camp. You know what's happening there. How can you see the misery of those people, your people and mine, and be indifferent to it?" I went over and sat down on the foot of her bed. "You know I'm not indifferent to it," I said quietly. She had her back turned to me and was working on her hair in front of the mirror. "You may not be indifferent, but you're not going to change anything by teaching people English and French and associating with foreigners." I caught her eye in the mirror. "You think you're going to change things by going out and shooting somebody?" Thirith shifted her eyes. "Not somebody," she said. "The enemy." I stood up but kept my eyes squarely on her. "Which enemy?" I said. Thirith went on combing her hair. She now had a little half-ironic smile in place. "Sometimes I really wonder," she said. "If you don't know who our enemy is by now, how can you teach anybody anything?"

So I'm trapped these days somewhere in the desert ground between the two people I care about most, my more or less objective lover from another country and my violently political daughter by chance adoption. And I find it increasingly difficult to imagine a road out of this for someone who can't possibly take up a gun or just fly away. I wish you were here to give me the comfort of your wisdom. And on the practical level of hope, I wish you could also tell me if the reports are true about a warmer policy in America concerning Southeast Asian refugees, a larger quota for immigration and a special appointment for the purpose in the Department of State. Is it more than show, and will it make your work easier?

Whom am I talking to? Really. This journal sometimes strikes me as the desperate chatter of a sterile middle-aged maniac addressing her own void. Maarten is right: I need the sea. He comes on Saturday to take me there, maybe just in time.

May 26. When one turns off the road to Bangkok and goes south on highway 317 toward Chantaburi, one enters an unfamiliar country. Very soon after the turn one realizes that on both sides of the highway there is a totally peaceful landscape of green rice fields and water buffalo loping toward their canals and farm huts with the wash hanging outside as though there were no threat to any living thing under that sky, even from the rain. One travels for kilometer after kilometer through that passive countryside, broken only here and there by the distant contour of a mountain rising up abruptly out of the plain, so abruptly that its shape seems not of the earth one touches but painted there for a while simply to break the long green monotony of its made-up grounding. There is no border anywhere. And there are no sounds even with the car windows open, except for the sound one makes penetrating the still air ahead or passing the mango orchards or the rows of planted teak. One does sometimes see a human figure among the buffalo and hump-necked oxen and dark birds, but the figures are serene, withdrawn, silhouettes with no apparent motion against a motionless set.

There is enough consistency in that landscape to work a gradual change in one's mood after an hour or two of its stillness, a return to forgotten possibilities maybe, anyway a settling in the mind. But of course for somebody as restless as I am, the mood doesn't last as long as it should. That first afternoon, well before we came to the turnoff for Kamput, where Maarten was to check in for a moment to establish the "official" excuse for our excursion south, I stupidly broke into what I thought was a lighthearted silence that had taken over our van, broke in to comment on the scene out there, and I must have done so in a tone that suggested more irritation than I felt. I can't remember exactly what I said, something about how very far from their violent border those Thai farmers seemed, though actually less than an hour away, and how that thought made this quiet landscape almost too unreal for me to bear—something along those lines.

Maarten didn't turn his head when he spoke—a bad signal with him. "What is happening along the border isn't the Thai farmer's fault," he said. "I must say, Sameth, sometimes you seem to lose all perspective." I just stared at him. Then I said, "It's sometimes a bit hard to find the right perspective from the sort of space I've been given to live in for almost four years." Maarten didn't respond. He kept his eyes straight ahead, focused on the empty highway. But of course I couldn't leave things there. I had to say, "And if the Thai farmer isn't at fault for what's happening along the border, his bloody government surely is. Even if the United Nations Secretary-General congratulates them for their humanitarian attitude toward all these displaced persons they are burdened with."

Maarten had never lectured me or anyone else in my presence as far as I can remember, but he lectured me then. He told me what Secretary-General Waldheim had actually said to the Thai government, not in secret, not just to those close at hand, but before reporters so that anybody capable of reading the newspapers could get this message and later verify what he'd said, and what he'd said came down to this: all people had a right to run away from a system of government that they opposed, and it was the duty of all countries to accept and welcome those running away, and not as displaced persons who could be asked to leave by the authorities but as legitimate refugees. And when the Thai Minister of the Interior remarked, again within hearing of the reporters, that other countries did not feel a duty to receive foreigners crossing illegally into their country and that every country, including Thailand, had a duty to survive, Secretary-General Waldheim simply ignored him. That is what Mr. Waldheim had actually said and actually done in public, whether the Thai government liked it or not, though he may also have said other things in private and though he may also have congratulated the Thai government for its humanitarianism. And as a matter of fact, Maarten said, there Waldheim had a point too, since the Thai government, for all its hysteria about the mass of new refugees coming in illegally by boat and on foot, had actually treated those arriving better than some other Southeast Asian countries had, and the Thai authorities were at least willing to feed the hungry and care for the sick as best they could despite the poverty they themselves had to deal with among their own people.

Maarten had the facts—the newspaper accounts, and the Bangkok talk among foreigners, and the connections with people in power. How could I argue with him? All I had was a feeling in the pit of my stomach. And when I didn't argue with him, he softened his tone and went off into regions that I guess he assumed would be safer, less likely to get up my irony or anger: what Waldheim, just back from his wide travels, had apparently said that Hanoi had said about Thailand's dubious neutrality, and what China had said about Hanoi's dubious neutrality, and what Hanoi had said about China's influence in the area, and China about Russia's and Russia about America's and what all of them had said about Cambodia being a special and very complicated case seen from any perspective, including that of Sihanouk, who was just waiting for Heng Samrin to kill off Pol Pot and Pol Pot to kill off Heng Samrin so that he himself could return to rule his country after free elections. And all the while Maarten was giving me his half-amused account of the mighty debating the fate of the special case, I couldn't help wondering exactly where he had gotten his information about Waldheim's intimate dialogues with these world leaders, whether from private or public sources, and if private, under the patronage of exactly whom.

Once that particular seed of doubt is planted, there is no possibility it won't sprout, not in my experience anyway. And of course it is out of the question to talk about its being there—in fact, it seems essential to cover up its traces. I sat there smiling, pretending to be terribly entertained by his clever style of presenting these confused perspectives, until he must have noticed something about the quality of my smile and shut up abruptly. We took the turn toward the border, now among hills, the tall mountains at our back and Cambodia and its forests our skyline ahead. It gave one a different feeling to come toward the country that way rather than to see it while living on its margins. Not an easy feeling—I can't describe it. Familiarity made ominous? I decided to wait in the van when we arrived at the Kamput camp. Maarten had parked well beyond the camp gate, so I couldn't be seen by the guards, but I found myself sliding lower in my seat as I sat there, as though I had reason to hide.

He didn't make me wait long, less than half an hour. As we turned back toward the main highway, I could tell something was working in him because he was driving too fast for that kind of road. "Wouldn't you know it?" he said. "Of course we had to pick Ho Chi Minh's birthday for our excursion to the sea." That made me smile. "I didn't know Ho Chi Minh offended you that much." Maarten glared at me. "You don't know what gets into these people. The Vietnamese have attacked the Khmer Rouge everywhere they can find them and now thousands of Khmer Rouge are crossing into Thailand. From Trat all the way north. And not just guerrillas with rifles but front-line troops carrying mortars and rockets and heavy machine guns." I tried to be casual about it. "So this means we have to go back to Aran, is that it?" Maarten looked at me again. "Aran? Not now that we've come this far. We probably couldn't get back to Aran if we tried to. There's a bloody alert the whole length of the border and they're starting to close off all roads leading there."

I gathered this could mean the road we were on, but I didn't say so. I hung on to the edge of my seat and let him drive as wildly as he felt necessary. The black berets were setting up a new roadblock by the time we reached the main highway, but they weren't quite in business yet and waved us on through, I suppose because our van didn't really look much like a threat to anybody's army. Maarten turned south and didn't slow down until we came to the outskirts of Chantaburi. It had been our plan to spend the night there in a villa that houses some ICRC friends of my Irish neighbor in Aran, but Maarten thought we might better keep going toward the coast and maybe come back to Chantaburi when things had calmed down a bit. I had no objection to that at all; my hunger for the sea was whetted by the changing landscape as we went south, more and more palm trees, fewer wood and bamboo houses on stilts and more touching solid ground, with painted walls and balconies, some, even before the town, with the air of villas made to smell the sea.

But I was in too much of a hurry. The town of Chantaburi was not on the sea, and though it is richer than Aran—more cement, more billboards advertising love and war at the cinema, shops where one might buy anything sold in Bangkok—there was too little of the mindless escape I was looking for. That had to wait until some distance into the road we took west on the far edge of town. The light was dying by then. Maarten had picked up a bottle of Mekong whiskey and some sort of fish on a skewer in Chantaburi, and when we had finished eating we started passing the whiskey back and forth with a fierce, silent determination to bring on a mood our spirits couldn't generate on their own. The result was that we were quite pissed—as my Irish friend would say—by the time we reached Kleong and angled toward the shore. I remember that stretch of highway lined by trees, I don't know what kind of trees but with tall thin trunks rising to a burst of leaves, the trunks planted very close together so that the leaves would merge at the sides and overhead to knit a canopy that seemed to shut out the light except where the naked sun came through the trunks in a low glare that covered the asphalt with long shadows. All I could see directly ahead was the coming dusk.

"Where's the sea?" I asked Maarten, petulant, half-angry. "I don't know," Maarten said. "Let's find it." And he stepped on the accelerator to bring the car to a speed that was exhilarating, terrifying. Then, suddenly, a few kilometers into that terror, he slammed on the brakes and turned sharply left on a dirt road that seemed to lead into a wilderness of pine and acacia and palm trees without visible boundary, and there, less than a kilometer along that rough road: the sea. It came on us so suddenly that Maarten skidded the van to a stop and just sat there gazing at it as though it were a thing seen for the first time. The water was absolutely still, a light-struck glaze. Beyond the last line of palm trees there was a beach, white sand, stretching to the right and the left in a long, long curve that vanished into dense headlands at the limits of the bay. We seemed to have come into the arc at dead center, but the road had no purpose beyond the trees, because ahead of us it became a track that turned into grass before it reached the sand, and there was nothing for it to lead to in any other direction.

Maarten was still sitting there with his arms crossed over the steering wheel, staring at the sea, when I climbed down on my side and ran to the edge of the water. There was a cluster of rocks far out in the bay, tall as a passenger ship, dark against the thin sunlight, and farther still the outline of an island. I stripped as quickly as I could, left everything there as it fell and ran into the water, thrusting hard against the sea's pressure until it brought me down and I had to give in and slide into it on my belly to take in the feel of it along the length of my body. Then I swam out and farther out in regular fast strokes without easing up or turning until I had to flip over on my back and float to catch my breath. Maarten was standing on the shore taking off his shirt by that time. I didn't wave but turned over on my belly again and kept heading out toward the rock ship in the middle of the bay, swimming with long and steady strokes as though it might be possible for me to go that far and beyond with the right pacing, but finally giving up when I began to get out of breath again, floating unhurried now because in my nakedness the feel of that water, cleaner and warmer than any I could remember, was liberation enough.

Maarten caught up to me as I lay there on my back gazing out at the swollen red sun. He didn't say anything. He waited for me to turn over and start back toward the shore in a long angle, as though I were aiming for a point below the headland at the far corner of the beach; then he came up to swim beside me, matching his pace to mine. I smiled at him. We kept going like that, turning more and more toward the land, until we reached shallow water. When it was only waist deep, I stood up, threw my head back and stretched my hair to wring it out. Maarten lay there waiting, staring at me—staring with what seemed a certain melancholy hunger. I eased back in the water and let myself drift over so that I could reach out and brush his blond hair out of his eyes, as though to help him make sure he could see all he wanted to see. That was enough for him. He picked me up almost roughly and carried me all the way in, still not saying a word, and he didn't put me down until he came to the grass at the inner edge of the sand. And that is where we stayed.

I'm a bit reluctant to talk about what happened next—anyway with the image of you listening to me, dear Tan Yong—but I have to, because it is essential in showing the rhythm of our time by the sea, the pattern of mixed expectation and threat, of release and confusion, that emerged from those hours and that left me where I am now. And if I speak about it too openly for your taste, though faithful to my mood at the time and its aftermath, you will have to forgive me or not as it pleases you. I was afraid that Maarten might be naive about making love on sandy ground, so when he came down beside me to kiss me and then to lick the salt water off my breasts, I told him he'd better get a blanket out of the van. He leaned back on one elbow to look at me, half-smiling, then went back to licking the water off me as though he planned to dry me that way from head to foot. He wouldn't stop. But at the same time he was careful about what he was doing, slow and gentle in the way he moved, letting his tongue do the touching and the fingers of one hand as though he knew he'd get into trouble if he turned too sharply or came against some part of me with any part of his body that had been against the ground. And I tried not to move at all as I lay there stretched out for him until that just wasn't possible any longer, and at that point he leaned back away from me and waited for me to spread myself open, then came over me very carefully and let me guide him in with the hand I'd kept clean.

The care we had to take, this hesitancy that imitated reticence, made us seem like new lovers then, lovers with the advantages of discovery, but of course it couldn't go on that way. Maarten finally led me down to the water, and when we'd washed the sand off each other he went back down the beach to get a blanket from the van and to gather up our clothes. I sat in the shallow water with my arms crossed to cover my breasts and gazed out to sea. I was tempted to go in again. I knew if I did that I'd keep going on until I was completely sober and tired out. When I finally glanced down the beach, Maarten was coming back with the clothes over one arm. I watched him the whole way back, smiling to myself as though seeing him come toward me that young and naked for the first time. And when he had the blanket spread out on the inner edge of the beach between a palm tree and some kind of thick green bush and was standing there obviously wondering what I planned to do next, I let my impulse to swim die completely and went back there to him, this time making him stretch himself out on the blanket so that I could kneel over him and take my slow fill of him as I pleased.

It must have been past midnight when we began to talk. I had been dozing for a while and woke up to find the moon out, blurring the clean brightness that had taken over the sky after the sun went down but at the same time now highlighting the few constellations I knew by dulling their messier background. I found Maarten awake too, gazing straight up at the sky, apparently unaware that I was watching him. I was ready to say something about what sea air did for the clarity of constellations even with the moon out when it occurred to me that saying anything about a night sky that blatantly open to both of us would spoil it all by turning the thing into a ghastly cliché. So Maarten was the one to speak first, still without looking at me. "It makes one think about the larger picture, doesn't it?" he said. I studied him. "What larger picture?" I saw Maarten's shoulder shrug almost imperceptibly. "Whatever there is beyond the things that make us so afraid." I was still looking at him. "You think there's something beyond those things?" Maarten now smiled at my probably excessive seriousness of tone or the touch of surprise in it or something. "I guess I think so," he said. "Does that so surprise you? Otherwise what's the point?" I tried to make my tone lighter. "I thought the point was fairly much one of surviving. At least in this part of the world." Maarten tried to hold his smile. "But surviving for what?" That made me shrug. "I don't know," I said. "Things like this. And for being enough in charge of one's life not to be afraid." Maarten turned away again and put his arms behind his head. "Maybe it's sometimes easier not to be afraid if you can believe in something beyond yourself and your own survival. Or even the survival of those close to you."

That made me sit up. I had a fairly good idea where he was trying to lead me now and I had no desire to go there—not at that time of night or maybe any other time. But I also didn't feel I could cut him short. What I should have done was take a short walk and come back when my sense of alarm had died down. Instead I turned to him without any effort at evasion and asked him point-blank if he was trying to tell me that he was a believer. Maarten seemed to hold back a second, then simply nodded. "And you want me to become a believer, is that it? Meaning, I suppose, a Christian?" He sat up beside me. "I don't want you to become anything," he said. "I just want to do what I can to help you. And to be honest with you about myself so you trust me again."

I knew Maarten's relief organization was supported largely by church groups in his country and elsewhere, but it had never occurred to me that he himself might be a believing Christian. I suppose there was every reason why it should have occurred to me, but it had never come up in any conversation about him or me or where we stood. Maybe it was a sign of the trouble between us that it never had. Anyway, discovering a thing like that about someone you've shared your life with intimately for some months is very disconcerting, unnerving, almost like learning that one has been betrayed. Which is absurd on the face of it—and that too doesn't help. I stood up and walked slowly to the edge of the sea, hoping he wouldn't follow me so that I would have time to think. My suspicion about his working for certain obscure interests that he hadn't chosen to reveal to me now seemed comically beside the point. And of course that too was absurd when one thought about it for two seconds: what more plausible motive for taking a levelheaded view of our violent game of nations, of seeing things from the larger perspective and maintaining an objective stance, than doing so in the name of Christ and the final vanity of life on this earth?

Maarten didn't come up beside me as I sat there, and soon I began to feel cold, alone, I don't know what. But I stayed where I was, looking out at the relentless gray sea. And when I went back to the blanket I got my clothes together and dressed before I lay down beside Maarten again. He was asleep or pretending to be asleep, in either case an act of charity, because if I'd had to go on talking at that point I would have had to admit to him how alone I felt, and there would have been no possibility of my hiding that what he'd told me in his effort to be honest was the main reason I felt that way.

We stayed on the beach the next morning lying out in the sun until it seemed unsafe to burn any longer. We talked about many things, none of which I can remember now, but of course not about the one thing that should have mattered. Before we picked up to leave, now red from the sun and hungry, we took a long walk almost to the headland at the western end of the bay. There wasn't much to see, really, just a few empty huts with grass roofs and a section along the beach that had been cleared for what looked like the foundations of houses or bungalows, ten or fifteen spaced equally apart along two strips of road leading back from the beach into an open field. That part of our wilderness had been discovered anyway, and so had a section of forest at the tip of the headland where there was a clearing for a radarscope that was surveying the heavens with the ominous hum of a giant bumblebee poised for evil.

On our way back to the van, Maarten took my hand. He said he had something on his conscience that he wanted to get rid of, and this was a report he'd received at the Kamput camp the day before, news that he was afraid might alarm me and that he'd therefore kept to himself, maybe out of mistaken selfishness. The report was that most of Cambodia had begun to suffer from severe famine partly because there had been a bad winter harvest, partly because the Vietnamese had shipped food away to their own people, partly because the fighting was in some of the richest farming regions, including Battambang Province. And the report went on to say that thousands on thousands were now gathered near the Thai border waiting to cross over in the hope of finding food, especially Sino-Khmer, but also Khmer Rouge and even those who had worked for the Vietnamese.

I did my best to put his conscience at ease. I told him he'd been right not to bring all this up the previous afternoon, but the news didn't really come as a surprise since I'd been keeping up with what the newspapers had to say on the refugee problem. Then he said the report mentioned specifically some twenty thousand Sino-Khmer gathered at the border near Ban Nong Chan—that was the detail that had worried him most, since Thirith might somehow get caught up in the mess of those thousands trying to cross into Thailand as illegal entrants against the wishes of the Thai military. The border was closed at the moment, but how long would that be effective? he asked. I had no answer for him, and I couldn't face another discussion of the rights and wrongs of allowing those starving Sino-Khmer to hover on the border, whether as displaced persons or as illegal entrants or as whatever they might be called to keep them in their nameless and stateless place. And I killed an impulse to ask him about the exact source of this report. I simply thanked him for sharing the news with me and for showing concern about Thirith, but I said that she was now quite outside my control, I couldn't make her stay home if I wanted to, and my one hope was that her new friends would provide her with the protection I no longer could.

Maarten was clearly much relieved by my response. I could tell from the fact that he didn't let go of my hand until we reached the van, in fact took me down to the edge of the water for a last sentimental survey of the beach that had been our reunion and our parting—though I don't think either of us realized it at just that moment. My realization came when we got back to Chantaburi and stopped in to visit the friends of my Irish neighbor, who were gathered in a hostel run by one of the relief agencies. Maarten and I were feeling very mellow by that time, having gorged ourselves on an early lunch by the shore near Ban Phe. We had shrimp and squid and two kinds of whole fish I had never seen before, and we drank beer after beer while we watched a family—a husband, wife, and six children—drag their weather-beaten boat up on shore for a Sunday cleaning as a city family might an old limousine. By the end of our lunch I was in love with that family and in love with Maarten again and with all the painted boats someone had brought out and lined up along the pier beside us to make us think we were on holiday, and back in the van I fell asleep against Maarten's shoulder totally serene and mindless as we rode on to Chantaburi in the rain which had come by then in great force to wash away, it seemed, all his sins and mine too.

But inside the hostel the mood was different—my mood especially. The people gathered there were a mixture of ages and nationalities, mostly young Europeans and Americans, mostly involved in relief work or training programs of one kind or another, all very friendly and hospitable, all much worried about what was going on along the border. The worry seemed to focus on what might happen to them if the Vietnamese actually decided to follow their Khmer Rouge enemies a certain distance into Thailand and wipe out some of the border camps as they advanced, for example the Kamput camp, where most of them worked weekdays. Where would that put them and the projects they still had in progress? Farther up the border in another camp? Somewhere in the northern provinces? Back in Bangkok? Or would they be forced to go back home and start working all over again in another country—if there was another job in another country?

Maarten's role in all this was apparently to act the informal emissary from the capital to the outlying regions, the visitor pretty much in the know, reticent about saying too much yet bringing late news meant to calm nerves and restore hope. When pressed, he said as far as he could tell, the Thai military had the situation very much in hand, the Prime Minister was reported to have urged the public not to panic at threats made against Thailand by the Heng Samrin puppet government because the threats were as hollow as the government itself, and the Prime Minister had apparently been cool enough to crack a bad joke about the tension along the border—something to the effect of "How can a little man like Khmer invade a country as big as yours and mine?" Besides, Maarten said, with all the problems the Vietnamese had these days, including that of trying to feed their own people after the fifth crop failure in a row, they were not likely to take on Thailand while still trying to run Cambodia, at least not for the time being. Of course during all this speculation, nobody, Maarten included, mentioned the refugees crowded into the border areas and what might happen to them if the Vietnamese invaded.

I listened to the talk as long as I could, trying to keep a pleasant expression on my face, trying to be as amiable toward the others as they were toward me; then I took a walk in the garden. It was a small garden with two outdoor chairs and a table made of cement with splotches of tile in it, quite ugly under its single mango tree, but I sat out there feeling more at home than I had felt inside. I don't know whether it was mostly a physical hangover from lunch or a spiritual hangover from the previous night, but I felt down, dispossessed, no longer capable of making the gestures that might bring me within range of people like that. I suppose they had every right to be worried about their safety and the threat to their work—after all, they didn't have to be out here in the filth and disease of the camps doing what they were doing—but their worry couldn't be mine, and I couldn't give much useful thought to the problems of packing up one's work kit and moving on to another country, any other country, whenever the borders one is facing become too vague or hot.

The problem of Maarten was more complicated and unsettling, not only difficult for me to grasp but painful even to have to recognize, because if I lost touch with him completely, what would I have left to sustain me? Yet I simply couldn't avoid it any longer. How could I pretend that I might come to see from a perspective as large as his, so otherworldly? I couldn't just dig up the Buddhism and superstition that had died with my mother or the folk wisdom and quaint ancient philosophy that had died with my father or—what no doubt would have pleased him most—my grandmother's harsh Anglicanism. And if I tried to believe in something up there or out there in his universe, where was I supposed to find some sort of tradition to give it solid grounding and keep it from becoming cheap? I no longer had any of my own, and I couldn't simply adopt his. The thing was hopeless, and my sense of that seemed to isolate me completely.

Maarten didn't come out to see why I'd gone off by myself, so I decided to take a walk down to the main square in town. There was everything and nothing there. When I got back I could hear music in the hostel, and from the doorway I saw that some of the people in there had begun drinking. Maarten found me sitting at the table in the garden. My face must have been wrong, because he said "Sameth" and ran his fingers along the ridge of my cheekbones. I didn't have to tell him that I wanted to go back to Aran. He took my hand and led me over to the van and said I should wait there for him; then he went back inside to say goodbye for the two of us.

It was dark when we reached my rooms on the edge of Aran. We came across more roadblocks than usual, but otherwise things seemed quiet. Maarten decided to spend the night with me and leave early the next morning for Bangkok. I didn't wake up when he left. The note on my writing table said "Call me." That was all. Now almost a week has gone by and I haven't called him yet.

June 1. Our stretch of the border seems to have become important again to someone besides Pol Pot and Heng Samrin. There was a report earlier this week that Her Majesty the Queen of Thailand had paid a visit last Saturday to both the Trat and Chantaburi districts to check on the condition of Cambodian refugees, and on the same day we in Aran received the American ambassador. There was a picture of the Queen in the paper breaking away from her entourage of military officers to talk directly to some of the refugees, I suppose with the aid of an interpreter. She was reported to have ordered doctors from the Red Cross to provide more care for those wounded by mines and for those suffering from skin diseases.

The American ambassador was here to gain firsthand knowledge of the border situation and apparently visited some of the new settlements to speak with the illegal entrants in person. What he saw must have touched his heart, because the paper says he promised General Kriangsak one million dollars in emergency aid, and now he is on his way to Washington to ask President Jimmy Carter for more. General Kriangsak is reported to have told the ambassador "in no uncertain terms" about Thailand's difficulties with the refugees and its need not only for financial aid but for an increase in American "intake" of displaced persons. It seems the ambassador had no comment to make on the intake question.

These visits by the Queen and the ambassador do not provide much excuse for celebration when one reads in the paper this morning what the Supreme Command Chief of Staff General Saiyud Kerdphol has to say about the situation on the border. Yesterday he warned a group of British businessmen gathered at the Oriental Hotel that Thailand must "prepare for the worst," and to him "the worst" means the arrival of perhaps one million more Indochinese refugees during the next two months. As General Saiyud views the situation, these refugees could easily become a "sixth column" of political, economic, and social liability for Thailand, a sixth column that actually covers a fifth column now in place and waiting to create a cause célèbre that in his view can somehow became the pretext for "any hostile country" to invade Thailand. By any hostile country he really means Vietnam, which he accuses of practicing "racist exclusion policies" that resemble those of the Nazis during World War II, different in method perhaps, but from his perspective even more callous. He apparently told his British businessmen that "if Adolph Hitler had been as indifferent to world opinion as the present Lao Dong Party, his 'final solution' for the Jews might have been more cheaply and effectively achieved by casting them off on leaky boats rather than by consigning them to the gas chambers of Auschwitz."

The General, who is described as an internationally recognized counterinsurgency expert famous for speaking his mind, was obviously in grand form. He went on to tell his British audience about the "double standard" that the United Nations has promoted in dealing with Cambodian refugees: "If a man is forced out of his country because he objects to something, the U.N. says that other countries should accept him. If the new asylum country were to treat him in the same way that his own country did and thereby get him to leave again, the entire world would rise in horror against the offending country and very effective sanctions could be invoked." I doubt it. The general ought to relax. Who in the wide world is going to rise up in horror to defend displaced persons on the Thai–Cambodian border, especially now that we have become a sixth column hiding Communist spies and agents?

The truth is that we have had a rather quiet week in this section of the border; at least that is the impression I have gathered, which may simply mean that I am cut off from what is actually going on, along with all the others here who are subject to the increasingly severe military restrictions—and that now includes not only "old" refugees, but journalists, foreigners, anyone without property here or a special pass or some invisible connection. We see only what we are allowed to see. The little first-hand news I get of circumstances outside our camp comes from the piece of road leading to my rooms in Aran and now from Thirith. She visited me here on Wednesday. We had a fine time together, a very relaxed conversation, the first in weeks. Maybe my letting her have more time to herself, more free space to breathe, has worked to diminish her hostility toward me or our situation in the camp or whatever it was that had begun to make me appear her enemy.

Thirith even spoke to me at one point about what she was actually doing in her new organization. It seems she isn't involved most of the time in anything directly military or political, not as she describes it. She said there were of course regular orientation meetings so that the organization could be briefed on political developments and on current strategy, but her duties at the front—I'm certain that's the way she put it—consisted mostly of helping to distribute sacks of rice to the new arrivals in the settlements near Ban Nong Chan. She says she has to do that three times a week, which seems to me more distribution than is normal, anyway more than one would expect in the regular camps. Either that isn't all she does, or the Thai military are allowing more relief work in the new settlements than most old refugees are allowed to know—but I wasn't ready to question her when she was trying to be more open with me than she has been. Nor was I ready to point out that the distribution of rice might not seem political in her innocent view of things but could certainly be used for political advantage, even recruitment, by those in charge of her organization.

One reason I found it difficult to be as open with her as I could have been was the joy, the intensity, that she showed me when she spoke about her feelings in being part of a group again. Her face seemed to take on an almost religious illumination. What she now felt, she said, wasn't only a new purpose in her life but something of what she had known in school, before the April 17 catastrophe brought death to her city and to most of her friends. I can't remember all her exact words, but I suppose the best way to put what she seemed to have discovered was a sense of community, though what she conveyed to me wasn't quite so abstract, it included a sense of family as well. This is what she felt with her friends in the new organization, what made her nights out with them, even if it meant sleeping in the fields among the hungry and the sick, so satisfying, not just an experience of shared belief and commitment but of warm camaraderie, etc. It was as though her four years in our camp had given her nothing— no sense of community, no family, nothing.

I was of course hurt at the time, though I tried not to let it show. But now that I've had two days to think about it, I've come to see that it's probably best for her to feel as she does. To the degree that it may isolate me, it liberates her—and her telling me about what she's now experiencing makes the thing finally less personal, finally perhaps necessary. I still don't know what this shared belief of hers amounts to exactly, or just how much satisfaction there ought to be in sleeping out among the desperately hungry and sick now that she is so well fed, but if it gives her a sense of purpose it may work to kill the more dangerous cast of mind that led to her withdrawal and then to her condition of—what shall I call it?—of reckless afterlife. In any case, I actually feel closer to her now than I did a week ago, and that means a gain for me as well.

Before Thirith came to visit on Wednesday I had two long mornings here completely alone to do some painting and decorating. I didn't get very far, because I found it hard to get into the proper mood. I've tried to give the rooms a touch of myself by bringing in the odd trinket and some extra clothing from what I've gathered over the years at the camp, but I can't get rid of the aura that now haunts the place, or at least my perception of it: the aura of its being temporary, a place to be passed on to the next susceptible refugee whom Maarten chooses to rescue for a while from the meanness of life on this border. I spoke to Maarten by phone on Sunday—not a long conversation. He was as warm as I could have expected in view of my not having called him for a week, but he didn't raise any objection when I suggested that it might be best if we didn't see each other this weekend so that we might have more time to find our bearings. He said simply, "Well, I'm here if you need me. All you have to do is call." I wish he had objected. I was really trying to test his feelings, stupidly I suppose. I'm not in a strong position to be testing other people's feelings when I'm so unsure of my own.

I did another thing that doesn't please me—this inspired, I imagine, by the American ambassador's visit to Aran and my insecurity about Maarten. I sat down at my desk yesterday and wrote a letter to our mutual friend in America. I wrote the letter without having a clear idea of what I would do with it when I had it written, because I had no address to mail it to. I suppose I vaguely had in mind letting Maarten help me find an official address through his American connections in Bangkok, but that did not become a serious issue because I decided in the end not to attempt to mail it. The letter was almost entirely about Thirith: a bit of history— my escaping with her across the border, our life here as she grew to become a more or less healthy woman, my hopes for her emigration to a third country, etc.—and then a description of what she is like today, how self-reliant if a bit proud, how essentially innocent, how beautiful if still on the thin side. But as I went on, I suddenly felt as though I were trying to sell my daughter to a stranger, almost pimping for her, and I had to give up. Who am I to play that role with a man who has shown no sign of interest in me for over four years, let alone in a young woman he has never met? And if I have to write a letter to ask for help with Thirith, why can't it be to you, dear Tan Yong, that I write instead of to an invisible American?

June 9. The worst has happened and there is nothing I or anybody else can do about it. The Thais are sending the Sino-Khmer back across the border by force. I came here to my rooms yesterday morning to do my laundry in the tub, and I had just begun to hang things up when the Irish nurse from next door burst in to say that something very strange was going on outside because she had started to walk into the market in town and had found herself facing a line of Thai soldiers with machine guns stretched across the road not far from our entrance gate. There was another group farther out on the road that leads into town and more in the distance. She of course turned back to the gate. And as she stood there watching, buses began to come down the road heading into Aran from the direction of the border north of here, bus after bus, crowded with people she took to be refugees because they were dressed that way: men, women, children, all ages, packed in like passive animals. She counted ten buses going by; then there were no more for a while but the soldiers kept their stations by the sides of the road, so she thought she'd better tell somebody about it, somebody who knew enough Thai to find out what was going on.

I went out to the front gate with the dreadful feeling that I knew exactly what was going on, though I thought at first it was just another attempt to move new refugees en masse from one settlement to another before they got too firmly planted in their bamboo-and-plastic shelters. The buses had started to pass by the gate again by the time we got out there, some of them beautiful aluminum buses with a broad red stripe lined by blue for decoration, and some with flowers and bright beads in their front windows, as though out for a holiday excursion. They were all heavily loaded, and one could see the occasional armed soldier on board, but the refugees inside didn't seem in a state of panic. Some even smiled and waved as they passed us—the children mostly—which meant that either I was too hysterical in my premonition or they didn't really know where they were going.

Cold suddenly but still calm, I decided I would try to find out. I took my friend the nurse by the hand and led her down the road with me to the line of soldiers nearest us. They drew back slightly as we passed, as though to make room, I suppose because we looked foreign in our slacks (my Irish friend also has fairly light hair). I don't know what kind of officer it was who talked to us finally, but he was very polite—and very much in charge, because none of the others apparently dared to speak. I asked as firmly as I could where the buses were going, and he told me not to worry about it, they were just going to Bangkok. And when I asked "Why Bangkok? Where in Bangkok?" he grinned and said I had no reason to be so suspicious, they would be going to a transit center there for a while and then on to another country. I tried to control what I was feeling so that my voice would stay neutral. "There are so many," I said. "Do you know where they are all coming from?" The officer was still grinning. "That's no secret. From Cambodia. From the border near Ban Nong Chan. Where else?"

He was only partly lying. They were in fact from the settlements near Ban Nong Chan, but they weren't on their way to Bangkok. I found out when I finally got through to Maarten late in the afternoon. By then more than fifty buses had gone by, at least that is how many I personally counted, and they were still moving past our gate, as they continued to do into the dusk. It took Maarten several hours to find out what was actually going on. He was taken completely by surprise just as most were here, and he was more angry than I have ever heard him, at least in part because he had been through Aran briefly the day before yesterday with a group of some forty diplomats from various countries, including the Netherlands, and it seems there had been no indication of any such mass movement of refugees in what the diplomats had seen or had been told. In fact the Thais had created the opposite impression, since a senior minister attached to the Prime Minister's office had made a public declaration that the government now realized fully that any measures taken by Thailand to deal with the refugee problem would have to take into consideration the image of the country in the eyes of the international community.

Maarten swore and swore. This statement and the visit of the diplomats were all just bloody camouflage, he said. All just bloody theatre. And the way he said it made me think he was taking it personally, as though he himself had been privately betrayed. Anyway, he finally learned from his sources, reliable or otherwise, that the refugees from the Ban Nong Chan area, mostly Sino-Khmer who had come across recently, would be transported by bus through Kabin Buri and then northeast to the border region somewhere below Surin or Sisaket, where they would be escorted by the military back over the border into Cambodia at points considered free of the current fighting. How many refugees? He didn't know. The operation was supposed to take five days at least. That probably meant thousands and thousands. Maybe everybody in this area who was camping out along the border.

I don't have to tell you what this news did to me, even if it wasn't entirely unexpected. We are forbidden to go anywhere now, not into town, not back to my camp. Apparently no one is allowed to enter Aran from any direction. Even if Maarten finds some way of getting here, he won't be allowed to go to Ban Nong Chan or the other settlements because he was told that nobody who is not in uniform, whether Thai or foreigner, will be allowed to use the border roads in our region. So I am completely sealed off. And Thirith could be in Cambodia by now.

I stood by the gate watching the buses go by yesterday evening until it became too dark to see clearly. My Irish neighbor tried to get me to come in for dinner, then gave up and brought me a bowl of food and a mug of tea. I couldn't really see into the buses, but I thought that at least I might be seen by Thirith if she were to go by in one of them. For whatever good that would do. And I went out this morning to watch when they started coming by again, until that just made me feel sick. There seems to be nothing one can do now that makes sense. Not even writing about it. Though maybe that's one way I have left to keep my mind from turning.

June 12. Maarten made it through to Aran yesterday afternoon. By that time maybe four hundred busloads of refugees had passed by here, something approaching one hundred a day during the past four days. And there were more going by this morning, though not at quite the same rate. We now know that the buses will keep coming this way until all forty thousand of the new refugees in the Ban Nong Chan area are taken to their so-called safe border point in the north for the forced crossing back into Cambodia, and then it seems the Thai army will move south to Chantaburi and Trat to clean out the refugees there as well. Certainly by now there can't be many left in our region, no new refugees anyway, no Sino-Khmer.

Maarten came here on a special pass with some other official working for the UNHCR. The news they brought was evil—for a start, from the English-language newspapers, where the government is shown to admit, more or less, what it is up to and to defend its new program of forced repatriation. "Don't preach to us," General Kriangsak tells the U.N. and the International Committee of the Red Cross, "this is our business, done to protect the national interest. All you international people do is talk, talk, talk, and what you say is unreasonable and shameless." And the General seems to have the support of most Thais, including student leaders from eighteen educational institutions, who issued a joint statement calling the "refugee influx" both a social and a security problem for Thailand created by its neighbor and demanding that Vietnam "review its inhumane policy of pushing its own people abroad." But the news that hasn't yet reached the papers and may never do so is worse. Maarten had trouble bringing himself to tell me everything he and his friend had learned in Bangkok until I convinced him that I'd had three long days by myself to prepare for hearing anything he might know and that I was certain I could take it without the kind of emotional excess that might embarrass either him or me.

The news that had him worried came from an "old" refugee who used to work for the Joint Voluntary Agency and who had just returned to Bangkok from hell by some miracle—so Maarten put it. This old refugee, former refugee, had gone to Ban Nong Chan early last week to search for a brother and sister he hadn't seen since the April 17 exodus from Phnom Penh when his family had been dispersed like so many others. The man was following a premonition that his brother and sister had crossed into Thailand recently after the evacuation of Sisophon, where other relatives of his had once had a business. It turns out that not only didn't he find what he hoped to in Ban Nong Chan but his premonition almost cost him his life, because he was forced to board one of the first buses to go out of the Ban Nong Chan area on Friday despite his protests about being an old refugee and a former employee of an international agency. The poor man tried to get off the bus every time it stopped, protested again and again that he had no business being on it (I gather he is a little man but made of iron), until the other refugees around him embarrassed him into shutting up. Most of the bus were apparently convinced that they were on their way to a transit center just as they'd been told. When they turned off the Bangkok road at Kabin Buri heading north, the center was to be in Surin, and when they passed that, some other northern town they didn't know, and even when they turned south again through Kantharalak toward the border, now well after dark, there was no panic, because the soldiers on board distributed rice and cakes and passed water around from a bucket and told them not to worry so much about where they were going, it was all going to be fine for them, at least they weren't in the army.

Where they were going was an escarpment on the Preah Vihear ridge that separates Thailand and Cambodia south of Ban Phumsaron. The approach on the Thai side is apparently easy, a grassy slope where the old refugee and his group were allowed to camp out for the rest of the night along with the others who had arrived ahead of them. At dawn they were made to move up the ridge in order, and at the top they were told to go on over the edge, one family to follow another and each to care for its own. What they were facing wasn't exactly a cliff, really a steep incline, maybe at a 60-degree angle, and covered with vines and brush strong enough to provide a good hold and a safe descent if you took your time. They weren't hurried once they got started, but no one was allowed to hesitate on the edge when the moment came, and though the soldiers were there with their rifles poised, nobody really needed to be prodded along according to the old refugee's account of things, maybe because the several busloads ahead of them seemed to be making it down the escarpment in reasonably good order though very slowly, the women and children helped by the men and all working their way step by step with desperate care.

The second hell was at the bottom. There one found an open field with a pond on one side and a forest beyond. The field was mined. Most headed for the pond when they reached the bottom, because they needed water for the uncooked rice they'd been given as a parting gift, and soon the way to the pond was littered by the wounded and the dying, and then the way everywhere. The sound of the wounded was the only sound. Those coming from behind could hope to make it through to the forest only by stepping on those who had already fallen or by trusting to the benevolence of spirits, and the way out soon became a single path protected by the dead.

By the time the old refugee made it to the foot of the escarpment some of those ahead of him had safely crossed to the forest, but he decided he'd seen his last minefield and heard his last cry of agony in that unknown place even if it meant forcing the Thai soldiers to shoot him when he reached the top of the ridge so that at least they would have to bury him whole and in a private grave. He scampered along the foot of the escarpment until he was exhausted, then crawled some more to the limit of his strength and lay low until it was dark again and he could begin a slow angled climb back to the top of the ridge. What he found in the darkness at the top was not the Thai army he'd expected but a group of refugees, twenty or thirty he said, who'd taken the same route he had and who were hiding there among the trees. They were more terrified of him than he was of them, probably because he was wearing his regular Bangkok clothes and looked like a Thai, even if the clothes were now a mess. He decided to keep going through the forest until he reached a road of some kind. This is where Maarten first spoke of miracles, because before the night was out, the old refugee had found not only a road but eventually a truck going along that road that was carrying wood to Buri Ram and willing to give him a ride, and from there he was able to get a bus back to Bangkok.

I wanted to tell Maarten that the man's not looking like other refugees and his being able to speak Thai maybe diminished the miraculous aspect of his return to Bangkok that quickly, but I was too taken by the old refugee's demonstration of will to let any irony of mine color Maarten's version. And I had reason to be grateful to my Khmer compatriot, because it was apparently his story, which Maarten picked up at JVA headquarters, that persuaded Maarten and his friend to use the full extent of their influence to get themselves out to Aran so that they could protest this atrocity at its source and offer me what assistance they could. At the very least they hoped to talk the military here into allowing the refugees to repatriate themselves by one of the several roads that cross the border into Cambodia in the region of Preah Vihear, this though they fully realize that the escarpment route is a deliberate attempt by the Thais to discourage those refugees who make it across that minefield alive from returning to Thailand by their own choice.

They of course found that there is nothing they can do. The people here are not in charge of policy. And they insist that many refugees want to return to Cambodia, have gone back on their own already, which is at least partly true. And when Maarten and his friend make their protest in Bangkok, that will surely prove as useless as the protests by the Red Cross and others during the first days of the forced repatriation. Mostly for my sake they did make one trip to the border area north of here before returning to Bangkok last night. The Thai military wouldn't let them close to the settlements near Ban Nong Chan, but they were able to visit my camp. There was no sign of Thirith there, and the camp leaders they approached either didn't know where she was or thought it best to keep what they knew to themselves. I no longer have any doubt where she is, but I didn't share my conviction with Maarten. I'll save that for his next trip here tomorrow, when the evidence should be final. I just hope Thirith has some of the iron will of our fellow April 17 refugee. I hope I do too.

June 15. The buses didn't stop coming through Aran until late on Tuesday, though the first phase of the forced repatriation ended that day. It seems there were extra buses, enough to carry several thousand old refugees from our camp to a new holding center in Buri Ram where these so-called legal displaced persons are to await resettlement in third countries: America, Australia, Canada, France. I discovered this on Wednesday, a day late, when Maarten returned to bring this news along with other developments reported in Bangkok, but it doesn't matter, I couldn't have gone to that center anyway without Thirith even if I'd had the right documents. Apparently this transfer of old refugees for processing was an effort by the government to appease various countries who have protested its action in the north, but the protests haven't yet put an end to its solution of the refugee problem because the second phase of the forced repatriation is scheduled to begin in the south this weekend.

It seems that a total of 41,020 illegal entrants from our area have been sent back to Cambodia through "safe exits" in the Preah Vihear district of Sisaket Province, and as the exodus now changes direction, the government is trying to put the brightest shroud it can over the horror that has happened. We are told in the papers that the operation in the north went smoothly and that there was little resistance from the refugees. An official in Sisaket Province reports that "they seemed to be happy going back to their homeland again." And the procedures at the border are shown to have been humane. Each refugee was provided with rice cooked and uncooked, dried meat, and sufficient fish to last for five days. Then according to one high-ranking member of the government, "we simply informed the Vietnamese officials on the other side of the border by loudspeaker that we were going to send back the refugees, and when they okayed this, we allowed the refugees to walk across."

Government sources do admit to one tragic incident. "A refugee, apparently believing that he was being bused to his death, attacked the bus driver, causing the vehicle to plunge into a deep ravine in Nadee Subdistrict of Prachin Buri." And in another unexplained episode, some kind of disturbance aboard a bus full of refugees made it collide with a six-wheel truck coming from the opposite direction. So at least a few of our compatriots offered enough resistance to ensure that this phase of the government's operation didn't end as smoothly as it had begun.

On Wednesday Maarten was able to drive me back to the Wat Koh camp in his van. I decided to take advantage of this to pack up my things, my essential things and anything of value that Thirith had left behind, and to bring them back here to my rooms in Aran. Everyone at the camp was excited about the transfer of the day before and the prospects for the many left who hadn't been chosen to board the buses going to the transit camp in Buri Ram. There was very little talk of the Ban Nong Chan evacuation except among those of us who were missing relatives or friends. I learned that Thirith had not been seen at the camp since the day before the first buses began to take the Sino-Khmer away from Ban Nong Chan to the northern border. Since others of her group were also missing, I had to assume that she and they were caught up with the new refugees and carried off to Preah Vihear, as was the Khmer who used to work for JVA in Bangkok. Those now camped in Ban Nong Chan are only a few new arrivals who crossed over from Cambodia this week, too late for the bus ride north, and if Thirith had been hiding out somewhere else along the border in our area she surely would have made an appearance by now. I don't want to think anymore about where she may be at this moment or how she got there. I have to count on her luck. What I want to think about now is simply getting things ready so that I can go look for her.

Maarten has promised to help me—at least so he pretends. He says that he is not yet ready to give up on the idea that she may have boarded one of Tuesday's buses for Buri Ram, presumably unseen. Yesterday and today he is supposed to be doing what he can to track her down there if he can find anything to track. But he is not prepared to take me to the Preah Vihear district even if he could get permission to drive me there. He says that if he fails to find Thirith on his own and if I still insist on going to that section of the border when the situation there is back to normal—whatever that means—he will see to it that I get there. But he will not take me there personally, because he thinks the idea is mad.

I've tried to explain to him why I have to go. Admittedly my chances of finding Thirith are not good now that she has had who knows how many days to make her way ahead of me with or without enough to eat. But how can I not try? And once I'm over the border, maybe my plan of turning south to Battambang to see if my sister may have come back to her home doesn't offer much hope either. But the fact is that I have to turn somewhere. Anyway, I can't simply sit here in my rooms in Aran doing nothing. I no longer belong here. The truth may be that there is no other place I belong either, but there is still a place where I once did. And if it turns out there is nothing for me in Cambodia, no Thirith, no family, nothing left for me to give myself to, I will at least be completely free to find a new beginning. I suppose the first move then would be to make my way back here, but I'm not ready to tell Maarten that.

He is at least willing to provide me with recent maps. And if he won't take me to the border himself, he says that he can see to it that I'm allowed to leave Thailand where there is a road across the border and where one can presumably arrange a guarantee of safety from the Vietnamese. He told me that the government had not totally misrepresented the situation in the Preah Vihear region, since the Vietnamese were actually seen to be guiding some of the refugees through the forest beyond their minefield and since there seems actually to have been some contact between the Thai and Vietnamese military. They are after all not formal enemies, he said. The formal enemy of the Vietnamese is still Pol Pot.

I don't know who the formal or informal enemy is any longer and I don't care. Separation is the enemy, and betrayal, and not belonging anywhere. Maarten obviously thinks that I have quietly gone out of my mind under the stress of recent days, and I imagine he hopes I will gradually return to reality if I am humored a bit and given time to settle down. I have never been clearer in my head. I know what I have to do, and if he won't help me finally, I'll have to do it on my own. I have to go home any way I can. It may strike you as some sort of comic distortion for a Sino-Khmer to go on calling Cambodia home, but at least one no longer has to pretend that the word has any meaning here.

I'm going to end this journal now. When Maarten next comes I'm going to give it to him in a sealed envelope addressed to you in care of our friend at the American Department of State. Who knows if it will ever reach you? And if it does reach you it may not matter to either of us by then. But now it is yours, dear Tan Yong, for better or for worse.

FOUR

They had just passed the first klong in open country beyond the Bangkok suburbs when Dubois winked at Tim and leaned forward to tell the driver that he could begin looking for a place to stop.

"Christ," Garfield said. "We haven't been on the road an hour yet."

"You have to clean the tubes right away," Dubois said. "Get the Bangkok atmosphere out of your plumbing before more corrosion sets in."

"You won't make the border before dark that way," Garfield said.

"So? The border isn't going anywhere. The border is one of your eternal verities, out there day or night. You should know that by now, Garfield."

"The only verity I'm sure of in terrain like this is that you're a goddamn alcoholic. At least the minute you're free of headquarters and within smelling range of Mekong whiskey."

Dubois turned to Tim with an expression of pained sadness. "What do you say to that, Tim, my boy? Is our friend here being accurate even in a piss-assed way? There must be other verities he believes in besides my devotion to Mekong whiskey. He must still believe in America's manifest destiny out here in Southeast Asia, don't you think?"

"I don't know him well enough to say," Tim said. "But I'm ready for a stop. I picked up a bad case of Southeast Asian blues at the Nana Hotel."

"Mekong will fix it for you," Dubois said. "If you give yourself to it with absolute faith, see it for the true Thai blood of the Lamb, it can cure even a case of what you get at the Nana Hotel. Believe me."

"Believe him and you'll end up believing anything," Garfield said. "Which is what happens to just about everyone who stays out here as long as our friend has."

"He's right," Dubois said. "Better to get your ass back to Washington at least once a year for a refresher course in policy. Helps you figure out where you are so you can go elsewhere with a clear conscience."

"Not where you are so much as who you are," Garfield said.

"Anyway, helps to keep you steady on the promotion ladder."

"Instead of falling off on your fat behind smelling of Mekong whiskey."

"Ah, yes, ill fate and abundant wine may do you in, but a man of no fortune can still have a name to come, while a frustrated general fades away to nothing. So the poets tell us anyway."

Garfield turned around in the front seat. He was smiling now. "What the fuck are you talking about, Dubois?"

"I'm just quoting poetry, Garfield. A touch of poetry for your desert places. And if it's all the same to you, I'd appreciate it if you'd pronounce my name the French way to keep my ethnic fathers at rest. Rhymes not with 'boys' but with 'pourquoi.' "

"Well, it rhymed with 'boys' last time I was out here."

"I don't want to shock you," Dubois said, "but I've given all that up. Along with my inscrutable and sometimes dangerous local wife. So I'm as straight now as your best career diplomat trained at West Point."

"Except for the local whiskey."

"You ought to try it, Garfield. Really. It'll keep your pecker hard as steel and polished bright the whole day long, I promise."

Tim decided Dubois's dislike for Garfield went deeper than he'd thought at first, and it was beginning to look like the feeling was mutual. The two of them had been at it now pretty much from the moment Tim had climbed into the van to take a seat in the third row back, where he figured those hitching an unofficial ride properly belonged. At the same time, he was fairly sure their dislike for each other wasn't about to take them anywhere that would do either of them damage where it counted. As far as he could tell, they both finally served the same side, maybe different ends of the diplomatic establishment, but anyway not his side.

That didn't mean Dubois hadn't been as friendly as you might want during their quick lunch in the Embassy canteen, initially maybe just out of indebtedness to old Tom and their time together in Cambodia, but as things warmed up a bit, out of what seemed at least a half-serious interest in helping him solve the letter-delivery problem that had finally gotten him over to that Embassy, despite his reluctance to cash in on the old man's connections. He figured Dubois might at least get him started on the right track without demanding anything in return once they got out there to the camp. And the man had done his best to make him feel at home during the ride by sitting in back with him even though he was supposedly in charge of the van, a thing Garfield wasn't likely to have done had he been in charge, you could be sure of that. Sit next to a guy with hair that long and a week's growth of beard?

But from another point of view, Garfield probably wasn't far off target about Dubois's having been in Southeast Asia too long, not so much because the man had gone native and morally casual, but because he seemed to have turned hard. You got the impression that his kicks came from the hopelessness and absurdity he could find in just about anything. And you never quite knew what direction he thought worth a trip because it seemed from his angle of vision that anywhere one might look was desert country. Garfield, on the other hand, knew exactly where he'd come from and where he was heading: West Point to the Defense Department to the State Department and off into the wild blue yonder. He wasn't about to waste much time getting his medals, either, which meant not one hour of cruising the Thai–Cambodian border beyond what his special mission called for. He'd put it right up front. There were hotter areas, more productive areas, for a man with a grasp of the realities: the Middle East, or Eastern Europe, or even Central America.

Dubois didn't seem to be in any hurry to get back from the border, and he had no special mission other than the one they'd worked out at lunch, but at the same time, he hadn't held out much hope of the two of them tracking down the people Tom wanted them to check out. Too much shifting sand out there was the way he'd put it, too many movements this way and that among the refugees, especially earlier in the summer, when the Thais had sent some forty thousand—could you believe it?—back into Cambodia by force and had moved most others at one point or another from where they were to someplace else so they didn't get adjusted to the idea that any place in Thailand was really home. But at least the man had offered to stay with him as long as it took to check out the territory around Aranyaprathet. And he'd been free and easy with background information, what you might call the cynic's short history of modern Cambodia: each new regime worse than the one it had overthrown, back to the time the French had pulled out and left the politicians to their own corrupt devices so that Pol Pot could finally come in to murder his own people en masse and prepare the way for the Vietnamese to invade the country and flood poor Thailand with unwanted refugees.

Garfield tried to play it closer to the chest. He wasn't interested in history, good or bad. What did interest him was the present, and since there wasn't what he'd call a crisis situation in the area at the moment, he wasn't going to waste too much time on talk: just do what was required to get another quick look up and down the border so that he could report back to State on how they might best implement Jimmy Carter's promise to double the American intake of local refugees. Then back to Bangkok, and as soon as he could arrange it, off to where the serious action might be during the month ahead. Maybe it was his not wanting to talk about the local situation as much as his style of looking at things that was getting to Dubois. He was still trying to smoke him out.

"So that's the way you people in Washington think you're going to fix things up over here," Dubois was saying as the driver cut to something near normal ground speed. "When the Thais send forty thousand refugees back home down a cliff and across a minefield and then threaten to send another forty thousand across the border farther down the road, you get Jimmy Carter to take an additional one thousand Cambodian refugees and spread them as thinly as possible around various of our United States."

"We didn't get him to do a thing," Garfield said. "You can probably blame that on Rosalynn. Anyway, you won't push me into taking credit for anything Jimmy Carter does."

"Well, credit due or not, you can tell the boys back there that even raising the quota to several thousand a month as they now seem to be contemplating isn't really going to impress the locals over here, whatever it may do to the people in the great American heartland. Because these days the famine beyond the border will get you more than that number of new refugees crossing over in a single week even during the rainy season when the traffic is supposed to get waterlogged."

Garfield had no comment. He was gazing out the side window as though helping the driver find a place to stop.

"Why isn't several thousand a month better than nothing at all?" Tim said.

Dubois smiled at him with glowing gentleness and placed a hand on his knee. "May you always be so ready to stroll down the sunny side of the street, my boy. That kind of puny benevolence by a country that is after all made up entirely of refugees, which now includes even the remaining Indians, will do no more than entice a few thousand extra Khmer into the border area every month in search of greener pastures that nowhere exist."

That got to Garfield. "So what in your wisdom do you think we ought to do to handle the situation over here?"

"No idea, friend," Dubois said. "Not a thing I'm much consulted about any longer. But you people in Washington might want to give a few minutes' thought to what Jean-Paul Sartre recommended the other day with fading breath before a packed room of astounded reporters."

"What was that?" Garfield said.

"That Europe take in all the Indochina refugees and hold them until America comes around to being America again. He thought France might want to accept the seventy thousand now in Malaysia, and West Germany all the thousands still in Thailand. What do you say to that, Garfield?"

Garfield had nothing to say to that. He just stared at Dubois, shaking his head slowly as though the man had told a dirty joke that no stable person would think funny, certainly not in the company they were keeping. That look gave Tim the clue that not only was he traveling with allies who had no use for each other, but one of them wasn't likely to come down off his high horse before they reached the border, because it seemed to make him very uptight having an outsider sharing the back seat with an insider whose tongue was too loose and thick for a Foreign Service officer representing America in an area of shifting values.

But the outsider was not in the mood at that point to get on the man's case or on anybody else's for that matter. It had taken three days of sitting out Bangkok at the Nana Hotel to break down his resistance enough to let himself be drawn over to that Embassy for help in getting himself out of the city and moving in some direction that didn't lead to a dead-end street with a freak sex show that made you want to puke in your bandana, or a hot massage off a dark hallway that was aired and fitted out to cultivate really unusual and private kinds of incurable disease. He wasn't about to lose himself the rest of his free ride into the country over questions of who belonged where and who should do what for whom in the kind of abstract argument that was surely more old Tom's territory than his own. These were people they were talking about, for God's sake, hundreds of thousands of people. He just wanted to make his best effort to get out there and do the job he'd promised the old man he'd do, and then be on his way someplace where he could be of actual practical help to somebody, wherever that might be. Maybe Garfield was at least half-right: talk just didn't take you far enough in any useful direction.

Dubois put his hand on the driver's shoulder to stop the van. He got out and stretched, then crossed the highway to check out a place he'd spotted. Apparently satisfied, he signaled the driver to come on over.

It struck Tim that the place Dubois had chosen wasn't even up to your local version of Burger King. There were a lot of flattened-out headless fish hanging from a wire on one side of the entrance, chalk-dry and dusty-looking, and another batch that had tentacles dangling out one end of them like a cluster of fuse cords. Under the mud-stained canopy an old woman was working up something green and stringy in a shallow frying pan, and beside her a younger woman with dark skin that looked as if it had been Cloroxed was browning skewered chunks of some kind of meat on a grate that seemed to have once been a car radiator.

Dubois chose a table under the cement section of the roof where it was cooler. He ordered Mekong whiskey. Tim decided on a beer. Garfield ordered a Pepsi-Cola and asked Dubois if he didn't want a second one sent out to the driver. The driver didn't drink Pepsi-Cola, Dubois told him, just tea, and the driver would prefer to get that himself. Nobody wanted anything to eat. Garfield sat back in his chair and for a minute looked almost relaxed. When the rice whiskey arrived, Dubois filled his glass halfway up and raised it to Garfield.

"I drink to Jean-Paul Sartre. Even if you two gentlemen may think he's full of shit."

"I didn't say he was full of shit," Garfield said. "He's a philosopher. Nobody would expect a man like that to have a sense of the political realities. It isn't his business."

"And how do you see the political realities, Garfield? Do you think America is ever going to become America again and accept a huge quota of Indochina refugees into its great melting pot?"

"No way. Why should we? We've already taken more than anybody else."

"Because we're the great melting pot. And because we came out here a few years ago and messed things up a bit for the people in question."

"We're a great sucker as far as I'm concerned."

"How's that, Garfield? Who are we sucker to these days? Surely nobody in Southeast Asia, unless you have in mind the Chinese and their Khmer Rouge protégés."

"I'd say we're sucker to just about every country in the world that can't solve its own problems."

"Is that so? My, my."

"Instead of leading the free world the way we think it ought to be led, we try to buy everybody's favor—right, left, and center—by sending our money over to bail people out the minute they get themselves into an economic or political crisis."

"So you think one way or another the great melting pot is destined to lead the free world, is that it, Garfield?"

"Don't you? Who do you think ought to be leading the free world?"

"Jean-Paul Sartre."

"That's the trouble with you, Dubois. You haven't had a serious thought in ten years."

"Oh, I'm serious," Dubois said. "Deadly serious. I think it's time the great melting pot got out of the business of leading the free world before it's too late. Both for us and for the others."

"Better let the Russians take over the business of leading the world, free or otherwise, is that it?"

"And the Chinese. Don't forget the Chinese. Let the two of them fight it out until they kill each other off."

"While we just sit home and cultivate our garden, right?"

"What's left of it," Dubois said. "Not so much left of it these days. Wouldn't you like to cultivate what's left of your garden, Tim, my boy? You and the rest of your generation to the last dregs of the great melting pot?"

"I don't have a garden any longer," Tim said. "My old man took it away from me because I dug up his rosebushes to plant zucchini fertilized by honest manure I'd hauled in from Maryland."

"Your old man was once a reasonable fellow," Dubois said. "I'm sorry to learn he's become a prig."

"He had a point," Tim said. "The neighbors complained all the time."

"You see, Garfield? Even in the great melting pot you can't cultivate your garden any longer with honest manure the way an honest man should."

Garfield took a last swig from his Pepsi-Cola bottle and set it down at arm's length. Then he raised his right hand and with his extended thumb and forefinger shot the bottle dead with a little "pow." He got up and crossed to the van without turning and climbed into the front seat. Dubois, staring straight ahead of him, poured out another half-glass of rice whiskey.

"You don't much like that man, do you?" Tim said.

Dubois looked up at him. Then he shrugged. "He's all right. Just a little too full of himself. And of America's role in world affairs."

"I thought for a minute there he was going to turn and let you have it."

Dubois smiled. "He wouldn't do that. I'm his senior in this business. Besides, he halfway agrees with me."

"About what?"

"About how we helped fuck things up over here. Maybe even about how little we're doing to make up for it these days. I'm still working on that with him."

"I didn't get the sense he agrees with one thing you said."

Dubois smiled again. "Most of that brave talk of his was just for your benefit. He probably hopes you'll let your old man know what a staunch citizen he is."

"I don't get the impression he gives a damn about me or my old man. The impression I get is that he's not too happy I'm tagging along for the ride."

"Relax," Dubois said. "He's all right really. Just a little young and eager. We'll let him sit out there in the van for a bit and simmer down."

Dubois reached over and offered to pour some rice whiskey into Tim's empty beer glass. Tim shook his head. Then he signaled what the hell. The rice whiskey was weaker than he expected, and sweeter, almost a liqueur.

"So what's the game plan, my boy?" Dubois said. "Looking to get yourself a job once we reach the border? They've got plenty of use out there for people ready to work their asses off for too little pay and a lot of humanity."

"The only plan I've got is to deliver my two letters and have a talk with the lady's daughter and then clear out. Thailand doesn't really grab me all that much. I thought I might head for the main action, say in Cambodia itself."

"That's what you thought, is it? And how do you plan on getting there? Somebody's flying carpet?"

"I figured I'd apply for a job with one of the agencies they're letting in there these days."

"Well, so far they've let in about as many Americans as you can count on one hand. Only agency officials or medical specialists, as far as I know. So you've got a bit of training to go through first."

Tim shrugged. "Whatever. Time is a thing I've got plenty of."

"Well, while you're checking into other possibilities you might think of a job on the border here. I mean you're not going to find your people overnight, I can guarantee you that. Assuming you ever find them."

"I'll find them eventually if it's at all possible," Tim said. "No question there. The only thing I can't be sure about is how long it's going to take me."

Dubois laid a hand on his knee again. "If you weren't such a sweet kid I'd say you remind me of Garfield sometimes. May the Lord in His infinite mercy shine down with goodwill on your infinite confidence. I mean it."

"Don't worry about me," Tim said. "I'll just do whatever can be done. I'm not a masochist. Just a little stubborn once I get my mind set on a thing."

"I'm not going to worry about you," Dubois said. "I just thought you'd better be prepared for the worst. That border area's some kind of desert, only overpopulated by alien people and trees."

He offered to empty the last of the half-pint into Tim's glass, and when Tim covered the glass with his hand, he poured what was left into his own. Dubois studied the empty bottle, turning it slowly as though its shape held a sobering mystery.

"You know, I met the lady you're looking for," Dubois said. "Just once. In Phnom Penh."

"You're kidding," Tim said. "You actually met her?"

"It was purely by accident," Dubois said. "Your father kept her under pretty tight cover. None of this parading your local mistress around while the wife is under evacuation orders to stay clear of the post."

"Yeah. My father was always a fairly careful man. Not one for letting scandal interfere with his career."

"Not one for sharing a good thing either," Dubois said. "That lady was something to look at. I mean if you go for the Oriental type that isn't quite one thing or another. I myself prefer straight Khmer or straight Thai. Better chance of knowing where you're at."

"So did you get an idea of where she was at? I mean in those days?"

Dubois shook his head. "I didn't even get a chance to talk to her. They were having a drink in a place where the French hung out and I'd just popped in there to look for a friend. Your father introduced me to the lady but he didn't ask me to sit down."

"So how come you're so sure it's the person I'm looking for?"

"He didn't have any other lady friends in Phnom Penh as far as I know. Anyway, all the long-termers knew about her, at least those in the political section, because he'd met her while she was giving French lessons at the Embassy and in the beginning he was like a school kid about her. But I bet I'm about the only one who ever saw the two of them alone together in public once they really got involved."

"The problem is, I don't even know what she looks like. He didn't keep any photographs of her. All I've got to go on is the name she's living under these days."

"That isn't your problem," Dubois said. "Your problem is that they've shifted the refugees around so much in the past six months you have no way of knowing what camp she's in at the moment. If she's in a camp at all."

"Where else would she be?"

"God knows. Some third country. Back across the border. That is, if she isn't dead. And the same goes for her so-called daughter."

"Neither one of them is dead," Tim said. "I'm willing to bet on that."

Dubois studied him, half-smiling. "What makes you so sure?"

"Just a hunch," Tim said. "They're survivors. Both of them. I could tell from the diary the old man gave me to read."

"You may be right," Dubois said. "But your problem is still exactly where they're surviving."

"Well, wherever it is, I'm going to do my damnedest to find them," Tim said. "It's just a question of starting at the beginning and working your way forward."

"And where exactly is the beginning?"

"I don't know," Tim said. "I thought you might at least be able to show me that."

"The only thing I can do is show you the camp near Aran where she and her Cambodian journalist friend used to work. What's left of it, anyway."

"That's a beginning."

"But if there's no trace of her there, I really don't know what more I can do for you. Given my own time restrictions."

"Whatever," Tim said.

"Though I can put you in touch with one person who knows the area as well as anybody out there these days. A young fellow they call D.J. for reasons I can't fathom. Actually, you remind me a bit of him at times."

"What's he doing out there?"

"Finding himself. More or less. Like a few others in your generation."

Thirith was bored. Even sentry duty alone on one or another edge of the outpost was better than lying there silently among off-duty soldiers who had nothing new to say to her, lying there fighting against sleep just in case Tao Lom got through his strategy meeting in time to stop by her hammock and take her for a walk to the one spot they'd found within the camp boundaries where they could have a bit of privacy. Waiting on Tao Lom's pleasure so many empty hours wasn't exactly her idea of serving the Khmer Serei cause to the full extent of her talents, though Tao Lom might think it was. And waiting like this was especially boring when the outpost continued to be as quiet as it had been in recent days, when there wasn't even a sound in the jungle around them to remind one that an enemy actually existed somewhere out there. They hadn't seen any action for almost three weeks now, and except for routine patrols within easy reach of the border, Tao Lom said they weren't likely to see any until the rainy season began to die out, even if the guns and ammunition they'd been promised arrived in the meanwhile. That could mean mid-September before they got under way again, another whole month of waiting, another month of just sitting around talking politics, the same endless politics, and no chance to test whether or not one's heart was still in the struggle.

It wasn't the first time she'd felt herself questioning where her own heart might be, but she knew it was too much inaction and too much talk that made it happen, not the struggle itself. When the action started there was no time to think. If one had courage, then the sense of what to do, the right thing, became instinctive, and that was how one separated the weak from the strong, the reliable from the dangerous. But lying around in a hammock or even taking another uneventful turn at patrolling the safe boundary of a sleeping outpost that had no reason to wake up, that made one wonder if the juices that kept life interesting weren't gradually drying up to make one an old woman in a body that had just begun to enjoy its ripeness.

Everything along the border seemed to go from one extreme to the other these days. At first there had been the excitement of joining the movement, of finding people one's own age who believed in what they were doing and made one feel necessary, part of something important. Then it became clear that a Khmer Serei settlement beginning to overflow with refugees of every age and condition and every kind of hidden past wasn't the best place to train healthy recruits, much less to build a full company that had the right pride even if not enough guns to keep order in the settlement. But out of that disillusionment came the new outpost inside the homeland, where one could at least feel a bit of one's native soil between one's toes and sometimes taste it in the air one breathed, even if it was only a few kilometers from the border.

But that hadn't worked out quite as one hoped it might. It may have been far enough beyond the border to save the movement from forced repatriation, but it wasn't far enough to have convinced even sympathetic Thais that the new soldiers in training deserved heavier arms and more supplies and not just the same old moral support. She was sure that was because too many of the most recent recruits would crawl back across the border into Thailand and wait out the shooting whenever it got uncomfortably heavy. Which just meant that the others had to prove where their hearts lay by testing themselves more severely, the men by going out on patrol farther and farther into the enemy's zone until the bravest were gradually sifted out, and the women by carrying ammunition almost as far or by treating the wounded along the forest paths as soon as they were brought back out of range, removing the shrapnel when possible and cleaning up the wounds, or if one didn't have the hands for that, helping to hold the men down when there wasn't any more anesthetic to inject.

If she was to be completely honest, she'd have to admit that those few women who finally earned the right to go on patrol with the men had an easier life most of the time—better rations when they were available, and certainly more hours to themselves when the action was over. And how many times had there been a patrol really worth going on, especially after the ammunition began to run short? The several times she'd had a chance to fire at the enemy, she hadn't actually seen what she was firing at, so that one came away wondering if it wasn't at least half a game, some danger of course but much noise and show, a way of convincing oneself that one had more courage than most but for no purpose that seemed to last. In her case she sometimes felt that what had earned her a place with the men was foolish recklessness more than pride or skill. Or a mixture of these and the fatalism she sometimes sensed but didn't really understand, something anyway that made her appear fearless to others when most of the time she was actually as frightened as anybody else and often in doubt about the value of what she was doing.

Of course there were those in the movement who thought she'd been chosen not so much for what she'd proved in the forest as for the influence she had with Tao Lom, and her knowledge of French and English, and her supposed connection with Thais she'd come to know in her four years at the old Aran camp. Tao Lom had told her what some people were saying. And he had actually done everything he could to persuade her not to join the patrols. As for her knowledge of French and English, that might earn her an occasional trip back across the border to act as interpreter for Tao Lom or one of the other camp leaders, but it didn't help with the problem of keeping a wounded man from bleeding to death. And the Thais—she didn't even know the few Thais whom Sameth had known, so far was she from establishing a useful connection.

It was suspicions like these that gave the movement a sour taste at times, suspicions that had really come in with the wave of new refugees whom the Thais had sent into the settlement after the forced repatriation and who had become the source for bad recruits. They were largely the children of people who belonged to a different class from hers, old city people who had supported Lon Nol and who distrusted anybody whose family had once worked as farmers or laborers in the provinces, even though they themselves had been forced to work with their hands in remote places under the Khmer Rouge. Most of them were not really interested in the movement and its aims. Most didn't really care about restoring true freedom and independence to Cambodia so much as recovering the property their parents had lost or maybe using the settlement and even the training program as a stepping-stone to a third country. That was why they were so jealous of the languages she'd learned from Sameth in the old camp, and of her occasional trips back across the border to meet with foreigners.

But the truly serious problem in the movement wasn't these new recruits and their lack of heart—there weren't enough guns for them anyway—but the new strategy that had resulted so far in nothing but waiting and then more waiting. How could there ever be a united front among all the Khmer Serei movements when half of them couldn't even agree on who the common enemy was? It didn't take a military genius to realize that one couldn't fight both the Vietnamese and the Khmer Rouge at the same time. And those who thought Sihanouk the enemy, if not right at the moment then in the long run, were training themselves to fight a ghost.

She herself considered any one of these enemies about as bad as the others, but the simple fact was that Vietnam happened to be the one that was occupying Cambodia at the moment, and it seemed to her merely common sense to think of fighting that enemy first. If one didn't get the Vietnamese out of Cambodia soon, there wasn't likely to be any Cambodia left. And if General Din Del and his group weren't prepared to make a deal for support with the Chinese because that meant having to cooperate for the time being with the Khmer Rouge, then maybe the only solution was for the other independent Khmer Serei movements to form a second coalition that would work with anybody willing to supply arms and rice for the struggle against Vietnam, whether the supplier was China, America, Thailand, or the various displaced politicians of one or another old regime who had managed to get their money out of Phnom Penh and off to Paris or some place else equally safe. And even if that might mean having to work for the moment with the Khmer Rouge, who seemed to have the support of everyone but the Russians and the Vietnamese, Pol Pot's hour would come around eventually, and in the meanwhile one would simply have to live with his smell whatever it did to one's stomach.

That was still her basic disagreement with Tao Lom. He didn't have much love for General Din Del or even Son Sann, but his hatred of the Khmer Rouge made him lean toward working within the Din Del coalition rather than attempting to create a second one that might have a better chance of foreign support. So the debate went on, and each of the movement's leaders spent his days trying to keep a pure line of one kind or another while cultivating whatever supposedly unattached source came along that might provide more guns and thereby more prestige for whoever was finally successful in getting the company armed well enough to go back into the fighting zone.

She couldn't really blame Tao Lom for his hatred. The poor boy had seen his parents clubbed to death in cold blood while his own hands were tied, and then had been forced to leave a younger brother behind for certain execution when he had to break away with what remained of his Mobile Group and lead them across an impossible river and through the jungle for the fourteen days it took them to get to Ban Tapey and the base camp at Wat Koh. He was obviously much bothered still by what he'd been forced to do, but if he could look at it impersonally there would be no doubt that he'd made the right decision, because if he'd gone back to guide his brother and the two others with him, all four of them would have been shot on the far side of that river, and who else would have proved strong enough to lead the remaining fifty-six in his group without a single loss as far as they finally went?

Despite his stubbornness, his fanaticism at times, Tao Lom was really softer on family questions than she herself was. Of course that might be because he still had a family to think about, with two sisters in Cambodia and an older brother in France—and it was clear his sisters in Pailin kept his will alive with images of a grand reunion when Cambodia was free again. Her own family was gone, and gone long ago, even if one counted Sameth. She had loved Sameth for a time, something between what one might feel for a sister and what one might feel for a mother, but it had finally become impossible to live with her. They simply didn't look on things the same way. She still thought about her often, wondered whether she'd found the relatives she was looking for after Maarten helped her cross back in the north. He said she'd planned to go to Battambang first, where her sister once lived, but what if her sister wasn't there? She wasn't really worried. Sameth would find a way to survive, she was strong, with her own kind of unshakable determination. Maybe that was the basis of their problem: two strong wills facing in different directions. Anyway, she realized now that if the confusion of that forced repatriation hadn't come along to separate them in the unhappy way it had, something more personal would have separated them all too soon, and that might have been unhappier still.

She couldn't help wondering now if there might not be something missing in that area of her heart that was meant for family feelings. Maybe something had gone dead in her as a sort of protection from insanity after her mother died of malaria and her father disappeared in the forest, a feeling that Sameth couldn't quite bring back. She certainly sensed that something was missing when she thought of having children. That idea left her completely cold. And the coldness had only been deepened by the one experience of that she'd had close at hand, the only excitement that the outpost had known during the past three weeks, and that a failure too since Sokhom's daughter had come out stillborn. Though she'd stayed back just watching through most of the night, she'd been the one who ended up holding the wet and gray and lifeless little animal that had come out of so much almost silent pain and that had to be buried before Sokhom even got a chance to see it closely. She remembered holding the thing out by its feet and hitting it again and again as she tried to beat some life into it after the others couldn't get the suction tube to bring out any sound beyond its own slurping, until they finally took the thing away from her and wrapped it in a towel to carry it out to the back edge of the camp. And when she'd gone outside exhausted to wash herself up, she found that somebody had already brought a white monkey into the courtyard and hung it upside down from a stake with its skull split open and its brains draining out into a black pool on the ground to pacify somebody's fear of evil spirits, and that had made her throw up out of an empty stomach until she tasted bile.

She couldn't understand how that kind of pain was meant to be associated with love even if it didn't end in such an ugly failure. But then again, she didn't know much about love. She knew what her body felt when she was lying naked next to Tao Lom in the forest and when he entered her, and she knew the calm feeling that sometimes came when they weren't even touching any longer but had been together through the night and wakened side by side to look out at the daylight arriving. But she couldn't always connect what her body felt to Tao Lom personally, and there were times when she felt nothing at all. There were also times when she resented him, resented his freedom to come and go as he pleased, resented his relation with other women in the movement and his expectation that she would always be there when he chose to come to her or to take her off with him. Even if he had been kind to her usually, and had looked out for her interests, and had been as gentle as she could want when they were alone together. So long as they didn't talk politics.

Of course the political disagreement might be covering something that went deeper and remained unspoken: a conflicting vision of Cambodia itself. Tao Lom was nostalgic about the country in a way she no longer was. His hatred of the Khmer Rouge, the passion he showed on that subject, was matched at the other extreme by his sentimentality about the old Cambodia. It came out in his attempt to keep past history alive—distant past history from the time of the French protectorate—through the weekly talks he'd organized for newcomers to the settlement. It reminded her too much of what the Khmer Rouge had done to indoctrinate the New People in the villages they created after April 17, even if Tao Lom's history lessons were meant to create an ideology for Free Khmer in a Free Khmer movement. And then came his attempt to revive lost traditions by arranging for music to be played that nobody really understood and training the children to dance the forgotten dances before they'd even learned to read and write Khmer.

There was no old Cambodia as far as she was concerned. Old Cambodia was dead. And the country Tao Lom seemed to have in mind bringing back was more Sameth's country than her own, a thing that couldn't really exist any longer, except maybe for those prepared to go on being displaced by living in the wrong time. Too much had happened during the past four years. She wondered if Sameth had discovered that by now. And if the old country was somehow still there despite what the

Khmer Rouge had done to it and now the Vietnamese, she didn't want to think about the implications of that for the future, at least not unless there was another kind of radical change. The roots of the present evil were to be found in the old history, in the superstition and the passive religion and the dominance of foreigners and the corruption of politics, royal and otherwise. She'd rather go to a new country than back to all that. And it was this kind of thinking that had her most worried of all.

———

Polk figured from the outside look of the new Aran headquarters that the place must have been somebody's villa once upon a time, but even though it had been more or less repainted recently, it still showed signs of the activity that came and went with the seasons so close to the border. The water tank that had been abandoned to rust beside the entrance gate was full of bullet holes, and the front yard was crossed by what seemed to be a partially filled-in trench or a series of foxholes that had collapsed. You could see a splintered shutter hanging loose at one of the side windows, and the iron railing around the terrace on the second floor had a gap in it ragged enough to have been caused by a stray shell. But as far as he was concerned, the look of the outside was beside the point. And however unprofessional the inside, the building had one major advantage over his having to work out of the motel down the highway closer to Aran: there was nobody out here to hassle him from any direction. The place would be completely his until Bangkok got around to sending out the volag group that was supposed to help him set up the expanded relief operation. That would take ten days to two weeks at least. In the meanwhile, with any luck, he could get his own unofficial business organized in a way that would allow him to ease it into his official business for their mutual benefit. You had to use some criteria for deciding who got what portion of rations that were anyway too short to take care of all those who needed them, so why not give the benefit of the doubt to those who were both helping you and making at least some effort to fight the common enemy?

He put down the suitcase he'd been using as his temporary filing cabinet and studied the layout from the front hallway. One thing he knew for certain from his experience in Korea: when you're doing business with Orientals you have to establish your authority right from the start, or even before the start, basically from the signals you send out regarding where you're at. As his first move in that direction he had picked himself out the room that would work best for the group leader's office, what must have been the old dining room, private enough for serious conversation but big enough by comparison with other potential office rooms to show who was in charge of the place. Now it would be a question of setting up the furnishings so that they carried the same message. He decided to put the dining-room table at an angle to make it look more like a desk. Then he took a stack of folders out of his filing suitcase and a dictionary and a pile of paperback thrillers he'd picked up in a Bangkok bookstore. What was needed now was some chairs from the living room, a straight-backed wooden one for the desk and a couple of those crazy bowl-and-swivel easy chairs that made you think of a bamboo radar beacon set to turn on some kind of fruit basket. Anyway, the natives apparently liked them, so they'd do all right for putting your local visitors in a relaxed mood while you tried to work out exactly where they stood.

He brought in the desk chair and an easy chair and tried out the easy chair in several positions until he found the right angle for dominating it comfortably from behind the desk. Then he went back to fitting out the desk top: a standing clock in one of the outer corners to balance off his statuette of an Oriental warrior in the other, a plate from the kitchen to serve for an ashtray in between. The desk looked busy enough now, but something was needed for the blank wall space behind the desk, something like a photograph or poster, preferably American. That would have to wait for his next trip to Bangkok.

At least the immediate problem had been pretty well solved: getting the place to look half in business by the time this Tao Lom arrived on the scene, hopefully with some concrete orders in hand from one or another of the local warlords who were backing whatever faction of the new resistance movement the man was supposed to represent. If their mutual Bangkok connection had things right, there was plenty of private money coming in these days via Paris, enough to keep the movement well oiled for a while so that you didn't have to worry too much about whose government might be behind which faction at a particular moment. Besides, whatever the faction—Sihanouk, Son Sann, Khmer Rouge, who knew what other crazies—the enemy was still Vietnam, and that was an enemy he had no trouble believing in heart and soul, along with everybody else except the Russians, who were in there as usual helping to fuck up somebody's economy so they could run things from behind the scenes for their own profit.

Of course what counted most in this business once you had your loyalties straightened out was organizational know-how: getting things set up so that you yourself were never exposed to what could become the dangerous outer fringes of the operation. You always had to make sure you used secondaries for the actual delivery work, while you remained at the center with your flanks covered, ever alert that nothing got out of control yet mostly out of view, what you might call the invisible man in the middle. Korea was still the best model he knew, the way he and the others had set things up at the 8th Army headquarters for the quartermaster corps in Inchon. Naturally that was less complicated than this operation because most of the time you were dealing with your own people and on the whole they liked what they were doing, bringing a bit of morale to the boys at the front, especially those in the outfits that had a puritan asshole for a colonel with a negative attitude toward booze, gambling, your occasional whore, anything that might bring the poor bastards out there a minute or two of R and R while their lives were on the line. Not that the truck drivers who brought the stuff out there didn't pick up some healthy cash for their trouble. With a twenty-buck markup on a bottle of the hard stuff, you could figure on taking enough to make it well worth their while and still have plenty left over to distribute around headquarters as was necessary.

Cash flow had never been a problem at his end of things. The problem you ran into sometimes was overenthusiasm, so that you had to get the drivers to calm down and play it cool in a way that would earn them a little respect for the service they provided. You had to tell them sometimes to just take their orders and make their deliveries and no fucking salesmanship along the way, unless they had in mind ending up like that spaced-out idiot who walked in on a squad still hot from a patrol that had cost them two casualties, sauntered in there with his smile from ear to ear and his line about anybody around here still live and kicking enough to want some real booze. As the story went, he didn't even get a chance to change the smile downward a bit before the top of his head came off as though his skull had burst its lid. Or those two local types who got themselves blasted into Buddha land for being greedy enough to take their whore back and forth to the front through artillery going off like the fourth of July.

Polk smiled to himself. The moral was clear: Never let a service to mankind bring in so much profit that it goes to your head. It wouldn't be a bad idea to get that printed up in the local languages for a motto and put it up on the wall behind his desk, maybe in a two-way frame with one side in English so that you could switch it around depending on who needed to get the message. And then a standing mirror beside it. He had to practice liking his appearance these days. His fringe of gray hair was coming in wildly now, so that it called for regular work with Vitalis to keep himself from looking like a clown. And it was time to trim back the mustache. He might actually get used to the thing if he could just keep it out of the way, but whatever shape he finally made it take could never have the class of what he'd made himself give up. And as far as he was concerned, his whole head still seemed to belong to a different human being.

He was on his way to the upstairs bathroom to check himself out when the front doorbell rang. The man he led into the dining-room office couldn't have been more than twenty-five, thirty at most, but some of his front teeth were already missing and some of the rest had turned brown. He was wearing blue jeans and a pink silk shirt. Polk tried to keep his smile steady as he motioned the man into the swivel chair. He went around behind the desk and balanced himself on the wooden chair so that he could lean back at ease with his hands behind his head.

"So you're Mr. Tao Lom," Polk said. He sat forward suddenly and turned the desk clock at a new angle as though he planned to begin timing his visitor.

"Yes. You Mr. Ball?"

"Baugh. As in Sammy Baugh. But you wouldn't know about that, not being a Washingtonian."

"English no good," Tao Lom said. "French good."

"My French is exactly zero," Polk said. "So you're one up on me there."

"Pardon?"

"Forget it," Polk said. "I'll talk slowly and I'll try to come right to the point. Our mutual friend in Bangkok says you can be trusted absolutely, and since I have to trust him absolutely or drop the whole deal, I'm ready to put my cards on the table."

"Cards?" Tao Lom said.

"All right, facts," Polk said. "Plain facts. But you're going to have to listen real hard, Mr. Lom. The first fact is, I think I can handle what you're looking for. Some of it, anyway. And the second fact is, if you and your people decide to do business with me, I'm pretty sure I can arrange a bonus as well. You understand?"

"Bonus?" Tao Lom said.

"Let's say an extra quota of rations," Polk said. "At the very least some extra rice. Through my agency."

"No rice," Tao Lom said severely. "Guns."

"You're not listening, Mr. Lom. Guns first, rice second. That is, if there are enough guns involved to make it worth my while and if our mutual friend in Bangkok comes through as promised."

"If?" Tao Lom said.

"That's it," Polk said. "The big if. He's got the stock, I've got the channels and the transportation. It's just a matter of getting it all together. You get my meaning?"

"You have guns?"

"He has guns. I have trucks and rice. You have money. Basically it's that simple."

"No rice. Guns."

"Christ," Polk said. "You sure have a one-track mind."

"One truck mine?"

"Look," Polk said. "Can you get your people out there to send me somebody who speaks English?"

"No English. French."

Polk looked at the ceiling. "What have I done to deserve this? Everywhere else in the world where people do business, English is your international language. But not on the Thai–Cambodian border. It figures."

"Parlez-vous français?" Tao Lom said.

"Parlez-vous my ass," Polk said. "It's got to be English or nothing, okay?"

"Okay. Please. You have guns, Mr. Ball?"

———

Tan Yong knew well enough where this meeting with Macpherson had to arrive before it was over, but exactly how he was going to get to that point remained a problem. He decided to use the few minutes more he might be made to wait in the State Department lobby to work out just what strategy he was going to bring to bear in handling an obligation as complicated and delicate as the new one Sameth had presented to him along with the package that Macpherson's secretary had handed over the previous week. Though there was no return address, he assumed the package had come from a place that he and Sameth had more or less created together but that she had left some time since for a new adventure in regions that were certain once again to test her capacity for living with despair.

In one sense it was already too late to do anything useful. With the season turning past mid-August, one had to conclude that Sameth had been back in Cambodia some two months now, and wherever she might have settled specifically, her fate was now sealed. Where Thirith might be was equally indefinite and equally final, whether or not the two of them were together again. The only thing left to do was let Macpherson know where things now stood with Sameth and her adopted daughter, and then it would be up to Macpherson to act accordingly, which at that point presumably meant notifying his son that there was no further need to look for Sameth in Thailand. The problem was how to let Macpherson know what it was necessary for him to know in some diplomatic way that wouldn't require his having to share the journal Sameth had mailed via State Department auspices.

Tan Yong couldn't help feeling the element of irony in his predicament, one that he hoped would escape his onetime rival—if that was the term for a relationship between two people with a common attachment whose paths had actually not crossed until shortly before that attachment became irrelevant to both of them for all practical purposes. The irony was that his own reticence about any further contact with even the fading edges of that rivalry had been the cause of the delay in his receiving that package with the notebook in it: he had gone out of Macpherson's office after delivering his letter to Sameth those many weeks ago without leaving a forwarding address and without any promise of sending one until he got himself finally settled in the Washington area. The delay was entirely his fault; he'd left Macpherson no way of forwarding the envelope Sameth had addressed to him inside the one addressed to the State Department until he'd finally checked back the previous week, almost on impulse, to see if there had been any concrete results from the trip Macpherson's son was presumed to have made to Thailand.

Of course, as Tan Yong had anticipated, Macpherson hadn't even begun to arrange his own trip there, while the son, though supposedly still on his way to Southeast Asia via Europe, and maybe actually there by now, hadn't yet communicated his exact whereabouts to his father. And from what one could gather about that particular relationship from the father, the son wasn't likely to do so until there was some very special reason for it—some emergency, financial or otherwise. Given this difficulty in communication between them, just how one got a message to the young man indicating that he would be wasting his energy on a useless search short of entering Cambodia itself—and that, one would hope for his sake, was out of the question—remained a problem Macpherson himself would have to solve without benefit of outside advice.

The delicacy wasn't there. It lay in whether or not he had an obliga-

tion to let Macpherson see any part of the journal itself. He really preferred to call it a journal rather than a diary, because the latter term suggested a document that was essentially self-addressed, as in the case of the
yellow notebook he'd brought from Thailand and presented to Macpherson on Sameth's behalf. This document was clearly addressed to a confidant throughout, a role that he was pleased to regard himself as having
filled for more than merely personal reasons, given Sameth's forthright
rendering of certain events that he felt needed to be recorded—and this
quite outside his own involvement in some of the history that had led up
to the painful denouement in which she was now alone. This was what
made his predicament especially awkward. If he thought there was any
chance that the document might move Macpherson to try to influence
refugee policy in some way, whether here or in Thailand, he would swallow his reticence, but on the basis of his experience with the man to date,
what were the likely prospects for that? And in view of the journal's very
personal tone in places, could he simply hand the document over to Macpherson for him to read at his leisure, whether with amusement at moments, or chagrin, or possibly even horror—whatever the emotions that
might pass through him as he read an account that he would of course realize was no longer addressed to him even indirectly?

Tan Yong had to admit that from one perspective it wasn't fair to
deny Macpherson access to the journal when they'd both had access to
the diary. Yet his having read that diary even before Macpherson had a
chance to do so was not only with Sameth's consent but at her urging, to
give him the background that might make it easier for him to approach
Macpherson for help in person. Sameth had not consented to anyone's
having a look at this new journal other than the person to whom it was
addressed. In fact, her having sealed it very carefully in a second envelope
addressed to Tan Yong, Esq., inside the one apparently addressed to
Macpherson at the State Department indicated her intention indisputably.
And as far as it was possible to determine a thing of that kind, her intention had been honored not only by Macpherson but also by this lover of
hers in Thailand who had been given the responsibility of mailing the
notebook for her after he'd apparently escorted her to the border. What
right did he himself now have, confidant or otherwise, to disregard her
wishes without any further evidence of what she might think proper?

It struck him that in any case it was rather precious of him to spend
so much mental energy debating this question of decorum when the substance of the document was what ought to be the object of concern. He
could certainly outline the essentials of that for Macpherson's benefit

without violating anybody's confidence, and it was surely among his obligations to do so at some point during their meeting. What had led Sameth to feel that she had no choice but to return to Cambodia in search of Thirith was not just a matter of personal conviction that some might think eccentric. It was at least in part a matter of historical determination, the consequence of policies that had their origin in events antedating by some years the cruel solution that Thailand had finally imposed on the refugees. And Macpherson's country—his own adopted country—after all shared some of the responsibility for the tragic pattern of those events. As Macpherson was already well aware. The question now was whether both he and Macpherson might still play some role in bringing about a further liberalization of the American government's policy regarding Southeast Asian refugees, especially in view of the modestly favorable turn in that direction that he'd read about recently. And a further question was whether a mere summary of the relevant parts of the journal was sufficient for this purpose, or whether he had to offer Macpherson a chance to read those parts as they were actually written.

Tan Yong suddenly felt unwell. He recognized what the trouble was: the pressure of an inner dread that sometimes came with his lying to himself, with hearing himself articulate so well what was mostly beside the point, really a diversion to cover some truth too difficult for him to face. Macpherson wasn't his problem finally, nor the American attitude toward refugees, scandalously indifferent as it might be. Sameth was his problem: where she now was in comparison with where he himself was. He couldn't bear to think of that. And he had hoped to avoid doing so by casting venom here and there, hiding from how much he'd managed to do for himself and how little for her by making himself feel superior to those who had done even less. The truth was that he had failed her at the same time that he was ensuring his own comfort, settling in an apartment with every conceivable American convenience located on a bus route between Baltimore and Washington that made it easy for him to explore whatever opportunities might come his way in either direction. And Sameth? Sameth had nothing ahead of her but some sort of undefined trial in a wilderness that could not be much healthier than the one she had left four years ago, at best another unfamiliar version of hunger and displacement. And what made this difference in their circumstances so very hard to face was that she no longer provided any outlet for the guilt it roused in him. There was nothing he could do for either her or Thirith now, no maneuvering on his part that might bring relief, no effort that might lead others to do something that could touch her personally. She was gone, out of reach, as simply and finally as by death.

He felt himself now to be a ridiculous figure—self-absorbed, insensitive—for having worried so much about what he was going to do with the relic she had left him. What possible difference could it make to her where she was now? How was it conceivable that she might care who saw her journal and who didn't? And suddenly he didn't care either. In the pain he'd begun to feel, his concern over diplomacy struck him as ludicrously academic, a crude irrelevance. Who was he to make such judgments on behalf of another whose soul was likely to be cleansed as his could never be? Under the image he now had of Sameth, he actually began to see that he and Macpherson were not so far apart as he might have preferred to think. Both were inconsequential lovers who mourned at the same shrine. And that being so, the gracious thing for him to do would be offer Macpherson Sameth's journal without any reservations. If there was a question of diplomacy involved, he would let Macpherson the professional try to cope with it. That was no longer an issue he could bring himself to care about in the slightest.

Tan Yong decided he had to sit down. He turned to grope for a chair just as Macpherson came up smiling broadly, hand extended.

"I'm sorry," Macpherson said. "I got held up outside the elevator. One of my colleagues seems to feel that the solution to the Cyprus problem lies in some sort of exchange of populations on both sides such as the Greeks and the Turks arranged in 1923. That would presumably leave the island an uninhabited wasteland."

"I'm afraid I'm not very familiar with the Cyprus problem," Tan Yong said.

"Well, don't worry about it. The thing looks increasingly insoluble. Much as Cambodia, though perhaps less dramatically so."

"Yes, I suppose dramatic is a term one might use," Tan Yong said. "If a bit too neutral in its coloring."

"Well. I'm really very pleased to see you again. Would you like to have a bit of lunch in the cafeteria or would you rather try some place a little more intimate and decorative?"

"As you wish," Tan Yong said. "I don't eat as much at noon as I once did. I'm still not really back in the habit."

Macpherson hadn't moved since they'd shaken hands. He was studying Tan Yong.

"Are you all right?" he said. "You look as though you're in pain."

"Not something I can do anything about," Tan Yong said. "Unless you wouldn't mind just sitting here a minute. We won't be disturbing anybody, will we?"

"Would you rather go up to my office? There's a couch where you can lie down."

"No, if we can just sit here for a minute I'll be fine, I'm sure."

Macpherson hauled a chair over so that it was at right angles to the one Tan Yong had sat down in abruptly.

"Well," Tan Yong said, "that's really much better. And maybe it's just as well that we settle a few personal matters before we make the effort to enjoy our lunch."

Macpherson was still watching him, clearly worried. Tan Yong began to unwrap the package he was carrying, slowly, meticulously, as though the thing contained layers of paper-thin crystal. He let the wrapping and string drop to the floor, then brushed the notebook cover with the flat of his hand before handing it to Macpherson.

"What's this?" Macpherson said. "What I think it is?"

"Read a page or so for a start. You'll see. It was in the envelope from Thailand that I picked up from your secretary last Friday."

Macpherson opened the cover and started reading, his expression sober, concentrated, the look one might think of him bringing to confidential material handed him by a colleague. The expression began to change as he moved into the second page. Halfway through the third page he glanced over at Tan Yong, then closed the notebook and passed it back to him.

"I wonder if this is really meant for my eyes," he said. "I rather doubt it."

"In one sense not, I suppose," Tan Yong said. "But in another sense most certainly."

"Maybe you can summarize what you feel might be relevant for me to know. At least before lunch."

"Yes. Well, first of all, the fact that Phal Sameth is now back in Cambodia."

"Back in Cambodia?" Macpherson said.

"Yes. She felt she had to go there in search of her adopted daughter. The daughter was apparently sent back across the border at an earlier point in the forced repatriation of many thousands, an event with which I'm sure you're familiar."

"Indeed," Macpherson said. "A terrible business. Unbelievable."

"Yes," Tan Yong said. "Most terrible. So there doesn't seem to be much point any longer in your son spending his time looking for either Sameth or the daughter."

Macpherson looked distracted. "No. I suppose not."

"A thing you may want to let him know."

Macpherson shifted in his chair. "Yes, but how the hell am I supposed to do that when neither my wife nor I has heard a word from Tim since he went off how many weeks ago is it now?"

"That is a problem for you, I see."

"I mean short of getting on a plane and going over there to track him down in person."

Tan Yong didn't say anything.

"Of course I can send a message via telex to the Embassy over there, but how do I know if he even checked in with them? Or if he did, that they have the slightest idea where he might be from one day to the next?"

"That is certainly a point," Tan Yong said. "But I suppose until you find you can go over yourself you'll want to be in touch with them in case they can trace his whereabouts."

"I mean my orientation trip to southern Europe and the Near East isn't even scheduled yet. And it would be awkward at this point, to say the least, for me to request leave in order to make a special trip to Thailand on strictly personal business."

"I understand," Tan Yong said. "Unless of course you choose to consider the business in Thailand not merely personal but also an opportunity to look into the refugee situation over there."

"I don't think that would be appreciated down here in Foggy Bottom," Macpherson said. "The Thai–Cambodian border is strictly outside my area."

"In any case," Tan Yong said. "That is an administrative consideration. The pertinence of which you alone can judge."

"The only way I could get out there at this particular moment is by requesting special leave. Without trying to coordinate it in any way with my official trip."

"Whatever you feel is necessary," Tan Yong said. "What can I possibly say? It is your son after all."

"I mean it really wouldn't be easy at this point any way you look at it."

"I'm sure," Tan Yong said, beginning to wrap up the notebook, then changing his mind. "But if you do decide finally that the only way is for you to go over to Thailand yourself, there is one person in particular

I'd like you to contact for me once the problem with your son is taken care of."

Macpherson wasn't looking at him. He seemed distracted again. "Who would that be?"

"The last person who saw Phal Sameth alive," Tan Yong said. "Unfortunately I know only his first name at this point, but I would hope to have more detailed information to give you before you leave."

D.J. put the left wheels of the pickup truck in the dirt on the edge of the highway, raising a wake of dust that curled back from Tim's door in a swirl to spread across the dry rice field at their side. The car approaching kept the center of the road.

"Give them plenty of room when they come at you like that," D.J. said. "And not just the Thais. Who at least have the excuse of not knowing how to drive. Give the foreigners plenty of room too."

"What's the foreigners' problem?" Tim said. "Besides having to drive on the wrong side of the road?"

"Border madness. You've got to be half-crazy to come out here in the first place, but however healthy you are when you come out, chances are you're going to be half-crazy by the time you go back."

"You seem to be doing all right," Tim said.

"Are you out of your mind? I'm as crazy as all the rest. At the moment I happen to be mad with unrequited horniness, which is a gentle form of the border disease, but who knows what evil is lurking out there to wound us some other way tomorrow?"

"I thought you told that nurse out at the camp that D.J. stands for Don Juan."

D.J. stared at him. "You'll believe anything, won't you? That was just a desperate attempt to be lighthearted about the sure failure looming ahead. D.J. really stands for Doomed Joystick. Pure irony. My roommates in college stuck me with it after a disastrous weekend and now the thing won't go away. At least not in its purified form."

"I don't think irony's the message that nurse got."

"She will in the end. D.J. never makes out. Guaranteed disastisfaction. Even out here where there's not much to hold a soul back and where you'd think the horn of plenty in that area might be generous enough to provide for a man with no talent but the grubbiest intentions."

"I'd say that's all talk to make the odds come out on your side," Tim said.

"It's no good. Optimism won't help. Not when it comes to D.J. and women. The only way to avoid disappointment is to concentrate on the black side of things. Of course you're still a solid piece of flesh and your experience is no doubt different from mine."

"I've never had any luck with nurses that I can remember," Tim said. "And those were the first native Irish people of either sex I've ever met."

"Well, I've got news for you, friend," D.J. said. "You're way ahead of me with regard to this evening's outing, because the Irish love blonds. And they can't stand anybody with a pointed head."

D.J. looked out at the landscape on his side with an expression of deep melancholy. His head *was* pointed, Tim decided, no way around it: D.J. was wearing a soiled seaman's cap with the rim turned down so that it peaked to a cone. Tim had spent less than a day with the guy, but he felt completely at ease with him now, really comfortable. He hadn't been so sure of him at the start: too laid-back, almost spaced-out at times—that was, until he actually got down to the business at hand. Dubois had just dumped Tim on D.J. that noon at Ban Nong Chan and had split to meet up with Garfield and head for regions south, pretending that it was a real pain for him to have to do so, especially since he'd been to the camp down there at Kamput just a few weeks previously. That hadn't seemed to be his plan when they'd all headed out there together from Bangkok, so Dubois must have gotten bored with Tim's problem after two days of getting nowhere with it, or else he figured he'd done his duty by Tim's old man and now he had to turn official again to keep his other diplomatic flank protected, the Garfield flank.

Whatever was behind it, after the visit to the old camp in Aran hadn't produced any trace of the people Tim was looking for or any lead that seemed worth pursuing, Dubois had simply shifted his focus from tracking down the woman and her daughter to tracking down D.J., and that was obviously to get Tim off his hands. Given the fact that D.J. seemed to live in a sleeping bag in his truck when he wasn't shacked up somewhere undeclared, they'd managed to find him a lot sooner than Dubois anticipated, if only because they'd hit distribution day at Ban Nong Chan. And once they'd found him, that was it, Dubois was over and out, back to Aran to link up with Garfield and no talk about anybody's further plans, Tim's least of all.

What had won him over to D.J. was watching him go to work at Ban Nong Chan: unhurried, full of loose banter in his half-English, half–pidgin Khmer, but in the end sure of where he was going. Distributing rice to that many hungry refugees was no easy responsibility. And D.J. must have been doing the job right with his lighthearted approach, because most of those refugees who weren't already starved into expressionless passivity ended up smiling at the funny man in the funny hat as they moved up from the square of dirt they were squatting in to another square of dirt in that endless line of patient squatting women waiting for a ration of rice that surely couldn't feed each of them and their children and all the grown men who depended for survival on a ration that small.

Whether or not D.J. could solve Tim's problem was another question. At least he'd been out there in one capacity or another for almost two years now and, according to Dubois, knew the border area as well as anybody else still around. But after the dead end they'd come to at the old camp in Aran, Tim had a pretty good idea what he was up against, and he didn't much like it. Nobody was going to stick his or her neck out to give you solid information, none of the current camp leaders, none of the older more-or-less-settled refugees. Not unless they could figure out first exactly what might be at stake. You asked one of them a question and they would look at you with keen attention, even sympathy, but very little coherent language, so the interpreter said. At least not when it came down to who was where when. Yes, the woman had been there some time ago and the so-called daughter also, but that was a very long time ago, who knew exactly how long? One had headed north at some point to another camp and the other had headed south at some point to Aran and maybe Bangkok, who could tell? Where either of them might be now was truly a mystery. And how could you blame them for taking that line given the way refugees had been shuffled around from one camp to another and one temporary settlement to another and sometimes back across the border only to pop up again in another temporary settlement farther up or down the same stretch of jungle? Why say more than you had to when you had every excuse not to know a thing? All that mattered finally was where you might be safe today and where you might be headed tomorrow.

He still liked to think that if anybody might have the nose for taking him in the right direction through that labyrinth of vague information and uncertain leads, D.J. would have it, even if the guy hadn't seemed much interested so far in grabbing hold of the question the several times Tim had tried to bring it up. Maybe it was just D.J.'s mood at the moment. The guy had come away from that rice distribution clearly exhausted, physically and mentally, though also on some kind of private high, the way an actor or surgeon might be after doing his thing too long but well. The man wanted to talk, but along the line of his psyche, not anybody else's, and Tim knew he had to ride out that mood until it was over. What you had to hope was that it wouldn't be followed by some kind of low that was equally difficult to break into.

"It's no joke really," D.J. was saying. "You see it beginning to happen about ten months into somebody's contract. The eyes take on a glaze at times. The concentration falters. And first thing you know, there's been a bad car accident, or a mental breakdown, or a crazy blowup of some kind."

"Some people must beat it. Dubois told me you've been out here almost two years now."

"I've been through it once already and out the other side. Six months ago I had to take a trip to Nepal and do some serious climbing. I figured the one thing that might cure me was very high air, getting up there close to the source. Naturally that has its dangers."

"Yeah," Tim said. "So I've heard."

"I don't mean that kind of danger. You get tempted to begin believing in things again. Another world. Not always the best medicine for the daily dose of inhumanity you have to cope with down here."

He was studying the landscape again, gazing out every now and then at the hills to the east. The sun had just begun to change color over the low plain to the west, but you could tell that it was already at work on those hills, coating the dense green with a mauve haze. D.J. leaned forward suddenly and reached under the dashboard to pull out a joint he had stashed away in a pack of cigarettes.

"It's mostly Cambodia's fault," he said. "Or Kampuchea, as they now call it. Anyway, it sits over there like an untreated wound. Since we can't get rid of it or do very much about it, we end up taking it out on ourselves."

He lit the joint and passed it to Tim. Tim took a hit and passed it back.

"Maybe I'm just beginning to know that," Tim said. "I get a weird feeling out here. Like the smell in the camps you can't quite identify."

"That's the smell of waiting," D.J. said. "Waiting to find out where you are. And I'm not talking just about the refugees."

He drew on the joint and passed it again, then closed his eyes for a second. "You know what happened to two of the guys I used to work with during my first year out here? Nice guys. Reasonable guys. Came out here with the best of intentions and worked well for a while. One night about a month before they were due to go back, they started throwing things at each other in their agency's Aran headquarters—stuff they'd brought in there for a late snack? Food fight, college-fraternity style. Maybe they were stoned or drunk, but I don't think so. Anyway, they just kept on going until they had the whole place torn up and emptied out into the yard—typewriters, files, books, furniture, medicine waiting to be checked in, the whole shebang. Trashed the place completely. Why did they do it? Nobody could ever find out because they didn't know themselves."

"I guess it sounds naive to wonder what the refugees must have thought watching a thing like that."

"The refugees?" D.J. said. "After what they'd seen already? Most would think it was just some sort of mad game the foreigners play every now and then to keep away that smell you mentioned. Exorcising evil spirits."

"I guess you could look at it that way."

"No, you couldn't, not really. You don't want to romanticize the thing. Madness yes, but the stupid kind that doesn't do anybody any good. Even if you believe in evil spirits. As I happen to. At least some of the time."

He passed the joint, but Tim shook his head. "I figure I better cool it," he said. "I've got to begin working out some plan of action or I'm going to end up wasting your time as well as mine."

D.J. took another hit. "Plenty of time to worry about that tomorrow. Tonight we relax and turn our fate over to the goddess of love and the goodwill of the Irish."

Tim didn't say anything. He was watching the tuk-tuk ahead of them weave its way down the highway with too many passengers in back, including a leather-skinned grandmother propped up on a crate in the middle facing the rear, her head above the canopy as rigid and uncurious as royalty.

"It's all right," D.J. said. "I haven't forgotten about you. Tomorrow we sit down and put together every bit of information we have about the people you're looking for, and if that doesn't give us a clue we take a short trip to a wat I have in mind just on the border southeast of Aran and visit the shrine there for advice. It's worked before, believe me."

"I believe you," Tim said. "What choice have I got?"

"None," D.J. said. "What choice has anybody got out here?"

Maarten took no pleasure any longer in visiting Aran. The main roads these days sometimes dried out so quickly in the heat that one could get a lungful of dust as though it were the height of the dry season. But whenever he had to turn off the beaten path to visit a settlement along one or another of the new dirt roads that they'd cleared to the border, the van would be lucky to get out again the same day without the help of a bulldozer or tank. And however short the trip, one arrived back in town looking like a pig farmer in the habit of riding his pigs. Then there were the stray volags of every imaginable type and nationality whom you had to pick up either on the way out or on the way in, whether or not you might be in the mood for conversation, because to pass one of them by was to condemn the poor sod at best to a sudden bone-deep drenching at at worst to a blast from some mine that one or another faction had planted along the new road. This particular nameless young fellow whom he'd picked up halfway in brought with him the additional disadvantage of smelling like a goatherd with too much unwashed hair and talking too fast in some kind of regional American accent that was not the easiest to comprehend.

"So what's the situation out there from where you come at it?" the young fellow was saying. "Is it basically an economic problem or political problem or what? And basically whose problem is it?"

"It is basically everyone's problem," Maarten said.

"I know it's that. Goes without saying. But whose specifically?"

"There's a problem for the Thais, the U.N., the foreign agencies, the refugees. For everyone."

"And what's the problem exactly?" the American said.

Maarten shrugged. "It's complicated. They all have right on their side, but they are all receiving an unfair share of justice."

"They can't all be right. Somebody's got to be wrong in this thing. Otherwise, why are we out here?"

"It depends on whom you talk to," Maarten said. "If you talk to the Thais, you learn that they have their own economic problems yet have to take in hundreds of thousands of refugees whom no one else seems to want and who may never go home again. And this provides an excuse for hostile activity by Vietnam."

"So why doesn't the U.N. get in there and do something about it?"

"What can the U.N. do? It has its own problems. For example, the economic problem of having too many new programs to support under too many new agencies with diminishing funds, and the political problem of not being allowed by the Thais to function openly near the border, where they are needed most. Not to mention the moral problem of still recognizing the Khmer Rouge as the legitimate government of Cambodia under the continuing persuasion of China and your country."

"My country?"

"I'm afraid that's right, my friend. Your country supports the Khmer Rouge representative in the United Nations. And from what one can gather, also the Khmer Rouge–Khmer Serei guerrilla coalition."

The American scratched his beard. "I'll be goddamned. Of course from one point of view, what else can they do? Support Vietnam and their invasion of Cambodia?"

"That's why I say it is complicated. And of course the refugees have the hardest problem of all. The first of which is survival and the second of which is having too many dispossessed leaders with no country to lead. And then there is the more long-range problem of finding a home somewhere that they can believe in whether or not they are truly wanted there."

The American was shaking his head. "It's a mess all right. I've been out here a month now and I just can't get a handle on the thing. I'm supposed to be a vocational-training specialist, but I still don't know exactly who I'm supposed to be training in what. Let alone for what kind of future."

"I have something of the same difficulty," Maarten said. "And I've been here almost ten months."

"Yeah? What's your line of work exactly?"

Maarten was suddenly very tired. He had no desire whatsoever to tell this young fellow what his line of work was. He really wanted to be rid of him and all his questions about the same old issues and the same old career problems and the new attempts at solution. It just made him that much more depressed. He simply wanted to be alone now—and well before they reached the town itself. He decided he had to be abrupt. They were close enough to the outskirts now so that it would be no serious hardship for the young man to walk in the rest of the way if no one else happened to come along to offer him a ride, and that was unlikely.

"My line of work," Maarten said, turning to look out the side window. "My line of work is much like everyone else's out here, but I'm afraid I don't have time to go into it right this minute. I'm stopping off at the Red Cross headquarters over there, so I'd better let you off out here on the highway."

"Any idea how I can get into town from way out here? Short of walking?"

"We're very close really. You'll find a tuk-tuk coming along any minute, I'm sure. Or another agency car."

The American stared through the windshield. Maarten pulled over to the side of the road and waited. The American reached over suddenly and slapped him on the knee. "Well, don't take any wooden nickels, okay?"

"I beg your pardon?"

"Just an expression. Are you English or something?"

"Something," Maarten said, trying to smile.

"Right," the American said, climbing down. "See you around the bloody neighborhood. If you don't mind a newcomer calling it that."

A month or so ago he would have driven off feeling quite guilty about this fellow and no doubt would have actually turned into the Red Cross headquarters driveway to cover himself, but not today. He didn't even bother to slow down. What was the point? The truth was that no sentiment, warm or cold, seemed to work for him now as it used to. And the country wasn't working for him either—certainly not as it had in the early days. Admittedly that was before the aftermath of the Vietnamese invasion had overwhelmed the border area, before his responsibilities had become exhausting, before his relationship with Sameth had become too confused for him to understand or to deal with. Of course even in the beginning there had been certain complications in getting his agency properly established. He'd had to learn to work with officials who were not always cooperative and to get help to the right people aggressively yet diplomatically. And of course he had made mistakes. But he had been his own man, with no one he had to supervise except himself, traveling as he pleased, getting out there to Aran regularly where he could actually see the positive results of his efforts. And there had been Sameth.

What was it that had sent that woman to him suddenly out of nowhere? Certainly in that camp they'd known all along what they had, some of the leaders anyway, but they'd had no intention of sharing it easily. They'd kept her hidden away back there in the YWCA School the way monks hide away a special treasure to be brought out for only the most important visitors. He'd been in and out of the camp on business at least three times before he'd happened to notice the YWCA sign across the front of the new building. So he'd been moved to ask toothless old Ponlok what a Christian organization like that had to offer mostly illiterate refugees who still had their home cures and their superstition and perhaps a little Buddhism left over for spiritual food but certainly no room under their restricted diet for the kind of athletic games and jolly fellowship the YWCA might be trying to teach them so close to the non-Christian country they'd only recently lost. Old Ponlok had smiled at him ambiguously, he'd thought at the time simply because it might have seemed odd for one Christian agency to be talking about another that way, and said finally, "You are free to see for yourself."

So he had. Even the building was special: as simple and monotonous as the wooden-sided barracks that went row on row to the far edge of the camp, but with walls made of cement blocks and ample window space. He could hear the children reciting something in English before he got to the door, a wonderfully strange chorus in a place as primitive as that. There must have been over a hundred in there, lined up the length of the room in two files of plank benches and desks resting on upended logs. Sameth had been sitting behind her own plank of a desk, with a blackboard at one side. She was wearing tight black slacks under a burgundy dress with loop buttons down the length of the front, her long legs tucked back under the chair, the dress unbuttoned below her waist so that it spread open to fall back from her thighs in two bright wings.

She was sitting there listening to the recitation with her hands pressed against each other between her breasts as though for prayer. Then her hands opened suddenly to hold the room between them for a second and came back together in a single satisfied clap. No sign that she'd noticed anybody at the door. She then got up to write another sentence on the blackboard, smiling to herself, but he didn't remember what she'd written. All he could recall was that first image of her, the face especially, forehead and cheekbones high and the eyes Oriental, but those Eastern elements toned down subtly, the dark hair with a touch of bronze, the coloring paler than what one found in Khmer women, the face not so round, the nose, though delicately shaped, too long, and the lips too broad. Not pretty exactly but very sensual. Anyway, so it had seemed to him. Yet before he'd gone any distance with that thought, he was struck by the thing that made it truly unusual, at least when she was listening to the children without smiling: an unexpected conjunction between the turn of the eyes and the turn of the mouth that gave it what in anybody else one might have called some mixture of sadness and defiance, but in her appeared as a kind of tragic dignity.

He was quite sure that he wasn't now reading into his memory of that look what he had come to know about her later, because a minute after her back was turned to write on the blackboard, his mute sense of what he'd seen in her had made him back away from the door as though he'd been intruding on mysteries that were not meant for his eyes. And it had taken another visit to the camp before he'd found the courage to approach the woman directly and talk to her. As well as he got to know her after that, he had never mentioned his secret visit to her classroom, and though he'd seen that look often again, he'd never spoken to her about it, even to make light of it. Sameth of course would have laughed at him whatever tone he might have chosen, called it another sign of his boyish romanticism, his latent Dutch gloom, who knows what—she could never take herself as seriously as he took her. And so it remained unspoken along with that part of her thinking which she kept private from him to the end, that part which had seemed to grow and grow in the last days until it darkened not only her feeling for him but his for her, and to work relentlessly to make their separation inevitable.

It wasn't only the business of her discovering his Christianity that night by the shore, he was certain of that. There had been problems during the excursion before that one, and at times there had been what one might have called political differences, had they ever been spelled out precisely enough for such an unambiguous designation. In any case, the distance between them had begun to show clearly before any question of religious belief became an issue, and if she had only given him a chance during their trip south to talk it all through as he had honestly wanted to at one point, he might have been able to convince her that none of these supposed problems was as important to him as she herself was.

Of course with Sameth that approach might have proven more dangerous to his case than any actual difference over politics or religion. She might pretend otherwise, but she expected one to take seriously what one believed in or professed not to believe in. And she was not the kind to be satisfied by what one man's devotion might give her. She was restless for something beyond that, something he had finally come to realize he couldn't possibly give her. How could he describe it? Maybe that too was part of the problem: he was always afraid that she would make fun of his language, call it sociological rhetoric or something like that, so the serious matters on his mind usually remained unspoken. But if he had to put it into words he would say that she seemed to be searching for some sort of firm tradition to put her faith in, some kind of stable community to belong to, a system of values permanent enough to be rooted in a place. Yet even that might not have satisfied her. Maybe what she wanted was nothing less than a country. Her country. And how could he or anybody else give her that?

She was intelligent enough to know it too. He wondered if that was the secret behind the look he couldn't talk about. Anyway, he might not have understood everything that she held back from him in her privacy, but one thing became clear at the end: he, Maarten, wasn't enough to stop her from going back across the border. The most he could do was see to it that she set out over a reasonably safe route. That he had done by convincing his one substantial contact with the Vietnamese military of the lady's potential value as a linguist. But he hadn't found the courage at the end to tell Sameth that he'd at least begun to understand what was behind her decision to go back. Still too much pride for that. And of course it wouldn't have done for him to suggest that Thirith's disappearance, however profoundly it might have touched Sameth at the time, wasn't the only reason or even the main reason, whether or not she was conscious of it. And if she herself suspected, as she surely must have, that the country she was looking for wasn't there any longer, then maybe even that wasn't the most important reason. Maybe it had simply become time for Sameth to fly again, fly until she could land—God knows where—on solid ground. Who could finally tell with a woman like that?

Maarten took his foot off the accelerator out of habit when he saw the sign marking the group of so-called apartments just outside Aran where he'd managed to settle Sameth for those last very unsettled weeks. He decided not to stop there, even if her rooms were still technically his. He would rather stay at the motel, as he had done the last time he was in Aran. Those rooms were dead, as far as he was concerned. So was her camp. If it hadn't been for Thirith's coming out of the jungle to pick up whatever Sameth had left behind, he wouldn't have had cause to visit either place again. He was ready now to leave Sameth's camp to the Norwegian Refugee Council and the International Rescue Committee and the Planned Parenthood Association of Thailand. His business was now elsewhere.

He had actually come to admire Thirith for being tougher and more realistic than he on the subject of Sameth's decision to return to Cambodia. When Thirith had finally tracked him down in the Aran apartment, she'd been very cool about it all, though not really at ease with him—or perhaps with his admittedly emotional account of the border parting and his sense of futility after the fact. He couldn't remember her exact words, something about Sameth's having to do what Sameth had to do, and there being no point in thinking about what he or she herself or anybody else might have done to make her change her mind. Thirith didn't even want to think about the part her disappearance might have played in Sameth's decision: if that was the cause, unhappy as the mix-up was, one had to see it as an act of fate that no one could have prevented and that therefore no one should really feel guilty about.

She was of course largely right, and her attitude was no doubt a healthy one under the circumstances. But it couldn't be his. That parting from Sameth had killed something in him, some sense of his own possibilities, and he wasn't likely to turn rational about it quickly. Of course Sameth herself had tried to make light of the transfer arrangements—the border trip was to be seen as just another outing in the country for illicit lovers who would end up taking separate roads home. She had even been unnervingly affectionate during the time they were alone in the van waiting for his Vietnamese contact to show up. But while he followed that military jeep with his binoculars as it moved off in the distance until it was finally swallowed up by the Cambodian forest, he had felt something go through him like a premonition of death—his, not hers—as though a part of his life had gone out of him with that vanishing image.

Now, two months later, the remnant of that feeling made him hate Aran. The town itself had never appealed to him, but as he slowed now to avoid the tuk-tuk traffic and the assortment of patched and peeling vehicles remade for local commerce, he felt suddenly nauseated by the town's ghastly mixture of poverty and modern enterprise—its old one-storied concrete structures of no recognizable style and never appearing completely finished. The only thing that had made it at all palatable in the old days was its being Sameth's town. Even the wooded places beyond the last of the houses and then the hills out along the border, one or another of what had been their pleasure gardens in the early months, now left him cold as well—simply part of the same monotonous landscape that was brought to life these days not so much by the change in seasons as by the violence of one or another army's attempting to establish its credibility or to keep possession of what it didn't own.

Fortunately the new relief work that had emerged from the UNHCR conference in July would give him as much to do in Bangkok as he could possibly cope with. That meant he could virtually bypass Aran from now on. Except for this Mr. Baugh. It was clear one had to begin keeping a closer eye on him, and that might still require the occasional trip out to the new headquarters near the border. However good Baugh's credentials in terms of previous experience and the references he'd produced, especially in comparison with several others who'd applied to him on short notice, there was something about the man that had given him an uneasy feeling from the start, something in his look and manner. And this latest request for more lorries—"trucks," the man insisted on calling them—without precise specification of their purpose was really a bit high-handed. In fact, quite unacceptable. But he was too tired and bored to worry about that until tomorrow. Whether he liked it or not, he would have to spend the night in the Aran motel fighting mosquitoes as usual, maybe treat himself to a quick meal at what they called the local Maxim's—the fish there was sometimes just passably edible—and deal with Mr. Baugh as best he could in the morning.

Polk had begun to sense that time was running out on him. Getting the two aspects of his current operation organized during the same short period had not proved as simple as he'd expected. He wasn't about to lose any sleep over it beyond his normal insomnia—that old unfading battle scar that he'd brought back from Korea—but he could feel the pressure building up so that it got his mind working too fast every time he felt himself finally drifting off into dream country. The new volag group would be out breathing down his neck in less than a week now, and even before that, he'd have to deal with the head of the Bangkok office, who'd promised to drop in on him during his next trip to the border, supposedly to see if anything more was needed before the group settled into the new headquarters, but you could bet your ass to check him out as well. He wasn't at all sure now that he could get things set up in time unless he got himself some local personnel in a hurry, people working directly for him and responsible to him alone. And it wouldn't hurt in the meanwhile to get a little more cooperation out of the Bangkok office, don't hold your breath.

The problem as he analyzed it was partly administrative, partly logistical. From the administrative point of view, the border area was bad news. It was almost impossible to sign up a contact who seemed capable of making a decision on his own initiative, even if you finally managed to break through the language barrier. You never knew just how much authority the man had on his own and exactly who he was representing behind the scenes. Of the five people who'd come to him so far through his Bangkok connection, people supposedly in a position to act as middlemen to his middleman, only two were ready to make a concrete offer without further consultation, and even in those two cases you couldn't be sure who would finally show himself at the other end of the tube you were talking through. All five were happy enough to tell you how important their particular movement was for the liberation of the fatherland—whether Khmer red, green, or yellow—but no one of them was ready to come up with the name of the character in their outfit who guaranteed final payment when the goods were on their way to their ultimate destination.

Of course that wasn't really his concern. His cut came out of the first installment, and he was completely out of the picture once the truck was on its way north to pick up and deliver its load. The major problem for him was still the initial logistical one of getting the truck out to Aran and handed over to the party who took it on from there. You wouldn't have thought that a couple of extra trucks added to the increased allocation of an agency expanding its activities significantly in an area of desperate need would raise the issue it had. The ICRC had at least a dozen new trucks of various kinds parked out there in the front yard—anyway the white paint and the red crosses on them were clean enough to let you think they were new—and that wasn't counting those in the field on a given day. So what made his agency so second-rate in the eyes of the UNCHR or the church groups backing them that they couldn't afford to up their allocation to six or seven if you please?

Administration, in a word. And leadership. It had taken three phone calls to Bangkok to persuade his so-called boss back there to initiate a request for a further increase to five trucks and a couple more phone calls to persuade him that two trucks were needed immediately for interim use, while the new headquarters was getting itself organized. Even so, the man had short-changed him by sending only one, with some kind of idiot for a driver who wouldn't let go of the thing and haul ass back to Bangkok until there'd been a whole new series of phone calls, with the driver doing most of the talking in some language he couldn't understand. That had really brought home his need to have a minimum of two low-key personnel he could use for special assignments in the field, Thais who spoke a Christian language and could drive a truck decently, people on a local payroll under his supervision so that there was no argument about who they were working for and no question about where their trust belonged.

At least he'd managed to get that one truck into action right off. Besides checking out the credibility of his Bangkok connection before he got himself more deeply involved, it would test the feasibility of letting the occasional truck go out on a drive-yourself basis. There was naturally a certain gamble involved—where wasn't there?—but he hadn't seen the point in delaying the start of the operation until he could hire himself a trustworthy local driver, especially since this Khmer Rouge representative, without question the most forceful and reliable-looking of the five border people he'd interviewed, insisted on providing his own driver. Which was just fine by him as long as that outfit got the truck back to Aran in one piece and ready to head out again the minute he had his schedule of rice deliveries worked out efficiently enough to allow him to release another truck to meet his second order for military hardware without causing anybody undue strain.

Of course there would have to be a separate expense budget for each of the two options, since it was one thing to give out the truck on a self-service basis simply for the equipment and the cover his agency would provide, and another to offer equipment, cover, and the personnel for getting the shipment where it was meant to go. But it wasn't really the budgetary issue that had him worried in the case of the second order. He was pretty sure this Tao Lom would understand relative figures if you put them down on a pad in different columns, and the man was clearly hungry enough for the shipment not to argue with him over a reasonable adjustment of the cost. What he couldn't be so sure about was whether he could make the man understand the logistics of getting the truck on the road heading in the right direction, and more important, the full responsibility of his outfit out there—Khmer Whateveritwascalled—for seeing to it that the shipment reached the final destination his outfit had in mind. He himself didn't want to know anything about that. Mr. Baugh could assume no responsibility—overt, covert, or otherwise—once the truck was outside the front gate of the new headquarters. From there on out, he knew nothing about nothing. But how do you get that across to a man who barely speaks your language? Hopefully at least the message had gotten through to him that he had to bring along a half-decent interpreter when he showed up to finalize the deal. But could you really count on the mother?

In fact, could you count on anything along that border? Anyway, as compared with Korea? And he didn't have only Orientals in mind. There were some very weird folk in the region, some really spaced-out types, very casual, very disconnected. He had hardly run into anybody out there he would call truly disciplined, with the kind of leadership qualities and self-reliance you would like to see in an area of conflict. People were either do-gooders or do-badders, nothing in between. And half the time you couldn't figure out where people stood. With the Khmers at least you knew they all had Vietnam as their common enemy, whatever the particular color of the outfit they were in. But these volag types, who was their enemy? Half of the time it was their own country. One thing you could bet your ass, they wouldn't have made the grade in anybody's army over in Korea, friend or foe.

The case of Vietnam he wouldn't argue. Something had gone wrong in Vietnam, that was for sure, but he wasn't about to point the finger at anybody. You fought the best fight you could and didn't knock the poor fucker in the next foxhole, however screwed up he might be, or beyond him, those who wouldn't—

Polk suddenly swung his legs out of his bunk and stood in his bare feet, listening. He was certain that somebody had come into the yard. The sound out there had been of feet moving but not meant to be heard. Silently, with no extra motion, he crossed to the chair and put on his pants, then picked up his shoes and made his way to the room next door so that he could look out on the front yard. He approached the window very cautiously, along the wall, though he had no clear idea why so much caution was needed—just a feeling, jungle sense. He eased a slanting look outside. As far as he could tell there was nobody out there, unless they were around the corner or flattened up against the front of the building inside the line of his vision. But if they were burglars, why would they stalk the place that way? In the middle of the night, with his pickup truck parked out in front? Maybe they'd cased the place quickly, figured somebody was home and moved on. Still, he couldn't get over his sense that somebody was out there.

He squatted by the window and listened again a long time. There was no single sound specific and clear-cut enough for identification, but inside the silence there was a pattern that wasn't quite right. And now the crickets, or whatever they were, had stopped their racket entirely, and so had the dog who'd been howling a ways down the road. In the vacuum they left he could now hear a scraping sound, so slight it was hard to tell exactly where it was coming from but surely from somewhere down front and in a rhythm that said it had to be man-made. He decided he'd better ease his way down to his office and pick up the .45 he had stashed away in the suitcase he used for filing, then maybe reconnoiter the front yard by circling around it from the back.

He had gotten as far as the office doorway, still holding his shoes in one hand, when the front door came open with a kick and a man burst in, followed by a woman, both holding Kalashnikov automatic rifles. The man he recognized as Tao Lom, though he was now wearing fatigues with a green-brown-white camouflage pattern and a green cap low on his forehead. The woman, or girl—it was hard to tell her age—had on the same fatigues with a single belt around her waist and a red-and-blue bandana around her neck Boy Scout fashion. Polk was certain he'd never seen her before, but it was clear she was not very pleased to see him.

"You could have rung the doorbell," Polk said. "No point in crashing in here like I'm hiding snipers or something. Now I'm just going to have to get that door fixed."

"You won't need the door," Thirith said. "You are going to come with us and we are going to execute you."

Polk smiled. "What did you say you're going to do, lady?"

"Execute you. For sending Tao Lom's guns to Tao Lom's enemies."

"You must be out of your mind," Polk said, the smile gone.

"*You* are out of your mind," Thirith said.

Tao Lom had moved up now to put the barrel of his Kalashnikov against Polk's belly. Polk stepped back into the office and kept backing until he nudged the desk. The woman came in to stand beside Tao Lom with her rifle now aimed at Polk's knees.

"Hey, you people are making some kind of crazy mistake," Polk said. "Tao Lom's shipment is coming up. Just give me a little time."

"No mistake," Thirith said. "Our patrol intercepted your truck. On the road to the Khmer Rouge camp in the north. The driver has already been executed."

Polk was shaking his head now. "I don't believe this."

Tao Lom turned to say something to the woman.

"Put on your shoes, Mr. Ball," Thirith said.

Polk just stared at her. Then he shook his head in disbelief. Thirith raised her rifle to the level of his hips, then moved it a fraction to the right. In a single continuous burst she made a short sweep of the area beside him, almost clearing the top of the desk: clock, a group of folders, ashtray, mirror, the head of the Oriental warrior, the top of the paperback pile beside it. Tao Lom gave a delighted little laugh.

"Now I will begin more to the left," Thirith said.

Polk sat down on the floor to put on his shoes.

Tim and D.J. hadn't even gotten started toward the border until some time after they'd downed their noon portions of rice and local greens, and then the rain had come along to stop them dead in their tracks. It had been a long, quiet morning, at least for Tim. D.J. was not in a mood to be rushed. When he'd finally woken up sometime around mid-morning, he'd explained to Tim that it normally took him twenty-four hours to get his spirits back in shape after distribution day, and he was doing his very best to cut that short for Tim's benefit, but it was not a matter entirely within his control. He'd stripped then and gone into the bathroom to stand in the middle of the concrete floor facing the wall and pour bucket after bucket of water over his head from the cisternlike bath-tub in there. Then he'd come back to lie on the bed again, staring up at the ceiling wide-eyed but with no other sign that he was really awake.

They'd spent the night side by side in that bed and a half, D.J. on his sleeping bag, because that seemed the most sensible solution when the nurse D.J. had courted late into the evening made it clear that he either moved into the empty room next door with his friend or spent the night in the back of his truck, there surely not being room enough for him in her narrow bed unless she had more reason to share it with somebody else than her heart seemed to allow that particular evening—so D.J. had re-ported to Tim with full melancholy after waking him up so that he could spread out next to him. Then Tim had had trouble getting back to sleep while D.J. slept right on, noisily, with what sounded like some bad dreams, but without any evident break. And Tim had been up by day-light. So had all the nurses who had to go back on duty, emerging from one or another of the rooms down the line to cross to the open-air dining area for their morning tea and rice. He'd waited until they'd cleared out in the white trucks that presumably took them out to one of the border set-tlements northwest of the town; then he'd gone over there to see if he could find himself some coffee. He'd settled for the strongest tea he could make and some rice with a mango concoction that was all right if you could get over thinking about it as a substitute for jam. Then he'd taken a long walk as far as the open country beyond the edge of the town.

His mind was a bit confused at that point, and though he wasn't really worried yet, he'd begun to wonder seriously if he wasn't going to end up having to go back and face the old man empty-handed, whether it meant giving him the message in person if Tom actually managed to fit a trip out there into his schedule before winter as he'd said he might or if it meant having to send it out via Dubois. Either way, the thought of having to deliver a message of that kind really depressed him. Just one more fail-ure for the old man to chalk up on his ledger of things Tim had set out on with serious commitment only to end up abandoning along the way for one reason or another. But even more depressing was the lack of focus in his getting work in the area. The way D.J. talked, picking up a job along the border was a sure way to drift either toward some kind of breakdown or, possibly worse, toward a real hardening in your ability to sympathize with what people were going through out there. Especially if you didn't have some special skill that could keep your mind on the job at hand or enough management experience to earn you a chance to organize something that was really useful. He couldn't quite see where his skills and his experience might fit in out there. And the more he thought about possibilities beyond the border, the further away they seemed.

He'd tried to raise these questions with D.J. over their quick lunch, but he couldn't be sure how far he'd penetrated the haze that still appeared to be clouding D.J.'s usual clearheadedness. He'd outlined what incomplete and unconfirmed facts he and Dubois had come up with from their visit to the old camp near Aran, and when that didn't seem to jog the guy out of his dejected mood—if you thought about it, how could it?—he'd moved on to talk about possible job opportunities in the area, only to find D.J. studying him with something that looked like somber bewilderment, as though he weren't about to believe that somebody with a free spirit would seriously consider any kind of work that might get him stuck in that muddy border territory, let alone in the unmapped marshes beyond. The only thing D.J. had actually said was that he wanted to show Tim a bit of landscape before they got down to candid talk about job possibilities in the region, and what he had in mind specifically was giving him a glimpse of Democratic Kampuchea. That could be connected with this wat he had in mind visiting anyway, so they could kill two birds with one stone, and if the local Buddha out there was on their side, they might come back from the border not only with a program for attacking Tim's mail-delivery problem but with some new insight into how he might want to think about his plans for the future in the days immediately ahead. There was no way you could rush these things, he added. The gods demanded their hour, their focus, their portion of contemplation. And sometimes more than that—more than an honest man could give.

They were well east of Aran and halfway to the wat when the cloudburst hit them. D.J. pulled over to the side of the road to wait it out. Tim had never seen rain like that, grand in its way, the steady rush and beat of it exhilarating at first, cooling the air in the car and filling it with its sound, then turning oppressive as it came on relentlessly against the roof and windows, mercilessly, so that you felt there was no way that you could get out from under it except by curling in on yourself like a fetus.

Then it lightened and vanished almost as suddenly as it had come, and the air became rich with the smell of settled dust and wet grass. They opened the windows all the way to take it in. The klong beside the road had a current now, and bits of driftwood and trash bobbed through the surface here and there and gathered in pockets along the bank. Up ahead, on the far side of the klong, you could make out a hut on pile stilts that seemed slightly bowlegged, but the hut had a new roof that glowed when the sun passed over it. A woman came around from the back, looked up at the sky, decided to spread her laundry on the thick grass at the side of the hut. A humpbacked ox moved in behind her and turned east, dewlap swaying. Closer by, a black water buffalo rose from the brush along the bank and loped to the edge of the water, smelled it, then walked in to face the current with its horns laid back and its ears opening out like fins.

D.J. started the engine and pulled out into the road. Waiting out the rain seemed to have relaxed him a bit.

"So it comes, so it goes," he said. "The gods turn violent one minute to put us in our place, then release us back into our domestic tranquillity. But don't you believe it."

"I believe it," Tim said. "I feel very released."

"That has nothing to do with the gods. That's because you made out last night the Irish way."

"I didn't really make out. Just a long friendly conversation."

"Three hours long? You and your friend Catherine Barkley disappeared for at least three hours."

"There was much to learn," Tim said. "Much history to explore. My ancestors, many mutual roots."

"You explored mutual roots for three hours?"

"Mostly," Tim said. "It seems mine go deep and far. Into both the north and south of Ireland, I'm told."

"Well, at least you had something mutual to explore," D.J. said. "Without roots, I was at a total loss with my lady. I mean it's clear that there's no way you're going to make out in this world when the only roots you've got are sunk into the shifting soil along the Thai–Cambodian border."

"You have other roots," Tim said. "You just haven't dug down deep enough."

"How can I have other roots when I don't even have a name to work with? D.J. is no name."

"Dig, man, dig. Know thyself. Find a name."

"This conversation is too close to the bone," D.J. said. "I'd rather concentrate on domestic tranquillity. You want to know how deep that goes around here? Look over yonder."

He slowed down and pointed at a rice field that was backed by a grove of mango trees which in turn dissolved into a forest rising against the low hill they were heading for at the edge of the border. There were three figures in a row at the back of the rice field, just visible against the trees behind them, all wearing straw hats.

"Watch this," D.J. said.

He edged the car over to the side of the road and stopped, then reached for Tim's camera. He got out and walked around to the front of the car and aimed the camera toward the three figures. They disappeared instantly, as though he'd knocked them all over at once with a click of his camera. D.J. came back to the car shaking his head.

"Dirty trick," he said as he started up again. "I'll have to ask forgiveness for that someday when I'm sure there's somebody out there listening. But it does prove my point."

"I don't get it," Tim said. "What makes them so jumpy?"

"Being Khmer. Doesn't serve to build up your sense of domestic security. Or feed your roots."

"How do you know they're Khmer?"

"Because they did that. Migrant illegal entrants you might call them, as distinct from more-or-less permanent illegal entrants. They come across the border for the day, pick up what work they can cheap or sell a thing or two, then head back home to their starving relatives and the pleasures of the hearth. That is, if the Thai army doesn't get to them at this end or the Vietnamese army at the other end or the minefields in between."

"You wouldn't think it was worth the risk."

"My sweet lad, forgive me if I ask you a direct question. When was the last time you were hungry? I mean really hungry?"

Tim didn't answer. There had been a time just after he dropped out of college when he'd gone for—how many days was it?—without anything but water and a single slice of pizza for his one meal a day because he couldn't get work and didn't feel like writing home for help, and boy, did he ever remember the taste of that pizza and the feel of some of the hours in between while his stomach was still shrinking. But he'd just better keep his mouth shut now in case what came out turned D.J.'s mood in some new direction. D.J. still hadn't glanced over at him. He was staring straight down the road, driving faster now, too fast.

"Talk about risk-taking," he finally said. "It all depends on where you're coming from and where you're going to end up. I've seen some of these people hobble into one or another of the settlements north of here with a shredded pantleg where a foot used to be a few hours before, and man, they are smiling. Can you believe it? And a few weeks later you'll run into one of them standing in the line outside a workshop for artificial legs and other devices for the handicapped and they're still smiling. I guess they figure nobody's going to waste his time trying to make a one-legged man with a peg for a foot walk his way back home across the border."

The klong became irregular suddenly, narrowing in places and finally opening out to shape a kind of pond maybe fifty yards long before closing to its normal width. A family was fishing at the far end, the man and woman in knee-deep water holding huge scoop nets slung from triangular hoops, the children around them—three, four—paddling water toward the nets with the kind of intensity that would surely drive away any fish with life still in it. The nets dipped in unison, hovered underwater, rose empty, then dipped again, and the children paddled away. It was hard to tell whether they were into serious business or just on a family outing, but they made you think that kind of distinction didn't matter to them. The car with foreigners in it didn't matter either. Tim figured they must be Thais, because D.J. didn't even turn his head to give them a look. He seemed to be in some other country anyway, back where he'd been most of the time since they'd gotten up. He didn't speak again until he cut speed abruptly and turned to park against the barbed-wire fence at the foot of the hill that he'd told Tim would give them as deep a look into Cambodia as they were likely to get without traveling where no man in his right mind would go except in a tank.

"From here on up it's sacred ground," he said. "Somebody may think we don't belong here, so you just follow me to the top, and if there's a problem, let me do the talking. Unless we draw fire from across the border once we're up there, in which case you're on your own."

The gate to the wat was open, but the clearing beyond seemed to be inhabited only by images: a field of steepled grave markers, a life-size Buddha with two attendants under a corrugated canopy, a smaller shrine on stilts at the far right where the trees began again. Directly behind them was a stone stairway that climbed the hill steeply until it disappeared over the top into heavy foliage. As D.J. started up, a young monk in saffron robes, head newly shaven, came into the clearing from the right as though out of thin air and stopped near the smaller shrine to sit on his heels. He gave no sign of having noticed visitors. Tim headed on up the stairs, then looked back to see that he was being watched shyly, as though out of curiosity. The monk turned back the way he had come and vanished into the trees around the hillside.

D.J. stood there waiting at the top. The peak of the hill had been leveled off so that the place had the look of a campsite, with a wooden structure in the center that appeared to be something between a cabin and a barracks, a small shrine on one side of it and a huge bunker partially covered by earth on the other side. Through the trees at the back you could just make out the main shrine on a rise above the campsite, a complicated formation of square columns in brown brick, two stories high and arranged to suggest a cube without exactly shaping one from any angle. The roof had become a garden of untended plant life. D.J. was checking out the cabin to see if anybody was home. Through a window you could see a kitchen with a stove and scattered pots and a table with a single plate on it, but no other sign of life. In another room beyond the kitchen there was a smaller-than-life-size Buddha partly covered by gold-leaf squares that must have been stuck there at some point by visitors to the wat. But you couldn't get in there now: all doors were locked. The whole place had the feel more of an abandoned outpost than of a holy sanctuary.

D.J. went over to the edge of the site near the head of the stairway and stood there looking out between a break in the trees. He didn't say anything when Tim came up beside him, just stood gazing out at the level spread of the plain they'd crossed as though it were supremely fascinating when actually there wasn't much out there to catch the eye, no rise in the landscape for mile after mile, no hill or man-made structure taller than a house, just the scattered trees and low huts and endless rice fields cut here and there by a dirt road or a canal until you got to the cluster of buildings that meant Aran and then the same open landscape until it dissolved into a loose horizon. But you could hear no sound at all, see no evidence of motion, so that after a while it seemed a great stillness had taken over the country below. That was what D.J. had been watching.

"The official name is land of the free, and you might want to smile at that," he said. "But I can see why people from across the way would be willing to risk killing themselves getting through to that kind of scene, hungry or not. What I can't see is why a few of them turn around eventually and head back across the border. Voluntarily. Come over here and I'll show you what I mean."

He moved off between the bunker and the cabin to the opposite side of the hilltop, where there was a path heading down through the forest.

You couldn't find a clear break in the trees to one side, just the spread that came with the path. But through that you could see where the hill ended below and where the first range of mountains began to rise beyond, and there was nothing else to see in that landscape but jungle leading to more jungle, range on range.

"See what I mean?" D.J. said. "Would you want to head down that path into the dense unknown? For my money it's the proverbial road not taken."

"That's Cambodia out there?"

"Cambodia. Democratic Kampuchea. Land of the still not free at all. Land of the who knows what."

D.J. left Tim standing there and headed up toward the mound with the overgrown shrine. When Tim finally turned away and followed him up, he found D.J. squatting there beside the entrance Buddha-fashion, his eyes closed. The sober expression on his face didn't go along with the pointed cap he was wearing, but it worked to keep Tim from speaking to him.

"It's all right," D.J. said, opening his eyes. "I'm not really meditating. Just brooding over your problem. And I think I've got a lead that may put us on the right track."

Tim sat down beside him. "So clue me in, for God's sake."

"Okay, now. Let's review what facts we have. You and Dubois checked out the camp where the woman and her daughter were last known to have been, according to this Khmer friend of theirs in the States, right? And the people you talked to in the camp said the mother had moved to Aran at some point and the daughter farther north at some point to join one of the Khmer Serei movements."

"What's Khmer Serei?"

"Free Khmer, so-called. Son Sann and some of the old pre–Khmer Rouge crowd. You know, part of the anti-Vietnam guerrilla operation that we and the Chinese are supporting these days along with the Khmer Rouge."

"Well, nobody in that camp was ready to tell us exactly what group the daughter may have joined."

"After what she went through getting out of Cambodia, you can be pretty sure it isn't a Khmer Rouge outfit. Anyway, the point is that neither one of them had been seen back at the camp for over a month, right?"

"The mother for longer than that. Two months maybe."

"And some of the people you talked to told Dubois that the mother had cleared her things and the daughter's things out of the camp completely at one point because the mother thought the daughter had been sent back to Cambodia as part of the forced repatriation in early June, correct? So what do we conclude from that?"

"That the mother and daughter weren't communicating very well. Or maybe that the people in the camp have things a bit confused."

"No doubt both true, but neither of great significance for our purpose. What is of great significance for our purpose is that the woman was allowed to clear her things out of the camp and live in Aran before she disappeared. A Khmer refugee? Even a Khmer refugee from way back?"

"Yeah, but as I told you, this lady was no ordinary refugee. She spoke at least three languages fluently and her Cambodian friend in the States told my old man that she had some kind of special status in the camp."

D.J. started rocking slowly. "More important, she must have had connections. You don't just pull out of a refugee camp and get yourself a place in Aran without connections."

"If she pulled out and disappeared, what great difference does it make? She could be in Paris by now. Or Australia. Or God knows where."

"Because if we track down the connections, we may be able to find out exactly where she disappeared to. And once we know that, we can decide whether there's any way of getting your letters to the lady. Or any point in bothering."

He was still rocking back and forth slowly as though the motion served to wind up his mind.

"And what about the daughter?" Tim asked.

"The daughter's easier. At least we know she's still somewhere in the neighborhood. Though I don't much fancy wandering through the war zone north of here trying to track her down."

"That you can leave to me," Tim said. "I mean if it's at all possible. You just get me headed in the right direction."

"Well, let's start with the mother first. If we can find some trace of her, that might tell us what direction to go looking for the daughter. Who are your connections in Aran?"

"My connections? I don't have any connections in Aran. Except for our Irish friends."

"Exactly," D.J. said. "Our Irish friends. Among whom we may find someone who's been in Aran long enough to know who else may have been set up there three months ago when there wasn't as much going on as there is now. So tonight you might think of spending less time exploring your roots and a little more time fulfilling your duty to your father, okay?"

"I don't think our Irish nurses would be much help. Most of them arrived this summer. And they claim they don't often get a chance to come into town except to crash."

"Then we'll check out all the foreign agencies that were operating in Aran three months ago. She must have had some connection with one or another of them. Or with some local Thai who did."

"Well, it's a start," Tim said. "I've got to admit I can't think of any other way to get things moving at this point."

"Good. Tonight the Irish nurses, tomorrow the foreign agencies. Now give me a few minutes alone to see if I can clear my head of all temptation to think myself unusually clever, because that way hubris lies."

He had his eyes closed again. Tim left him there. On his way down he spotted a saffron robe moving through the trees by the path to Cambodia, but it was gone before he could tell whether it was the same monk he'd seen below.

The clearing at the bottom was empty, crossed by long shadows, remote, almost eerie. Somebody had closed the gate. Tim let himself out and moved down the fence to sit in the car, now feeling more out of place than he'd felt at any point since arriving at the Nana Hotel a week ago. If he felt that way here, in territory that had at least begun to make some sense to him, how would he feel in a place like Cambodia or Burma or Vietnam? For the first time he began to wonder if Dubois hadn't been right. Maybe he was trying to hurry things too much. Maybe he ought to settle back for a time and get himself some kind of special training that would qualify him to do serious work in the region, something in agriculture or medicine, even if it meant having to go back to college for a spell. D.J. seemed to have survived college, at least in a manner of speaking. Otherwise he could see himself just drifting from one ineffectual job to another until some version of the border disease got to him. Besides, the job he'd already set himself was work enough for the moment, and worrying too much about what came after that could cloud your focus so that you lost your sense of direction before you were really on the way somewhere. He eased back against the seat with his arms behind his head and tried to relax. First things first, then play it cool until you see what the gods have in store. Wasn't that the way you were supposed to look at things out here in mango land?

Thirith's problem was no longer doubt so much as growing certainty. This Mr. Ball was an animal, no argument about that, and the bamboo cage they had him in was, from one point of view, as good as he deserved—not really that much different from the kind of hut that a new refugee might build for himself out of bamboo rods and thatched roofing and blue plastic sheets. But from another point of view, the man could be considered innocent, and if he was innocent, it didn't make sense for him to be locked up at all.

The question had been circling in her mind since their short political debate during her first period of guarding him late that morning, after her quite tiring attempt to explain to him why the committee would surely vote in favor of his execution. Actually she still wasn't at all sure that the vote would go that way, a thing she of course couldn't admit to Mr. Ball, but in any case the committee's deliberation was not likely to include her line of thought. If they voted not to execute him, it would have to be because the man was an American working for an international agency that had a certain diplomatic standing in Thailand. But then what would they do with him? They couldn't keep him locked up forever, with or without a judgment. Even if he was now technically inside Cambodia in a military zone and therefore subject to whatever military justice prevailed in the region, his crime had been committed in Thailand, and he had not come to where he now was voluntarily. Some might even choose to say that he'd been abducted and tried without proper defense. There would certainly be embarrassing repercussions from the Thai authorities if his bullet-filled body were sent back across the border or otherwise disposed of by the committee's decree, and if they kept him locked up as a prisoner, how could the justice of that be explained to the Thais or the Americans when they came looking for him?

Of one thing she was certain: now that the committee had taken up the issue, this Mr. Ball would not be released for some time, and if he finally was, it wouldn't be on the proper grounds, namely his being a political idiot. That he was so in fact had become clear to her early in their really absurd dialogue when he revealed that he had no sense at all of the difference between the Khmer Serei and the Khmer Rouge, except that one was to the right in its economics and the other to the left. They were all just Khmers as far as he was concerned, and they were all fighting the same enemy, which he insisted was his country's enemy as well. He seemed quite incapable of understanding that for some in the Free Khmer movement, the first enemy was not Vietnam but the regime he'd sent his shipment of arms to, the regime that had slaughtered its own people so thoroughly that it even seemed to have created a certain excuse for the Vietnamese to invade Cambodia—not that the Vietnamese hadn't been waiting eagerly so many years now for any excuse they might find.

This American had absolutely no grasp of the history he was meddling in. In his ignorance he could see only his particular black and white when it came to politics, and everything else was simply a question of business. His country was supporting both the Khmer Serei guerrillas and the Khmer Rouge guerrillas, so why shouldn't he? And to do business with both was a matter of free trade—how had he put it? free enterprise?—in keeping with the economic system of his own country and that which he understood the Free Khmer to be defending. So what was the great crime he was guilty of? From his point of view, he was merely a patriot helping foreign allies fight a common enemy. And his sending a shipment of guns to the Khmer Rouge before he sent one to the Khmer Serei was simply an accident of timing while he was getting his office organized. How could he be held responsible for failing to make political distinctions that neither his agency nor his country nor even the United Nations chose to make?

The difficulty was that it seemed to her the man had an argument. Given his political stupidity, which certainly wasn't his alone, could one condemn him to death for what he'd done? Could one in fact condemn anybody for committing an evil act if that person was totally ignorant of the evil involved or mentally incapable of understanding it, any more than could one condemn a child or an animal for taking something that pleased it when it couldn't know or care whom the thing belonged to? And if the man was making a profit from his so-called free enterprise, which he surely must have been, was he any more guilty than those who for their own purposes brought him the business that created his profit?

These were questions she wouldn't dare bring before the committee even if she were given the chance. They would call her soft, naive, a girl who still hadn't become a woman, with too little heart for the duty she was assigned and no subtle political sense. But would that make them right in the case of Mr. Ball? And if they were wrong, why should she be afraid to raise these questions, if not with them directly, then at least with Tao Lom? She knew the answer to that without having to brood over it.

If he'd been ready to listen to reason instead of following his own peculiar political instincts, his fanaticism coupled with his apparent need to avoid any action that might jeopardize his standing among the other leaders in the movement, the two of them wouldn't have brought the American back to the camp at all but would have either released him after scaring him half to death or fulfilled Tao Lom's impulse to do away with him on the spot. Now there was no turning back. The committee had to cope with their prisoner and face whatever incriminating complications might lie ahead—unless she could find it in herself to save the movement from the predicament it was now in by taking justice into her own hands.

Of course as well as being stupid, this Mr. Ball was an animal, there was no doubt about that. A thing that belonged to the jungle. And as such he was dangerous whether or not one considered him guilty from the political point of view. All cunning, all manipulation. When he'd seen that he wasn't going to get anywhere with her simply by arguing, he'd turned to flattery, and when that didn't work, he'd tried to bribe her with promises of money and employment and a suitcaseful of pretty things that would all be waiting for her back at his headquarters anytime she decided to collect them, if she'd only let him out of the cage and show him the way back across the border. The more tense she became listening to him, the faster he talked: there would be no problem about her people, he would take care of that once he was safe, see to it that she received any protection she needed, do everything he could to get her out of Thailand, arrange for her to go off to any country she chose—France, Switzerland, even America. He had connections in Bangkok, connections in the American government. On and on that way until she'd felt she had to tell him that if he didn't shut his mouth that instant, she would report his attempt to bribe her to the committee and they might then choose a slower method than bullets to carry out his execution.

But once an animal like that is trapped, there's no limit to its craftiness. Silence was his next tactic, complete silence for over an hour, this surely to make her think that something was wrong so that she'd open the door to the cage and look in long enough to allow him to spring at her like a jungle cat and take her rifle away. She wasn't so stupid. But of course she'd become curious enough to work her way silently around to the back of the cage where she could climb on a log to look in through the slit above the plastic sheeting to make absolutely certain that he was all right. She had found him sitting on his haunches gazing up at her the way a startled monkey might. And since she'd discovered him with his eyes wide open that way, he'd been forced to try another tactic, pretending this time to be in great pain, moaning, then bellowing out that he was sick, poisoned by the food, required the camp doctor immediately, had to get out and go to the toilet, all sorts of nonsense. When she'd answered that there was a perfectly good hole for a toilet right next to where he was squatting on the ground, he'd begun his mad raving about the Geneva Convention and the rights of prisoners of war, until she'd decided to move away closer to the edge of the forest and watch him from there so that she wouldn't be tempted into losing her temper and talking back to him.

There had been no talk out of him so far during her second watch. That could be because he hadn't yet realized that the watch had changed and the guard who spoke English was back. It was better this way. If he started blabbering nonsense again she might change her mind about what she now realized she had to do for the sake of both the movement and her own peace of mind. The more she thought about it, the clearer it became that the movement was bound to get into trouble whether the committee sent the American back dead or kept him in prison or sent him back alive. Once Tao Lom had decided he couldn't take justice into his own hands without losing his standing with other leaders, once he'd made the mistake of bringing the man back to the camp for the trial, there had been no way of hiding the fact or the movement's complicity in the disposition of the case, whatever the committee now voted to do with the prisoner.

The only clean solution of the diplomatic problem would be for this American to end up finding his own way back, a thing she couldn't see the committee agreeing to permit, Tao Lom least of all, especially now that their deliberations had reached a stage that was bound to set pride against pride. But if the man were to find his way back across the border somehow, her sense of the situation told her that he wasn't likely to complain to the Thai authorities or even to his own people unless he was cleverer than he seemed, anyway clever enough to explain acceptably the kind of business he'd organized and just why he'd been held by the Khmer Serei. And his chances of making it back through the jungle in one piece were hardly very good without his having a guide and without more favor from benevolent spirits than he was likely to find. The chances were better that he would disappear without leaving any trace behind him. That would be the best outcome from the movement's point of view. But whatever happened to him, in this way the movement would not be responsible for having either condemned or released him or even for having determined his innocence or guilt. She would be responsible for that. It was the only way she could see of saving the movement from the dangerous predicament that Tao Lom had placed it in by his rather self-serving political conscience.

Of course Tao Lom and the committee might not recognize the sense of what she'd decided to do, and the committee would surely resent her way of having done it. They would probably accuse her of failing in her duty, assuming authority she didn't have, disobeying orders, and so on, and from one point of view they would be right. But disobedience, if that was what one had to call it, was sometimes simply necessary. She could make up a story about the American's having overpowered her after pretending to be sick or after pretending to commit suicide, something that might appear credible on the surface. But she wasn't good enough at lying to make it hold. She would have to tell Tao Lom the truth and hope that he might make up whatever story he thought would convince the committee. And if she found him turning against her for what she'd done, that would at least solve the other, more personal problem that had her mind going back and forth: exactly what future her relationship with him might have now that she'd begun to lose faith in his judgment.

She circled around the cage now and eased up to it from the rear to listen. Mr. Ball was making a strange sound, as though he were talking to himself in a language not meant for human beings to understand. Then she realized that he was sound asleep, fighting with bad dreams. She looked to see if anybody was watching her. The few off-duty people she could make out at the back end of the camp were taking the heat in their hammocks, and the area between the cage and the forest was deserted, the tall grasses there moving just slightly under the still-insufferable afternoon sun. It was the right time to make him go.

"Wake up, Mr. Ball. I have something for you."

Polk came awake with the moan of someone startled by sudden new terror. He blinked at the strip of light above the plastic sheeting.

"I'm going to give you something special," Thirith said. "Because you've been such a quiet prisoner for so long."

"I refuse to eat," Polk said. "Until you bring me the American consul."

"Like Gandhi, is that it, Mr. Ball? Only water from now on?"

"I insist on my rights. I insist on seeing the American consul."

His voice sounded strained, unnatural. She wondered if he might actually be going mad.

"I will give you something better than the American consul. I will give you light."

She moved around to the front of the cage and unwound the wire that held the door shut. She swung it open and stepped to the side.

"All right, Mr. Ball. Come quickly."

Polk appeared in the doorway, blinking.

"Now go," she said, motioning with her rifle.

"Where?"

"There," she said, pointing the rifle toward the forest.

"I can't go there," he said. "I don't know the way out."

"You'll have to find it," Thirith said. "Now go quickly. Unless you would prefer that I shoot you for attempting to escape."

The gun came around to point at him. Polk studied her. Then he looked at the forest. He took off in a low crouch, his legs at an awkward angle but moving fast and easily, his back barely visible above the tall grass. He was nowhere to be seen by the time she had the door of the cage wired shut again. As she turned back toward the camp she was smiling to herself. She had no idea why an image of Sameth came into her head at that point, but once there, she found herself wondering whether Sameth would have been as pleased, and at the same time as amused, as she was by what she'd done. Would she have thought it clever and courageous, or merely irresponsible? And why in the world was the question at all important to her?

_____

Tim was sure they were now on the right track, no doubt about that, but the way things had been going most of the time out there in Aran, it really wouldn't surprise him if the thing turned back on itself at some point and led them to a final dead end. The break in their search, and the omens that went with it, had come with their dinner at the headquarters canteen the previous evening, when the lively redheaded nurse who emerged at D.J.'s side from his wide-ranging, increasingly frantic, finally triumphant pursuit of prospects for the evening turned out to have news for them. D.J. had been very possessive with the lady, clearly not pleased that Tim had decided to go it alone after spending too much time asking the wrong kinds of questions of the nurses who'd come in off duty. But late in the dinner Tim had managed to break into the developing romance to get in one more boring question about the business at hand and had struck pay dirt. The redhead had indeed been in Aran since late May, but in the early days, before she knew a bit of Thai, she'd met very few of the local people and couldn't talk to them when she did without an interpreter—except for one quite lovely Cambodian woman who spoke fluent English and who'd lived for a brief period in the apartment next to hers, a few doors down the line from Tim and D.J.'s room, having been brought there to work for one of the international relief agencies by her Dutch boyfriend. This woman had disappeared before the nurse really had a chance to get to know her. And then she went on to tell of a vigil she'd held with the woman during the period when the Thais took it into their heads to clean out the local refugees by forcing many to go home again, the two of them watching busload after busload pass the front gate until it was "fock all" for some forty thousand of the poor souls, and the Cambodian woman, quietly hysterical by then, had become convinced that her own daughter was among those who'd been sent back. The nurse hadn't seen any trace of the woman since or of her boyfriend, though one or the other of them had apparently appeared at some point to remove her things from the apartment next door, because the place was empty now except for the bedding.

That had been all she knew, but it was enough to keep Tim from sleeping easily that night and enough to put D.J. soberly to work the following morning. Tim had gone out to clear his head as soon as the sun came up, but instead of taking a walk right away, he'd checked out the empty apartment down the line from their room, the woman's apartment, glanced into it through each of the windows. The bed was made up with a sheet but there was no pillow, and the table in there had no chair in front of it. The other room had a larger table and a straight-backed chair on either side of it as though the thing had been set up for a dinner without plates or cutlery. There was nothing else in the apartment—no rugs on the floor, no curtains, nothing on the walls except clean green paint. There was nothing especially feminine about it either, God knows nothing you'd call erotic, except maybe the style of the bathroom. The place looked like a green cell that hadn't yet taken in its first prisoner, woman or man.

It made him wonder about the woman, what it was exactly that had brought her to live there alone, or mostly alone, without anybody to talk to except a few foreign nurses completely new to the territory. Her own private space? The camp he'd visited with Dubois outside Aran, her old camp, was surely grimmer: rows of barracks made of wooden slats and plain tin roofs, the floor in each a platform well above the ground doubtless to make room for the nesting rats and other unwanted things living down there, the platform thinly partitioned every few yards to give you the illusion of private space. While he was out there with Dubois he'd learned that at one point the woman and her daughter had been assigned a room in the staff area, but there was no area in that camp that looked much above what you'd expect to find in a temporary prison, and that was what it must have been for her, even if she'd had someone to talk to regularly and work to keep her fairly busy and people who knew what she'd been through because they'd been through it themselves. This green room created a different image of her, more remote in a way than she'd seemed after his visit to her old camp, where it had been difficult enough for him to picture the woman in that diary settling down to live for four years. The two rooms here were as clean as you might want, but so bare and isolated, so clear of any connection with her other life, that it almost made you think she'd come there to hide out from her past, daughter included.

But what did he know? Maybe she'd just come there to be with her Dutch lover. If so, they hadn't left any evidence behind to show that the place had been a love nest. Whatever it was that may have taken her there initially, the look of the rooms made him feel that she'd ended up living there alone, with only the bare essentials. And if so, where did that leave her now? The whole thing was pushing him to see the woman in a new light. Maybe she wasn't so much the clever seductress with charm enough to draw in whatever man she might need to keep herself secure for a while, the image of her that had come to him at times while he was reading her diary. Maybe she was more a woman regularly under threat of being abandoned and therefore always ready to move into smaller and smaller circles of self-containment in order to survive as best she could on her own. And one of the first circles would have been the one she built to protect herself after old Tom and the other Americans had left her behind in Cambodia without the support they'd once provided for her. If so, the old man really owed her one, that was for sure, but at the same time you couldn't say he was the only one who did, not even the only American.

Tim had told D.J. about his look-in on the apartment and the feeling it had given him once they'd gotten out on the road that morning, but by that time D.J. had his mind fixed on one thing only: tracking down the Dutch boyfriend. That had taken them a while, because they'd had to check out several agencies before D.J. pinpointed exactly what they were looking for. He was still furious at himself for not having picked up the clue right at the start, and now, on their way out to the man's headquarters, Tim couldn't get D.J. to focus on what Tim saw as the major obstacle still ahead: how to bring up the question of the letters diplomatically with a man they presumed to be the Cambodian woman's current lover. Wouldn't he want to know exactly who these people were in America who were apparently so closely related to his lady that they could send a personal messenger halfway across the world to search her out, not to mention what plans they might have for the woman from then on? But D.J. still hadn't calmed down enough to take up questions of diplomacy. Beyond his irritation, he seemed to be getting light-headed with the feel of imminent success. He had the pickup truck going in and out of every bend in the road as though some clock in his head were driving him to fly, and he couldn't stop talking to himself.

"I've known Maarten Ruyter ever since he first came out here," he was saying, his head shaking away. "Not well, but God knows well enough so that it might have occurred to me to check him out right from the beginning."

"What difference does it make?" Tim said. "We've caught up with him now, that's the important thing."

"Look at the time we lost farting around. Half the morning."

"The way I look at it, if he's really our man, we're way ahead of the game at this point. Considering where we were this time yesterday."

"He's our man all right. Only I should have picked up on it immediately. As soon as our sweet pink-faced friend with the rich vocabulary came on with her bloody story about the bloody Thais."

"Not our friend. Your friend. You wouldn't even let me get close enough to find out if she and I might have mutual roots back in the mother country."

"Forgive me. My head was rendered insensitive and dull by the suddenness of romance. Still is that way, it seems."

"At least it hasn't changed its basic shape."

D.J. gave him his melancholy look, then his middle finger, then reached down between the seats without cutting speed to pick up the beer he'd parked in front of the four-wheel-drive gearshift. He took a long swig of his Kloster, then studied the bottle as though it had somebody else's warm specimen in it. The truck hit the shoulder and went on as it pleased until D.J. got it back into the center of the highway. He returned the bottle to the floor, shaking his head again.

"I knew we had our woman when my sweet redhead told us the Cambodian lady spoke English and Thai, but the Dutch boyfriend just didn't ring any sort of bell in my love-struck brain. I guess I've always thought of Maarten as being English because he has that kind of accent."

"Well, now that we're all agreed he has to be our man, why don't you just slow down and relax before we end up over there pulling rice stalks out of our teeth."

"I mean we had to check out damn near every agency out here before it came to me to see if there was one that had a base in Holland. Three months ago, that's where I would have started looking. So maybe it's really time for me to take another trip to Nepal. Say with our Irish friend for company."

"I promise to see that the two of you go off into the sunset heading in any direction you choose if you'll just get me safely to this Dutchman and his woman so I can prove America is no longer cop-out land."

"Prove for whose benefit? I bet the Dutchman couldn't care less. And the woman must have given up on that issue some time ago."

"Okay, for my old man's benefit then."

"You ask too much," D.J. said.

"Just a last chance to live in domestic tranquillity. Is that too much to ask?"

"All right," D.J. said, cutting speed. "But the minute you slow down, you give them an easy target."

"Give who?"

"How do I know? Whoever's out there trying to get you."

D.J. reached for his bottle again, then changed his mind. He edged over to avoid a bus that was emptying its passengers into the line of those waiting to get through the checkout point. The line was already a good half-mile long. Two soldiers in black berets were doing the checking while another group of soldiers watched from the guardhouse. Off to one side there was a clean line of squatting villagers, twenty-five or thirty of them, held there by a single guard who was walking casually behind them, the barrel of his rifle dipped to crease their backs as he moved down the line.

"Poor bastards don't know half the time what's legal to carry home and what isn't," D.J. said. "They keep changing the rules on them, hoping that way to stop all trade across the border."

"So what do they do to the ones they catch—shoot them?"

"No room for wasting bullets on civilians. Just scare the shit out of them."

"Those soldiers?"

"They look meaner than they really are," D.J. said. "They only rough them up a bit, kick the bejesus out of them if they're carrying too much of one thing."

"Like what?"

"Too many shirts or shoes or spare bicycle parts. So the villagers just go back and try again, hoping to get it right the next time. I mean it's a free country."

On the far side of the road, a short distance beyond where the bus was unloading, there was a fenced-in villa off on its own, seemingly unconnected to anything else in the landscape. D.J. pulled up outside it and killed the engine.

"This should be it. The UNHCR man said it was sitting out there by itself beyond your local commuter checkpoint."

"Well, hold up there a minute," Tim said. "We've got to work out some kind of strategy. I can't just go in there and hand the man my two letters as though I'm some kind of private international delivery service."

"So what do you have in mind? Asking to see the woman herself?"

"That's one possibility," Tim said. "Another is to give the man a little bit of background and see if he's willing to take it from there. I mean I don't want to put either of them in a difficult position."

"What kind of background d'you have in mind, lad? The sad tale of your old man's departure from Phnom Penh? If I were you, I'd let bygones be bygones in this particular case."

"I just don't want the man to get the idea that I'm out here to interfere in his private life. We've got to make him understand that what we're really after at this point is seeing if we can help the woman's daughter get herself settled in somewhere. Maybe get herself some education."

"Well, why don't we just tell him that?"

"I was planning to," Tim said. "I just don't know how to handle the business of my old man. I mean why he's involved. Even if it is only by way of me at this point."

"Why don't we let the woman handle that if she thinks it's still necessary once the letters have gotten through to her? I mean there are certain times in life when it's best to play dumb."

"I'm not too good at that."

"Well, I am," D.J. said. "Besides, I know the man. Sort of, anyway. I mean he's always seemed a reasonable type to me. So why don't you let me have a go at him first, and we'll see where that brings us out, okay?"

The gate was open and there were a white pickup truck and a white van parked in the yard, but no sign of life inside the villa. The doorbell didn't seem to be working, and since the front door was ajar they decided to go on in.

"Ho," D.J. said. "Anybody home?"

Maarten came to the doorway of the room on their right and stared out at them. He finally recognized D.J., but his bewildered expression barely changed.

"I thought it was the police," he said. "Look, my dear Mr. D.J., at what they've done to my new headquarters. Before I've even had a chance to get the place properly furnished."

He motioned them over to the doorway and showed them Polk's office with a sweep of his arm.

"Jesus," D.J. said. "Who would do a thing like that?"

"I hope that is a thing the police will tell me when they finally get here," Maarten said. "The man who was supposed to be in charge of this place has simply disappeared."

"Well, if he was sitting behind the desk, there can't be much left of him now."

"I've checked carefully," Maarten said. "There is no blood anywhere."

He crossed to the desk as though about to have another look behind it, then turned to sit on the edge of it with his arms crossed in front of his chest. He was smiling now, a bit stiffly.

"Well, my friend," he said. "You didn't come all the way here to help me solve the mystery of this disaster. Which I'm afraid is primarily my fault for not checking into this place sooner than I did."

"You know how things go out here," D.J. said. "Whether it's sooner or later, they're going to get you in the end. As I was telling my friend Tim here, who's new to the territory. Let me introduce you, by the way. Tim. Maarten. Last names don't really matter out here where life is so transient, right? Which is why I never bother with mine. I mean this isn't Bangkok. Or some other social center. Whatever. Anyway, Tim here is just over from the States, you know, sort of looking to find himself, among other things. One of which you may actually be able to help him with if you can give him a moment of your time."

Maarten was studying D.J. with the same steady half-smile, as though nothing D.J. said made the slightest sense to him.

"Tim, the letters please," D.J. said.

Tim handed D.J. the letters out of his back pocket. Maarten smiled at Tim now. Then he lowered his eyes and as a kind of nervous gesture leaned to pick up a statuette lying on its side at the corner of the desk. He set it upright on its base, though it looked seriously damaged. Tim thought the thing was vaguely familiar, probably a copy of something he'd seen in a book, but this didn't seem the right moment to go over there exploring.

"Okay," D.J. said, shuffling the letters. "You've got enough problems of your own this morning as anybody can plainly see, so I'll come right to the point. We wonder if you happen to know a Cambodian lady refugee called Phal Sameth."

Maarten's smile faded. "If you ask the question, you must know perfectly well that I do. Nevertheless, may I ask why you want to know?"

"Because my friend Tim here has some letters he'd like you to deliver to her if it's at all possible. As a favor to some mutual acquaintances in America."

D.J. handed Maarten the letters. Maarten looked at the envelopes carefully, studying the name on each as though it were written out in script that was both beautiful and terribly difficult to read, then handed the letters back.

"Phal Sameth is in Cambodia," he said. "I have no way of getting letters to her."

"Cambodia?" D.J. said.

"Indeed," Maarten said.

"Do you hear that, Tim? Our lady's in Cambodia."

"I can't say I'm exactly surprised," Tim said. "Though don't ask me why I'm not."

"Our lady?" Maarten said. "I don't think I understand."

"Just a manner of speaking," D.J. said. "And what about the lady's daughter, or adopted daughter? Whatever you might call her."

"Thirith?" Maarten said. "Thirith is also in Cambodia. Only not so far inside. Maybe twenty kilometers from here."

"Twenty kilometers?" D.J. said. "That's about where the Vietnamese army is hanging out these days."

"She's actually in a Khmer Serei military outpost just across the border," Maarten said. "But of course that would be in the war zone."

Tim and D.J. looked at each other.

"So what do we do now?" D.J. said.

"I don't know," Tim said. "I guess we'd better take a little more of the gentleman's time to get a couple of things straightened out. And then we'd better have a close look at the map."

———

After three hours of moving through the forest as fast as he could, Polk was tired and thirsty, but one thing he knew he had to talk himself out of was sitting down to rest. He had to make it at least to the top of the

———

ridge ahead, where with any luck he'd get a clear view of the terrain beyond and maybe even find himself a road heading out in the right direction. The trees had begun to thin out; that could be a good sign. He figured he had about two more hours before the sun went down, and he needed the sun, not only for orientation but to see where he was putting his feet. Once it got dark, he would have to give up completely until morning. In a forest where the going was that heavy, he didn't think it likely that he'd run onto any mines, but once you found yourself moving through country that had been crossed regularly by who knows how many different armies, one more insane than the next, there was no telling what kind of shit you might walk into. And at some point he was bound to hit a trail. That was where the fun and games would really begin. But without a trail, there wasn't much chance of finding a road leading out to civilization, in whatever direction civilization might be.

The trouble was, even with the sun to orient you, it helped to know where the fuck you were when you first looked up at it to get your bearings. All he'd had to work with was a general idea. They'd brought him out there in the middle of the night, traveling who knew exactly how long on a dirt road that wandered all over the place and got rougher and rougher, and then they'd locked him up in a human rat cage with no view and so little light he might as well have been blindfolded. All he knew was that Khmers of that color were mostly well north of Aran, and jungle like that meant they'd crossed the border at some point and were well inside enemy territory. East meant Cambodia, west meant Thailand. North and south could both mean trouble, but the only roads leading out of Cambodia in that area that he could remember from his office map were due east of Aran, so common sense told him to head southwest, using the sun to keep him on track as long as the sun allowed.

Once he reached a road out, he had in mind traveling straight to Bangkok. His connection there owed him one. The man might have kept his word in one way, but in another way he'd given him the royal shaft. He must have known that there'd be a problem of diplomacy in handling those crazy Khmers; he could have provided him with a little more background. Anyway, from now on Sam Baugh was staying out of politics. No sweat about Khmer This, That, or The Other. As far as he was concerned they could shove it, one and all. He was not interested in their war anymore, or anybody else's war, for that matter. From now on he was a pacifist. And from now on, business had to be pure business: no more charity work, no more problems of diplomacy, no more confusion about loyalties, political or otherwise.

What he had in mind working out once he got himself safely to Bangkok was some kind of link to the Golden Triangle operation. There was a lot going on up there, and it was completely clean of politics. The local warlords ran things the way they always had, and whatever country in the Triangle they might belong to, they all had the same thing in mind: cultivating their poppies peacefully and getting their crop where it would bring the best price—in short, keeping the lines of trade open and the traffic moving. He was certain he could find a way to contribute his know-how to their operation if his man in Bangkok just gave him a few honest leads. Transportation was still his area of special competence, after all.

Polk saw the light coming on strong up ahead. He figured it must be a clearing of some kind. That could be tricky: easier turf for a while, but you never knew what might have been laid out there by somebody's army to keep people on this side of the border. He decided to stick to the edge of it, circle around it until he had it cased. The sun was coming right at him now through the lower branches ahead as the trees thinned out. He veered south and eased up on the clearing with trees still protecting his left flank. It looked like just a small natural opening in the forest, no purpose that he could see, surely not man-made. It might have had a water hole once, because there was a dip in the middle where the tall grass just seemed to give way, but from where he was standing there was no sign of any water out there now. Still, there might be a trickle of a stream leading into it that wouldn't show unless you were right on top of it. He decided it was worth a look if he took his time getting there, anyway a chance to give his aching legs a minute's break.

He hit the first spread of bones just as he was coming out of the tall grass, stumbled right into them because his eyes were on the dry hole ahead of him. He tried to work around them, but it was hard to find a clean place to step, and in his hurry to get out of there, he struck a skull with his foot and broke off the jawbone. The feel of it stayed inside his shoe as he cut to the left of the hole, heading for the trees on that side of the clearing. He'd barely made his turn before he came on another group of bones, laid out like a skeleton with the skull in the right place but some of the bones half in the ground and others at a weird angle, as though some animal had come along and messed with their natural shape. And they were white, whatever was aboveground, whiter than any bones he'd ever seen.

He was panting when he hit the cover of trees again. He wouldn't want to think he was superstitious the way the local natives were, but a trip like that really freaked him out. He'd seen plenty of dead soldiers in his day—white, black, yellow, whatever—but the bodies of fighting men were one thing and civilian bones that had been lying around unburied long enough to turn that white was another thing. You came out feeling like you'd violated an Indian graveyard full of spirits where no man was meant to tread—no white man anyway. He didn't like that feeling at all. There was no way you could take it for a sign of good luck. On the other hand, thinking about it too much could just mean more trouble. He tried to swing himself into a different rhythm by concentrating on getting himself up to the brow of the ridge with as little expense of energy as possible, one step after another, brushing the foliage clear with his hands as calmly as he could but keeping a sharp eye on the ground immediately in front of him. You just had to take what came and go with it. There was no other way.

The climb to the ridge made him seriously thirsty. He still hadn't managed to pace himself exactly right in his eagerness to get up there and beat the sun. Now it would be mostly downhill for a while. He would take it very slow, go as far as he could but at a much more relaxed pace, try to get his body back to where water was just an idea and not physically essential. He decided to keep to the brow of the ridge for a short distance even if it meant turning due south, because that way he could stay with the view he now had of the slope opposite while the light still held in case something turned up that could pass for a road. His luck came back with his first concentrated sweep of the landscape through a break in the trees: a ribbon of brown winding out of the east and curling into the hill he was looking at for maybe a mile, then vanishing into heavy green. He started angling down there at full speed, then held himself back. Easy. Stay loose. Don't press the thing when it's going your way.

About halfway down he spotted a pickup truck coming out of a bend just before the long curve that brought the road around the base of the hill opposite. He figured the truck was less than a mile away. That made him lose his cool. He took off, careening down the hillside as fast as his tightening legs would move, and when he saw there was no chance of making it to the road in time, he began to yell his head off until that put him completely out of breath. He paused near the bottom to watch the pickup truck grind by and head on around the hill until it was out of sight. He sat down and stared at the road below him. Then he figured what the hell, if one truck had gone by there would be another, and anyway, from where he was sitting you wouldn't have been able to tell whether the thing belonged to a friend or foe. He decided to amble on down there and find himself a lookout point that would give him plenty of time to make up his mind on that score before the next one came down the pike.

He was just about to ease himself into the ditch at the side of the road when he heard a sharp command behind him in an unknown language. He whirled around to find four of them standing there in a row with legs spread, all but the lead man aiming their Kalashnikovs at him where it would hurt most. They looked like regular soldiers, because they were all wearing exactly the same outfit and green berets with a red star, the kind of outfit you sometimes came across during TV news coverage of the Vietnam War. The wrong side of the war. Polk raised his hands halfway and tried to smile, as though with recognition. The lead man looked tired. His eyes above his high, protruding cheekbones had deep rings around them, and when he finally bared his teeth to smile back, what Polk saw was a skull.

———

They had stopped short of the first T.F. 80 checkpoint to switch seats so that Tim could pass himself off as D.J.'s driver both going out and coming back and have a piece of decent road on which to get acquainted with the truck before they headed into no-man's-land. As D.J. opened his door to climb down, Tim reached over and put a hand on his shoulder to hold him there. D.J. slumped back in his seat.

"Now look here," Tim said. "I'm serious. I really don't want you to go out there if your heart isn't in it. I mean this is my private thing and there's no obligation on your part from whatever angle you may care to look at it."

"Heart? How can anybody put his heart into going where at least three different armies are getting set to take pot shots at each other and move in on each other's territory the minute the rains let up enough to allow heavy travel?"

"Well, then, I'd just as soon go by myself."

"Go by yourself? You're mad with border fever. You've got a pass that will get you through the next checkpoint and the one after Ban Nong Samet and then what have you got? Diddly shit. You don't know two words of Thai or Khmer. And even if you knew some relevant language, how do you expect to get yourself into a Khmer Serei military outpost with enough of your head still in place to explain what an American is doing out there beyond the border in a truck he doesn't own looking for a

Khmer girl he's never even met but hopes to send to college in the land of milk and honey?"

"I'll find a way," Tim said. "You don't have to worry about me."

"No, you won't find a way. Not without D.J. you won't. So as things have now worked out, it seems I don't have any choice but to go along with you. Only I'm not going to pretend I like it. In fact, the idea scares the bejesus out of me."

"Well, I can't say I like the idea much myself," Tim said. "But after coming this far, I'm not going to give up. I mean the idea of giving up sits worse with me than going out there into no-man's-land."

"Good," D.J. said. "I'm glad you've got your priorities straightened out clearly like that. If I had any choice my first priority would be to head back to Aran and spend a long evening trying to figure out why this trip is so goddamn necessary."

"It isn't necessary for you," Tim said. "I mean that."

"I'm sure you do mean it, lad. But let me ask you just one question. Suppose you make your way out there and luck into finding somebody who speaks English and who's willing to dig up the girl for you. What do you do then?"

"I just give it to her straight. No problem. Your friend Maarten said her English is pretty near as good as his. So I just tell her that my old man would like to arrange for her to get herself an education in America."

D.J. smiled at him. "So she says what a lovely idea, puts her gun away and packs her things and climbs in your truck to head for the cherry blossoms of Washington, D.C., or the California sunset or whatever, right?"

"I don't see what's so funny about that," Tim said. "You're the one who claims you haven't yet met a refugee out here of either sex who wouldn't give an arm and a leg to get themselves to the States. California most of all."

"I'm not talking about whether she wants to go. Sure she wants to go. Who wouldn't? Burger King Whoppers and Dairy Queen Specials to go with all the rice you can eat? The point is, how do you get her there?"

"That's for my old man to figure out. Maybe with Dubois's help. I mean they're in the visa business."

"So what do you do with her while you're waiting for your old man to take her off your hands?"

Tim studied him. "I don't know. I figured you might have some thoughts on that score."

245

D.J. shook his head. "You're really something else, you know that? One minute you say you'll find a way all by yourself and it's not necessary for me to go along and the next minute you're handing me the not-inconsiderable problem of transporting an illegal entrant from no-man's-land to Bangkok and getting her settled in somewhere."

"Bangkok? Who said Bangkok?"

"Well, just tell me where else you figure on hiding a refugee you've more or less kidnapped from a military outpost beyond the border and brought back into the country more or less illegally. You wouldn't want her hanging around in Aran, would you?"

"I don't know," Tim said. "I guess I hadn't figured that far. But Bangkok is all right by me if you think that's best."

"Good. I'm glad we're in full agreement about that. Now, where in Bangkok would you suggest we take her?"

"I wouldn't want to presume to suggest," Tim said. "I mean you obviously know Bangkok a hell of a lot better than I do."

"But you could always find someplace to put her if you had to, right?"

"Well, if you really have to do something, you haven't got much choice but to do it, as far as I can see."

"Okay," D.J. said, "I guess there's no way I can win. You probably would find someplace, too. The fact that I happen to have an in at the Transit Center on Wireless Road is just a piece of luck somebody like you wouldn't consider really necessary but maybe a thing that could come in handy once you've arrived at the point where you've got to do what you've got to do, right?"

"You don't have to get all worked up about it," Tim said. "I'm perfectly ready to look around for a place once we get to Bangkok."

D.J. was staring at him. "You know, there just aren't that many places you can safely hide a refugee in Bangkok. I mean even the place I have in mind will depend on our being able to bribe the right people. But what do I know? With your luck you'd probably find you could shack up with her at the Oriental and get away with it."

"I don't know why you keep saying that I'm so lucky. I'm really no more lucky than the next man. The next American, anyway."

"No? Well you're lucky enough to have found a sucker like me to go along with you on this crazy trip. Which is more luck than you can say I've had in many a moon, my friend. Except maybe what I've picked up since I started traveling with you."

246

D.J. climbed down and came around the front of the truck. He stood outside Tim's door until Tim finally slid over into the driver's seat. Once D.J. was settled in he took off his seaman's cap and tried to brush his hair flat with his hand. It still looked like cat fur that had been in and out of a serious fight, so he borrowed a comb to work on it some more. Then he took off the blue bandana he was wearing around his neck.

"Okay, from now on I'm the volag official and you're my driver," D.J. said. "You don't talk in the presence of others. You just smile back very sincerely when anybody smiles at you."

"What do I do about my pass?"

"You show it at the checkpoints and then you forget about it. Where we're going, passes won't do either of us much good. Once we're out there beyond Samet and the Thai military, we rely on my Naval Reserve card. Or my American Express Card. Or any luck that you happen to have left that you can share."

Tim gave the gears another dry run, then checked out the four-wheel drive. The clutch gave him trouble as he started off, coming in so late that he had to grant it a lot more faith than he was used to. D.J. was watching him sideways, his nose crinkled.

"Now try it with your shoes on," he said. "And for God's sake start smiling."

There was no problem at the first checkpoint. While the soldier on duty was still struggling to read the passes, the officer in charge recognized D.J. and came over from the guard stand to wave them on. D.J. said something meant for a joke, but the officer wasn't in a mood to smile back. And even the mood of the landscape seemed to change as soon as they turned off the main road and headed up toward the Samet encampments on a narrower dirt road that had been wounded in places by the heavy rains. There was a canal by the road and rice fields out there, but for some reason there were no people working in them, and though the hills were kilometers away in any direction, allowing for open country, there didn't seem to be much planned cultivation, the trees sparse and casually placed—here papaya, there banana or coconut—no sign of animals, the whole giving you the feeling of land that had been taken up for a while and then suddenly abandoned. And the village they came to had the bleak look of one of the older refugee camps now being evacuated, except that the wooden houses were on pile stilts and there was fencing around them to keep the cattle in. You could see the occasional dog or chicken running free through the village dirt and naked children playing in the mud where rainwater had gathered, but the working villagers were elsewhere, either asleep inside the houses or out in the fields in makeshift huts still trying to escape the afternoon sun.

Beyond the village they turned east toward the encampments, and the farther in they went, the more desolate the landscape became, the sense of openness closing in on you gradually as the trees began to show up in clusters and the fields became smaller, hedged in by brush left to grow wild. Tim slowed for the black-market checkpoint, but that too seemed deserted, and when they crossed the dry moat meant for a tank trap, the gun emplacements along its rampart all looked empty. The only life on that section of road was at the last T.F. 80 guard stand, where there were more than the usual number of soldiers watching the invisible border ahead. This time D.J. decided to wear his hat in case that roused somebody to recognize him. When he stuck his head out the window on his side and saluted the stand, the soldier in charge came out and waved them on. But he wouldn't smile either.

They hit the first encampment just before the trees thickened into a forest. It was a new encampment, D.J. said, another spillover from the main one that had cropped up before his last trip out there, and people were still coming into it from the border area to the north, a line of them two abreast held to the side of the road by what looked like armed civilians wearing fatigue caps. Tim slowed and then stopped to let them pass. The first rows were made up mostly of young women, all carrying heavy sacks on their shoulders or sometimes on their heads, all standing up very straight and moving with a graceful swing as though to show that the weight they were carrying just made for another asset, no sign of any emotion in their faces. They turned off the road as they were about to come alongside the truck and entered the field they were heading for, half of it already filled with the young and the old huddled in groups under swaybacked canopies made of blue plastic sheets held up by bamboo poles. D.J. was watching the line of marchers at the point where it turned off the road.

"You see a thing like that," he said, "and it makes you think it's worth any trouble trying to rescue one of them for the land of the free and the home of the brave."

"A thing like what?"

"The way they walk. They don't know where on God's earth they're going, at this point surely no place you and I would want to go, and still they walk like that."

When the road split in front of the main encampment they took the northern branch, and when it split again they turned east into what had become dense forest on both sides of the road. The sun was in back of them now, and the shadows had started coming in to slow them, forming a messy patchwork with the ruts left over from one rain or another. Keeping east at the next fork meant that they had to choose the branch that was hardly wider than the truck itself, a rough swath hacked out between the trees that would have given an oxcart trouble if it was a place oxen might go. There were tree stumps here and there and loose logs lying around, and the ground underneath was not always firm. When Tim had to go into four-wheel drive to make it up the first short incline, D.J. decided to take time out for a look at the map.

"We're well beyond the border now for sure," he said. "So if Maarten knows what he's talking about, the guerrilla outpost shouldn't be more than a few kilometers farther in. That is, if we're on the right road."

"Well, he said to keep going east after the encampment, and that's what we've been doing if the sun is in the right place."

"Unless we turned too soon. But I don't think so. The Khmer Serei military never lets itself get too far out from base camp, so I say we go with it another kilometer or two."

Less than a kilometer down the road they hit the first really wet spot. Tim put the truck into four-wheel drive and gunned it through, swinging sideways and then back and sideways again as though on a Dodgem track. He made it out heading in the right direction but had to cut to one side suddenly and found himself moving sideways again. At the next wet spot he gave himself more speed coming in and blasted on through almost in a straight line until he hit a stump hidden by the mud and got his front wheels at a bad angle. He had to work hard to keep from thinning out trees along the side of the road as he came onto firmer ground again.

"Maybe you'd better take over," Tim said. "I've never had to drive through a logging operation like this."

"You're doing fine," D.J. said. "You can't help what you can't see."

Another five hundred yards and the road ended in a crude turnaround. Off to one side there was a cleared strip where two military trucks and a jeep were parked in a row. Through the trees ahead you could see huts with thatched roofs and a grove of what looked like suspended hammocks. Two soldiers with automatic rifles were standing in the trees just beyond the turnaround. The rifles weren't exactly aimed, but it was clear the pickup truck had them interested.

"Welcoming party doesn't seem to know who we are," D.J. said. "I'd better go out and greet them and you'd better just keep low."

He took off his hat and ran a hand through his hair, then opened the door on his side and jumped down. The soldiers hadn't moved a muscle. When D.J. reached for his wallet, both rifles came up to the ready.

"Okay," Tim heard D.J. say as he raised his hands wide. "No American Express Card. Just love and kisses."

Whatever banter he came up with worked to get his hands lowered again. The three of them went off through the trees to the clearing with the hammocks. Tim relaxed back in his seat. He closed his eyes and tried to talk himself into being cool enough to doze off, but there was no way he could make himself cool. His idea of what he was going to say to the girl was one thing, but the actual language he might use, the approach you made to somebody so completely a stranger, seemed out of reach the more he thought about it. And he wasn't even planning to get very far into the business of how she might get herself to the States and what she might do once she got there. That was really up to his old man after they got her to Bangkok. It was enough to have to persuade her to go where D.J. had in mind putting her up for a while. How was he going to do that? Sure, playing it cool, taking one step at a time, waiting to see what the gods had in store was fine until you got down to facing the live stranger you actually had to talk to. D.J. might be able to dance his way through it. There was no way he himself could.

When D.J. came back there were three soldiers with him. The one walking ahead beside him didn't have a gun. They held up at the turn-around. D.J. stood there talking to the soldier beside him, glancing out at the forest every now and then as though wary of an ambush, then came over to the truck on Tim's side.

"The lady you're looking for is apparently in some kind of trouble," he said. "That fellow over there seems to be the camp leader in charge of her. And he won't let us in there to see her."

"Jesus," Tim said. "What's she done?"

"Can't tell exactly," D.J. said. "My Khmer isn't good enough to get the whole story. Seems she disobeyed orders, whether this guy's or some-body else's. Anyway, he's very curt about her. His way of explaining where she's at is to point at his head. Which could mean that she's crazy or could mean that she thinks too much, I suppose equally dangerous for a lady soldier trying to make a life of it out here in the jungle."

"Well, what do we do now? Head back empty-handed?"

"Maybe I could bribe our way into seeing her for a minute. If you think there's any point."

"Well, it's better than heading back completely empty-handed. I mean how much do you think it will cost?"

"No idea. I'll have to check it out with this Mr. Tao Lome or whatever his name is."

D.J. turned away from the truck and motioned the unarmed soldier to come on over. The soldier hesitated, then came partway into the turn-around. D.J. went over to talk to him, the two of them standing there half-facing each other, D.J. gesticulating to the air around him as he searched for vocabulary, the soldier gazing at the military trucks one minute and at D.J. the next. The more they talked, the more it looked as if they were bargaining over some kind of black-market exchange. One of the two armed soldiers became restless, shifting feet, every now and then glancing over a shoulder toward the camp. The other had his eyes square on the pickup truck, standing at the ready with legs spread as though he thought it might take off over his head any second and have to be brought down like a helicopter. When D.J. finally turned back toward the truck, the two armed soldiers came over to flank the third, though a good step behind him.

D.J. climbed into his seat. Then he reached for his hat.

"Mr. Tao Lome seems to be a man of principle. Much offended by any talk of money. So having a word with the lady is a definite no-no."

Tim studied him. "Well, I guess that's that."

"Not exactly," D.J. said. "I told you the gentleman is a man of principle. He said the only way we could talk to her was by putting her in our truck and taking her away from here. He didn't seem to care where."

"You're kidding."

"That's what the man said. I get the distinct impression that the problem he's got with her is a problem he'd just as soon get off his hands as quickly and quietly as possible. And the problem is more personal than military."

"Well, let's grab her and get out of here."

"Not so easy. That's just what we can't do. He's got to get the lady's consent. Anyway her cooperation. And then he's got to get her out of the camp the back way, I suppose to make it look as though she took off on her own. He said we should go a kilometer down the road and just wait. If she doesn't show up inside the next hour, we're to keep going and forget the whole thing. So what do you say?"

"I don't see that we have any choice but to go down there and wait."

"Well, you've got to realize that relieving him of his problem puts it right back on your head."

"Not mine. My old man's."

"No. Yours. You'd better face it. Once she's in the truck you're stuck with her whether your old man helps out or not."

Tim looked at him. "Whatever, then."

"So we go for it? The point is, if I don't get down to tell the man otherwise, we're in business."

"Sure," Tim said. "We go for it. I mean we really can't do anything else at this point."

As he turned on the ignition, D.J. leaned out and saluted the soldiers. The three of them backed up and stood there watching the truck maneuver out of the turnaround. In his rearview mirror Tim saw the unarmed soldier heading back through the trees toward the camp. D.J. leaned over to note their starting point on the odometer.

A kilometer down the road put them nowhere in particular: a fairly straight stretch with the usual dense forest on both sides and nothing to distinguish the place that either of them could see. Tim pulled over as far as he could and cut the engine.

"So now we just sit?" Tim said.

"Did you remember to bring along the Parcheesi?"

"The what?"

"You're no fun," D.J. said. "Too young for me and the wrong upbringing. I'm going to catch a little shut-eye in case something as lovable as last night's angel drifts into my life again."

He put his hat over his face and leaned into the corner. When he started breathing heavily, Tim realized he'd meant what he said. He tried out his own corner, but it was no good. He kept finding reasons to look out at the forest so that he could end up looking at his watch. Forty-five minutes into D.J.'s snooze he heard something moving through the trees behind them, the sound a deer might make easing into the open. In the rearview mirror he saw her come out on the road a short distance back and head toward the truck with a bundle of clothes on her head. She was in uniform, with bandoliers crossing to form an X between her breasts. He recognized the style of her walk, the bearing, but the look of her face was another thing: girlish in its roundness, no rough lines that he could see, the lips and cheeks full, the whole distinctly Khmer but prettier for his taste than what you normally came across, and then a sharpness in the eyes, a sternness, that gave the face what you had to call authority—ten, fifteen years beyond the age the features made it out to be. There was no way he could tell how old she actually was, surely older than he'd assumed, and he found that look of hers a little frightening. He reached over and nudged D.J. awake.

"Our lady soldier," Tim said.

D.J. looked in the mirror on his side. "Isn't that something? You see what I mean about the draw you get? Now haul your ass out there and help the lady climb in back so the two of you can get acquainted. You're going to have to spend a lot of rough time together."

Thirith stopped in her tracks as Tim hit the ground. She stood there rigid watching him. He sauntered over and put out his hand.

"I'm Tim," he said. "And that's my friend D.J. hanging out the window."

She stared at Tim's hand as though it were half eaten away by leprosy.

He put out the other hand. "Let me take your things."

"No," she said. "I want to know where you are taking me."

"Well, that all depends," Tim said. "I mean it's really a thing we ought to talk over a bit."

"I must know," Thirith said. "I can't believe what Tao Lom tells me anymore."

"Well, let's say Bangkok," Tim said. "At least for a start."

"And then?"

"Who knows?"

"No, I must know. If you can't tell me, then I will have to go back and kill him."

"Well, let's not get ourselves too worked up here. How about America? I mean as a general idea."

"America," Thirith said. "So he didn't lie to me completely. And what am I to do in America?"

"We'll have to chat about that. Why don't you just let me help you climb in back here and maybe we can talk about it on the way to Bangkok?"

She lowered her bundle to the ground but didn't move an inch.

"What do you mean by general idea?"

"Well, that's the thing," Tim said. "The specifics will require a little working out."

"He said I was to train to become a doctor and then return here."

"A doctor?"

"You see. I knew he was lying."

"It takes years to become a doctor," Tim said.

253

He reached down and took up her bundle and hauled it to the rear of the truck. He let the back down and stood there waiting. Thirith finally came up opposite him.

"He said in America people can study to become whatever they want to be. Of course I knew he was lying."

"Well, now, let's not jump to conclusions," Tim said. "I mean anything is possible. Even these days."

D.J. had crossed over to the driver's seat and was leaning out the window again on that side.

"Yo, there," he said. "I mean whether or not America the beautiful is still the land of opportunity, we'd better haul ass out of here before the Vietnamese move in to make the whole question beside the point for us. So anytime you people are ready."

Tim stood there looking at her. Yes, she was something. He felt himself going shy when she looked straight at him even if her look wasn't shy at all.

"So," he said. "What say we climb in?"

He made a half-gesture toward helping her up. She gave her head a little sideways motion, a kind of shrug that seemed to mean the thing was more or less settled in her mind, then raised herself up to sit on the back of the truck and swung her legs in neatly as though she'd been traveling that way all her life. When D.J. started the engine, Tim climbed in and sat on the bench opposite her, the bundle on the floor between them. Once they were settled in, there didn't seem to be anything more for the two of them to say to each other, though she kept on looking at him with what he read as a mixture of curiosity and suspicion, as though he were a new kind of animal with really interesting fur but possibly dangerous. D.J. now had the truck weaving down the road at such a fast clip that each of them had to hang on to the open grillwork with one hand and the bench with the other to stay upright. D.J. took the truck through the first wet spot mostly sideways, but he made it out hardly slowing down. His luck gave out on the second one: the truck glanced off a stump on the way in, and recovering from that slowed the thing down enough to get it stuck just as it was about to clear the last patch of deep ruts. D.J. got down and took a turn around the truck to have a look. Then Tim and Thirith got down too He'd put them in there up to the hubs on the driver's side.

"I guess there's no way but to fill in the patch behind," he said. "So I can back well onto it and get up some speed."

"How do you plan on filling it?" Tim said. "Looks to me like that would eat up a truckload of dirt."

"One uses branches," Thirith said. "One doesn't use dirt."

"The lady's right," D.J. said. "So let's get with it. Go for whatever you can find that has a lot of leaves."

The three of them turned off in different directions. Thirith took out what looked like a hunting knife and went for a tree beside the truck. She had an armful of small branches laid out on the patch by the time Tim got back with the load he'd picked up. D.J. had found himself a small tree thick with leaves that had been cleared from the side of the road ahead and dumped back into the woods. He was dragging it back to the road by one of its branches when the thing happened. The trunk end must have run over a mine and set it off, because D.J. was suddenly knocked clear of the trees and out to the edge of the road holding only a piece of the branch he had a grip on. When Tim and Thirith got to him, he had dropped the branch and was holding his left leg with both hands just above the ankle, his face tight with pain.

"I don't want to look down there," he said. "Is it as bad as I think?"

"Jesus," Tim said, squatting.

Thirith was already beside the leg cutting the pantleg free to the knee. The bones above the ankle were broken through and exposed, but the foot was still attached. The blood was pumping and flooding out now, and you could see other wounds farther up the skin. Thirith had taken the bandana from around her neck and was twisting it into a tourniquet.

"It's going to be all right," Tim said to D.J., "don't you worry," but his voice didn't come out the way it should have. D.J. had his eyes closed. His face had begun to change color.

"A stick," Thirith said. "Any stick."

Tim took the branch D.J. had been holding and broke off the end. She had his leg in her lap now and was tightening the tourniquet just below the knee.

"Hold it there," she said.

He held the stick where she had set it, and as she raised the leg he could see that the blood had slowed. She took off the sash that was wound around her head and began to tear it into strips, using her knife when she had to. She positioned the ankle on her thigh so that it was supported there and cut the laces on D.J.'s jogging shoe, then eased it off. D.J. was moaning now. She used the first strips to bind the ankle so that the foot was held in the right place; then she reached back and searched the ground around her until she found two sticks that could serve for a splint. When she had them bound to the ankle and the shin, she let the leg lie across her thighs and undid her belt so that she could take off her bandoliers. Tim reached over to help her with that but she shook him off. She tied the bandoliers together at both ends, her hands working with fast precision, then took the tourniquet stick from Tim and fixed it so that it wouldn't unwind. She handed him one end of the tied bandoliers.

"We use this to get him to the truck," she said.

She eased out from under D.J. and knelt to pass the bandoliers under his back, then gave one end to Tim so that the two of them could work the bandoliers down in rhythm until they were under D.J.'s buttocks and spread to shape a sling. Then she raised D.J.'s back so that he was sitting up and knelt beside him to put his arm around her neck and to hook the sling around her inside elbow. She motioned to Tim to do the same. They lifted D.J. together until he was sitting in the sling with his legs hanging free; then they moved off carefully to the rear of the truck. D.J. still had his eyes closed, breathing fast, his face pale now, grayish, but you could see it come alive every now and then to tense against the pain.

"He is very lucky," Thirith said when they got the back of the truck lowered. "If he had struck the mine himself, there would be no foot left."

They edged him up on the truck and Tim held him there while Thirith climbed in to lay out the two bench cushions as a mattress. Gently but steadily she swung his legs in, and with Tim hoisting at his end, got him partly on the mattress. Then she took the sling and rigged it to the grating to help her keep the leg high. She sat on the floor and worked her hips gradually under his thighs to cushion him against the road.

"You know the Red Cross center near Aranyaprathet?" she said.

Tim nodded. "I think so."

He was down working on the branches, getting them placed up against the rear wheels.

"Go," Thirith said. She sounded irritated.

"I want to get this set up so we don't find ourselves stuck again."

"Go," she said. "There is no time."

But he didn't head for the driver's seat until he had the branches laid out both close up and far enough back to give him the distance he knew he needed.

The first twinge of something like nostalgia hit Macpherson soon after he turned into Wireless Road and headed down toward the American Embassy. Returning to the Erawan Hotel after four years had done nothing for him but dredge up disturbing recollections from his short stay there after the evacuation, when, fresh off the rescue aircraft carrier, he'd been cut by a sense of belonging to a world that was not only out-of-date and irrelevant, but sometimes conspicuously indifferent to its anachronism. Yet back then he had nevertheless found himself taking tea by the pool as though tea in the British mode were plausible for an American with French perfume still alive in various corners of his flesh, walking in white ducks down corridors that smelled of empire-building and obsequious service, paying exorbitant prices for simple, unnecessary souvenirs as though out of noblesse oblige, all because he'd been too disoriented and soul-sore to care about resisting the style of the place.

Not doing any of those things this time, playing the disinterested observer, had merely made the stodginess more pronounced and boring. Then the traffic out front, the bad air, the streets filthy even though the rainy season wasn't quite dead. Once out there he'd decided against taking a cab because he was early for his meeting with Dubois and it looked as though he'd get to the Embassy faster by walking there anyway, but as soon as he'd started to take in the stench of the morning rush hour—when wasn't it rush hour in Bangkok?—it struck him that he'd made a serious mistake not to have accepted Dubois's offer of an air-conditioned car for the few days he planned to be in that fume-ripe city, even if his brief business was essentially personal.

On Wireless Road things had opened out a bit and he'd begun to sense that he was in more tolerable territory, not only more comfortable but somehow directly familiar. And then, as he'd looked around, he'd suddenly felt a sensation that was totally inexplicable in that context: it was as though he'd come into a known neighborhood and passed a house he'd forgotten was there but recognized as one he used to go to when he was in love with somebody who lived behind windows where the blinds were now closed. Nothing that he saw around him had any possible reason to be suggestive in that way, though he did recognize the guardhouse at the gate to the Ambassador's Residence, and instead of taking his cue from that to begin weaving a path through the stalled traffic beside him and across to the Embassy side of the street, he decided to stick to the side he was on for a while to see if that might clue him in to what he'd felt.

He was down opposite the Embassy by the time he'd worked back through the thing to its source on that first day in Bangkok following the evacuation, when he'd taken the same route for a long walk after checking in at the Embassy and then returning to the hotel to rest up for his evening at the Residence. The walk had not been pleasant. At that time there had been no way he could win the argument with himself about the necessity of leaving Cambodia, however unassailably logical the idea was. And the logic was still there: if you believed the United States should get out of Southeast Asia before it did more damage to itself and others, then there was no choice in the matter but to get out of both Vietnam and Cambodia as quickly and cleanly as you could, and that was exactly what he had done his damnedest to arrange in his area of responsibility. Yet the logic of it, the moral and political and whatever rightness of it, did not jibe at all with the emotion that had been building in him that day from the moment he got into that evacuation helicopter. What he'd actually felt was not even a remote hint of moral righteousness—that had come much later, when the rationale for his action had jelled over a period of some months—but a large measure of guilt at having to abandon a people he'd come to love.

And of course not just a people. That admission to himself had been the turning point in his walk. He'd managed until that point, maybe through some process of psychological self-protection, to carry on his inner debate in general terms, national terms, which no doubt made the guilt more abstract, more impersonal, finally more bearable. But it hadn't held that way long enough, because a block or two into Wireless Road on that first afternoon, the day's long effort to keep some distance collapsed completely. A sharp mental picture of Chien Fei had interrupted his train of thought to kill all further abstraction. She was standing at the window of her apartment looking out on Phnom Pehn under siege with her back turned to him so that he couldn't see her face, and she wouldn't turn around, as though too proud to show him what she might be feeling, or simply indifferent now to what he might think. And that picture had led to others, some made up and some not, until he'd found himself straining with whatever self-control he had left to keep the tears back.

He'd suppressed this painful moment on Wireless Road in the aftermath of his transit stop in Bangkok four years ago, again maybe out of necessary self-protection—the quick cure you had to go through if you were going to move on to a new post and work there effectively. Its return now was without passion, for all the remnant hurt and self-doubt in it. He'd gone his way as he had to, and she'd gone hers. The fact was that if he'd somehow tried to follow through on the wild impulse to stay behind with her that had come to him during their last night together, she would surely have talked him out of it before he'd gotten very far. That kind of choice was not in his character, she would have said, not at all in keeping with his Anglo-Saxon sense of responsibility, and she would have been right. The fact that it might have been in her character, that it was much more her kind of thing than his, would no doubt have divided them eventually anyway.

He'd been tempted to say something along those lines to Tan Yong after learning that their friend had made up her mind in mid-June to go back to Cambodia in search of her adopted daughter—a thing that could be taken to prove his point. But he'd decided then, and still thought it right, that any comment from him about the relation of character to hard choices might be misinterpreted by Tan Yong as belated self-justification. The mood that noon had already become tense enough by the time they'd moved on to the cafeteria. From the start Tan Yong had obviously been nervous about how to handle what he seemed to think was a new and embarrassing revelation of his continuing link with Chien Fei—or Phal Sameth, as he still insisted on calling her—and he himself had been equally nervous about how to show the right mixture of surprise and indifference when he really felt neither.

Anyway, he had to admit that it had been gentlemanly of Tan Yong to let him have a look at the second installment of their friend's diary in view of the personal coloring that she'd brought into at least a part of what he'd read—even if Tan Yong kept on calling it "the document" to cloak the fact that it was a rather intimate account specifically addressed to him alone. But the decency behind the gesture had been rather muted by the man's implicit expectation that he become pushy enough to move into State Department areas strictly not his own. Besides, he could hardly push the sort of case for mass refugee relief that Tan Yong apparently had in mind without raising laughter that would be heard all the way from Foggy Bottom to Capitol Hill.

Tan Yong wasn't naive. He knew that the great American frontier had closed long ago. Macpherson figured all that talk about large-scale refugee resettlement had really been a plot to get him on the defensive so that he couldn't refuse to follow up on the other, more personal issue that had occupied them during their brief lunch: what this volag director who had been Chien Fei's last "contact" in Thailand—to put it euphemistically—might know about her travel plans once she'd crossed back into Cambodia. Tan Yong had left him no way out on that issue after he'd been maneuvered into showing himself ready to explore the feasibility of a quick personal trip to Bangkok. At that point anything less than a promise to visit the border if necessary to look the man up and check out the situation would have made him appear more indifferent than he was regarding the fate of both Chien Fei and the refugees in general. So whether or not he managed to track Tim down before he had to get himself back to Cyprus and points west, it seemed he was now committed to spending at least a day in the border area so that he could first find and then interview this Maarten Ruyter.

He had to give Tan Yong credit for instincts that were purer than his own: when a situation is hopeless, a loss irretrievable, final gestures are all that remain to show where your heart could have been. Talking to this Maarten Ruyter was apparently the only gesture, vicarious or otherwise, that either of them could still make in the lost cause of Chien Fei, alias Phal Sameth. And if talking to him might not prove the easiest of assignments, this last trip to the Thai–Cambodian border nevertheless could be seen to have a certain symbolic value, the essential completion of the circle, however inconsequential in practical terms. After it was over, he might be able to put both Thailand and Cambodia behind him once and for all, if not exactly with a clear conscience, then at least with a sense of finally having done the best he could to avoid simply sweeping the last of the dirt under the carpet. It was now up to Dubois to see to it that getting hold first of Tim and then of Maarten Ruyter didn't become an ordeal that made you think new furies had been unleashed out there to collect some ultimate installment due for those necessary betrayals four years ago in another country.

Macpherson crossed over to the Embassy side of Wireless Road and headed on up to the guard post at a fast pace, not because there was any particular need to hurry but because he always moved faster than normal when he'd put something at rest in his mind, as though a fast pace were the physical evidence of his mental resolution. The guard was apparently expecting him: he gave a sharp salute after returning Macpherson's diplomatic passport, then told him by name to sign the register, then put in a call to Dubois without being asked to as he handed him a pass. Macpherson changed his pace to business as usual for the walk over to the chancery. Dubois was waiting inside at the foot of the stairs.

"You can relax," he said, extending his hand. "I've found Tim finally. And I've traced your Maarten Ruyter to his new headquarters outside Aranyaprathet."

"I knew you'd track them down," Macpherson said. "Don't I look relaxed?"

"You look fine," Dubois said. "Really fine. But then, you always did."

"You're looking pretty good yourself," Macpherson said. "Lost some weight, right?"

"Well, let's say so," Dubois said. "Lost some hair, anyway."

He led him on up the stairs and down a corridor to a room with a secretary at either end of it, then into a smaller office off to one side. It was overcrowded with filing cabinets and papers stacked on chairs. Dubois cleared a seat and gestured Macpherson into it.

"If it's all right by you, let's sit here a minute and take care of the personal business before we make our courtesy rounds and get into matters of state, capital S or otherwise, okay?"

"Absolutely," Macpherson said. "So tell me how you finally managed to track Tim down."

"He's at the Nana Hotel," Dubois said. "But just how he got there is a tale I'm not sure I fully understand myself. The boy wasn't exactly loquacious on the subject, I have to say. Probably still thinks of me as part of the military-industrial complex or something."

"The Nana Hotel? Isn't that supposed to be a glorified brothel?"

"Only on the lower floors. If you get up high enough, you're fairly safe if you really want to behave yourself."

"Why would he choose to hole up in a place like that?"

"I think it's the only place in Bangkok he really knows," Dubois said. "And I suppose it's just as well, because otherwise I might not have found him until he got around to showing up here for help of one kind or another."

"He might at least have taken the time to make a phone call to the Embassy. To let you know how things were going. I mean after you went to the trouble of getting him out to the border."

"Anyway, when word finally came in from Aranyaprathet that he'd left for the big city several days ago, the Nana Hotel was the only place I could think of to begin looking for him. And there the dear boy was."

"Doing what exactly?"

"That's the thing," Dubois said. "How can I put this in the best possible light? With one hand he's helping a friend recover from a serious accident that he seems to think was partly his fault and with the other he's helping to harbor an illegal entrant."

"Then I can't really blame him for wanting to hide out."

"I don't think he wants to hide out from you," Dubois said. "In fact I think he's sort of counting on you to help him out of his—what shall I call it?—his awkward situation. You see, the illegal entrant is the so-called daughter of your former lady friend in Phnom Penh, if I can call her that without offense."

"Tim found the daughter?"

"So it seems. Not only found her, but got her settled into the Lumpini Transit Center just a little ways down the road from here."

Macpherson was staring at Dubois. "Now how the hell did he do that?"

"I'm afraid I can't really tell you because that's the part of the story that isn't entirely clear to me. You'll have to get the details from Tim. If he's willing to tell you. All I know is that the three of them turned up at the ICRC headquarters in Aran after the accident that almost cost the friend his foot. Then they were taken in by a group of Irish nurses out there until the fellow with the injured leg, who goes by the name of D.J., could be transferred to the Police Hospital opposite your hotel. My guess is that D.J.'s the one who somehow arranged for the daughter to get herself into the Transit Center, since he knows just about everybody in the refugee business out here, Thai, Khmer, or otherwise. My assumption is that he bribed—"

"Okay, okay," Macpherson said. "Let's not worry about the details for the time being. Do you happen to know where the daughter is in transit to?"

Dubois sat back in his chair. "I'd say nowhere at the moment. She hasn't got any legitimate papers. But I get the impression Tim thinks you might be able to help change all that."

"I guess that doesn't really surprise me," Macpherson said.

"I think he has in mind trying to get her settled into the great melting pot."

"You mean as a resident refugee?"

"I don't really know," Dubois said, sitting up again. "You'll have to check that out with him yourself. I took the liberty of suggesting that he drop in on you at the Erawan for afternoon tea. That should give you plenty of time to figure out what line you're going to take."

"Well, I don't quite see how he thinks he can get her a green card when she doesn't have any relatives over there. I mean a student visa is one thing and refugee status in anticipation of citizenship is quite another. As I don't have to tell you."

"I get the impression he hopes you might take the place of a relative. Act as her sponsor in one way or another. I tried to explain that it isn't quite that simple when it comes to refugees under a strict quota, but you know Tim."

"Well, I do and I don't. But that's not really for you to worry about.

I mean this is really none of your problem. I'll just have to handle it as best I can."

"I appreciate your letting me off the hook," Dubois said. "Because I need your help with another problem that really is mine and that also involves you in some way I can't explain."

Macpherson turned to look at him. "What's that?"

"Have you ever heard of a character named Sam Baugh?"

"Sam Baugh? As in Sammy Baugh?"

"That's it. He came out here a short while ago and got himself a job as a kind of field director out in Aran for your friend Maarten Ruyter."

"Never heard of the man. Baugh, I mean."

"Well, a report crossed my desk from one of our people monitoring the Vietnamese radio out of Cambodia, and it seems the Vietnamese military across the border from Aran claim to have captured an American spy named Ball. Since this Baugh disappeared from the new headquarters out there recently after some kind of raid that still remains a mystery to the Thai police, we figure Baugh and Ball must be the same man."

"Sounds plausible to me," Macpherson said.

"But you're sure you've never heard of him."

"Not that I can remember. Anyway, the name sounds a bit phony. The Baugh part, anyway."

Dubois reached into his top desk drawer. "You may have something there. Which is why I need your help. Because here's one of the items found among the man's personal effects that were left behind in the headquarters after it was raided. You'll see that your name appears in that book with the address changed several times. Just about all the addresses in there are from the Washington area."

He passed the address book across the desk. Macpherson turned to his name and studied it. Then he started going through the thing page by page. He finally looked up.

"Jesus," he said. "It must be Polk."

"So you do know the man?"

"Yeah, I'm afraid I know the man. Under a different name."

"Well, if he's one of ours, meaning the boys who hang out upstairs, we have a serious problem on our hands, though not an insoluble one. If he isn't, I'm afraid there's not a damn thing anybody can do for him."

"No, he isn't one of ours in the way you mean it," Macpherson said. "At least not as far as I know. Besides, the FBI was looking for him."

"Would you care to tell me off the record how your name got into his address book and how you happen to know so much about him? I mean I thought I'd better check that out with you before heading upstairs with some of this stuff."

"I appreciate that," Macpherson said. "What are you doing for lunch?"

The waiter was standing several discreet paces away from the table and slightly behind his new customers, trying to keep his eyes neutral, neither on them nor on the two girls in bikinis by the poolside, their long legs and tight bellies so white for that late in the summer that he couldn't imagine any climate northern enough to produce skin like that and keep it so pale. He also couldn't imagine what sort of relationship there might be between the two men he was waiting to serve, the older, gray-haired one dressed in a light blue summer suit of the kind Americans wore, with a clean white shirt and a red silk tie, and the younger, blond-haired one wearing a yellow T-shirt with a red-and-white bandana around his neck, tight blue jeans, and green shoes of the kind foreigners used for running. He hadn't seen the two of them come in together, but they'd been sitting there talking for a while, and they never seemed to look each other straight in the face except for a glance now and then. He decided that they were pickup lovers and things were not going well between then, good reason to keep his distance until they actually called him over.

"You don't have to have tea," Macpherson said. "You can have anything you want."

"Well, then, I'll have a beer," Tim said. "A Kloster. Or Singha. Whatever."

"And how about something to eat? A sandwich or something?"

"Can't say that I'm really hungry," Tim said. "Carried some lunch over to D.J. at the hospital and ended up having to eat most of it myself."

"That's your buddy with the injured leg? How's he doing?"

"He's doing all right," Tim said. "They've got him strung up so that he can't move too easily, but the leg will come out okay in time. So they say, anyway."

"Well, that should be a relief to you," Macpherson said. "Though our friend Dubois doesn't quite see why you should feel it's your fault."

"He didn't really want to go out there," Tim said. "He went out there just to help me out."

"Anyway, I gather it could have been a lot worse if you hadn't gotten him medical assistance as quickly as you did."

"It's Thirith who deserves the credit for that. Without her there's no telling what might have happened to the leg."

"She sounds like a very capable girl," Macpherson said.

"She's not a girl. She's a woman. All woman. I mean you should have seen her take over out there just the way a doctor would. All they had to do was kind of reset the thing when we got him to the Red Cross clinic and then put in some pins once he was in the hospital. Of course there's a lot of damaged tissue and some other shrapnel wounds. I mean one part of that leg really looked like raw steak that you'd—"

"I get the picture," Macpherson said. "You sure you don't want something to go with your beer?"

"I'm fine," Tim said.

Macpherson signaled the waiter to come over. He ordered a Kloster and a coffee with milk. Then he took off his jacket and hung it on the chair beside him.

"Anyway, I think you deserve a lot of credit for going out there in the first place. Not to mention actually finding the woman and getting her out of a military camp."

"That was really D.J.'s doing," Tim said. "I wouldn't have gotten anywhere on my own."

"Still, I appreciate what you did."

"Yeah, well the problem is, what we do now that we've gotten this far?"

"That's the problem all right," Macpherson said.

"The point is, I've got some ideas on that score if you'd care to hear them."

"Sure. Shoot. But I'd better warn you that after talking it over with Dubois, I can't see any easy way out."

Tim stood up as though to stretch but turned instead to push his chair back, then took a step away from the table and stayed there facing out as though gazing at the poolside sunbathers.

"I get the impression that what Thirith would like to do is go to medical school in the States," he said.

"Is that right?"

"And personally I think she'll make a damn good doctor someday."

"Very possibly," Macpherson said. "But don't you think we might start off considering something a little less ambitious?"

"Like what?"

"Well, maybe some kind of language program here once we get her status straightened out. And then maybe some sort of local nurse's training course."

"She doesn't need a language program. She's already had a language program for almost four years via her mother. Or whatever. Which reminds me."

He reached into his back pocket and brought out the two letters he'd been carrying, each now folded in quarters, the corners bent. Macpherson stared at Tim's hand as though he were being offered a wad of used Kleenex. Then he took the letters and flattened them out without really looking at them. He leaned over to tuck them into his inside jacket pocket.

"There was no way I could deliver those," Tim said. "Your lady friend is back in Cambodia."

"So I've learned," Macpherson said. "Only I don't think it's quite right to call her my lady friend at this point."

"Well, whatever you care to call her, that woman really has guts to have gone back across the border the way she did, I can tell you that."

"Guts she has," Macpherson said, gazing across the pool. "She always did."

When Macpherson didn't say anything more, Tim turned away again as though it made him uncomfortable to see that particular look on his father's face.

"Anyway, I figure there's no way anyone can help her now," Tim said. "But the daughter's another matter."

"True," Macpherson said. "But to be realistic about the daughter, you've got to realize that all refugees are under a tight quota system these days, and even if we manage to get her status straightened out, she very likely hasn't got what it takes to qualify for entry into the United States. Either as a student or as a refugee."

"She's got brains and talent and willpower. What more does she need? I mean we're talking about the great U.S. of A., the land of golden opportunity, right? Not some poor country out here that hasn't got all that much going for it and can't take care of its own people without outside help."

"Will you just quiet down a little? The point is, she's a Cambodian refugee who's now in Bangkok illegally and who hasn't got a single relative of any kind in the United States. So we haven't much to work with at the moment. Get the point?"

266

"So because she lost all her relatives in Cambodia and lost the woman who was taking care of her, she's now supposed to go on rotting away in a refugee camp, is that it? I mean who in the States isn't descended from a refugee at some point in his or her past? So what's so great about us that we can start turning our backs on a potential citizen of that caliber?"

Macpherson sighed. "Look," he said. "I'm not trying to argue principles. I'm just trying to explain the realities of the situation."

"Well, fuck the realities of the situation," Tim said. "The realities of the situation are that a person with unusual talent is sitting out there in a filthy barracks that you can smell a mile off with no future ahead of her, and instead of thinking about what you might do about it, you try to tie the thing up in a lot of bureaucratic Foreign Service red tape so nobody can move. I mean Jesus Christ."

The waiter was hovering in the background with his loaded tray. He couldn't decide whether it was all right for him to go in there and interrupt the two of them. When Macpherson shook his head and then just sat stiffly gazing at Tim's back, the waiter went in and unloaded his tray as quickly as he could and got out of there.

"Your beer is here," Macpherson said.

Tim didn't turn.

"Can I ask you just one question?" Macpherson said. "Even if it's a bit personal?"

"What's that?"

"Are you in love with this girl? Woman, I mean?"

Tim still didn't turn. "I'm not in love with her. I mean I barely know her. I just have tremendous admiration for the way she's turned out after what she's had to go through."

Macpherson was smiling to himself. "Well, it sounds to me as though you're at least half in love with her. But what does an old fart like me know about the mysteries of the human heart, right?"

"I didn't say that. Anyway, my feelings aren't the point one way or another."

"Well, they could be one factor," Macpherson said. "If you'd just sit down a minute and try to be unemotional about all this."

Tim turned back and sat down. He stayed on the edge of his seat as though one wrong word would catapult him up again.

"I gather you're determined to get her out of Thailand by hook or crook," Macpherson said.

"Who wouldn't be? I mean what future has she got in Thailand?"

Macpherson poured some beer to top up Tim's untouched glass. "Well, there may be a way out of this sub rosa. Strictly confidential. At least as far as anybody outside the family goes. So the idea didn't come from me, understand?"

"What idea is that?"

"It's the sort of thing I spent no little time and energy trying to prevent in my early years when I was stuck with consular work, so it really goes against the grain for me even to suggest it."

"Well, I wouldn't want you to do anything that goes against your conscience," Tim said.

Macpherson leaned forward a fraction. "Have you ever heard of marriages of convenience?"

"Sure," Tim said. "I'm just not sure what the term means exactly. At least in this connection."

"As I mean the term, it's a marriage that's arranged to get somebody into the United States not otherwise entitled to entry through marrying a U.S. citizen who can get him or her in as a spouse. Sometimes for money, sometimes not, but anyway to get around what you call Foreign Service red tape, which is actually our immigration laws."

Tim reached for his beer and took a sip. "So what's needed to arrange a thing like that?"

"The first thing that's needed is the consent of both parties. Consent to the marriage and consent to the divorce. The rest can probably be worked out fairly routinely via our contacts at the Embassy. Filing an I-130, medical exam, and so forth."

"The divorce?"

"Well, the idea is that you don't stay married. Not once the party without citizenship has a green card in hand."

"We'd better go over this again," Tim said. "Slowly."

Macpherson sat back, smiling more easily now. "So the idea interests you, does it? Maybe the old man isn't a total fart after all."

"Sure it interests me," Tim said. "Theoretically, anyway. I mean wouldn't it interest you if you'd managed to get yourself into my shoes?"

The hospital gave Tim a serious case of hypochondria every time he went in there, first from the sweet-and-sour smell of the place that surely meant the air they had you breathing was being polluted by the battle between drifting bacteria and weak antiseptic, then from the sense that every surface you came up against had planted germs on you belonging to diseases you couldn't name and probably nobody else would be able to recognize from the strange welts or chancres they would eventually produce after it was too late to do anything about it.

Still, as long as D.J. was in that ward, he wasn't about to let his squeamishness keep him from seeing that the guy got three squares a day and a little friendly dialogue to keep the Bangkok blues from moving in on D.J. to undermine what had so far proven to be really good morale for somebody in D.J.'s condition. Besides, this particular off-schedule visit was for his own benefit as much as D.J.'s. He needed solid advice from someone who could understand his point of view. And though he'd promised the old man to keep the thing inside the family, as far as he was concerned D.J. qualified as family after what he'd been put through on behalf of the Macpherson clan.

Anyway, now that they had Thirith tucked away at least temporarily where they'd hoped to put her all along, again thanks to D.J.'s connections, and now that Tom had come up with a plan, he had to give the old man due credit. Never in a thousand years would he have believed that somebody so generally uptight about his professional responsibilities would come out with a proposition that might be legal in the strictest sense but surely wouldn't be regarded as ethical by anybody in the business, in fact could get the old man in trouble with some of his friends over at the Embassy—Dubois maybe excepted—if they knew that the idea had actually come from him. But even more important, it meant that if they now went through with this quick marriage thing, and that was still the big if, old Tom was more or less committing himself to helping Thirith get herself started on a career once she got herself legally settled in the States. Otherwise, who was going to take care of her after she got the divorce he said she was supposed to agree to in advance? Considering the years it would take her to pick up the education she needed, however bright and ambitious she might be, this was no little thing the old man had in mind giving her.

But what might or might not happen in the long run wasn't worth thinking about until you got at least halfway there. His problem right now was trying to make himself believe that he had the guts to put the question to Thirith in the first place. How do you get to a woman as independent as that with the proposition that she seriously consider marrying somebody she's known for less than a week and then divorcing him as soon as she gets herself into a new country on the other side of the world, a place that is after all not much more to her than some lines on a map?

Even if the two of them had gotten to the point where she was behaving a degree better than neutral toward him, no longer suspicious and willing to engage in a little conversation, it was hard to take that as enough to go on when what would be needed was a substantial amount of trust. And the fact that he was far from neutral toward her might not be exactly reassuring from her point of view, depending on how you came at the thing.

Tom had been pretty shrewd to pick up on whatever it was in Tim's tone of voice that had shown him to be very much on her side, but the old boy had been way off base to suspect him of being in love. Sure he'd been thinking about her a lot, but not the way a lover would. She kept too much distance between them to make for that. What he felt was more an urge to protect her, to take care of her the way a brother might a sister he was close to, though how could you tell whether that was right without actually having had a sister? He really couldn't explain it, especially since he'd been around her such a short time. All he knew was that he couldn't call it love, not in the ordinary sense in which he'd use the word, because it didn't have to do with sex, it was different from the way that made you feel—outside it in a way. Not that she wasn't something to look at and God knows could surely turn him on in two seconds if she had a mind to. But the main thing he felt when he thought about her was this intense urge to put his arm around her and tell her everything was going to be all right, he wouldn't let anybody harm her.

If he had to trace that feeling back to where it had started coming on strong, it would have to be that first night after they'd settled in with the Irish girls while D.J. was over in the clinic still groggy with the painkillers they'd given him. Thirith had seemed finally to relax a little in that atmosphere, as though being among nurses put her with people who might really understand her, and he'd sat there listening to her telling those girls about her experiences back in Cambodia: her town's being emptied by the Khmer Rouge, her trip into the countryside where she'd ended up working like a convict and watching her mother slowly die of malaria, and her really weird trek through the jungle until she reached the Thai border. Of course some of it he already knew about from the diary the old man had given him to read, but to hear her tell it, to watch her face soften with what she was bringing up out of her past, and to hear her voice change however much in control of herself she tried to be, that had really gotten to him. In the end, underneath all the distance and self-assurance that she'd come on with at first, he began to see another person who was younger and gentler, not easy by any means but more approachable, like a wounded animal that needed special attention and care. So from then on whenever she looked at him in that direct way that had given him a sinking feeling from the very start, he now had this added urge to comfort her, shield her, make her know that it was going to be all right after all. And whatever the old man might think, that was not the kind of thing you called love. Even if he himself didn't know exactly what you did call it.

D.J. was lying there in the ward apparently dead out. Tim stood at the foot of the bed waiting, hoping his just being there would eventually work to wake the guy up because he didn't have the heart to do it himself. Then the man in the next bed down the line began to wheeze and cough as though air had started coming in through the bandage around his throat. Suddenly D.J. opened his eyes and blinked.

"Ho there, old buddy," Tim said. "How you doing?"

"Lord. Is it dinnertime already?"

"No, I just popped in betweentimes because I need a little advice. How's the leg? Still hurting?"

"Not like a church door fell on it, but enough, 'twill serve."

"Should I get the doctor in here?"

"Not for me. I plan to live a while longer. Maybe for the poor guy next door."

"He's all right. He just smiled at me. At least I think it was a smile."

"So what's this advice you need, lad? Your old man has finally disowned you for getting an unwanted alien pregnant through parthenogenesis, right? A real no-no down at the Embassy."

"Not exactly," Tim said. "But he wants me to marry her one day and more or less divorce her the next."

"When you haven't even kissed her yet?"

"He says it's the only way I'm going to get her into the country. Though it isn't really kosher and I'm not supposed to tell anybody outside the family."

"Aha. Very interesting. So your old man isn't pure red-white-and-blue after all."

"I never said he was. I just couldn't be sure what he was most of the time. But in this thing I've got to admit he seems to be coming out all right."

"How do you more or less divorce somebody? Divorce is supposed to be terminal."

"The point is, you marry her here and then divorce her over there as soon as she's a legal resident. By agreement in advance."

"Thirith agrees to all this?" D.J. said. "That beautiful cold girl who saved my life?"

"Well, that's the thing," Tim said. "I don't see how I can get her to agree to an arranged marriage, let alone a divorce the minute she gets her green card in the States. The old man says you should have a clear understanding in advance so there's no misunderstanding later."

"Like Thirith maybe deciding after she's married that she's into a good thing, right? Got to put it on the line with these refugees."

"Yeah. That's the problem. I can't face spelling the whole thing out to her. She's bound to be offended."

"Well, how about getting your old man to marry and divorce her? He's had more experience handling these things."

"Be serious, will you? He's already married. At least as far as I know."

"Yeah, I forgot," D.J. said. "And to a legalized alien. Which I guess is as much as one American nuclear family can take."

"My mother's not an alien. She's a U.S. citizen."

"Well, she used to be an alien. Like some of my best friends. So no offense meant."

"Anyway, it looks to me like there's no way I can win this one," Tim said. "And we can't leave Thirith sitting in that barracks indefinitely however cooperative your friends out there might be."

D.J. wiggled himself into a new position. His face showed the strain.

"You know, these painkillers they're giving me must be doing strange things to my head. For a minute there I thought you sounded half-serious about this marriage idea."

"You think I ought to be?"

"Maybe," D.J. said. "Anyway on a trial basis."

"What kind of basis is that? With a girl like Thirith?"

"Well, you don't have to tell her it's temporary," D.J. said.

"So what do I tell her?"

"You just tell her you want to marry her to get her a green card and let things develop from there."

"I couldn't do that," Tim said. "I'm not in love with her and she's not in love with me. Besides, my old man probably wouldn't agree to go along."

"Your old man isn't marrying her. You said he couldn't. And as for his going along—"

"Can't you be serious for five minutes?"

"I'm deadly serious," D.J. said. "The point is, you're not marrying the girl to please your old man. You're a big boy now, remember?"

"I'm not marrying her to please myself, either. I'm doing it to help Thirith."

"So what's your problem? Marry her and to hell with it. Leave the rest to the gods."

"I can't do that."

"Why not?"

"I don't know. Now you've got me confused. I just don't think I can."

"Get out of here," D.J. said. "You're making my leg hurt."

"I mean she'd never agree to just marrying me. Trial basis or otherwise. I'm sure of that."

"Fine. So what's your problem?"

"The point is, we've got to do something."

"Well, do you want me to marry her? I've already damn near sacrificed a leg for her, but I suppose the least I can do is offer to marry her on behalf of my bashful friend, especially after she ended up saving the best part of my leg."

"You're a real comedian, you know that?"

"I have to be. Otherwise I may end up looking like our friend next door here. He's clearly lost his sense of humor. In fact, it looks to me like he's dead."

"Should I call somebody?"

"No. If he's really dead they'll show up in a flash. They need the bed. But I think he's just bored with Western Hemisphere marriage counseling."

"Okay. I'm going. But if I get her to go through with this, you're going to have to act as best man for the wedding and witness for the divorce. I'm warning you."

"You'll never find me. I'll be in Nepal. Or on my way home where the buffalo roam."

"Not with a leg tied up like that."

"Sure. Because with a head like yours, you may end up marrying the girl while I'm still in the neighborhood, but by the time you get around to even thinking about divorcing her, I'll have won the Boston Marathon."

He had his eyes closed now, and Tim could see his face fighting to keep the discomfort from showing. He went around the bed and put out his hand to brush D.J.'s hair back off his wet forehead. D.J. caught his hand and gave it a squeeze, but he didn't open his eyes.

Tim could feel the turn toward September in the changing light as he crossed over from the hospital to Ploenchit Road and put the sun at his back. The traffic looked as though it hadn't moved since he'd gone in there. He knew in general where Thirith was on Wireless Road from having looked in on her the day after they took her to the Transit Center in the ICRC van, but he'd come at it then from the opposite direction, the Nana Hotel side, so he figured he'd better not try any shortcuts getting down there or he might end up facing a klong that gave you no way out except through sewage and drifting plastic.

Anyway, that first trip down Wireless Road had brought on a cheap thrill that still embarrassed him and that he'd just as soon wipe out with a second clean go at it. What had cut into him unexpectedly was a sensation from the old gone life he'd known as a spoiled Foreign Service brat when you'd go down embassy row in one post or another and feel that you belonged to a privileged society that couldn't be touched by any foreign disturbance that might be going on around you, what at a later point you might see coming out of poverty or injustice or imposed corruption but not then, because there was always somebody at hand whose job it was to protect you from any heavy local realities and there was always a safe way out to a better country, namely your own. And even though you were a kid, people you didn't know treated you like a princeling, all respect and attention for no reason you could understand at first but grew to accept anyway. You were an American. That was justification enough.

Of course you eventually came to see that all the attention was unearned, the privilege phony, just a product of where you happened to have been born and where you happened to be at that time. And soon enough you found out that any so-called status that wasn't based on something you yourself had done or at least could be thought to do wouldn't hold up for a minute in the street. But the street was back home, where they might start you out thinking you were something special from the day you were born, inheritor from your forefathers of the inalienable right to this, that, and the other, but where it took only a few months of unemployment and a continuing diet of pizza slices to bring some reality into that great dream.

Abroad it was sometimes more difficult to see things the way they were. And some of those who went overseas to work for the government or in business came on weird for Americans with inalienable rights. When they found themselves in a place where the local people hardly had any rights at all and had never heard of the right to pursue happiness, or who couldn't make it any sort of way no matter how much they might try, these American types got defensive or something, closed themselves off

where they could eat their own flown-in food and go to their own restricted schools and mix only with their own kind. And because they were
basically good people at heart, some of them at least, they would begin to
feel guilty about the way they looked down on the foreigners around them
even though they themselves were actually the foreigners. They'd try to
get their government to reorganize the place they were in so that it became more like the way things were back home, introduce whatever it
was that made their country God's country. And when they saw that most
people abroad didn't really want to become other than what they already
were and had been for years, that turned the local foreigners back into a
threat of some kind.

Maybe it wasn't all that different back home in many ways. Even
though you and everybody else around you except the Indians had started
out overseas at some point, you found people who looked on all foreigners
as foreigners, some kind of enemy unless they became like you, and you
didn't want too many of them around even then, especially if they were
too brown or yellow. The point was, Americans actually were luckier than
most, they did have more rights and opportunities and a better country to
live in than most—God knows he himself wouldn't live anywhere else on
a permanent basis—so why not relax with what you had? Why not let
people come to you the way they used to in the old days instead of going
out there trying to change the world so that it came out the way you liked
when there was no way it ever could, with or without violence?

Okay, maybe it wasn't that simple. With the Russians and the Chinese out there doing the same thing in their fashion, you might not be
able to play it so cool on a given Sunday. And maybe you had to take care
of your own people who were out of work and sometimes living like refugees before you opened your doors all the way to everybody else in need.
Nothing was simple these days. If you tried to take in the big picture,
what you saw out ahead was a confused mess of special interests pointing
every which way and nobody with the whole truth on his side or even a
clear road out. And God knows, he couldn't pretend to have any answers
himself. All he had was a gut feeling that things had taken a wrong turn at
some point on the side he believed in most.

Anyway, at this juncture he had enough of a problem getting his
own life to make sense without taking on the whole of U.S. foreign policy
as well. He had to focus on what he was going to do immediately ahead.
Now that he was well into Wireless Road he realized that in any case he'd
been stretching things to call it embassy row when all he could really see
was the Vietnamese Embassy early on and now the American Embassy

down the road on the same side, as though two old enemies had decided that once the hatchet was buried, there was no harm in retiring to the same neighborhood as long as they kept some open air between them. Of course the hatchet wasn't really buried, at least not as far as Cambodia was concerned, but he wasn't about to get into that subject either. He had to concentrate. What was he going to do about this beautiful displaced person waiting up ahead for some kind of answer regarding her future that was straightforward and easy to understand?

He decided he'd just lay it all out in front of her. He'd go in there and get D.J.'s friend Prak Chim to call her over to his office, and when she was settled in there comfortably on a chair, he would put the issue to her straight. And no mention of the old man at that point. D.J. was right about that, it had to be all Tim's baby from now on. He would simply spell out the options: if she wanted to stay in Thailand to train herself, he might be able to work out something through his contacts at the Embassy and elsewhere, but once he'd done that, she would be on her own, because he had places to go, his own education to worry about, etcetera. If on the other hand she really wanted to go to the States, there was only one way he knew that it could be arranged, and that was as follows, take it or leave it. There was no other route by which to go at the thing but the direct one, head on.

He'd planned to take a stroll into Lumpini Park to get his mind fully organized, but he didn't see any point now. That would just be further evasion. And the more time he had to worry about it, the harder it would be to get himself into the right mood to say what had to be said. He cut over and went up to the guardhouse. Prak Chim was in but apparently busy. Tim got the message that he was supposed to wait. He sat on the ground and crossed his legs, then closed his eyes, hoping that would clear his head completely. All he could see was Thirith, so he opened his eyes again. Then Prak Chim was there above him, flashing a single gold tooth.

Tim followed him past the wooden barracks to one of the large concrete buildings that he figured was used for administration. They ended up in an empty office opposite the one he'd been led to for his previous session with Thirith, when he'd come out feeling more than a little on the defensive after she'd described quite openly some of the domestic horrors she and the others in her overcrowded dormitory had to put up with, from the special smells of the food and bedding to the unholy quality of the squat-plate toilets that flushed by pouring, whenever the person ahead left you something to pour. This time Prak Chim must have thought he was setting up D.J.'s friend for a meeting of lovers, because he disappeared without a word, and when Thirith finally came in, she came in alone. She looked pale, tired. She stood there and watched him without smiling.

"Hello," she said. "You look so serious. Do you have bad news? Your friend's leg is worse?"

"No, he seems to be doing all right. I was just sitting here thinking."

"Then the bad news is about me?"

"No, just sitting here thinking. Really. You all right? You don't look too good."

"I'm sorry," Thirith said. "They came for me without warning. I didn't have a chance to wash and fix my hair."

"I just mean you look a little tired. Otherwise great. Really."

"I am tired," Thirith said. "I have slept everywhere, as you know, but I can't sleep here. It's like a cage, but with many people in it. I don't think I can stay here much longer. I don't know what I'm going to do."

"Well, that's the thing," Tim said. "I don't think you're going to have to stay here much longer. It's just a question of where you go next."

"You mean it won't be America," she said. "I knew it wouldn't be."

"Let's not jump to conclusions. It might be. I mean it could be. The point is, you might decide it's better to get your training here in Thailand."

"As a refugee? How could that be better?"

"Well, it isn't so easy to get to America these days. In fact, it's very complicated."

Thirith looked at him squarely. "I knew America was impossible. From the first minute Tao Lom said it. I am just as foolish as all the others who have thought it might be possible."

Tim had to look away. "It isn't impossible. It's just very difficult. I mean the only way you could get there is by agreeing to marry somebody who's already a citizen."

"That is what you call possible?" Thirith said. "You've come to tell me that is what is possible?"

"I don't mean marry forever. Just until you get your residence credential. Your green card. It would only take two or three months once you got over there."

Thirith's face began to change as she watched him. She seemed almost about to smile.

"And who is this person I'm supposed to marry for two or three months?"

"Well, it could be anybody who's a citizen," Tim said. "I mean anybody who's willing to go along with the idea."

"And what would be my obligation to this citizen?"

"No obligation," Tim said. "Just as he would have no obligation to you."

Thirith was smiling now. "You Americans are very strange. How can you have a marriage without obligations?"

"I'm not saying you'd be dumped once you got over there. Something would have to be worked out. All I'm saying is that there wouldn't be the normal personal obligation, so to speak. At least there wouldn't have to be."

"Living as man and wife for three months and no personal obligation? Where am I going to find a man like that?"

Tim looked at her. "Well, I wouldn't have brought up the idea if I didn't think you could find a man like that."

Thirith was studying him again, still smiling. "Is it because I don't look too good that I'd find such a man?"

"I told you, you look great. I mean it."

"How can I be sure, then?"

"It's a matter of trust. I guess you'd just have to trust him."

"Is that really possible?" Thirith said.

Tim had to shift his eyes again. "Sure it's possible," he said. "Though God knows you don't make it easy when you look me over that way."

This time when he glanced back at her, she was the one who ended up shifting her eyes.

———

The driver was quite irritated at that point. He was of course not in a position to complain, especially when both passengers in the van were strangers, but there was no chance now that they would be able to return to Bangkok before dark, and it seemed increasingly likely that they would have to spend the night in Sisaket or Surin, a thing he did not even want to take responsibility for suggesting in view of what they were certain to end up exposing themselves to in either place if they were obliged to look for overnight accommodations. And if he might actually succeed in convincing his wife that he had in fact been held up out there along that desolate stretch of border so late in the day, he would surely return to her with lice or some other vermin on him that would require special treatment and bring a heavy dose of irony down on his head. Working for the Americans had already created enough problems with her family and some of her so-called friends. Bringing in lice from the provinces to spread among the children would cost him more than debate about one's political allegiance ever could.

When he found hard to understand was the need for a special trip to Ban Phumsaron and that particular stretch of the border. They had visited the principal refugee centers, new and old, that the few officials from Washington who traveled out as far as Aran normally chose to visit, and they had seen more of the temporary encampments north of Aran than was necessary in order to obtain a complete picture of human misery. Just getting through that area had been trial enough for anyone who might think they were out there on a pleasure excursion: unfamiliar roads every way you turned in the thick forest, none leading in any certain direction, some of them still heavily damaged by the rains and no assurance that the next bend in a given road wouldn't bring you to a full dead end where the van had to be turned around very carefully to avoid the mines on both sides of you so that you could reverse your path who knows for how long and try to find a new way out. And all for the purpose of reaching another field that might have been some Thai farmer's only means of support in a better season but that was now a muddy desert given over to the sickness and hunger of foreigners from across the border who didn't quite know where they were and certainly had no idea where they were going next.

In any case it was fortunate for him that one of his two strangers seemed to have some grasp of the area they'd crisscrossed the previous day, because without his help they'd still be trying to make their way out of that no-man's-land to the main road. And this stranger—was he American or English or something else? How could you really tell from the way he talked?—might be counted on to take responsibility for where they spent the night, whether or not it was his idea to take an extra day for this long detour up to the Preah Vihear region. There was no way of knowing whose idea it was because the decision had obviously been made over breakfast, while the two of them were beyond his hearing. There had been no discussion of it in the van and no consultation with him at any point: the decision was simply presented to him as a change in the itinerary by the American visitor from Washington who was in charge of the trip.

He glanced into his rearview mirror to see if that might tell him what it was that had kept his two passengers silent for so long. One was gazing out the window at his side over the empty fields toward the rise ahead. The other was gazing at his knees. Both looked rather melancholy—though he couldn't be sure he was reading that expression correctly.

Could you ever really tell what was behind the inscrutable look of foreigners such as these, so frugal about revealing their true emotions, at least to one another? They had even decided to sit in separate rows back there for this leg of the trip, each to his own window seat, as though in an airplane.

The younger one with the odd accent suddenly looked up front. He must have noticed that he was being watched. When he turned to speak to his companion in the seat behind him, his voice was so low that his words were incomprehensible. And so was the response he got.

"We don't have to explain all our movements, of course," Maarten said. "But we should perhaps at least tell him that we don't want to go right up to the border. We should tell him to stop well this side, where we can climb up to the escarpment on foot."

"Tell him whatever you feel you have to," Macpherson said. "My policy in general is the less said the less room for misunderstanding. But you've had more experience in this country than I have."

"Perhaps you're right. I will just tell him to stop at some point that I recognize, and then I will say that we simply want to take a brief walk to stretch our legs."

"You'd better tell him in Thai," Macpherson said. "His English strikes me as rudimentary."

"Yes, in Thai, of course."

"Not that we're going to fool him for a minute. He must know the recent history behind this place. After all, the forced repatriation here was in the papers."

"The history he surely knows. What he doesn't know is why two foreigners might want to visit this place specifically at this moment. And that is what we don't want the Thai authorities to raise a question about. For your sake, not mine. I couldn't care less."

"Well, I couldn't care less either. They did what they did. There is no hiding the fact or the cruelty of it."

"Which is of course the point," Maarten said. "I mean from their perspective. And that is why our presence here three months later might raise a question."

"We'll just have to take that chance," Macpherson said. "Anyway, I don't mind telling anybody who might try to make an issue out of it that my motives are purely personal."

"Indeed. As are mine too."

"And I don't mean only our friend's point of departure into Cambodia. I mean taking something back that I can share with her other friend

Tan Yong. Who isn't in a position to make this trip himself and who more or less suggested the idea."

Maarten studied him. "I find that interesting," he said. "What is it exactly that he suggested? If my asking this doesn't embarrass you."

"He didn't suggest anything specific," Macpherson said, looking away. "I just mean the idea of a gesture. Visiting the place where a thing like that happened to his people might have meaning for him."

"And the last road Sameth took? That wouldn't have meaning for him, as you put it?"

"I suppose. It clearly does for you."

"But not for you?"

Macpherson smiled and shook his head. "I guess it's natural for you to think in those terms. Is there any way I can convince you that my view of Sameth, as you call her, is quite neutral after all these years?"

"No," Maarten said. "There is no way you can convince me."

"Maybe, then, I'm just not expressing myself well. The point is, you have no reason whatsoever to look on me as a rival."

"I don't look on you as a rival. I don't even look on this Tan Yong as a rival. What would be the point of that? Sameth is gone."

"Then I don't understand what you're implying."

"If you knew her as I knew her you could never be neutral about her," Maarten said. "I'm sure this Tan Yong isn't."

"Of course in one sense I'm not at all either. I meant in the normal sense."

"In no sense," Maarten said. "But I wasn't quick enough to realize that myself. Or to do enough about it. Because had I been, she might not have returned to Cambodia."

"Do you really believe that?"

"I don't know," Maarten said. "I'd like to think it."

"Well, then by all means think it," Macpherson said. "My own view is that nothing could have stopped her. But who am I to say?"

"Who is anybody to say?" Maarten said. "I mean neutrally speaking."

He turned back to gaze out at the fields ahead now rising in a gentle slope that ended sharply at the skyline. Suddenly he stood up and moved forward to tap the driver on the back.

"I think this is a good place for our walk," he said to Macpherson over his shoulder.

He spoke to the driver in Thai. The driver glanced at Macpherson in the rearview mirror to make sure that the man's suggestion had cleared the chain of command, and when Macpherson nodded, he pulled over to the side of the road. The driver sat rigidly minding his own business when Macpherson followed Maarten out the side door.

The field they headed up was grass-covered, with occasional patches of brush. It struck Macpherson as thoroughly bucolic, innocent, untouched by history of any kind, almost ground for a picnic. He kept a pace behind Maarten so that he wouldn't have to talk on the way up.

They were both sweating when they got to the top of the ridge, though the sun was low. Another ridge was visible not far off as the crow flies, but to get there would mean climbing down a steep incline maybe two hundred yards long to reach a clearing that was bordered by a dense forest. There was no sign of life below them or in any direction they might look.

"I can't be certain but I think it happened down there," Maarten said. "I know there is a ruin some centuries old not far from here to the east. That is supposed to be a point of orientation, so we must be close."

"If it is down there, it looks as though it's been cleaned up by somebody," Macpherson said.

"Perhaps. We're really too far up to tell."

"And that was Sameth's route too?"

"Not exactly. I wouldn't have allowed her to cross the minefield down there, of course. She went by road."

"Our road?"

Maarten nodded. "An extension of it. Which isn't visible from here."

"And do you know where she was supposed to be heading after the border?"

"She said if she didn't find Thirith she would go to Battambang to look for her sister again. But who knows if there is a Battambang now?"

Maarten moved off along the line of the ridge with the sun at his back. Macpherson decided not to follow him. He sat down at the edge of the incline and looked out over the landscape below and beyond. It was green, lush, empty: forest that might be called jungle if there were more definition to it but that seemed only a thick spread of foliage now, shaping a ridge to the east and then nothing. He had seen stretches of Cambodian jungle from a helicopter, but this didn't have the same look. There wasn't enough confusion of freewheeling nature and open spaces and man-made things. The landscape down there was too regular, silent, dispossessed. It was neither the Cambodia he remembered nor the devastated Cambodia he had imagined. And it was the more ominous for being that secret, that cold to the eye. But if what he sensed in its silent regularity was an aura of death, that could be just his imagination, fed by the history he'd been told. The truth was that he felt totally a stranger to the place, too disoriented now to know what it really was.

A breeze had come up as he sat there, and the sweat in his shirt now chilled him where it clung. He stood up. Maarten was a good hundred yards off, his arms folded in front of him, studying the landscape. The image of the two of them standing there so far apart gazing out at the same spread of silent country amused him for some reason. It occurred to him that it might have amused Chien Fei too. He decided it was time to head back.

As he came up, Maarten spoke without turning. "It's obvious that I've been out here too long," he said. "There is too little about this setting that moves me now."

"That seems to go with the territory," Macpherson said.

"I don't feel I have any place here now. Quite aside from my recent failure."

"You mean the Polk business? The Baugh business, rather. That was hardly your fault. The man was a casualty of wars you're too young to remember."

"That and so much else. I'm not in touch with things any longer."

"Well, I can't say that I am either. Not out here."

Maarten sighed. "In my case it isn't only a question of place. It's a question of what one believes, what one believed. I'm not even sure about that any longer."

"Well, maybe it's time to go home," Macpherson said.

"Yes," Maarten said. "Wherever home may be."

FIVE

1983

It may be foolish of me to think that there is a useful precaution in my not addressing you by your name, dear lady, but this impulse perhaps tells you how uncertain we who have been so far from you for so long remain about the situation in the home country. To say your name again to myself in private with an assurance that you are still alive, to know that it is not merely a sort of exclamation that signals my hopelessness about ever seeing you again as it so often did during the past five years, this is in any case enough pleasure from the sound and shape of it to fill the moment.

I cannot be confident that the English I choose in writing you will say what I mean to say in the right tone of voice. I write in English because that seemed to you safer at the time you sent your journal from Thailand, as it always seemed when we were together and must still seem to you now, but also, let me confess, because this allows me to show off to you a bit. I have my own English typewriter now, and I have taught myself after much practice to use it with perhaps just enough grace to get by. So forgive me if the tone comes out in a way that does not please you. I want you to know that nothing has happened to me since I last saw you so long ago that could possibly equal the joy that came to me with the slip of paper that reached me a few days ago bearing your name and address, even if the name was not the one you gave me to call you (is this because you now wish to separate yourself from that part of our shared experience which neither of us wants to remember?) and the address an unfamiliar street in our old city.

It is rather awesome to think of that little slip of paper carrying the only news I have had of you since your journal arrived through the same intermediary three and a half years ago, but it tells me in its undecorated way the essential facts: you are alive, back in Phnom Penh, healthy enough to write with a steady hand, generous enough to remember my name. That is all, and though it whets the appetite for more, much more, it brings with it as much as I could have imagined possible in those moments of highest hope before almost any hope began to seem self-indulgent. Of course the thing made me excessively greedy. I did my best to get more news from the representative of the American Friends Service Committee here, but free as she was with her time and patience, she proved to be of no further help. As she explained to me more than once, I'm afraid, she could not tell me anything beyond what the slip told me because it had come to her with many others like it by way of an unidentified source in Phnom Penh, and there was nothing else with it except the instruction that it be transmitted to me via our mutual friend in what the local people call Foggy Bottom.

This means that I am too ripe with questions to be at ease behind this typewriter now that I have found a means of sending this letter to you that seems to me as safe as any I could possibly use. If it reaches you, if you are indeed at the address I have, it will arrive almost directly from my hand to yours, by way of two couriers who could not be more trustworthy: Thirith's husband, son of our mutual friend, and the companion who helped him bring her out of the jungle north of Aran, where she was once encamped under circumstances that I will not elaborate upon here. Please excuse me if I pass over the story of their getting together, since these two young men can tell it to you in person when they deliver this letter and answer the various questions that this news is certain to raise in your mind. Yes, Thirith is now married to an American and has been for three and a half years—that is the essential fact. And to the extent that I can judge, the two of them are happy. In any case, she is safely here, with someone to take care of her and with work that she finds most rewarding (a skilled nurse assisting surgeons now). And he is doing good work with an agency that will shortly send him and his friend on a brief mission to Phnom Penh that they will describe to you themselves. I leave it at that for the moment.

I am sure you realize how difficult it is for me to decide what you may or may not want to hear, what might compromise you in some way or simply cause you pain. At the same time I want you to trust what I say absolutely, as you always used to. But the difficulty isn't only because of my unsure sense of how you might choose to respond to me in a personal way. I cannot escape another sense: that I am writing into the unknown. It is impossible for me to measure your current circumstances, to weigh them justly, sound them deeply enough, so that I can be certain no harm comes to you from writing. Though part of my work here is to collect and distribute news of the situation in Cambodia, I have only a hazy picture of it: what one gathers from the wire services and agency representatives and those few who have crossed into Thailand fairly recently and found their way to this part of the country, no source entirely objective, no source at all complete. Much propaganda comes out from the current government against the Khmer Rouge, but you and I know all that too well from our own experience in the country and our years on the border. What does not come out clearly is the actual quality of life since the Vietnam invasion, the nuances that would permit one who has lived there to judge the situation with exactness and certainty—though there have of course been accounts in various journals here, some from eyewitnesses, most too colored by public information, government information, to seem reliable, all of which suggests that private sources are not freely accessible or perhaps even available. And of course we are well aware of the recent border activity that destroyed Nong Chan and made twenty-five thousand of our homeless compatriots that much more homeless once again (I will enclose some clippings relating to that). So we know the war and the displacement go on.

Perhaps I have already said too much that touches on politics. I will resort to other questions, then. My first is to ask if I may hope that you will give my couriers a full answer to this letter, one that they can bring out of Cambodia with them, thus ensuring that it will be seen by my eyes alone. Will you do that for me? I want to know anything and everything that you feel you can tell me about the life you have been living since your last communication so long ago (one that I tried to answer by letter at the time with no luck, as my couriers will explain). And I want to know what your life is like now, today, and the condition of the country you chose to return to, as I did not. May I count on you to tell me whatever you can that will not put you into some sort of jeopardy? I do not see how there could be any danger in the route I have described, but of course you will have to be the judge of that. And let me say that I will be disappointed if you find that you cannot be as candid with me as you once were, even if I might understand the reasons why that would be difficult for you now, with so much having gone by—so much harsh personal and general history—since we last talked on the edge of our camp, your hand between both of mine.

If you discern a shading of guilt behind the tone that comes through this language I have to use, you will of course be correct. I do not feel guilty about my decision to come to this country, don't misunderstand. The guilt comes from my having had so much good fortune while you were having so little. And this inhibits me from writing about my situation here. I suppose it is only proper for me to outline my own circumstances after I have so insistently asked that you outline yours, and if there is presumption in my thinking that you might be interested in learning about my life here, you will have to forgive that along with all the rest that needs forgiveness.

The truth is that I am generally content, if not what one might call happy. My work provides a good income for someone with my limited requirements, and it gives me the feeling most of the time that I am doing something to help those who have suffered more than I have, which in turn saves me from that unacceptable sentiment of having abandoned my people. Along with the newsletter that I am responsible for preparing, I act as one of the coordinators in the Washington area for the resettlement of Cambodian refugees, helping them find employment and a place to live. There are problems always: difficulties that grow out of the barriers of religion and language, out of communal indifference and labor competition. But we have not had the degree of discrimination against us that has been shown in other areas, nor the violence—the beatings and muggings and robberies—that greeted some of those who originally settled in Brooklyn, New York. (You will see from an enclosed clipping that a number of Cambodian families have now been transferred to Harrisburg, Pennsylvania, where they have finally found a place to rest that has no fear encircling it beyond the ordinary kinds.) So my work can be called satisfying, it has a purpose, but of course that is not enough.

I suppose the problem in my situation is as old as what the Christians' Adam knew while he was naming every beast of the field and every fowl of the air—surely hard, useful work—but could not find a helpmate. I live alone as I have these many years. It is not that I lack for companionship. I am welcome in many homes here, and I visit people—our people mostly—more than enough to fulfill my need for social company and talk. I even have dinner on occasion with Thirith and her husband just to keep in touch with her and to provide a generally silent audience for her complaints about her mother-in-law, who has accepted her into the family with what seems less than a full embrace—at least so Thirith would have us believe (she has never complained about her father-in-law, by the way, who has apparently done as much as anyone could expect in providing for her education and her support in other respects). What I do not have is that which only a very few friends can provide, none here: the unspoken intimacies and the secret sharing.

I feel I am becoming embarrassingly personal, perhaps more so than I should have reason to expect you to tolerate. I think I had better shift to another theme. I told you that I did not feel guilty about coming to this country. That puts it too blandly, too negatively, as you will realize when I tell you that I have now become an American citizen. There were of course thoroughly practical reasons for my doing so, but it would be disingenuous of me to pretend that these alone formed my motive. I have become sincerely attached to many things here. Though I can probably never have the same feeling for this country that I once had for the old Cambodia, I can now celebrate the virtues of this place while accommodating its failings, and I find that the former much outweigh the latter. It seems banal to mention the freedom one has here in speech and movement, but for those of us who have been denied these in the cruel ways you and I have known, there is reason to hymn the banality until the false note in it vanishes. And one can say the same for eating well (I spare you the specifics out of my uncertainty about what you have and do not have these days, except to mention the quality of the meat, including our local hams, extraordinary hams if sometimes a bit too salty). And the people too can be unexpectedly generous, at least in this part of the country, as hospitable as one needs. But what I must tell you about in more detail is the beauty of the place.

When one imagines this country from your side of the world, one usually creates a mental picture of the cities with tall buildings and the open stretches of flat field that go on and on for kilometers in great squares and that are cared for by giant machines, and of course these are here in abundance. But what I have come to know is on a smaller scale, less pretentious and overbearing but for my taste a landscape grand enough: the hilly countryside southwest of the capital. I am friends with a large family of Cambodians who have settled on a farm several hours by car from this city—among the first of the families I was responsible for orienting after I myself settled in this area—and I visit them for a weekend every now and then when my work schedule allows me this luxury. They live in a reconstructed barn on a hill that opens to other hills in the north and west and to a great green valley that finally comes out to the sea in the south and east. The land around them in every direction belongs to the horses and cattle they tend for the owner, who is rarely there, and they also have all the land they can use for their own garden and much left over for the wheeling hawks. When I leave them, they send me back to the city with my arms full of the vegetables they grow, and they give me all the honey and sweet preserves ten men might eat in a month.

I have traveled with this family in my small Japanese car and their slightly larger truck the length of the Blue Ridge Mountains to the west of their farm, and I can say that their situation is not an accident of good fortune only but fairly typical of the farms one sees in this section of the country. And I can also say that the mountains near them are not blue, nor is it a ridge—at least not as we know it—that the highway to the south offers one: it is a broad park that is richly green in one season and bright yellow and deep red in another, and it goes its way for some hundreds of kilometers, open to anyone's wandering, bringing the traveler into and out of high vistas that I will not attempt to describe for you but that must have made the early settlers of this country think they had come into some new Eden that even their courage and ambition had not justly earned.

I have also taken more than one trip with this family to the home of Thomas Jefferson called Monticello, where there is an ingenious house that is both entertaining in its inventiveness and audacious in its command of the surrounding landscape. The lady who escorts one through the house told us that this Jefferson was known to say that he felt he owned this world of ours and half a world again when he would look out from his hill across all the Virginia he could see. It seems he also owned some slaves to help him manage his very special lookout on so much of the world. But I will not dwell on that curse of a ghost in his cellar (there is actually a photograph down there of a talented slave of his who once made carpenter's nails to supply one of his business enterprises). In any case, this Jefferson was a genius, there is no doubt about that, and part of his genius was knowing the value of where he had arrived. The brochure they give you there says that he promised one lady visitor that he would show her a flower here, a tree there, a grove near a fountain, a hill on one side of his hill and a river on the other side, because "indeed, madam, I know nothing so charming as our own country."

I have gone on too long. May I conclude by asking if you think there is any chance that I might someday be able to show you the same flower and grove and hillside? I often imagine how much someone with your knowledge of our lost history and culture, your facility with the right languages, could contribute to our work here—and I will not mention your more personal qualities for fear that you will think me a flatterer. The newsletter could be yours entirely, or any other part of my work that might appeal to you, and this would free me to give more time to my old profession. I feel there is much I could write that might bring the experience we have known during the past decade to a broader circle outside our own. What I am suggesting could all be completely on a professional basis if that is what you would choose. I think I can say with confidence that I would find a way to arrange for your admission to this country, if necessary via the route that Thirith took. And you know that you could trust me to leave you free of any obligation toward me that was not of your own making. But if—how can I say this with grace?—if it should prove that our arrangement might go beyond one of professional convenience, beyond that of fellow workers and even close friends to the final stages of companionship, I would welcome that more than I know how to say. I therefore say no more.

Goodbye, dear lady. I do hope it is goodbye for the moment only. But whether or not I receive an answer to this letter, there has been joy for me of a rare kind in writing to the beautiful image of you that I still hold unaltered after so many years and that has now been given new life again, even if the image no longer carries the name I knew.

Faithfully yours,
Tan Yong

April 15. I hope you will not mind, dear Tan Yong, if I choose to answer your warm letter in the seemingly colder form of a personal journal. It is one measure of where we have arrived in our People's Republic of Kampuchea after four years of so-called Salvation Front rule under the Vietnamese that your worst fears are justified and that it still strikes me as politic to write in a notebook that appears to be some kind of diary so that what I write may pass for something other than a secret communication to be sent abroad were it to fall into the wrong hands during the next two weeks—that is, if the English of it remains untranslated. Two weeks is about how long your couriers, as you call them, those two quite amusing young Americans you sent me, say that their business in Phnom Penh is likely to keep them before they are required to return to your country. Also in this form I can attempt to answer your questions—you do ask too many, my friend—as my leisure allows each day, and I can take what time I need to consider the most important question you ask, the very personal one about our possible future together, because I can't answer that satisfactorily for my own sake, let alone for yours, without much careful thought. I promise you an answer before I have to hand this over to our young American couriers, and at that time I will try to include a special message for Thirith as well.

There is one thing I want to make clear at the start to set my mind at rest. I did not give my name and address—my old name and new address—to the person who contacted the American Friends Service Committee in order for these to be used in a plea for help, a kind of message of last resort sent out to sea in a bottle. I would be dismayed if that were the impression you received from the representative who tracked you down through our State Department friend (does it still make sense for me to call him something so impersonal?—this my first question in return for one of another of yours, though I may become bold enough at some point during the next two weeks to put it directly to his son, who is now after all some sort of unofficial relative of mine also, it seems). I passed on that slip of paper because I felt it was my first chance to use an unconditionally safe route to let you know that I was still alive and, by implication, reasonably healthy. Nothing more. And of course I hoped you might find a way, through them or otherwise, to let me know that all was well with you. That I would get so much news so quickly, including the still quite startling news of Thirith's marriage three and a half years ago to this blond American, would not have occurred to me even in a wild flight of fancy, and I assure you such flights are in any case a rare indulgence these days. So my attempt to reach you has had wonderful results from this point of view, better than I could have hoped for. But I want you to know that I had no hidden motive in mind, no larger expectation, certainly no coyness regarding the future. I learned some time ago to be guarded but entirely candid with myself regarding the future in the light of our country's—my country's—recent history. So coyness in this respect would be a particularly despicable sin in approaching an old friend.

You say you want to know anything and everything I may care to tell you about my life since my last communication with you four years ago as I was about to cross back into this country in search of Thirith after the forced repatriation. (I gather my Dutch friend Maarten served me faithfully to the end by forwarding what you strangely call my journal, even if that was also really a long letter addressed to you. I wonder if you have news of him—but why might you more than I myself?) I really want to meet your interest in where I've been during these four years because I know it's honest—mere courtesy was never enough for us from the start,

294

so how could it be now, after so much lost time?—but I have to say that it would be no pleasure for me to go back into what have now become blessedly forgettable if not entirely forgotten regions of my past. And I'm not sure I can write about the early days of my return here without that touch of self-pity which would add unnecessary sweetness to the true flavor of their horror.

You must have heard reports about the bad harvest here in the winter of 1979, the stocks of food that were gradually swallowed up by one army or another after the Vietnamese invasion, the administrative chaos that followed, then the weakness of the irrigation system and the loss of seeds and tools and draft animals that resulted in a ridiculously inadequate planting that spring and summer, and finally the severe shortage of rice and fish that year. I crossed back over the border in time to meet this dangerous situation at its worst—dangerous especially for those who had to travel. Maybe I can give you a sense of my feeling about those early days by saying simply that there were times when I was hungry in a way that I will not allow myself to be again ever if I still have the strength to make myself die. And there were also times when I did things to avoid being hungry that I refuse to believe I could do again and still face myself. Can you who knew me as I was in the camp believe that I would work for the Vietnamese military in Battambang to ensure a healthy rice ration while I was there, that I would steal what I had to from wherever I could in order to survive the road back to Phnom Penh, that I would allow myself to become the occasional mistress of a Heng Samrin official to get myself through that difficult winter in our capital? Yet I did these things. And I do not want to tell you, even you, what else I had to do in those early days.

Let me talk about the places we used to talk about in the camp, our cities—I think I can do that without passion. Battambang first of all. At the time, I thought I was choosing to go there as soon as I did out of convenience rather than the logic of my search for Thirith: the driver who took me across the border (Maarten's doing again) convinced me finally that it would be hopeless so long after the fact to follow any one of the several routes that Thirith might have taken after the Preah Vihear escarpment, and he had orders to go on to Battambang. The one bit of logic in that route was the possibility of Thirith's having gone there herself to look for my sister on her way back to Pailin, which I assumed to be her final destination. Of course it wasn't, and all this speculation seems quite ridiculous after the fact of Thirith's apparently having been on her way all the while to a border military camp north of Aran. But in those first days I had to live with the feeling that I was abandoning the search for her before it had fairly begun.

I found nothing in Battambang: no Thirith, no trace of my sister, no evidence that the city might come alive again that summer or the next. In the center it was the same great vacant film set that I had taken it to be four years earlier, but it was overgrown now with weeds, and the refuse everywhere had become rooted in the ground, sometimes partly covered by earth as though a planting natural to the landscape. People had of course returned to recover their homes, and large numbers had gathered on the outskirts, but the Vietnamese had evacuated the heart of the city, and the presence of so few there only heightened the dead, outland aura of the place, as though one were living in an indifferent archaeological site, off the main route, only partially excavated and rarely visited. I found my sister's house a shell, all its hated furniture gone, only the fixtures that could not be easily carried away still there to prove that it had once been a home.

I stayed in Battambang two months before deciding to move on to Phnom Penh. My work there was some translating of English and French documents for the military authorities to whom my driver had introduced me, trivial documents really, newspaper reports and journal articles and a few public dispatches that any educated European might have worked through without need of help. But this doesn't change the fact that it was the enemy my work served and that it did so in payment for food and lodging under his roof. And when I decided to leave Battambang, it was not out of some crise de conscience about this work but in response to rumors that international relief agencies were arriving in the capital and schools were opening again and the new government there was searching for assistance from anybody with a higher education or technical training who had managed to survive the Khmer Rouge massacres (even if the government itself included many Khmer Rouge defectors who had taken part in those massacres at some level of responsibility). Phnom Penh thus became the city of hope for a few of those who could still feel hope. Exactly what the new government there was looking for never quite emerged from these rumors, but the assumption was that better rations than we were getting went with it, and every day one heard from people passing through Battambang that some former schoolteacher or technician or petty official who had hidden his or her identity from the Khmer Rouge was now returning to the capital to reclaim a place there or to try out a new position that carried some of the old respect.

I joined this sporadic migration south—the principal migration was actually in the other direction, toward the border—with hardly a thought about what I might be doing, almost as casually as I had allowed myself to drift into working for the occupying army in Battambang. I didn't try to find out what the conditions really were in the capital. I simply got myself an official pass from my employers, packed what I could comfortably carry, and let one of the Vietnamese drivers deliver me beyond the outskirts of a city I'd never liked even in the best of days.

I would prefer to think that it was malnutrition eating at the brain that caused this carelessness in me, but I was not really undernourished at the time even if my diet was hardly balanced, and compared with what my body became after six weeks on the road to Phnom Penh, it was quite healthy in those first days. Something must have happened to the health of my will soon after I reached Battambang. Instead of being resolved to the extent I could be, I found myself becoming nonchalant, no longer resourceful so much as aimlessly reckless. Of course I couldn't have analyzed it at the time—that was part of the problem—but I now suspect that it had to do with finding my sister's house in that condition. My last blood link vanished with that beautifully pretentious furniture, as the city had vanished before it along with the country my sister and I had known. But the loss was no longer so abstract and general, no longer an image of passing history and dying landscape but something too intimate for the mind to bear openly, and perhaps this brought a tic into my psyche, an uncontrollable perception that nothing existed which could hold one anymore except the impulse to survive. Survive for what? Nothing that one could define beyond the only thing left: me.

If I turned south for Phnom Penh with this unexplained psychic disturbance and a certain rumor of hope, the way there gradually pared my psyche down to the bone in a ruthless cleansing. There are long stretches of that trip that I don't remember at all. What I remember is mostly isolated days and isolated events, days of work in the fields to earn enough extra rice to go on eventually to the next village or town along Highway 5—Muang, Pursat, Krakor—stealing from an unprotected sack in one marketplace and later from a house that seemed abandoned only to be beaten for it by someone stronger than I, a man the first time, a woman the next. And I remember the hunger when there was no work or nothing anywhere to steal. Though my pass got me through the roadblocks, it made me suspect to others who had to make their way around them, and I found myself mostly traveling alone. There were times when I didn't think I could possibly get to Phnom Penh. And then I would hear from those heading north that the shortage of food in the capital was surely worse than where I'd come from. I would sit by the highway and hope that a passing truck might turn its wheels enough to run me down or that somebody strong might come down the road to take what I was carrying and beat me to death. Then I would pick myself up and walk on again until an empty or sleeping house appeared that I could try to rob or until I came to a camped group willing to give me enough rice or Russian wheat grain to keep me alive a while longer. But my conscious will had gone out of me before I reached the capital. It no longer mattered to me if I stayed alive, I had anyway made up my mind that I wouldn't, and what it was that moved my body long after it stopped making sense to me to go on was a thing I neither understood nor cared to understand.

The first image of Phnom Penh that I remember was the graveyard of cars outside the city, untouched by the weather after four years, a slice of my past that I confused at first with the graveyard of cars outside Battambang, where I'd recovered my suitcase after leaving the convoy of foreigners en route to Thailand in 1975. I stood there contemplating those animal shapes in rusted metal, smiling to myself for the first time in many days over the irony of having walked so long and so far only to return to where I'd started out. And another image I remember as I pushed on from the crowded outskirts into the still-uninhabited streets closer to the center: the trash, alive, constantly in motion it seemed, floating by barricaded stores and wounded apartment buildings and dense overgrown gardens, this trash surely a mirage because it included swirling banknotes that nobody was bothering to gather up. I caught one; the thing was real certainly, though it looked unfamiliar as I gazed at it. Then I realized it was Khmer Rouge money and not real at all. Was the city itself? I sat down on the pavement, bewildered now, drained to the limit, and that is where I stayed, it seems, until they came to collect me.

I'm going to leave you for the time being, dear friend. I promise to return to this when I next have a free moment, but I'm sure you realize that it's still something of a burden for me to think about those days and what I had become. Let me leave you with a warmer picture of our city to hold you until I come back. It is the end of the New Year holiday for us, and I assure you that if you were here you would see very little difference in the open air from the holiday mood you knew before Pol Pot. And I don't mean only the housecleaning and fireworks and activity in the wats. The small shops are now back in business, many more than last year even, and one can now buy not only traditional things but much new merchandise, especially in the open markets, where one finds imports from Thailand—silk blouses, sunglasses, cosmetics—on the west side of the city and duller things from Vietnam on the east side. Cars and motorcycles and bicycles are back in the street, and so are women in broad-brimmed hats rather than bandanas and children in blue-and-white school uniforms rather than black military dress. One still finds buildings boarded up and much rubble and even some barbed wire, but the city would seem to you almost as it was before the Americans left eight years ago. Except, of course, that it still isn't our city.

April 17. I have seen your young friends again. They came this time with some more recent newspaper clippings as they had said they might when they brought me your letter. We had a Nescafé on my balcony (they invited me to their hotel, but I think it best that I not be seen with them in a place as public as that for reasons that will become clear to you in due course). We talked a bit about their work here. It seems that they have already begun to encounter obstacles that they had not anticipated, first of all severely restricted travel outside Phnom Penh and then a definite lack of understanding on the part of the local authorities, both the government and their Vietnamese "advisers." They told me that the main object of their visit here was to explore the possibility of helping this country to become self-sufficient in the production of certain vegetable seeds—tomatoes, chili peppers, Chinese cabbage, cucumbers, squash, I can't remember what other rare, exotic things—by coordinating the production, collection, and distribution of these seeds through the international church agency they represent. But apparently the government seems eager for help with the production aspect and not at all with the collection and distribution aspects, which means that if the program is established, the international agency may have no way of ensuring that the seeds go to the areas that most need them or even that they do not go largely to Vietnam.

The failure of understanding is of course quite standard in our part of the world, especially when one is subject to this particular kind of foreign occupation, and it is not likely to be resolved in a week or in a month. But I didn't want to discourage your friends by telling them so. They both seem so determined to do something that will benefit our country, to "pay their dues here," as the older one with the funny hat put it. It's very touching, if a bit naive. Are most Americans their age so conscious of a past in which they were really too young to play a role and so generous in spirit toward a people on the other side of the world who could easily remain forgotten? Is Thirith, for example?

The clippings they brought are alarming, if not truly surprising, for all the distortion in the news we are given by our leaders. It is painful enough but hardly difficult for me to believe from the clippings you sent that the Nong Chan camp, which was not much more than a field densely covered with bamboo poles and plastic walls at the time of the forced repatriation, has now been burned to the ground by the Vietnamese army and the camp's twenty-five thousand refugees sent scurrying for safety elsewhere after four years of trying to root themselves in that border desolation. Has anything really changed that would allow those refugees to find more solid ground than they've known all these years? No third country has become very much more hospitable than it was, and the Khmer Rouge and the Khmer Serei are still on the border in large numbers with their international support to keep them armed and active; the Thais still care for Thailand and the Vietnamese for Vietnam. I read now that fifty thousand Cambodian "volunteers" under the direction of Vietnamese "advisers" have built a wall of earth and a tank ditch thirty-five kilometers long opposite the tank trench that the Thais dug on their side of the border sometime after you and I reached the old Aran camp. Does this suggest that the Vietnamese are going to leave our country soon and go home so that the refugees can return in peace? Not in this generation, dear Tan Yong. At least not until the occupiers have swallowed all that they can comfortably eat from the table of the occupied, including, perhaps, a portion of the table itself.

Forgive me for telling you what I'm sure you fully realize without my having to declaim it. I'm avoiding what I promised you: the rest of what I can tell you about myself to bring you up to date. I'm not sure how much more there is that would really interest you. I rediscovered something of my former self lying on the hospital bed between a pregnant woman less than Thirith's age who had anthrax and a boy maybe ten years old who was suffering from acute malnutrition, not my kind which had brought me down to bones covered mostly by skin only but the severe kind which bloats your legs and stomach. They both died before I left the place. I had been picked up by people working for a French committee that had come to the capital to distribute medical supplies and sanitary equipment—I still don't know exactly how or where because those who had found me were gone by the time I was allowed to leave the hospital. I don't even know exactly how long I lay in that ghastly ward, some weeks certainly, most of those around me in much worse condition than I was, someone dying every day, usually without a sound. The woman next to me would turn her head so that I couldn't see her swollen jaw and her white lips, and every morning she would tell me that she was much better, but the poor thing couldn't hide the sound her dry breathing made and the unnatural rhythm of her breasts with their nipples still firm under her shirt. Unlike me, she wanted very much to live, and obviously not for herself alone, so that watching her die made me ashamed.

That was maybe the beginning. Anyway, my will began to return gradually and even my resourcefulness. I was released from the hospital apparently without lasting damage from the malnutrition, and through a doctor who came regularly to my ward, I managed to get work with the French agency that had brought me in there. I took inventory of medical supplies that arrived, keeping records in French and translating them into Khmer when necessary, and this work provided ample food and a place to sleep in the committee's so-called headquarters. But of course that couldn't last. Even a simple position of that kind in a starving city under foreign occupation becomes a matter of politics. I was dismissed in favor of a Khmer woman who had returned to our country from four years in Vietnam and who pretended to know their language as well. In fact what she knew was a Vietnamese official, one of our proconsul "advisers." But the loss of this work is what quickened my pride and made me resourceful again. I had made my own contacts during the month I worked in the headquarters, not with the Vietnamese but with lower-level officials in our puppet government, those responsible for liaison between the French committee and our Vietnamese occupiers. One of these officials found me a place as an interpreter for a Khmer representative with inadequate French who was responsible for checking the committee's supplies as they came in from abroad.

Of course one pays for favors of this kind. I was not so naive as to have thought I would be granted steady work that actually carried a wage without being called on to share some of my spoils, and I was perfectly prepared to hand over what was expected. It had not occurred to me that I would also be called on to hand over my body, even occasionally. In the first place, I didn't think that in my emaciated state—I still had no true roundness to show—anybody would be interested in having me. And then my own interest in my body, along with anybody else's, I assumed, had died on the road to Phnom Penh. But I found that my patron in the government not only began to court me whenever his schedule allowed, taking me out for tea and bringing me this or that delicacy, but finally made it clear that the apartment he had found for me was not to be regarded as purely private property, at least not every night of the week.

He wasn't a particularly cruel or lecherous man, and difficult as it was for me to believe, he was evidently much attracted to me, but of course I could feel nothing but indifference toward him however well he behaved. Still, I let him stay with me his one or two nights a week throughout the winter and into spring. I have no excuse. I simply didn't know what else I could do. And I wasn't strong enough to decide that it was better to give up my work and my apartment rather than allow myself to be used in that way. That is, not until I realized I was pregnant.

You can imagine what kind of unacceptable surprise this development was for me—or not being a woman, perhaps you can't. I don't know how to explain the thing delicately. I'm sure you're aware from your experience with the refugees in our camp what effect malnutrition can have on a woman, and it certainly had that effect on me for some months, beginning during the summer even before I left Battambang, though at that time I thought it was simply a matter of nerves, as it may well have been. Anyway, pregnancy could not have seemed more remote to me after I came out of the hospital here—I suspect it would have seemed so even without this false menopause—and during the months that followed I foolishly took no precautions nor asked for any. Then for a while I refused to believe what was happening to me until the symptoms were inescapably clear both to me and to the doctor I finally consulted.

It embarrasses me to dwell on all this. Let me say simply that within a month I had lost the child by miscarriage and was free of my demoralizing relationship, if I can be allowed this small euphemism. The man never even knew I was pregnant. After the miscarriage, I simply told him one evening that I couldn't any longer make love with someone I might originally have felt I owed a certain gratitude but now felt I owed nothing but contempt. The man was stunned at first, then hurt, then sullenly angry. For some days after that I couldn't sleep a full night through without waking up abruptly with the expectation that daylight would bring my dismissal notice. But it never came. I assumed in the end that my former patron had simply decided to call it a day and leave me to my fate, too proud maybe to use his power to get back at me for my having rejected him, noble personage that he was. I proved to be quite wrong about that, too generous, but in retrospect I take that as another sign of my having turned back toward the rediscovery of some sort of—what shall I call it?—inner stability.

My work and my apartment were saved through the intercession of the man I now live with (more or less)—a very different type, I have to add, and a very different relationship. His name is Chantha, and he's the gentleman I served as interpreter during the winter and spring I've been writing about. I didn't know that he'd interceded for me until almost a year later, when our association had become such that he knew he could tell me a thing like that without my feeling any obligation toward him that I didn't really feel for more personal reasons. This is the kind of man he chooses to be, which is why I can still love him in some fashion after almost three years.

Will it seem patronizing to you after this confession if I say that he actually reminds me of you in many ways? Not physically (if he is handsome at all, it is not in your style), nor intellectually, since his mind doesn't extend out very far in several directions that would interest you and me, but in the delicacy that he brings to our relationship and in his sensibility. Also in his political orientation—but I will save that for later. What I found out almost a year after the fact was that he had more or less blackmailed my patron into withholding a dismissal notice in my case by threatening to reveal some of the graft that the patron had gathered from his early liaison work with the ICRC-UNICEF relief mission that had set up business here in October of 1979. The two of them had worked together a short while for that mission, but when Chantha began to notice too much of what was going on, those in the Heng Samrin government who were stationed along the line of profit saw to it that he was transferred to his position with the French relief committee, a less ambitious enterprise from everyone's perspective. Fortunately for him, his own political connections elsewhere in the government were strong enough to protect him in his new work, and by extension, me as well.

Why did Chantha care to save me, even at the cost of jeopardizing his own security? I asked him just that when he finally told me what he'd done, and he insisted that at the time he considered me so essential to his work, so necessary in covering his deficiencies, that without me he would eventually have lost his new position anyway. It was a smart explanation, one that he assumed would flatter me enough to be acceptable, but I didn't swallow it whole. I think he'd been truly offended by what he must have seen as my patron's crude way of exploiting my need, though I'd never spoken to him directly about my personal situation in those early days. And maybe he was beginning even then to fall in love with me; maybe—given his high, if generally hidden, moral seriousness—he began to look at me in a way that made love possible when I came to him that day and told him that I expected to lose my job as his interpreter because I couldn't any longer accommodate the man who had arranged the job for me. I remember, just before I shifted my own eyes away, that the business-only mask which Chantha invariably kept in place during our work hours suddenly softened enough to nullify the effect it was meant to create, and I think that was the first time I realized that there was actually a thing made of flesh and bone behind it.

As I implied, it took some months before we came to know what we could know of each other. He was wonderfully reticent, I suppose his own emotions controlled so that they could be finely tuned to the wavering fragility of mine, and my sense of that, as my body gradually wakened to his unselfish affection, finally won me over. We used to walk along the bank of the Tonle Sap talking about everything under the sun that was personal without being intimate—our past under the Khmer Rouge, our lost relatives, our shared disenchantment with the current situation in our country, our growing worry about where we might be led if the regime continued to become more and more repressive—everything except the one thing which brought most of the others to that riverbank and the barges along its quay that carried at least a memory of the restaurants they once were. And when we would fall in with lovers walking our route, Chantha would hold himself a touch more erect and allow a fraction more distance between us, I suppose so I wouldn't feel that our sort of friendship had to be in any way compromised by the company we happened to be keeping. Yet the Tonle Sap was where we always went, and if we went there presumably so that we could be alone in the midst of others who also wanted to be alone in public for their own reasons, those reasons enveloped us sometimes like a hot wind. After four or five months of these almost daily excursions through the byways of love, I simply couldn't stand it any longer and reached over one day to take Chantha's hand. He held on to me as though I'd reached out to save him from drowning, and when I finally wanted my hand back, he wouldn't let me have it.

I think I will leave you again at this point, my friend. I don't know why it is, but even after more than five years away from you, I still feel a bit shy talking to you openly about another lover, as I did after Maarten came onto the scene. Maybe that says something about this lingering attachment there is between you and me, a thing never adequately consummated when we were together and now carried forward in the imagination for so very long. Has it held strong for that reason? I wonder if it is still healthy for either of us to think so.

As I began to look this over before putting it away, I noticed the date. Isn't it strange that I slipped right by that at the start, as though it had no more meaning in my life or yours than any other date in April, for all our having lived as April 17 people from the time the Khmer Rouge evacuated our city through our first years at the camp? Is that what happens in a country's history? A cataclysmic event has its moment in time, finds itself a name, lives on for a while in that, is replaced by another event that has its moment, its name, its passionate recollection, only to be forgotten in due course except maybe as a classroom exercise because another event comes along, and so on? Is that true even when the event is the death of a city, of many cities, and the murder or displacement of a whole people? Can it be? If you and I let that be so in our lifetime, we have reason to die ashamed.

April 20. I have brought you almost up to date. I think I implied that Chantha and I decided not to live together in the literal sense but to keep our separate apartments. At the time, we agreed that this was for strategic reasons—namely, that if either of us fell out of favor again, there would still be a place we could share. The unexpressed reason was that each of us had become used to being alone by then and neither was quite ready to take on the commitments that living together would mean. And so it has remained. Two years ago I began teaching school again, and shortly after that, Chantha moved on to new work with the Kampuchean Red Cross because he decided he would feel less pressure from the government there. I became the one who started feeling pressure, though of a different kind from his, more pernicious in the long run than bureaucratic corruption, which after all was not introduced into our country by Heng Samrin.

In the beginning I taught at the elementary level and was allowed to do more or less as I pleased, though of course entirely in Khmer because study of foreign languages is banned now except for Vietnamese. I tried to work with my children here as I had with those in the Aran camp, bringing the good things in our past to life whenever I could in my teaching and in our songs and games, even if I had to do so under portraits of Marx, Lenin, Heng Samrin, and Ho Chi Minh, all brothers in what is now called a militant alliance for the development of Indochina. And the history I taught was the history I myself had known over the past thirty years, seen as I had seen it. Since the party line of our government and their Vietnamese advisers gives much attention to the evils of Pol Pot, at least part of that history could pass official scrutiny, and in any case nobody checked up on me initially in a systematic way. Then, at the start of the next school year, we were given new textbooks prepared by special government committees and printed in Ho Chi Minh City. The textbooks saw the evils of Pol Pot as the product of what are called Chinese "hegemonists," and these books reshaped our history to show the long-standing ties of friendship between Vietnam and Cambodia, based on an even deeper friendship with the Soviet Union, all making for a wonderful unity of progressive forces in Indochina devoted to the protection and expansion of Communism à la Hanoi. Of course no hint anywhere that the presumably once-progressive force called the Khmer Rouge had its earliest origins in the Vietnamese-dominated Viet Minh, and that relations between Pol Pot and Hanoi were at worst neutral until 1976, when Hanoi presented Pol Pot a draft map for negotiation that apparently gave Vietnam large portions of Democratic Kampuchea's territorial waters.

I found very soon that I couldn't teach this new history even when I tried in subtle ways to bend it back toward the reality I knew. The lie in it wouldn't go away, nor the bad aftertaste of the ideology it was supposed to promote, and these things gnawed at my mind until I began to show the old symptoms of nervous disorder. This was about a year ago, and it brought on the first crisis in my relationship with Chantha. He fully understood my predicament, and there was no disagreement between us on ideological grounds—after all, he had lived through the same years with an even closer knowledge than I had of our often chaotic and ugly politics. But his position, at least at first, was that I had to keep my job for the very same reason that I wanted to give it up: if I walked out of that classroom, I would be replaced by someone else who would simply follow the party line strictly, and where would that leave my children, who would have to grow up on a diet consisting entirely of distortion and propaganda?

Of course he had a point, a strong one that he knew would touch me, but I told him I simply couldn't go on without doing myself damage and in the process losing control of the classroom anyway. He must have seen that I was beyond persuasion. He let me brood over my problem alone for a solid week, and then he came to me to say that he'd found a way out: he would use his influence with the few friends he still had left in the government to get me promoted from the primary level to the secondary level, where there were still no new textbooks. I could go on teaching what I wanted to at that level, within the general requirements and guidelines. That would solve my problem, wouldn't it—at least for a while? The trouble was, I answered, that it would only be for a while. Wasn't I merely postponing the question that way? What would happen when the new textbooks from Hanoi arrived for pupils at the secondary level, as they surely must in time. Wouldn't these carry an even heavier load of false history and imported ideology to overwhelm the more developed minds they were constructed to seduce?

Chantha had an answer to that, but it wasn't the one I expected. He said that correct as my theory might prove to be, I had no choice for the time being but to keep my old job or accept the promotion he was prepared to arrange for me, because to give up my position as a teacher at this point might put both of us in danger. He went on to explain why this was so in a calm, matter-of-fact way that was almost more frightening to me than the news it conveyed. My predicament, understandable as it was, had unfortunately created one for him that now obliged him to reveal things he had hoped to spare me until sometime in the future, when all danger would be past. It hasn't yet passed, dear Tan Yong, and I suppose there is danger in my revealing it to you here, though perhaps not much more than in other things I have already put down in this new "journal." I place my trust in our couriers and the luck you and I have shared at other times. Anyway, I have to take whatever chance may be involved if I'm to write you as amply and truthfully as I feel you deserve.

The long and short of what Chantha told me that day is this: he is now a member of an underground group that has the ultimate mission of replacing Heng Samrin and his circle but on the way there plans to do whatever it can to sabotage the alliance between the current government and its Vietnamese advisers. This underground group, a kind of secret fraternity, is apparently made up mostly of lower-level officials already in the government who have become disaffected in the three years since the Vietnamese invasion and others not yet in the government or the military but gradually working their way in from any angle they can. According to Chantha, the members cover the political spectrum from former Sihanouk and Lon Nol followers to purged Khmer Rouge, and their shared ideology is a forcefully simple if perhaps unrealistic one: Cambodia has to be saved from Vietnam and saved quickly if it is to survive as a country with a recognizable national identity of its own.

As you will have gathered, I'm not out of sympathy with this point of view, and I'm sure you wouldn't be either if you were here to see what has been gradually happening to our country since the invasion and where we still seem to be headed. After four years there are still some two hundred thousand Vietnamese soldiers in control of our highways and our borders, our foreign friends tell us that any negotiation involving Cambodia and the outside world has to be cleared through the Phnom Penh of-fice of the Vietnamese Communist Party, and even our national ballet at the royal palace now dresses up in the traditional costumes of Vietnam and Laos along with our own. Once more our life here is being strangled by foreign intervention. But to be part of a secret conspiracy against a puppet government as paranoid as this one would have called for more courage or recklessness or political optimism than I would have chosen to exercise of my own free will.

The trouble is that I'm apparently implicated in the conspiracy whether I choose to be or not merely by virtue of my intimacy with one of the fraternity's members. Chantha didn't put it that way to me, of course, but this is more or less what it comes down to. Under a regime of the kind we have now, there is no association of the sort I have with Chantha that is likely to go unobserved, especially if the government becomes increas-ingly unsettled and self-protective, so guilt by association has to be taken for granted. Should something go wrong or be seen to be going wrong, we will suffer for it together. It seems my fate is now bound to his in a way that I couldn't have anticipated when we became lovers and that I have to believe he couldn't have anticipated either.

At the time all this came out, Chantha tried to assure me that I had no reason to be afraid so long as I didn't do anything drastic to call the government's attention to me as a possible dissident—by which he meant, I suppose, my refusing to teach the government's new mythology. He in-sisted that the group he belonged to was a very tight one that admitted only those with proven integrity and reliability, and they were all subject to the strictest security procedures, etcetera. He also assured me that the group was not nearly ready to become active. There was still much plan-ning ahead, much need for expanded membership in the right quarters, and when they were ready to become active, I would have ample warning. In fact, he said, if any sort of danger was imminent, he would make the necessary arrangements to get me out of Phnom Penh, and if I so chose, he would see to it that I got safely to the Thai border. I didn't end up very greatly reassured, but at the same time I didn't see how, under the cir-cumstances he described, I could refuse to accept the new teaching as-signment that he was prepared to find for me.

In one sense we've had a quiet time of it since that day. He never talks about what he is up to, and I see no evidence in his life of anything unusual going on, no changes in his schedule that might signal a secret meeting, no encounters while I'm with him that would make me suspect some member of his group had crossed our path. But of course I see him only in the evenings now that we are not working together, and there are parts of every weekend when we do not see each other at all. To make my association with him seem more casual than it is in fact, I now go to his place instead of his coming to mine, and I rarely stay through the night. In other ways I try to live as I have always lived so that my neighbors and my fellow teachers aren't conscious of any particular change. But what I now know influences me all the time. I seem to have developed that sixth sense which is supposed to come to conspirators out of their feeling of insecurity. I watch people with a sharper eye than I used to, I'm more careful about what I say in public, and I've become a bit wary of meeting foreigners in the open. I also wait with increasing anxiety for the day when Chantha tells me, "The time has come. Now we move." I can't help wondering where I will go then.

You must see now why it has been so difficult for me to answer the question you raised about my future, so difficult to answer it with care and honesty. There is one side of me that wants to leap at your offer, to spread my wings before the possibilities you've set in front of me and fly off to your city and the open valleys and hills beyond it that you paint in such bright, seductive colors. And the possibility that draws me on more than any other, dear Tan Yong, is that of renewing a life with you, whether the arrangement you propose were to remain one that would allow us to be together again as friends and fellow workers or whether we were to find it could become something else, as it has for Thirith and her young American. This side of me still believes in the richness of living, the rewards that come with working as you please; yes, even in a happiness that one can share with another when one has found a place where there are peace of mind and physical health and a full table to satisfy the beautiful cravings that our world has given us for our pleasure. And the other side of me, the darker side, says there is no such place. Or if there is such a place, it is not my fate to know it, not any longer, because I am a Cambodian woman with a past and a present that I can't possibly escape.

Let me try to be more specific about this division I feel in myself so that it doesn't seem as though I were giving in to a kind of middle-aged self-pity, a thing I'm sure you would be the last to accuse me of after the time we used to spend trying to sort out some of the contradictory thoughts that would come to both of us during our years on the border. You can see from what I've outlined of my life that it is still very much determined by the political situation in ways that are both imposed on me and that come from inside. I continue to believe in my country on some level that remains important to me, and I therefore can't simply stand to one side and accept what is again happening to it or entirely give up hope that there can be a change here for the better, remote as that may now seem. Yet there is another part of me that considers almost any politics we've known here or are likely to know as quite absurd, that anyway sees a terrible danger ahead for all of us if the usual politics aren't put aside at some point soon and if nations do not cease to be national in a way that can threaten others. Where does that place me? Can one be a nationalist without believing in nations? I want the Cambodia I once knew, or something like it, yet it is hard for me now to conceive of a Cambodia that doesn't have the threatening look of one or another of its neighbors, whether Vietnam, Laos, or Thailand. Even so, does this allow me to abandon my country for another on the far side of the world while it is still so directly threatened by the Vietnamese occupation?

And there is the other level on which no country is enough for one to believe in. You and I used to talk about this when we would sometimes search our border wilderness to see if there were any remnants of a faith and a religion that we could gather up and hold to securely enough to teach other refugees even more lost than we were. I don't think either of us found a truly solid basis for faith then, and I can't say that I've found it in this new wilderness created by the invasion, but that doesn't quite kill my impulse to go on looking. This being so, is there any point in looking if one doesn't begin where there is a history and a tradition one can identify with and build on, even if there are only broken pieces to guide one at the moment? That is the one side. The other side says that such searching is a dance on air, a flight into illusion, an escape from the more difficult reality where faith of this grand kind no longer has any place. One must cope by oneself. Will and choice are not to be confused by association with the names we give our superstitious dependence on something outside ourselves, whether we call it the Buddha or God or fate or simply good and bad luck. Both these sides are in me, and they are still at war.

Where does this leave us, my dear friend? I'm afraid it leaves you where you are, still holding your gift of possibilities, and me where I am, wings still folded. I can't move. I'm sure Chantha would arrange for me to return to the Thai border if I were to ask him to, but I can't bring myself to abandon him and everything else I would have to abandon simply because the chance to escape has suddenly come my way. Do you understand now why I have to say this? And will it make more sense to you if I also say that I don't exclude the possibility of changing my mind should things become truly impossible here and should there still be a way out? I am after all the same Sameth who crossed the border once and crossed back again, perfectly capable of contradicting myself to go off in a new direction, not yet so old and tired that I would turn away from a last chance to live. But now I choose to stay here, and I don't want to pretend any longer that there might be something else I can do.

April 23. Our young friend Tim was here again yesterday. He came alone, and we ended up having a long talk. It seems that his marriage with Thirith is not as settled as one had hoped it might be. You may already know about their problem, though you didn't say anything specific about it in your letter. I'll assume you do, so that I won't feel I'm violating any sort of confidence in mentioning it. I gather that it is a question of his wanting a child and Thirith's not wanting one—a classic disagreement of course, perhaps the most dangerous one. He had thought in the beginning that it had to do with her interest in becoming a doctor, the sort of endless road which that placed in front of her, but apparently she found the scientific studies needed impossible for her and has now accepted her role as a nurse specially trained for surgery—in itself a remarkable accomplishment, it seems to me. So her work is demanding, but not enough by itself to prevent her from having a child. At least so it appears to her husband. He finally came out and asked if I knew what it was that might be going on in Thirith to make her so very reluctant to have children, so reluctant even to discuss the question dispassionately.

What can I tell him, dear Tan Yong? What would you tell him, having lived in the same camp with Thirith for two years and having known all too well what she went through getting there? I did the best I could to fill in the background which might help Tim to understand that part of her which was fashioned by the history that the three of us shared, but of course I couldn't speak for the rest, the more important part which carries her private psyche. I promised him that I would write her and offer my unsolicited advice. Even if I can't believe that she will listen to what I have to say.

Tim and his friend return tomorrow to collect this small package for you and my letter to Thirith. Their work here is apparently done for the time being because they can't proceed without further instructions—that is how complicated and inconclusive their negotiations have turned out to be. Tim says they may be asked to come back at some point, perhaps during the summer. That was bright news for me. It means that I may have a chance to hear from you again. And this makes it so much easier for me to say goodbye, dear friend.

———

Phnom Penh
April 24, 1983

Thirith,

It is Sunday, and this city has a peaceful rhythm today, but I'm having difficulty taking advantage of it. Your husband, Tim, flies to Bangkok tomorrow. I must have this letter ready for him when he and his friend with the name I can't possibly spell correctly come to my apartment this evening for the last time, yet it is noon and I'm only now sitting down to the empty sheet that has been on my desk since early morning.

I woke early thinking I had much to say to you, but when I went over it to work out how I might write it down, I was overtaken by the sense that I was addressing a stranger, or what is more inhibiting, the ghost of a stranger. You are anyway no longer what I knew. It is almost four years since we last saw each other. I can imagine you only as you were then, silk blouse and military belt, barely twenty but very headstrong and already off on your own road, so that I feel we had actually separated some time before I lost touch with you and crossed back into this country with the rather irrational hope—as it seems to me in retrospect—that I might track you down somewhere.

I remember that while we were living together in the camp, I had to remind myself constantly that you were not my daughter and that I really had no business treating you as though you were or expecting any sort of unearned affection from you, though after what we had been through crossing out of Cambodia and getting ourselves settled in the camp, it was not easy for me always to be so objective in my feelings or to give up what must sometimes have seemed to you a too possessive sense of responsibility. It didn't occur to me until much later, long after I'd grown used to the idea of not finding you again, that even had I been your actual mother, I should have learned to let you go your own way with more patience and selflessness than I managed to show while we were together.

I suppose this realization has had its effect in giving me some of the distance that would have been useful earlier, but it has also cost me that sense of intimacy which might make it easier for me to say what I want to say here. You are a woman of twenty-four with your own work, a husband, a home, a new country much different from this one. We have little in common now except what will soon become a dying memory of our having helped each other survive to reach what we once were. But if this makes us in some sense strangers, I wonder if it might not allow us to approach each other again with less prejudice and passion than we used to indulge in at times. You no longer need feel you owe me anything, as I no longer feel that I have any claim to your affection. We are equals now; neither of us possesses any part of the other. You can be as free of me as I can be of you if that is what we choose.

I hope I will find it less difficult to write you honestly now and that you will accept this without anger or irritation, but of course no one is forcing you to read farther than you want to—and please don't go on for one second if what I have to say begins to sound like motherly advice. Your husband, Tim, has spoken to me rather openly about your marriage, maybe more so than you would have wanted him to (by the way, I find him an unusually decent person, and very handsome; if he were to stay in this city any longer, I would do my best to steal him from you, even if that might be a touch incestuous of me, as he will have to explain). Your Tim is obviously worried about the disagreement between you over having children, and he came to me to see if I might influence you in favor of having at least one child. I tried to tell him that a question of that kind was entirely personal, not only in the sense that it is private business between the two of you but also in the sense that a woman makes few decisions in her life that call for less influence from anybody on the outside. It would be terribly presumptuous of me to try to persuade you one way or another. At the same time I did promise Tim I would write you any thoughts on the subject that I felt I could share.

What I have in mind telling you is strictly between the two of us, and it has to do with my own failure to deal with the question properly before the time arrived when it was decided for me. I didn't start off with any inner conflict about having children. When I married, I was much in love with my husband and both of us expected to have a family in due course, but I was young enough not to be in a hurry. So I thought, at least. Of course I hadn't counted on the war's taking my husband away before I'd barely come to know who he was. I don't have to tell you what followed, how remote having my own children soon became. And in the wreckage of our country, I found you, and after we crossed the border, I had the children I taught in the camp, always something along the way to make up for what was missing. And when I crossed back, there was no room in the chaos I discovered to think of children other than those starving at one's feet. That is, until I actually became pregnant three years ago.

The details of how and why are no longer important. What is important for me to tell you—and this I've told no one else—is that I chose to give up the child. I've pretended to others that the pregnancy ended in accidental miscarriage, but it is not so. And I've said to myself that there was every reason for me to give up the child: my age and health at the time, my indifference (at best) to the father, my unsettled circumstances, and so on, all true, all finally not enough. What I can't quite hide from myself any longer—and again, you are the only one I've said this to—is that I could have kept the child after all, and more and more feel I should have. Now there is no possibility of my making up for that decision, because any chance of my becoming pregnant again has apparently vanished, sooner than I expected it would but perhaps understandably in view of what my body has known since I last saw you.

Don't think that I'm looking for any sympathy in telling you this. What is done is done, and it was my doing. Nor do I want to think that I consider your need and mine as necessarily related. Twenty years separate us, much past history, much expectation. I've told you what I have as a kind of warning that is yours to remember when needed if you find it helpful, so that twenty years from now you may be spared the feeling of perhaps having made the wrong choice through carelessness or through satisfying yourself in substitute ways, or, hardest of all to accept, not knowing yourself well enough.

I'm not sure that some of my reasons for feeling the way I do now are good ones. Can one really fill one's sense of emptiness by creating a thing one must learn gradually to lose? Can that really take the place of believing in something beyond one's self that lasts? And is it fair to a child to bring it into our kind of world—my kind, anyway—in an attempt to make up for what our history has cost us? As you can see, I have my own doubts still. Your reasons for not wanting to have a child may be sounder than mine for thinking I should have had one. I can't speak for what is in your heart, so I don't plan to try. But for your own peace, don't be casual about a decision of this kind, and don't let it cost you someone you might regret having lost the chance to care for.

I still have a few hours before my messengers arrive to pick this up. I've talked to them about my life here, so they can bring you up to date on most things you may want to know. And they keep insisting that I should take time someday to write down in detail all that I've seen since crossing back into this country and am seeing still. Who can say? If I ever do write something that can become public, I will of course share it with you. Now I think I will leave you, to take a walk down to the park by the Phnom. It isn't quite the same park I used to walk in with my husband. They have small jet planes now for the children to ride in circles, each with a symbol representing one or another of the four countries that make up our new militant alliance. At least they allow Cambodia to go on being one of these. And at least the old shrine beyond the planes remains what it always was. I find that a place where I can still feel more or less at home in my city.

Sameth

About the Author

Edmund Keeley is the author of five novels, twelve volumes of poetry in translation, and three books of criticism. His first novel, *The Libation* (Scribner, 1958), was awarded the Rome Prize of the American Academy of Arts and Letters. His second novel, *The Gold-Hatted Lover* (Little, Brown, 1961), was written while he was on a Guggenheim Fellowship in fiction. He has also had grants from the National Endowment for the Arts, the National Endowment for the Humanities, and the Ingram Merrill Foundation. His translations of poetry have earned the Harold Morton Landon Award of the Academy of American Poets and the Columbia Translation Center–P.E.N. Award. In 1982 he received the Howard T. Behrman Award for Distinguished Achievement in the Humanities.

Mr. Keeley teaches creative writing and contemporary literature at Princeton for part of the year and spends the remainder writing full-time in old and new places.